Stolen Magic

M. J. PUTNEY

BALLANTINE BOOKS
NEW YORK

Stolen Magic is a work of fiction. Names, characters, places, and incidents are the products of the author's imagination or are used fictitiously. Any resemblance to actual events, locales, or persons, living or dead, is entirely coincidental.

Published in the United States by Del Rey Books, an imprint of The Random House Publishing Group, a division of Random House, Inc., New York.

Del Rey is a registered trademark and the Del Rey colophon is a trademark of Random House, Inc.

Library of Congress Cataloging-in-Publication Data

Putney, Mary Jo.
Stolen magic / M.J. Putney.— 1st ed.
p. cm.
ISBN 0-345-47689-1
1. Wales—History—18th century—Fiction. 2. Monmouthshire (Wales)—Fiction. I. Title.

PS3566.U83S76 2005
813'.54—dc22
2004063400

Printed in the United States of America

Del Rey Books website address: www.delreybooks.com

2 4 6 8 9 7 5 3 1

First Edition

Text design by Julie Schroeder

In memory of Cheryl Anne Porter, with her grace, intelligence, and killer punch lines, and to Carol Morrison, my role model for selflessness and generosity

ACKNOWLEDGMENTS

My thanks to all the usual suspects, including John, for his understanding when my brain was lost in the eighteenth century, and my sister Estill and my friends Pat Rice and Susan King, who are very patient with my whimpering when the book isn't going well.

Thanks also to the triptych of editors who made this possible: Betsy Mitchell, Linda Marrow, and Charlotte Herscher.

Finally, my thanks to Susan Scott for guidance on matters eighteenth century.

Stolen Magic

Chapter ONE

MONMOUTHSHIRE
1748

As the Earl of Falconer, Simon Malmain traveled with an entourage of carriages and coachmen and most certainly his valet. As the chief enforcer of the Guardian Council, he walked alone, a darker shadow in the night.

The sky was dark with clouds, perfect for secret deeds. Simon wore black, even his fair hair covered by his tricorne hat. Not that he feared Lord Drayton, whose powers were less impressive than his ambitions, but a wise hunter left nothing to chance.

His horse had been left in a convenient field so that Simon could approach Castle Drayton unnoticed. He'd studied the castle from a distance and spoken with a former servant, who had fled Drayton's service in fear of his soul. The master of the house was in residence, recently returned from London, where Drayton held a cabinet post. Simon had considered confronting him in the city before deciding that this remote area was better. If there was a magical battle, the fewer who might be affected, the better.

The castle stood on a rocky rise cradled in the bend of a small river that ran into the Severn. The original building had been updated and expanded over the centuries, but its site remained an imposing hill chosen to repel attacks. Soldiers would have a hard time penetrating the castle. Simon didn't.

He met the first barrier near the top of the hill. It was a warning shield of surprising competence. Drayton must have been practicing. Simon sketched a series of symbols with one hand. A man-sized hole opened in the energy shell. He stepped through and closed the portal behind him, undetected. Though he could have taken the wards down entirely, there was no reason to warn Drayton prematurely.

The next barrier was the closed gates. Luckily a small side door cut through the wall, its position largely concealed by overgrown vegetation. Its bespelled lock was no match for Simon. He hushed the squeal of the door and closed it soundlessly behind him. Best to leave it unlatched. He doubted he would have to leave in a rush, but he never took anything for granted. Enforcers of Guardian law who made assumptions were unlikely to die in bed.

In the shadow of the wall, he used his inner senses to study the courtyard. A pair of bored guards stood watch in the turret that loomed above the castle gates. In a peaceable England, that marked Drayton as a most suspicious man. The product of a guilty conscience, no doubt.

Before entering, Simon scanned the keep. At this hour most servants were asleep in the attics or the stables, a separate building behind the castle. He wrinkled his nose in distaste as he felt the energy of the establishment. It was crude, corrupted, with most of the residents either fearful or brutish. He felt the quicksilver touch of a lighter female energy, perhaps a very young maidservant. He guessed she would soon have reason to curse her parents for putting her into service under Drayton. Perhaps literally under. Still another reason to confront the man, before he could do more damage.

A corner chamber on the second floor was brightly lit, and he sensed that Drayton was working there. The man's energy was untroubled; he didn't realize his castle had been breached.

Cloaking himself in a don't-see spell, Simon crossed the courtyard and ascended the steps to the keep. There was no reaction from the guards in the turret. If they noticed him, it was only as a shadow.

The lock on the door to the keep was old and primitive, easy to open. He stepped into the absolute darkness of the entry hall. After pausing to check that the space was devoid of any living presence, Simon conjured a spark of mage light in his palm. He kept it dim, just enough to illuminate his path across the great hall and then up the broad stairs.

His blood quickened as he ascended, knowing that the end of the hunt was nigh. Though he acted by will of the council to enforce the laws of the Families, the hunt itself fulfilled an ancient, more primitive need.

Cracks of light outlined the door to the corner chamber. The knob turned easily under his hand. As he had guessed, the room was a study, richly furnished and well lit. Lamplight glinted from gold-leaf decorations on the furniture and the frame of the mirror above the fireplace.

Simon wasted little attention on the furnishings. What mattered was Lord Drayton, the man behind the magnificent desk that faced the door. His powdered wig and brocade garments would not have been out of place at the royal palace.

Simon had found his prey.

Drayton raised his head at Simon's entrance. There was no shock in his expression. Only . . . a trace of satisfaction? Surely not.

"If it isn't the esteemed Lord Falconer, dressed as a highwayman," Drayton said dryly. "I've wondered when you would come after me. I expected you sooner."

"I take my time when I collect my evidence." Simon's voice was cool, but a warning bell sounded in his mind. It wasn't natural for a mage to be so relaxed when confronted by the Guardian Council's enforcer. "Not that it was difficult in your case. Lately you've made little attempt to conceal your transgressions of Guardian law."

Drayton leaned back in his chair, playing idly with the quill of his pen. "With what am I charged?"

Simon pulled a folded document from an inside pocket and dropped it on the desk. "Here is a listing of what I know and can prove, though I have no doubt there is much more. You have used your power with greed and selfishness, and injured many innocents in the process." He shook his head, still amazed at the other man's callousness. "How could you encourage the Jacobite rising, knowing how many would die? Didn't those sundered souls cause you pain?"

"Not particularly. Few of the dead were any great loss to mankind."

Simon clamped down on the anger triggered by the other man's words. Loss of control would put him at a disadvantage. "I suggest you consult the charging documents. If there is anything you would like to dispute, now is the time."

Drayton skimmed the pages. "Admirably thorough." His brows arched when he read the last page. "I didn't think you'd discover that. Well done. You're a credit to your lineage." He dropped the papers back on his desk. "As you suspected, this is not a complete list of my wicked deeds, but it's quite enough for your purposes."

This interview was going all wrong. Drayton acted as if he was invulnerable, yet his magical power had never been more than average. Silently Simon began to scan the room, seeking dangerous anomalies. Aloud, he said, "As you know, there are two stages of censure. You freely admit that you have violated Guardian laws. Are you prepared to swear on your blood that you will never do so again?"

Drayton smiled lazily. "You can't imagine that I will do that."

"And if you did, I can't imagine you keeping your word," Simon said dryly. "You leave me no choice but to forcibly strip your powers from you."

"Strip away, Falconer." Drayton's eyes narrowed. "If you can."

Simon hesitated a moment. The process of destroying another person's magical powers was not pleasant for either party, and was very seldom invoked. His intuition was also on high alert—Drayton's reaction to this confrontation made no sense. Simon detected a very small thread of energy running from Drayton to an unknown destination, but nothing else was out of order. Why was the other man so confident?

Drayton stretched a magic-hazed hand toward a desk drawer. Seeing through the spell, Simon stared incredulously as the other man pulled out a pistol. Did Drayton really think such a crude defense would be enough to protect him from justice?

With a swift gesture to channel the energy, Simon destroyed the pistol's internal mechanism—and in the same instant, he was blasted by a magic power unlike anything he had ever experienced. Every fiber of his being was under attack, ripping asunder.

As he gasped for breath, he realized that he was falling, unable to save himself, much less fight back. Drayton had pulled the pistol to distract Simon from the real attack. But where the bloody blue hell was the bastard getting such power? This was immense, far greater than anything the rogue had ever shown. Such power didn't come from nowhere.

He managed to evoke his inner senses and was startled to see that the fine thread of energy he'd seen attached to Drayton had become a river of fire. Raw power poured into Drayton, who channeled it into searing waves that enveloped Simon. Agonized, he thrashed about on the floor, feeling as if he were burning alive. His limbs were being torn and reforged as in a blacksmith's fire. His pulse hammered in his ears, almost drowning the sound of Drayton's laughter and a strange, ripping noise.

He tried to muster his own power but he was overwhelmed, voiceless magically and physically. His mind was fracturing, clarity melting in Drayton's magical flames.

"I have waited a long time to do this, Falconer," the other man hissed. "In your arrogance, you thought you could take me. Instead, I am taking you."

More energy scorched through Simon, shocking as a lightning bolt. Was this death? But he had always thought death would be a quiet welcome, not this hell of agony and flames.

The last jolt of transforming power knocked him into blackness. Then, mercifully, the pain began to ebb away. Guessing that he had been unconscious only a moment, he struggled to regain his feet. But his body was unfamiliar, awkward. He was pushing himself up not with arms, but—with forelegs?

Wondering if he was dreaming, he forced himself upright, and saw that his view of the room was curiously distorted. But no dream could feel so real. The scents of books and ink and dust were sharply intense, and he ached in every muscle.

He turned, and almost tripped over his own feet. His body was no longer his own. He looked down, having to turn his head to see. Impossibly, he saw four cloven-hoofed legs tangled in black fabric—the torn remnants of his clothing. Fighting panic, he looked around and saw that Drayton was visibly gloating.

Fear washed through Simon as he recognized vicious malice in the other man's expression. He backed away from Drayton, his tail lashing.

His *tail*?

Frantically he swung his head, somehow managing to bang his forehead on the bookcase behind him. Ignoring the pain, he stared into the mirror above the mantel.

Looking back at him was a shimmering white unicorn.

Chapter TWO

Simon gazed at his reflected image with horror. He saw no trace of himself, only a mythological creature with a pale coat, a silvery horn, and frantic eyes. The tail that lashed reflexively was long with a tuft of hair at the end—a lion's tail, not that of a horse, though he had a horselike body and flowing mane. It wasn't his head that had banged against the bookcase, but the spiral horn that rose bizarrely from his equine brow.

Despite the evidence of his eyes—eyes on the sides of his head, not in front—he had trouble accepting what he saw. Could Drayton have created an illusion so vivid it seemed real?

"You don't believe it, do you?" Drayton laughed. "You've become a legendary beast—one that will give me more power than any Guardian who has ever lived."

Simon felt the menace thicken suffocatingly. There was something important that he had studied about unicorns, but his mind was not working properly. The knowledge he needed lay just beyond comprehension.

"If you have enough wit left to understand your situation, you might want to say your prayers, Falconer." With a whispered word and a hand gesture, Drayton lay a binding spell over his victim.

Bands of pure energy spun around Simon, immobilizing him. Drayton gave a nod of satisfaction before turning his attention to other spellwork. It took only one long, murmured incantation to cause a braided circle of light to shimmer into view, enclosing Drayton and Simon within its circumference.

Simon's hazy mind recognized that Drayton had prepared in advance for a complex act of ritual magic, so he needed only a handful of commands to bring the spell to full, dangerous life. That knowledge triggered Simon's memory of unicorn lore: if a unicorn was slain by ritual magic, its horn would become a matchless instrument of power. Drayton intended to kill Simon and harvest the horn, removing an enemy and enhancing his own power at one stroke.

Rage suffused Simon. He began to fight the energy bonds that immobilized him, but they pulled tighter as he struggled.

His horn. A unicorn horn had magical properties. He swung his head around and stabbed the spiral into one of the energy lines that bound his hind legs. The tip of the horn scraped his leg painfully, but the line snapped. With short, sharp stabs, he severed the other bindings until his legs were free. Furiously, he charged at Drayton, horn lowered for battle.

He almost managed to impale the renegade mage, but Drayton dived behind the massive desk, throwing up a defensive shield at the same time. Simon stabbed at the shield without effect several times before he realized that Drayton was muttering another spell. It was time to leave.

He leaped across the study with a single bound, feeling a vicious shock as he broke through the ritual circle. But without hands, he couldn't open the door. After an instant of confusion, he spun around and bucked, using the full, coiled power of his body to slam his rear hooves into the door. The latch shattered. As he bolted from the room, he saw that he'd left deep cloven hoof marks in the elegant panels.

He reached the top of the staircase in seconds, then skittered to a halt, almost falling headlong. How could he go down the steps without breaking his legs or his neck? Backward? He tried to analyze the choices, but his mind was still fractured, unable to work properly.

"Damn you, Falconer!" Drayton's furious shout came from the study.

As magic thickened around him again, Simon unleashed instinct and sailed recklessly down the stairs in three bounds, relying on luck and four-legged balance to stay upright. As he thundered across the wide hall toward the entrance, a cluster of half-dressed male servants ran into the hall from a side door, blocking Simon's exit.

From above, Drayton shouted, "Stop the beast, but don't kill him!"

Simon lowered his head and charged. All of the servants but one scattered in fear. The exception grabbed a chair and brandished the legs in Simon's face. A horse would have backed off. Simon swerved just enough to hit chair and servant with one powerful, muscled shoulder. The chair shattered and the servant was knocked howling into a wall.

This time when Simon reached the door, he knew to spin and buck. The solid wood was much heavier than the study door and it didn't give at once, but he could feel it shudder under the impact of his furious hooves.

A dozen booming kicks broke the latch. Simon pivoted and shouldered his way out. The courtyard was a dozen steps below. He soared to the ground in a single leap. His rear hooves and legs stung from kicking the wood, but not enough to slow him down.

The gates in the outer wall were massive and towered far above his head. He swerved to the right, glad he'd left the postern door unlatched. Since it opened outward, he could leave easily—except that he banged his head into the frame, not used to the dimensions of his new body. He ducked, then bounded through the door, feeling the momentary bite of the wards on his hide.

Free of Castle Drayton, he galloped headlong down the hill, reveling in the power and amazing speed of his unicorn form. He was free. . . .

He was in a prison of dark magic. The small part of him that was still Simon fought the mindless exaltation of speed. He must plan, *plan,* what to do—yet the beast within yearned only to feel the wind in his mane and the turf beneath his swift hooves.

Knowing how visible his shimmering white coat was, he raced at top speed into the nearby forest that ran west into Wales. When he was a safe distance from the castle, he halted and took shelter under a tree, panting less from exertion than from shock.

With black humor, he allowed that he had a right to be shocked at his present state. At least he had escaped certain death for the time being. He found that despite his mental disorientation, he could still reason, albeit slowly and with difficulty. He was unsuccessful at recalling the mathematics that he studied for amusement, but memory of the events of his life existed. He was still more or less himself.

Could he break the transformation spell? He tried to summon his magic, but without success. Worried, he experimented to see if he could perform a small spell. Mage light came naturally to him—he'd created it in the cradle. Now, nothing. He tried other small spells with an equal lack of success.

How could he live a life without magic? He refused to consider the possibility. Somewhere was a solution that would return him to himself. He just needed to find it.

He rubbed his head against the tree that sheltered him. Thinking gave him a headache—a unicorn brain wasn't designed for rational thought. Which meant that he must think as much as possible in order to keep his humanity alive. The powerful, disciplined mind of Simon Malmain was in danger of being overwhelmed by the animal body he inhabited.

The annihilating rage he'd felt during his escape from the castle was completely unlike anything he'd experienced in human form. He had always been known for calm and the ability to keep his head under all circumstances. Now that calm had vanished as thoroughly as his human form. He flicked his tail with uneasiness, and then despised himself for the animal gesture.

What did he know about unicorns? They were considered legend, but legends often had a basis in reality. Tradition said that unicorns were fierce fighters and so wild it was impossible to capture one alive. They could outrun all other creatures, which was fortunate since the precious horn was so valued that hunters would trap and slaughter unicorns whenever possible. So perhaps unicorns had existed and been hunted to extinction. Whatever the truth, he was a unicorn now.

Were there female unicorns? Not that he'd ever heard of. Perhaps the horn was too powerful a sign of masculine potency for the myths to consider unicorns as anything but male. Or maybe the females of the species were hornless and hence of no value to the hunters, so they had disappeared from legend.

Slowly he began walking again, evaluating his new body. He felt swift and powerful. Even if Drayton sent riders in pursuit, Simon doubted any horse could catch him. He raised his head and sniffed the cool night air. His senses had become more acute. The scents of the forest had a layered density he'd never experienced before, and his hearing and vision were sharpened.

His stomach rumbled. What did unicorns eat? He imagined a beef roast, then shuddered. No meat. Grass? He twitched his nostrils, and realized that the patches of greenery under his feet smelled rather good. He lowered his head and began to graze. Not bad, though he would prefer a bucket of oats if he had the chance. He found that grazing soothed him, which also cleared his thinking a little.

What should he do now? Even if he could make his way unseen to the home of a fellow Guardian, he doubted that he would be recognized. Simon imagined himself scratching a message in the dirt with a hoof, and was sickened to realize that he couldn't remember how to shape words. Reading and writing were now beyond him, a loss as profound as that of his ability to perform magic.

Might a highly empathic Guardian sense his human essence? Perhaps a close friend like Duncan Macrae or his clever wife might recognize Simon, but they were far away, in Scotland.

His aching head could come up with no better plan than to stay in the area until he better understood his choices. Could he confront Drayton and force the man to release him from the spell? How the devil could he do that—stab Drayton with his horn? As if the renegade mage would stand still to be impaled!

Wanting to outrun despair, Simon abandoned his grazing and moved deeper into the forest. He increased his pace to a swift canter when he found a narrow, seldom-used track. He needed time . . . time to understand this change, to assess what power he still wielded.

Would he have time enough before the beast nature overwhelmed what was human? Heart pounding, he broke into a gallop and blazed into the forest.

Dark clouded nights were the best for poaching. The two roughly dressed men had done well and now they were heading home, game bags full. Hearing the sound of hooves, they wordlessly drew into the shadowed trees that lined the forest track.

Voice almost inaudible, the shorter man whispered, "What kind of fool is out ridin' at this hour, Ned? And at such a speed?"

Ned shrugged, wondering if the rider might get thrown and break his neck. He and Tom weren't no thieves, but if a man died right in front of 'em, they wouldn't refuse fortune's gift.

The clouds broke, illuminating a shimmering white beast that galloped headlong through the night, unhampered by bridle, saddle, or rider. Ned sucked in his breath, but he didn't speak until the sound of hooves faded. "Did you see that horn?"

"It was a horse!" Tom snapped, his voice shaking. "It was a *horse.*"

Furious, Lord Drayton radiated a dangerous magic that made his steward, Parkin, want to flee for his life. Though Parkin had a touch of magic himself, it wouldn't be enough to shield himself if Drayton came after him. Best he keep quiet and wait for his lordship to calm down.

It took a long time, but after scorching half the books in his study, Drayton returned to coherence. "Damn Falconer! I should have guessed that a mage of his strength would be able to break through my circle." He laughed harshly. "It was for his strength I wanted him."

"Aye, my lord," Parkin ventured.

Drayton scowled at Parkin. "The king desires my presence, so I must leave for London tomorrow. That means you are the one who must capture the unicorn. He *must* be captured, and he must *not* be killed. Do I make myself clear?"

His lordship's eyes carried a deadly threat. Parkin had never seen him so menacing. On the other hand, if Parkin could capture the beast, Drayton would be well pleased. "I understand, my lord. But . . . how does one capture a unicorn?"

"The traditional method is to stake out a virgin and let the unicorn come to her," Drayton said impatiently. "You and your men wait with nets and knives. Hamstring the beast if you must—that will prevent him running away again. I don't care if he's injured, as long as he is alive and his horn is undamaged when I return in a fortnight."

"Does the maiden have to be young and fair?"

"According to legend, all she need be is virgin, since purity is what attracts the unicorn." Drayton shrugged. "Do what you must to capture it."

That didn't sound so hard. Parkin bowed. "It shall be done, my lord."

Drayton made a sign of dismissal. "Make sure this door is repaired, too."

"Aye, my lord." Parkin backed out of the study, grateful to have escaped with his hide intact. Now he remembered the old tales of catching unicorns with a virgin, but where would he find one at Castle Drayton? The few female servants who lived here were either old and weary or coarse sluts willing to spread their legs for any man with a coin or a compliment.

Except for Mad Meggie. Parkin frowned. The girl must be well past twenty, but he guessed she was still a maid. For one thing, she was under Drayton's personal protection, so wise men kept away from her. If she'd been pretty, someone might have risked taking her just for the fun of it, but Meggie was ugly as a mud wall, scared of her own shadow, and spent all her time around the stables. The horses didn't mind that Meggie was mad, but everyone else at the castle avoided her, as if her craziness was catching.

Would Drayton mind if his loony ward was used as bait? 'Twasn't like they'd be hurting the wench. If she wasn't virgin, Parkin would have to look in the nearby village, and it wouldn't be easy to persuade parents to let him borrow one of their precious daughters. He'd best hope Mad Meggie was still untouched, and that the unicorn was near enough to sense her presence.

Wondering from how far away a unicorn could detect a virgin, he headed for his desk to make a list of the men and equipment he'd need. As soon as his lordship left for London in the morning, it would be time to arrange the unicorn hunt.

Chapter THREE

Life was easier when his lordship was gone. Meggie waited till his carriage left, then begged bread and cheese from the kitchen and went riding. Her mare had a fancy name, but she thought of it as Lolly.

They returned to the stable by mid-afternoon, draggled and wet from playing together in a shallow stream. Mindlessly happy, Meggie brushed mud and bits of grass from the horse's sleek chestnut coat. If the lord had need, he could reach her no matter where she was—the night before, he'd all but pulled her soul from her body, leaving her dead tired. Today he had other things on his mind, so she was free to do as she wished.

As she brushed Lolly's withers, the mare rubbed Meggie's back with her muzzle. Meggie sighed happily as the pressure soothed stiff muscles and Lolly's contentment filled her mind. In the warmth of Lolly's feelings, Meggie was also content.

"There you are! Where have you been all day?"

The harsh voice caused Meggie to shrink back in the stall as the steward, Parkin, impatiently strode down the center of the barn. He'd never hit her, but he was harsh and scary. Usually he didn't notice her, and that was good.

"R . . . riding," she stammered.

Parkin curled his lip. "I should have guessed. If you're not virgin, it's because you gave it to a stallion. Come along, I have work for you."

Her eyes widened. Only the lord ever used her—she hadn't known Parkin was capable of doing that.

Seeing her expression, he modified his voice. "This is simple work—just a game, really. All you have to do is sit in the forest for a bit, and a . . . a special horse will come to you. Easy." When she still stared distrustfully, he said, "I'll give you a new dress." His nose wrinkled. "After you bathe so you don't smell like a horse."

She didn't understand, but allowed him to take her wrist and pull her along to the main house. His manner was gruff but not mean. Something worried him. Meggie was only a small part of that.

Her tiny bedroom was high in the house and usually she washed herself there with cold water in a basin. Today Parkin took her to a larger bedroom on the second floor and turned her over to a maid with instructions that Meggie be bathed. Though Meggie liked the warm water in the tin tub—large enough to hold her!—she didn't like being scrubbed like she was a baby. But the soap smelled like roses.

Meggie dozed in the rose-scented water—then came awake with a jerk, heart pounding. She had dreamed she was falling from the castle walls, tumbling helplessly into a strange new land. The dream was accompanied by the chilling knowledge that she was going to be wrenched away from the only life she knew.

She thought of the endless days in the castle, her only pleasure the horses. She had no chores, no duties, not even scrubbing floors. Her only task was to be available when the lord clawed into her mind, ruthlessly taking what he wanted and leaving her half dead, like a broken egg. She had no word to describe the horror of those sessions, but she hated them. And him.

With sudden fierceness, she thought that if change was coming, she wanted it.

The maid, Nan, said, "Time to get dressed, Meggie. Out of the tub."

Obediently Meggie climbed from the tub and dried herself. The new dress Parkin had promised turned out to be a white nightgown trimmed with lace and far too large for her. The lace was pretty.

Nan sniffed in disapproval after she dropped the garment over Meggie's head and tied a bow in the tapes at the neckline. "If Parkin is going to do what I think, 'tis wicked cruel." Face set, she began brushing out Meggie's long dark hair.

Worried, Meggie slipped her feet into her shoes, wondering what the maid meant. Parkin chose that moment to enter her chamber. "Come along now, girl, we've wasted enough time. The sooner I catch that unicorn, the better." He shook his head. "You haven't the faintest idea what I'm talking about, do you? No matter. Just do as I say and you won't be hurt." Under his breath, he added, "At least, I don't think so."

"A moment while I put the girl's hair up," Nan said.

"Let it fall loose. It's more maidenly." When Nan glared at Parkin, he snapped, "I'm not going to bed the wench. Why would I want a plain skinny thing like her?"

Meggie might be simple, but she recognized contempt. Horses were kinder than men. Blinking back tears, she followed the steward out to the courtyard, where a pony cart waited. Not wanting him to touch her, she scrambled up to the seat, sliding as far away as possible.

Half a dozen men came out of the stables carrying nets and ropes and whips. Some were stable hands, the others laborers. Seeing Meggie's fear, Parkin said impatiently, "Stop your grizzling. You won't be hurt as long as you do what I say."

Biting her lip, she clung to the side rail as he drove the pony cart down the castle road and into the forest. The armed men followed, joking among themselves until Parkin ordered them to be silent.

They turned onto a rough track that led to a clearing surrounded by dense shrubbery. "I suppose this place is as good as any," Parkin said. "If this works at all."

Meggie sensed uncertainty in the man's mind. He had a task and wasn't sure how to do it. When he offered his hand to help her from the cart, she jumped down on her own, increasingly uneasy about what was happening.

"Sit over here." Parkin pointed to a spot under a tree on the edge of the clearing.

Meggie sat down, tugging the loose folds of the nightgown over her ankles. It was dusk and getting chilly.

Parkin took a rope from one of his men and tied it around the trunk of the tree, then deftly knotted it around Meggie's waist before she realized his intention. She tried to scramble away, but the rope was so short she couldn't even stand up. "What did Meggie do bad?" she said, baffled and frightened.

"The rope is so you'll stay put. We're going to hide in the bushes, so if you need help we're right here." He signaled to his men and they all withdrew into the thick shrubbery. Meggie could no longer see them, though she could sense their feelings. Parkin in particular burned with nervousness and anticipation.

Then . . . nothing. Time passed, night fell, and her fear faded away. She wrapped her arms close for warmth, and hoped this strange game would be over soon.

Simon woke from his standing doze. Now that night had fallen, it was time for him to start on his journey. He had decided that it was useless to stay near the castle and hope for a confrontation with Drayton. Several times he'd felt long-distance assaults from the renegade mage. Luckily, while Simon couldn't work conscious magic, his shields seemed strong enough to protect him. But the attacks forced him to the conclusion that he must seek help from other Guardians.

His best hope was to make his way to the estate of Lady Bethany Fox, the wise, elderly head of the Guardian Council. Her country house was perhaps a day's travel if he moved swiftly and evaded capture. Though he doubted she would be in residence, her servants would probably have the sense to summon her rather than trying to kill a unicorn that showed up on their doorstep. Simon and Lady Beth knew each other well enough that if the lady was summoned from London, she might be able to discern his identity, perhaps even remove the shape-changing spell.

He paused to drink from the small brook he had discovered. He was about to roll in the mud to disguise his white hide when he smelled an intoxicating fragrance. His nostrils flared involuntarily. A flower? No—nothing he had ever experienced before. This was the scent of . . . of innocence.

He turned and followed the ravishing fragrance. It was the promise of spring, of happiness, of the joyous simplicity of childhood before the dark complexities of adulthood. It was the celestial music of the spheres, as pure as angel song. As the tantalizing perfume grew stronger, he forgot his dilemma and his vague plans. All that mattered was finding this source of joy.

He reached the edge of a clearing and discovered that the source of the irresistible lure was a young girl in a flowing white gown. She sat beneath a tree, her knees drawn up and her arms wrapped around them. She rocked back and forth gently, her expression pensive as she gazed into the night. Waist-length dark hair spilled over her shoulders and gleamed in the reflected moonlight. His heart pounded as if he had galloped ten miles, for she radiated the purity he yearned for.

His instinct was to dash into the clearing, but he managed to contain himself for a moment, troubled by a memory that struggled to emerge from his inflamed mind. Though the maiden was purity and innocence, he sensed more than one kind of darkness around him. . . .

She turned and looked directly at him, and huge eyes widened in wonder. As soon as he heard her soft gasp, he was lost. Heedless of everything but blind need, he advanced into the clearing.

Meggie rocked quietly in the grass, deeply unhappy but unable to leave. She wanted this game to be *over* so she could return to her warm safe bed.

A faint movement caught her eye. She turned to see the most exquisite horse in the world at the edge of the clearing. It was pure white, its coat gleaming like silver in the moonlight. She inhaled sharply, sure she was dreaming. "Come, lovely one," she breathed.

The beast glided into the clearing, its steps so light they barely rippled the grass. As it approached, she saw a single horn spiraling from the creature's brow. She gasped again, understanding why Parkin had said this would be a special kind of horse. What was the word he had used? "Unicorn," that was it.

The unicorn's magical beauty made her ache. She tried to rise to greet it, only to lose her balance and sit clumsily again when the forgotten rope yanked her up short.

She muttered a word she'd heard spoken in the stables, then raised her hands in welcome as she marveled at the unicorn's unearthly beauty. The hooves were cloven like those of a deer, and the long tail was sinuous and tufted at the end like pictures she had seen of lions. It was male, she noticed. Very male.

The unicorn lowered his head, the sharp horn pointing straight at her, yet she knew he would not harm her. She sensed curiosity and a yearning that matched her own, and underneath, the pulse of a deeply wounded spirit.

"Come, sweeting," she whispered. She was good with horses, and perhaps she could soothe this one's distress.

With a last light step the unicorn bent his neck and stroked his horn against Meggie's cheek. Cool and smooth, the horn sent shivers of delight through her. It radiated a power unlike anything she'd ever known.

Murmuring endearments, she stroked the velvet-soft muzzle. The unicorn sighed deeply and lay down beside her, then rested his heavy head on her lap. Amazed, she caressed the silky neck, the warm flesh softer than the coat of any horse. Warmth radiated through her, heating places deep inside that had never known such feelings. She reached to touch the unicorn's spirit with her own.

Then the night exploded into shouts and violence. "Now!" Parkin roared, and half a dozen men burst from the shrubbery.

For a fatal moment the unicorn was motionless under Meggie's hands. Then he scrambled up, panic-stricken.

Meggie screamed, "Run!"

It was too late. A heavy net fell over the unicorn. As he fought the clinging cords, two men looped the ends of a rope around him, immobilizing the long graceful legs, then jerked the rope tight. The shining creature crashed heavily to the ground. Yet still he fought, hooves thrashing and horn stabbing.

A stable hand lashed the unicorn with a whip, then swore when his leg was grazed by a cloven hoof. He pulled out a knife. "Shall I hamstring the brute?"

As Meggie gasped with horror, Parkin replied, "No, it needs to be able to walk back to the castle. Put chokes around its throat."

The stable hands, used to dealing with troublesome horses, quickly tied enough ropes around the thrashing animal to completely control its movement. When they were done, the net was removed and the unicorn was allowed to rise. Again he tried to fight, but strangling ropes and freely applied slashes from the whips swiftly beat him into submission. Head down, he stood lathered with foam and blood.

"Time to go back to the castle," Parkin said. "There's a reward for all of you." He turned to Meggie. "You, too, girl. Guess you are a maiden still. Come on, now."

Too dispirited to flee, she climbed into the cart. But her long-clouded mind had begun to stir for the first time in years. The unicorn had been captured because of her.

Her fault. *Her fault.* Which meant Meggie must set the beast free.

There were advantages to being scorned and overlooked, Meggie found. She knew the castle and its outbuildings better than anyone, and no one took her seriously. In the day after the unicorn's capture, she planned how she would release him.

She thought it would be simple, since Parkin's precautions were aimed at keeping the unicorn from escaping, not preventing a person from getting in to see it. But the stone shed that had been turned into a unicorn jail was locked and guarded, and there were too many people moving around the courtyard.

Twice she tried to get into the shed, but the guards gruffly told her to go away, the beast was dangerous. Apparently his kicks had hurt some of the stable hands when he was released from his bonds.

Night would be quieter. After darkness fell, Meggie waited patiently in her room, wearing her darkest gown and her heavy brown winter cloak. Not until the great clock in the hall below struck three did she slip into the corridor. Earlier in the day, she had borrowed a handful of spare keys from a drawer in the steward's office. Maybe they would open any locks that might bar her way.

The night was cloudy and she smelled rain in the air. That might help the unicorn escape, if he could be freed in the first place.

With the lord away from the castle, the two watchmen on the gate were less alert than they should be. Knowing their positions, she was able to make her way through the shadows to the postern gate without being noticed. The unicorn would have to escape quickly, so she wanted this door to be unlocked and ready. The door had just been replaced because the beast had wrecked the old one two nights earlier, but they'd reused the same lock, and one of her keys opened it.

She made her way to the unicorn's shed. A guard stood watch outside. Meggie frowned. She hadn't expected the unicorn to be guarded all night. The fellow, different from the daytime guards, was broad and powerful, and he carried a shotgun. Maybe she should return to her bed and think of a new plan?

No. She squared her shoulders. She could feel the unicorn's anguish at his captivity. He must be freed, and more thinking wouldn't make it any easier. Worse, she had heard Parkin say the lord would return very soon to see his captive. She must act *now.*

Withdrawing to the castle wall, she found a fallen rock that fit her hand just right. She'd seen a man knocked witless when a branch fell on his head. If she had the courage, she could do that kind of damage.

Shaking with fear, she walked up to the guard, knowing he wouldn't be afraid of a small, weak female. "S . . . sir?" she asked meekly.

He tensed and swung the shotgun up. "What do you want, girl?"

"P . . . please, let Meggie see the unicorn?" For once, she was grateful for her stammer. No one could fear a simpleton with a stammer.

"Can't. I've orders this door isn't to be opened except by Mr. Parkin."

She tried the wheedling tone she'd heard a maid employ on a footman she was sweet on. "J . . . just a peek? Unicorn is ever so pretty."

The guard hesitated. "What will you do for me if I let you see him?" His gaze went over her with crude assessment. "All cats look black at night, and 'tis said you're a virgin, or the unicorn wouldn't have come." He lowered the gun, and stepped closer. "I like virgins. No pox."

Instead of fleeing, she stood her ground as he wrapped an arm around her and bent his head into a harsh kiss. Almost gagging, she slammed the rock in her right hand against his head, praying she would hurt him enough, but not too much.

Swearing, he staggered back, but didn't collapse. "You little bitch! You'll pay for that!" He lunged at her with bruising hands.

Terrified, she reached for his mind and *pushed.* Once she'd done the same when a sly ostler cornered her in the stable and put his hands all over her. He'd gone right to sleep, and she had run away.

When she pushed, the guard made a strangled sound and collapsed. Meggie felt a strange, distant twinge from the lord. He'd felt what she did to the guard, and it had caught some of his attention.

Blanking her mind so he would have no reason to look further, she tried the door to the shed. Locked—and none of her keys worked. Shaking, she searched the guard and found a key ring with a single large key. It slid into the lock and turned easily.

Before entering the shed, she tried to calm herself so that her fear wouldn't upset the unicorn. How intelligent was he? More so than a horse, maybe with enough wit to realize she had betrayed him. Maybe enough to stab her through the heart.

Praying that whatever attraction he'd felt for her would prevent that, she swung open the door and hoped.

Chapter FOUR

Immobilized by ropes and trapped in a windowless stone building, Simon had done his best to withdraw into the quiet of his own mind. Anger and battering at his bonds were futile. Better to inventory his memories of magic, and perhaps find a store of power to use against Drayton when the time came, for that time would surely be soon.

His drifting consciousness snapped to attention when he suddenly caught the scent of innocence that had enraptured him and led to his capture. Every muscle tensed and he instinctively moved toward the scent, only to be jerked to a halt by the ropes that held him in the center of the shed. He sniffed again, wondering if this was the same sweet female or another like her. The same, he decided. Her fragrance was so intense that she must be just outside the door.

She betrayed me to my doom. But not intentionally. Her cry of anguish when the hunters attacked had been genuine. Even if he knew that she would betray him again, he was unable to resist the sweet lure of her purity. He strained against his bonds, remembering the rapturous moment when he had laid himself at her feet.

The door swung open and a cloaked female silhouette appeared against the lesser dark of the night. "M . . . Meggie is sorry, sweeting," she said in an unsteady voice. "Meggie here to let you go." To his surprise, her words were accompanied by a distinct mental image of her releasing him from his bonds. She could mind-touch?

She stepped forward and banged into the rope that secured him on his right side. The impact jarred the cutting bit of the bridle that had been forced on him, hurting his tender mouth. When he shivered away from the pain, the maiden hissed a word that was not innocent, yet curiously endearing.

She must have brought a knife, for he could feel a blade sawing at the rope, accompanied by a murmuring of soft words. She was treating him as he would treat a nervous horse. He would have smiled wryly if he had been himself.

The line parted and she felt her way round him to find the left line. Once more the cutting. A quaver in her voice, she asked, "C . . . can you forgive Meggie for helping to capture you?"

He replied by rubbing against her affectionately, barely remembering to turn his head so he didn't stab her. He almost knocked her over in his enthusiasm. She laughed breathlessly and stroked his muzzle. The touch of her gentle fingers was exquisite. "N . . . nasty bridle. Will you be good if it comes off?"

He rubbed against her again, trying to indicate that he'd follow her anywhere as docile as a lamb. She must have understood, for she removed the wicked bridle and grasped a handful of his mane. "Must leave without being noticed."

Recalled from the fog of rapture she inspired, he stepped outside. A guard lay on the ground, moaning softly. Had his sweet maiden laid the fellow out? Impressed, Simon accompanied her through the shadows, his steps as light as he could make them. A light drizzle was starting to fall. Maybe that would aid their escape.

They were nearing the postern when the clouds broke and the light of a nearly full moon flooded the courtyard. A man yelled, "A thief is stealing the beast! Stop them!"

The blast of a shotgun pierced the night and a shower of vicious lead shot peppered Simon and his escort. The maiden flinched, then cried, "Go!"

Worried, he tried to see if she was hurt, but she released his mane and took off at a speed that proved she wasn't seriously injured. He followed, trying to place himself between her and the man with the shotgun. More shots blasted through the night, this time from the guard tower above the main gate.

The commotion had woken the castle and several men spilled into the courtyard just as Simon and the maiden reached the postern. She halted and said again, "Go!"

Aghast, he stopped in his tracks, nostrils flaring. She wasn't coming with him?

She made impatient shooing motions with both hands. "Meggie will be safe," she said bitterly. "They won't dare hurt the lord's pet simpleton."

Despite her words, he had no doubt that the approaching men would hurt her, perhaps very badly. He went down on one knee and imagined her mounting him.

She stared, shock on her narrow, angular face. Clearly she'd had no intention of leaving, perhaps couldn't even comprehend doing so.

Frightened for her safety and yearning for her presence, he whinnied and sent the riding image again. There was another ragged volley of musket shots, and this time he felt a searing pain in his left haunch, a wound far more severe than the birdshot.

His maiden bit her lip, radiating fear and confusion. Then she looked back at the approaching men and her expression changed to steely resolve. "Want to *go*."

She swung expertly onto his back. He scrambled to his feet and almost collapsed from the agony that blazed through his left leg. No bones seemed to be broken, so he tried to block out the pain as he bolted through the postern. A shiver of energy from the protective wards tingled his skin but didn't slow him.

The forest was less than a mile away, and they could lose themselves in its depths. He hardly noticed his maiden's weight, for even without a saddle she balanced lightly as a butterfly. Clouds covered the moon again and rain began falling harder, but his unicorn vision was uncannily sharp even in the dark.

They were halfway to the forest when he heard a thunder of hooves behind him. Some damnable person in the castle had organized a pursuit with wicked speed. If Simon was riderless and unwounded he could easily outrun the pursuers, but in his half-crippled state, they were gaining on him.

As thunder boomed and lightning lit up the sky, he dashed into the dark shelter of the woods. Branches lashed them as he followed an almost invisible track made by deer.

The pursuers followed easily, their speed barely diminished. One of them must have some magical tracking power. They would be on him in minutes, and what would happen to his maiden then? He had a horrible image of her raped and beaten, her sweet courage brutally crushed.

He tried to use his hunter's talent for concealment, but in his present form he couldn't wield his Guardian powers. Only the inherent magic of a unicorn was available. That gave him speed, strength, and heightened senses, but could not hide them from their pursuers. Frantic, he reached out mentally to his oldest friend, Duncan Macrae, the finest weather mage in Britain, perhaps in the world.

Help me!

Amazingly, he managed to reach Duncan, who was peacefully asleep at his home in Scotland. Jolted into wakefulness, Duncan responded with an incredulous, *Simon?*

Even as himself, it would have been almost impossible for Simon to explain the situation at such a distance. But desperation gave him the power to communicate a sense of where he was. He visualized a map of Britain where his position pulsed like a star. *Pursued! Storm?*

Duncan snapped to full wakefulness. *I'll see what weather you have to work with.* After a pause while he studied the weather patterns of Shropshire, he thought with satisfaction, *Excellent.*

Only moments passed before lightning slashed the sky and thunder shook the earth a bare instant later. The rain tripled in intensity, pounding with the force of a physical blow. Even though Simon was expecting this, for a moment he was thrown off his stride, slipping to his knees on the muddy track. His maiden lurched but maintained her seat.

He scrambled to his feet and resumed his flight through the forest, relying on his improved night vision to save him from crashing into a tree. Unfortunately his superior hearing could still hear hooves behind him, albeit at a slower pace. With his waning energy, he called Duncan again. *More?*

He thought he had failed to connect with his friend. Then he heard a faint, *More! Take care, Simon.*

The connection broke as Duncan concentrated all his power into his weather magic. The wind increased to near-hurricane force and trees began crashing to the earth behind Simon. A dead tree plummeted across the track too closely for Simon to swerve. Mustering all his strength, he leaped headlong over it. Scrawny branches scratched at his limbs but he managed to clear the trunk without falling.

Along with the turbulent weather, Simon sensed that Duncan was using Guardian magic to blur the trail. He must have guessed that for some reason Simon couldn't use shielding himself. Simon took advantage of the grace period Duncan had given them to run until his heart seemed nigh to bursting. Despite rain and wind, his precious rider clung like a burr.

When even hypersensitive unicorn hearing couldn't detect pursuit, Simon slowed to a walk, his lungs pumping like a bellows. Now what? He was cold, tired, and hurting, and the maiden must be chilled to the bone. They had to find shelter. In his previous exploration of the forest, he'd found a deep, rocky overhang. It was masked by thick underbrush, so there would be some protection from the still-heavy rain.

As he limped wearily through the night, he hoped his maiden knew something about treating wounds, or they might not be going anywhere in the morning.

Numb with cold, Meggie almost fell off the unicorn's back when he nosed through some underbrush below a huge overhanging rock and halted in the protected area underneath. She had thought their escape was doomed until the storm struck. Luck had been with them. Though she had been grazed by several shotgun balls, the hurts were small. She would be fine, if she didn't freeze before dawn.

The night was very black, but the unicorn's beautiful white coat made him dimly visible even under the rocks—except that part of him seemed to be missing, Worried, she touched the dark area on his left flank and raised her fingers to her lips, tasting the metallic tang of blood. He must have been wounded by a musket ball, which explained the increasing roughness of his gait during their escape.

The unicorn rubbed against her as if asking for help. The poor beast was trembling with fatigue, his sleek coat steaming from the cold rain that had fallen on his overheated body. "Meggie doesn't know what to do," she whispered, frustrated. "M . . . maybe if there was light."

Wait. She was wearing her cloak, and she usually carried a tinderbox in one pocket. She groped in the cloak and almost wept with relief when she found it. Now if she could find dry wood . . .

Cautiously she felt around in the dark under the deepest area of the overhang, hoping nothing nasty lived there. Once more her luck was in, and she found several dry, broken branches and a drift of leaves. She was responsible for the small fireplace in her castle bedroom, so even working in near-absolute darkness she was able to strike a spark onto the charred fabric from the tinderbox. When it caught, she carefully fed in bits of dried leaves, then twigs and kindling until she had a small fire burning.

She looked up to see the unicorn watching her. Was that worry she sensed from him? Aloud, she said, "N . . . no one will see the fire, and we need it."

Though the unicorn didn't reply, she suspected he understood her. He was far more than a horse. "Meggie will look at your wound after hands warm."

She held her numbed fingers over the fire and discovered that her right middle finger was bleeding, wounded by a ball from the shotgun. She sucked at the scrape to clean it, grateful the shot hadn't done more damage.

Later she could bandage the finger, but her injury was nothing compared to the gory slash on the unicorn's flank. Bending to avoid hitting her head on the stone overhang, she moved to his side. His horn caught the light of the fire, shimmering with rainbow highlights.

He nuzzled her affectionately and made a soft chirping sound. Touched, she hugged his neck for a long moment before examining his wound. It was deep and bleeding sluggishly. Though she'd always tended horses, she'd never seen a musket ball injury. "Ugly. Be still, sweeting, so Meggie can look closer."

She knelt by the unicorn's belly, not wanting to be behind those sharp rear hooves if he kicked. "S . . . steady . . ."

She leaned over and frowned, not liking the looks of the ragged wound. Was the musket ball buried inside?

She touched the gaping flesh—and the world exploded. A rush of heat blasted her backward as the unicorn vanished in a whirlwind of blazing energy and scalding light. The very air was warped, impossible to see through, but Meggie saw dimly that he was *changing.* Strange shapes were dimly visible as they twisted into stomach-churningly different forms. She cringed against the stone, terrified.

The blast of heat faded and the blurred air smoothed out, revealing the sprawled form of a human man. A completely naked man.

She pulled as far back as she could, whimpering. How could a unicorn turn into a man? How could there be a unicorn in the first place?

The interloper made no sound or movement. He looked like an angel fallen from heaven. Might he have been killed by that awful explosion?

Warily she forced herself to study the motionless body more closely. He lay on his side in a similar position to that of the unicorn. He was long and lean and fair, with blond hair spilling on the ground. His pale skin showed a peppering of small wounds like those made by a shotgun. And . . . and his left hip had a long, bleeding gash very like the unicorn's wound.

Not wanting to stare at his nakedness, she removed her sodden cloak and crept closer so she could cover him. There was a stark, honed beauty to his face and body. He looked intelligent and impatient and fatigued, but wholly human. He was also, to her relief, breathing.

Though she'd had no qualms when touching the glorious unicorn, she was reluctant to touch a strange man. Even one covered with goose bumps from the damp, chilly air. Carefully she draped the cloak over his long body.

His eyes opened.

Chapter FIVE

Simon was dragged from darkness by the touch of wet, heavy wool. When he opened his eyes, the maiden gasped and scrambled backward, her expression terrified. He couldn't blame her. The poor girl had experienced things that would have tested the mettle of an experienced Guardian.

He was lying on the cold ground, his left hand in front of him. His hand? Startled, he sat up. Pain seared through his left hip and he felt oddly awkward, not balanced in his body. But he had hands again, *hands!* With rising excitement he ran his hands over his bare torso. "God be thanked," he breathed. "I am myself again."

He felt a distant twitch from Drayton, who must have sensed this magical upheaval. Swiftly Simon covered himself and the girl with a blanking spell. Their escape would have been easier if he had been able to call such magic earlier.

Then he conjured a translucent, glowing sphere of mage light. It hovered just above his palm, final proof that his Guardian magic had returned. Delighted, he tossed the mage light upward to the stone overhang so it could light them both.

He turned his attention to his body. The maiden's wet cloak fell around his waist but kept him decent, barely. He donned the garment with care so his companion wouldn't be any more shocked than she was already. The cloak was cold and clammy, but loose enough to fit over his larger frame. A pity it wasn't half a yard longer.

Having sorted himself out, he studied his rescuer. She cowered under the stone overhang, her eyes wide with fear. The sight of her no longer produced intoxicated rapture, but he still found her distractingly attractive even though most men wouldn't give her a second glance. That must be a lingering effect of the unicorn spell.

Ignoring that attraction, he concentrated on mitigating her fear. Quietly he said, "My thanks for freeing me from a double captivity. Don't be afraid—I shan't hurt you."

She stared at the globe of mage light. "W . . . what *are* you?"

"Merely a man. My name is Falconer. And yours?"

"Meggie."

She was thin and plain and angular, with straight dark hair that fell in wet clumps around her narrow skull. Though her unfocused expression made her seem very young, the clarity of the mage light suggested that she was a woman grown. She had referred to herself as a simpleton, which would explain why she seemed so youthful. And yet . . .

Something about her wasn't right. He invoked mage vision, and saw a blurring of her features and form. Could there be an illusion spell overlaying a different reality? Such a thing would take great power if maintained indefinitely, and to what purpose?

Whatever the reason, she was certainly wrapped in magic. "You have been ensorcelled, Meggie," he said slowly.

She looked blank. "What?"

Given all the girl had seen, she deserved to know what was going on, but first he would warm them both up. He gestured toward the fire. It flared bright and hot.

Meggie drew closer to the flames, reaching out her hands eagerly. "What did you do? There was only a bit of wood."

He settled on the opposite side of the fire, so close that steam rose gently from the dark folds of the cloak. "Do you know anything of magic? The ability to draw power from nature and shape it to other uses?"

She shook her head.

"Magic is not rare," he said. "Many people have at least a touch of magic in their souls. I come from a group of families called Guardians. Most of us have a great deal of magical talent. Often we live in the wilder Celtic fringes of Britain, where the magic is strongest. When Guardians are on the verge of adulthood, we must swear oaths to use our power for protection and to help others rather than using it for personal gain."

"H . . . how does magic work?" She gestured toward the fire, which was burning merrily despite the shortage of fuel.

"There are many kinds of spells and rituals, but at heart, magic is about will. If one desires a particular result, such as a good fire, and has magical power, that desire helps achieve the result. With great power, one can do great and difficult things."

Interest glinted in her dull eyes. "There are other men like you?"

"Both men and women. Some of the most powerful mages—wielders of magic—are female. I am a Guardian, and so is Lord Drayton, your master."

Her expression closed. "If *he* has power, 'tisn't used to help anyone."

"Drayton is a renegade. I called at Castle Drayton several days ago to stop him from causing more damage." And damned overconfident Simon had been. "I thought my power equal to anything he might do. I was wrong, and he used his magic to turn me into a unicorn."

Meggie's jaw dropped. "You really *are* the unicorn!"

"Indeed, and I would like to know how I changed back to my real self, but I'll consider that later." Meggie was a vital part of this puzzle, that he knew. "I believe that Lord Drayton laid spells on you. Was there ever a time when you were near him, and suddenly you felt different?"

Her mouth twisted. "He found Meggie in a field. One touch and . . . and everything changed to *this*." Her gesture encompassed herself and probably her whole life.

"How long has that been?"

She looked away. "Long. Years."

"I would like to try to remove the spells that bind you."

She blinked like an anxious mouse. "W . . . will it hurt?"

"It shouldn't, but you might feel strange. Confused. Will you trust me to try?"

She bit her lip, then nodded.

He moved around the fire until he could sit next to her. His human feet noticed the rough ground far more than hooves had. "Just relax and let me hold your hands."

Her fingers trembled when she reached for his clasp, and her skin was cold despite the increased heat of the fire. He closed his eyes and cleared his mind of the pain and fear and humiliation he'd experienced since his confrontation with Drayton.

When he was centered, he laid a calming spell over Meggie and began gently exploring the magic knotted around her deepest self. The darkness of Drayton's energy was everywhere. Simon would have to work very carefully to avoid damaging her.

As he'd suspected, the highest layer of the tangled web was an illusion spell that changed the way people perceived Meggie. It was easily dissolved, since matter resisted being distorted by illusion.

He opened his eyes to see what she really looked like and caught his breath. Drayton had very cleverly conserved power by making only subtle shifts in her appearance, but those changes had warped what was delicate and graceful into a form and face that were awkward and angular. Meggie's coarse skin was now smooth, her dark hair had acquired thickness and gloss, and her features were well shaped and appealing. Her real self was an attractive young woman.

Closing his eyes, he resumed his work. The bindings on her mind and personality were far more complex and deeply rooted than the illusion spell. One dark knot of power strangled her intelligence, another subdued her natural personality. No wonder she seemed simple. It spoke well for her basic character that even crippling magic hadn't been able to suppress the courage that had led a terrified girl to free a unicorn.

When he finished untangling the web of spells, he was surprised to find a shielded sphere that shimmered like a silver apple. Simon explored it warily, wondering what it contained. He sensed that it held a part of Meggie rather than a trapped spirit entity that might be malevolent. A silver thread spun away from the sphere to vanish into the distance. Guessing that it connected her to Drayton, Simon visualized a silver knife and used it to cut the thread.

Then he turned his attention to the shining sphere. Destroying it would be a risk, but if he didn't try, Meggie would not be whole.

After encompassing the sphere in a bubble of his own power, he gradually poured in more and more magic. Rainbow hues glimmered across the bright surface. He was nearing the limits of his power when the silver apple exploded into a torrent of magic, like an unearthly butterfly smashing from its chrysalis.

With a wordless cry of anguish, Meggie jerked out of Simon's clasp and folded over on herself, burying her face in her hands. Silver light raged through her body, like a dam breaking. Only instead of contained water being released into its natural channel, this was a tidal wave of magic.

"Gods above," he gasped. "You are a mage. Or will be, with training." No wonder Drayton could afford the energy required by the illusion spell—he had been able to use Meggie's own power to maintain it. Her blazing magic equaled that of the most gifted Guardians Simon had ever known.

Though he wanted to comfort Meggie with a touch, he controlled the impulse. Her energy must find its own balance without interference from him.

Gradually her ragged breathing slowed. She straightened to face him.

Simon caught his breath again, for the transformation in her appearance was greater than when he had lifted the illusion spell. Her features had been reshaped, bringing her alive as a woman of force and intelligence.

Her gaze focused on Simon. "God *damn* the man!" she said in a bone-chilling whisper. "May he rot in hell for what he did to me!"

Her stammer had vanished and her accent was educated. Glad that her rage wasn't directed toward him, Simon asked, "How much do you understand of what happened?"

She frowned and rubbed at her temple. The wet hair was drying and firelight touched it with auburn highlights. "I know that I have been that monster's slave for many years, and from what you say, he used magic to do it. I have been living as a shadow under his roof, ignored and neglected except when he ravished my mind."

"Ravished your mind? What do you mean?"

She looked away. "He entered my mind and . . . and he stole my soul. Again and again and again. After the worst times, I would sleep for hours and have nightmares."

As soon as Simon understood what she was saying, he swore. "Damnation, he's been stealing your power and binding you so tightly that you didn't even realize your own abilities. No wonder he was able to overpower me when I confronted him—he was using your magic in addition to his own. He must have recognized your potential as it was starting to bloom, and he captured that power for himself."

She nodded slowly. "He said something like that the day he changed me—that I didn't know what I was. It made no sense."

"You must be a Guardian yourself, Meggie. Is that for Margaret?" He tried to remember if any Guardian children had disappeared under mysterious circumstances in the last few years. "You're tremendously gifted."

She thought, then shook her head. "My name is Meg, not Meggie. Not Margaret. But what you say makes no sense. I have no special ability. I am *nothing.*"

"That's not true. For years Drayton stole your magic, but he can do that no longer. Now you are free to soar." Since she was still shaking her head doubtfully, he asked, "What do you remember of your home and family?"

She closed her eyes and thought, then opened them again, expression stark. "I . . . I can't remember anything before the day Lord Drayton took me prisoner."

"You said you were in a field. Do you remember where?"

She shrugged helplessly. "Just a field. Maybe near here, maybe far."

"Your accent sounds as if you come from this border area between England and Wales, but you might have picked that up by living in Castle Drayton." Simon tried another tack. "Do you remember the date you were captured? Or at least the year?"

Her brow furrowed with effort. "I . . . I think it was the year of our Lord 1738."

"You have been his captive for ten whole years." It was an effort for Simon to keep his rage at Drayton from his voice. "If you were on the verge of coming into your power, you were probably thirteen or fourteen then. That would make you twenty-three or twenty-four now." She looked younger, but that wasn't surprising, given that she'd lost ten years of normal experience. "What was your life like? Did you ever leave the castle?"

"I wandered around the castle grounds, but never beyond." She frowned. "Whenever I approached the estate boundary, something always made me turn back."

"One of Drayton's spells must have been designed to keep you from escaping."

"I never thought to try. Mostly I drifted about like a . . . a feather in a pond. Usually I was with the horses or in the forest. The housekeeper made sure I received food and new clothing when necessary. The lord would enter my mind whenever he wanted—it didn't matter where I was." She shuddered. "Sometimes he summoned me to his study so he could experiment. Those times were worst."

Simon could only imagine the horrors Drayton had inflicted on Meg. Though her body might be virginal, she had lost her innocence the day she was captured.

Her fingers twisted together, locking in her lap. "Who am I? Why can I remember nothing except my Christian name?"

Hearing the pain in her voice, he said, "Your mind has been dampened for many years, so it's not surprising your memory is imperfect. Give it time to heal."

Her gaze met his. Her eyes were a smoky gray green. "Do you think it will?"

"I don't know," he admitted. "I've never heard of a case like yours. But your intelligence and understanding seem to have recovered immediately, so I think there's a good chance you will regain the rest of your mental faculties."

She rubbed her temple fretfully. "It feels like he's still in my mind even though he left for London two days ago. Can he reach me from such a distance?"

Simon swore again, this time to himself. In his haste, he hadn't taken the time to check that he'd fully severed the energy line that connected Meg to Drayton. He surveyed her energy field for the remnant of the silver thread.

Not only had he failed to fully cut the connection, but the line was intact and pulsing with a dark energy that had to come from Drayton.

Simon concentrated his power, then slashed at it. The thread continued to pulse no matter how hard he tried to sever it. Drayton was still hooked into Meg's energy—and growing more furious by the minute.

Since he couldn't cut the thread, Simon mentally grasped the shimmering strand and twisted a complex knot so that energy could no longer flow. Darkness vibrated angrily on the far side as Drayton hit the block. After a period of increasing tension, the darkness vanished, leaving only the silver strand. "I believe I've stopped Drayton from reaching your mind, at least temporarily," Simon said. "Is he gone?"

Her eyes widened. "I can't feel him anymore. God be thanked! I don't want him in my mind ever again." She frowned. "You said it's temporary?"

"Since I was unable to sever the connection between you, I created a block so Drayton can't reach you. The block should hold for a while, though I don't know how long. You're safe for now, and with help, we should find a way to cut the connection permanently. But now we must leave the area before he can find us." Simon glanced into the forest, where the downpour had settled into a misty drizzle. "Not that we would want to linger here anyhow."

She bit her lip. "I . . . I haven't thought about what I should do next."

"You are welcome in any Guardian household. We are about a day's ride from the country house of Lady Bethany Fox, head of the Guardian Council. When we reach there, I'll send a message to London and ask her to join us. Lady Beth will be happy to give you a home while you come to terms with your new situation."

"Thank you for not abandoning me."

"Of course I won't. You saved my life. Drayton had every intention of killing me when he returned to the castle."

Her gaze snapped back to him. "Why would he want to murder you?"

"He believed my natural magic was concentrated in the unicorn horn. By killing me, he could possess that magic for himself." Briefly Simon wondered why Drayton was so hell-bent on accumulating power, but that was also a question for another day.

His injured hip was paining him, so he raised the edge of the cloak and examined the wound. The bleeding had largely stopped, but it would start again when he became more active. He scanned lightly with his fingertips, using a healing spell that reduced the chances of infection. Luckily the musket ball hadn't lodged in his flesh. Or the unicorn's flesh. Whichever, he was fortunate that the wound wasn't worse, but it needed bandaging or he risked bleeding to death when he started walking.

"That wound needs binding," Meg said. "I can spare a petticoat."

He wondered if she was reading his mind, or just being practical. "Thank you. I will owe you a whole wardrobe when we get to safety."

A glint of humor showed in her smoky eyes. "I will need one."

He looked away while she removed the petticoat. A few rips, and she was able to deliver a double handful of damp but clean strips. "Do you need help?" she asked.

"I can manage." Though a hip was not easily bandaged, he managed to fix a heavy pad over the wound. The two of them were getting adept at doing intimate things without offending the other person's modesty.

When he'd finished with his bandaging, he rolled the kinks from his shoulders wearily. Apart from a phantom desire to stamp his hooves, he was as fit as he could be under the circumstances, so it was time to move on. "I hate to drag you out into the rain again, but we should leave now. I left my horse in a field not far from the castle, and that's a long walk from here. I hope we can reach him before dawn—we don't want to be seen in that area."

Meg cocked her head. "Why are you sure the horse is still there? I should think that whoever owned the field would have noticed and captured your mount already."

"I put a don't-see spell on Shadow. He's not invisible, but people will look away and not notice him." Simon grimaced. "Unfortunately, I left him saddled because I thought I would be gone a few hours at most and might need to leave quickly. There was grazing and water in the field, but he's going to be a very unhappy horse."

"I can call horses," Meg said. "I should be able to bring him right to us."

Simon blinked, but remembered how well Meg had communicated with him when he was in unicorn form. "Is it possible with a horse you've never met who is several miles away?"

"Isn't it worth trying? Your mount's name is Shadow. What does he look like and where did you leave him?"

"He's a tall dark bay with a white sock on his left fore. He's steady of disposition with tremendous staying power. And, as I said, saddled. The bridle I put in my saddlebags, so let's hope he hasn't rolled and managed to free himself of saddle and bags." Simon went on to describe the horse's location in relation to the castle.

Meg nodded and closed her eyes. In the flickering light, her face had the pensive sweetness of a Renaissance Madonna. He still felt an echo of the obsessive attraction he'd experienced as a unicorn. Like the desire to stamp his feet, that should fade now that he was himself again.

But in the meantime, he enjoyed watching her.

Though Meg had never called a strange horse from such a distance, it wasn't difficult. Shadow was restless and unhappy, so his energy stood out from that of the more placid horses in the area. She visualized the description Falconer had given her, then the location. All the facts resonated together: this was the horse. Gently she touched his mind. For as long as she could remember, she had been doing this from instinct. Now she reached out consciously. *Come to your master, Shadow. He needs you.*

The horse lifted his head as if he'd heard a physical voice. *Jump the fence and follow my call through the forest. Do you understand?* She sent an image of him flying over the fence, then trotting through the night to reach Falconer.

Shadow understood. Glad for action, he headed for the fence, his speed increasing with every powerful stride. Meg stayed in contact with his mind, not wanting the horse to get lost or confused. She also persuaded him to keep his pace moderate. It wouldn't do for him to reach their refuge exhausted.

When she was sure that Shadow was on the right track and happy to follow her guidance, she opened her eyes. "He's on his way. It will take some time. You covered much ground through the forest when we were escaping."

He smiled at her. "If you doubted that you have magic, doubt no more. I could have called Shadow for a short distance, but what you just did is much rarer. It will be interesting to see what you can do after you receive training in how to use your power." He smothered a yawn. "We might as well rest until he arrives. It's been a very long day." After a gesture that caused the mage light to vanish, Falconer pulled the damp cloak around himself and lay down on the opposite side of the fire.

Meg lay down also, but her mind churned with questions. "How do Guardians keep their abilities secret from everyone else?"

Voice drowsy, Falconer said, "We are trained from childhood not to use our powers in front of mundanes, which is what we call those without magic. If a mundane witnesses something he shouldn't, a mild spell of forgetting usually takes care of that. Our servants are from families that have served us for generations." He yawned. "Also, people generally see what they expect to see. They don't expect to see magic."

Meg had endless other questions, but she suppressed her curiosity since Falconer was clearly exhausted. Her mind didn't stop spinning, though. Her companion actually respected her abilities. That had never happened before. She had been somewhere between useless and a nuisance for as long as she could remember. The lord had used her mind, but that had been punishment. He had shown her neither courtesy nor respect.

Perhaps she should have been shocked by Falconer's talk of magic, but his explanation had made sense of a world she'd never understood—not to mention explaining why he'd been a unicorn mere hours before. She had never thought of her ability to call horses as magic, but perhaps it was—she knew no one else who could do it.

What had he said about using magic? That it was about desire and power. Frowning, she opened her hand and imagined a globe of mage light on her palm.

A softly glowing sphere appeared, the bottom tickling her palm. Pleased, she poked the sphere and felt a faint, not unpleasant, tingling. The ball of light didn't have a definite edge. Rather, it was like bright fog. She squeezed her hand and felt the tingling through all her fingers, while the light continued to glow around her fist.

Experimentally she tossed the light upward as Falconer had done. It vanished in mid-flight instead of attaching itself to the rock above. She gazed at the spot where it had disappeared. Though she had much to learn, she was beginning to believe that she really did have magical power. The thought was awesome and a little frightening.

She wondered what would become of her. Though she was now free, she could remember no home, no family, not even her last name. Thank God Falconer didn't mean to abandon her. The thought of calling on the aristocratic Lady Bethany was alarming, but not so alarming as being left alone with no friends or skills. The lord would surely find her again before long, a thought that made her shudder. She needed to learn how to protect herself from him, and she could learn that only from Falconer's Guardians.

Eyes closed, she explored the dimensions of her mind. She felt as if she had been drowning in molasses forever. Now her mind was swift and restless as a sparrow. Questions and ideas spun in all directions. It was hard to believe how slow and docile she had been. She hadn't even known what the word "docile" meant. She felt like a new person, but her new self was rooted in the stunted girl she had been for so long.

Falconer had said that her memory should heal. Praying that was true, she drew as close to the fire as she could get without scorching, and finally dozed off.

Restless dreams disturbed her. She was a swallow, soaring giddily through the sky. Then a great hawk swooped from above, rending her with cruel claws. The shock jerked her awake. When she dozed again, similar dreams plagued her to wakefulness.

The rain had stopped and the sky was pinkening in the east when a soft equine whicker announced that Shadow had arrived. Simon was awake and on his feet while Meg was still blinking blearily. She wondered if he was a soldier to have such alertness.

The horse butted his master in a demand for attention. "Your magic worked, Meg," Falconer said as he greeted his mount affectionately. "Shadow has done some rolling in the grass, which did the saddle no good, but saddle and bags are still here."

Meg stood and stretched, feeling stiff and grubby but happy. This was the first day of her new life. While much was uncertain, she had escaped from the lord and she had talents she had never known about. She moved into the shrubbery to relieve herself in privacy. By the time she returned, Falconer was properly dressed in the garb of a sober country gentleman. Even with wrinkled clothing and his fair hair tied back, he drew the eye. He had the same lean elegance as a man that he'd had as a unicorn.

"I'm particularly glad that Shadow returned with the saddlebags," he remarked. "Besides the bridle, they contained a change of clothing. No riding boots or hat, but at least I have a decent pair of shoes."

He shook out her cloak, now dry, and returned it to her. She donned it gratefully. Away from the magical fire, the morning air was chilly.

Falconer studied a handsome pocket watch for a moment, then snapped it shut and tucked it into his pocket. "I am fortunate that I left this in my spare breeches. Or perhaps it was intuition, not luck. I should have listened to my intuition more closely."

"Your magic didn't warn you there would be trouble?"

"Magic has its limits. If it didn't, we'd be gods." After slipping the bridle on the horse, Falconer dug into his saddlebags again. "I have a few currant cakes packed here. They might be broken, but at least they're food."

"Thank you." She accepted the broken halves of a cake eagerly. "Can you conjure up a cup of hot mint tea to go with it?"

"Ordinarily I'd say no because it would require a tremendous amount of power to create something from nothing. But as it happens . . ." He produced a flask with a flourish. "This contains China tea. It's several days old, but heated it should taste all right."

He removed the stopper and made a small gesture. Steam began to rise from the neck of the flask. He handed it to Meg.

"It's *wonderful.*" She swallowed to wash down the currant cake and almost scalded her tongue from the heat. "At the castle, we almost never had China tea because it was so expensive. Only the lord and the upper servants drank it regularly."

After a second, slower, sip, she returned the flask. Mint tea was nice, but China tea was better.

He took a swallow and was about to hand the flask back when he froze, his expression grim. "Searchers are leaving the castle to look for us. The rain washed out our tracks last night, but the leader of the group has some magic, and it's being enhanced by Drayton. Time we were on our way."

After Meg swallowed the last of her currant cake and washed it down with tea, Falconer stoppered the flask and put it into the saddlebag. He swung up onto Shadow's back, then offered his hand to help her up behind him. After she settled onto the saddlebags, they set off toward the north.

Shadow had such a smooth, steady gait that Meg hardly needed to hold on to Falconer. She glanced back toward their refuge, already concealed by greenery—and was startled to see that the horse left no tracks. "You're able to make Shadow's hoofprints vanish?"

"They exist, but a small illusion spell conceals them. A powerful mage would not be fooled, but the group from the castle might be. It will be interesting to see if Drayton's enhancement will enable our pursuers to see through my spell."

"This ability to enhance troubles you," she said tentatively.

"Drayton is using the energy of others in ways I have not seen before. That could be very dangerous." Falconer's voice was edged. "I shall not underestimate him again."

Meg kept a respectful silence for some time, but her curiosity eventually overcame her. "Can you tell me more about Guardian powers? For example, your ability to sense our pursuers leave the castle. With training, might I be able to do that?"

"You should be able to scry, but what I did was different. There are a number of magics that can be done by any trained Guardian. In addition, most of us also have some special talents—gifts that often run in families. Falconers have always been hunters. That includes skills such as sensing pursuit."

"What do you hunt?"

"Other Guardians," he said dryly. "Most members of the Families are thoughtful men and women who believe in our code of honor. But power is tempting, so the Guardian Council works to ensure that power is not misused. It is my task to ensure that the code is followed."

He said no more, but Meg guessed that he had always been successful in his work, until his encounter at Castle Drayton. When justice was administered to the lord, she hoped that she would be there to applaud.

It was a relief to finally reach Lady Bethany's estate after an endless day of riding and walking. The journey could have been shorter, but Simon preferred to take paths that avoided human habitation. After Meg's initial questions, they traveled in silence. Simon monitored their pursuers, who managed to come close to where the fugitives spent the night before they lost the track. The leader was frantic to find the escaped unicorn, but even augmented by his master's power, he failed. He would pay for that failure when Drayton returned home.

After they'd put distance between themselves and their pursuers, Simon slowed the pace and dismounted to lighten Shadow's burden. Later, Meg slid from the horse and insisted he take a turn riding. He protested—it seemed ungentlemanly to ride while a woman walked—but she was adamant. Given that his light shoes weren't designed for hiking and his wounded hip hurt like the devil, he appreciated the intervals on horseback.

Midnight was approaching when they entered the long, winding driveway that led up to White Manor, Lady Bethany's house. Simon had stayed there often, and the manor was a welcome sight.

Since lamps burned inside the structure, he wasn't entirely surprised when the front door of the manor was flung open and Lady Bethany swept down the steps, two servants behind her. A footman carried a torch and the other man was her head groom. "Simon, you rascal! What sort of trouble have you found for yourself?"

"Lady Beth!" He slid from the horse and bent to envelop her in a hug. "I thought you would be in London. You're a sight for weary eyes."

"I had a feeling that I should be here." She turned to Meg. "And who is this young lady?"

Meg was staring, unable to reconcile the aristocratic title with the warm, rounded, grandmotherly reality of Lady Bethany. "This is Meg, to whom I am greatly in debt." Simon helped Meg dismount. Voice low, he added, "She is one of us, and discovered that only last night."

Lady Bethany's eyes widened. "My, child, you positively glow with power. You must have tales to tell. Where have you been hiding yourself?"

"It's a long story." Simon handed his horse's reins to the groom. "Take good care of him, Wilson. Shadow has had a hard day and deserves to be pampered."

"It will be my pleasure, my lord."

Meg looked at Simon with shock and distrust. Maybe he should have mentioned that he was an earl, but when they were running for their lives, his title hadn't seemed relevant. Drayton must have given her a deep distaste for noblemen. He hoped it wouldn't take too long to change her mind. As they ascended the stairs together, he said, "Lady Beth, did your premonition about our arrival extend to preparing food and beds?"

"Only one bedroom was prepared, but another will be ready soon," she said imperturbably. "I'll allow you time to eat before I bombard you with questions. It's fortunate for your appetites that patience comes with age."

Their hostess gave them a few minutes to wash up before they assembled in the small dining room. A steaming tureen of chicken and barley soup was accompanied by platters of cold meats and cheeses.

Meg had made an attempt to neaten her battered gown and tangled hair, but she looked tense and very young. Her unease was forgotten when the footman served supper. Having had only two currant cakes all day, she attacked her food with enthusiasm, and surprisingly refined manners. Simon was equally hungry, but when he started to serve himself a slice of roast beef, his stomach clenched. He wondered if that was an effect of having spent time as a grazing beast. Luckily the chicken in the soup didn't bother him.

True to her word, Lady Bethany gave them a chance to take the edge off their hunger before asking, "Can we speak freely in front of Meg, Simon?"

He swallowed his mouthful of soup. "Yes—she's right in the middle of this situation. Plus, she knows nothing of her heritage, and the sooner she learns, the better. Meg, would you like to tell Lady Bethany your story?"

She glanced up. "You may tell her . . . my lord."

He winced inwardly at her tone when she used the title. "I am no different now than I was this morning."

"You may not be different, my lord, but I see you differently." Her gaze dropped to her bread and cheese.

Tersely he described Meg's life and her lack of memories of any earlier time. "But she's clearly a Guardian," he said to Lady Beth. "Do you know if any child of the Families disappeared or was stolen about ten years ago?"

His hostess shook her head. "I recall no such case. Perhaps only her father was a Guardian. Or perhaps she has wild magic."

"It's almost unknown for anyone to have wild magic of such strength." More likely, Meg had been fathered by a Guardian and was illegitimate. Guardians were seldom promiscuous because of their emotional sensitivity, but there were exceptions.

Meg asked, "What is wild magic?"

"Magical power that is found in people with no obvious magical heritage," Simon explained. "Wild magic is rare and seldom as strong as Guardian magic. It can also be unpredictably different from Guardian magic."

Meg's eyes narrowed. "What do you do with those who have wild magic? Eliminate them to prevent competition?"

"Heavens, no, child!" Lady Bethany exclaimed. "We usually adopt them into the Guardians. The Families have gained valuable new abilities that way." She glanced at Simon. "Your last letter said you were planning to confront Drayton about his misdeeds. What went awry?"

"He turned me into a unicorn so he could slaughter me with ritual magic."

The usually imperturbable lady gasped. "Surely he would not do anything so barbaric!"

"You're an optimist, Lady Beth," Simon said dryly before he continued his story.

When he described their escape, Meg said, "We were really lucky that storm came along to wash away our tracks."

Lady Bethany's silvery brows arched. "Was it luck, Simon?"

He shook his head. "I put out a call to Duncan Macrae for help. Woke him out of a sound sleep. Fortunately, he understood what I needed and was able to locate me precisely, and the existing weather was bad enough to give him material to work with."

Meg's jaw dropped. "You can control rain and wind?"

"I can't, but my friend Duncan can. Ordinarily I wouldn't have been able to reach him where he lives in Scotland, but sometimes desperation can increase power."

Looking thoughtful, Meg returned to her meal. Simon wondered how long it would take her to adjust to a world so different from Castle Drayton. Luckily, she had a quick mind now that she was freed from thralldom. "Meg not only released me from imprisonment, but she returned me to human form. I have no idea how."

Meg shrugged. "I didn't do anything. I was only looking to see how badly you were injured. As soon as I touched the wound . . ." She struggled to find words. "It was like a lightning strike. The air became strange, twisted, and you radiated heat. I'm not sure how long that lasted, but when everything returned to normal, you were a man."

"The heat makes sense," Lady Bethany said musingly. "When you changed from a smaller to a larger form, you must have drawn energy to create a larger body. When you returned to the smaller form, you would have radiated that energy back to the world. But how did Meg's touch break the transformation spell?"

"I had an open, bleeding wound, and Meg, you had received some grazes as well. Was there an open wound on your fingers when you touched me?"

Surprised, she said, "Yes. It was small, but there was blood."

"That's the answer. This young lady glows with raw magic." Lady Bethany's brow furrowed as she looked deeper. "So much so that when her blood touched yours, the spell was broken. Or rather, suppressed for the time being."

Simon frowned. "You think that the spell might be revitalized?"

The older woman examined him with unfocused eyes. "I fear so. The magic is still around you, and this sort of spell can be broken only by the mage who created it."

His mouth tightened as she confirmed his fears. "In other words, I might turn into a unicorn again at any moment."

She looked troubled. "I think the spell is unlikely to overcome you when you're aware and shielded, but yes, transforming again is a real danger."

"What if I meet Drayton face-to-face?"

"Be very, very careful and keep your shields at full strength."

This was not good news. "I shall have to keep you close if that happens, Meg. I found that being a unicorn was not good for mind or spirit."

Meg looked alarmed before recognizing that he wasn't serious. "Perhaps you should carry a vial of Guardian blood if you call on him again."

"That might actually work." Lady Bethany studied Meg thoughtfully. "What of you, young lady? Have you recalled more about your past?"

The girl set down her bread, expression bleak. "Nothing. The first thing I remember is the day the lord approached me in the field, laid a hand on my head, and paralyzed my will and spirit."

"Even though you have no earlier memories, are you finding anything familiar? Or unfamiliar? Do you think you grew up in a house like this one?"

Meg studied the damask-clad walls and fine furnishings before she shook her head. "No, this house is very grand and . . . and unfamiliar. Not like the castle, and not like any other place I've lived. I'm sure of that."

"Can you read and write?"

Meg hesitated. "I . . . I think so, but I didn't do either at the castle."

Lady Bethany rose and removed a slim book from a drawer in the sideboard. Handing it to Meg, she asked, "Can you read this?"

She opened the book warily, then relaxed. "Yes! It's difficult because I haven't read in so many years, but the words make sense to me."

"So you had some education."

"Her speech and manners are refined as well," Simon pointed out. "So she must have spent her childhood in a household of some substance."

"Can you help me find my family?" Meg asked, her expression hopeful. "You're mages—surely that can't be too hard."

"With ten years gone by and no idea of where to start, finding your kin won't be easy, but we will certainly try. I promise that," Lady Bethany said. "But not tonight. You're almost asleep in your chair, Meg. Let me take you to your room. A good night's sleep makes life look more possible. Simon, I'll join you in the morning room after I've settled Meg. We have more to discuss."

An understatement of major proportions. As he watched the two women leave the dining room, he wished he could believe that Lady Bethany would have all the answers he needed. But he knew better than to believe that, even for a moment.

SEVEN

Lady Bethany was right—Meg was ready to drop from fatigue. Nonetheless, she found it unnerving to leave Falconer, the only familiar person in this grand house. Though Lady Bethany had been nothing but kind, she had a degree of confidence Meg had never seen in a woman. During Meg's time in Castle Drayton, there had been few women in her life. The castle had been a coarsely masculine place. White Manor was very different, with her ladyship's feminine touch visible everywhere.

At the west end of the upstairs corridor, Lady Bethany opened a door. "This will be your room. Usually I put my granddaughters here."

Meg gave a sigh of pleasure when she entered the bedchamber, which was a fluffy, pretty confection of light colors and flowered fabrics. Wanting to see more than was illuminated by the single candle, she created a ball of light. "How lovely! I'm sure I'll be comfortable here."

Lady Bethany closed the door behind them. "Where did you learn to make mage light? Did Simon show you how?"

"Not exactly." Meg attached her first light to a post at the foot of the bed, then created another, larger light. "I saw him do it, then tried it myself."

In the gentle glow of the mage lights, Lady Bethany's expression was thoughtful. "He makes creating light look easy, but it isn't. I'm impressed that you are able to do it without any lessons at all."

Meg envisioned another glowing sphere on her palm, then examined it. "The first time was a bit difficult, but now it's simple. I think of light, and here it is."

"Your innate power is truly impressive." Lady Bethany gestured at the bed. "But for now, you need rest. Here's a nightgown, and there are some garments in the wardrobe that should do until we can have more made up for you."

Meg touched the nightgown, which was of fine white cotton with delicate lace trim. She couldn't remember ever owning anything so pretty in her life. Her room at the castle had been comfortable enough, but stark, and her clothing had been sewn by a woman in the village whose main interest had been in providing rugged garments that would last well. Meg had found beauty in the forest and the animals, but not in her daily life. "I don't know how to thank you," she said in a low voice.

"What we give is yours by right. Sleep well, Meg. Everything will seem easier in the morning." Lady Bethany kissed Meg's cheek, then quietly withdrew.

Meg raised a hand to her cheek, thinking that perhaps somewhere in the forgotten part of her life, there had been a mother who had kissed her with affection. Perhaps Meg had a living family.

Praying that her memory would return so she could find her beginnings, she explored the room. The carpet was soft beneath her feet, and when she removed her muddy garments and donned the nightgown, it whispered smoothly against her skin. A pitcher full of hot water stood on the washstand. She washed her face and hands, thankful for the luxury. The comb and brush on the vanity table were backed with silver. As she brushed the knots from her hair, she began to relax. This world might be strange, but it was welcoming. Somehow, she would find a place in it.

A glass of brandy in his hand, Simon prowled the morning room restlessly, tired but unable to settle down. When he reached the fireplace, he ignited the coals with a snap of his fingers. Though the night wasn't cold, the flickering flames were comforting.

Lady Bethany returned from taking Meg to her bedroom. "Did you know your protégé can conjure mage light as well as you do?"

His brows arched. "I didn't, but I'm not really surprised to hear it. When Drayton transformed me, he was drawing on a huge well of power, and most of it came from Meg. She'll probably be the fastest-learning mage in Guardian history."

"Which means she needs good training right away, before she damages herself or others." Lady Beth settled into a chair by the fireplace. "I wouldn't want her to discover how to burn the house down in her sleep. Speaking of Drayton, what do you think he wants? He must have known that he couldn't destroy you and not be punished for it. Even with Meg's power to draw on, he couldn't resist the force of the whole council."

"I wish I knew what he wants. He was stirring up trouble during the Jacobite rebellion and he seemed to be doing it indiscriminately rather than in support of the king or the Young Pretender." Simon lifted the poker from its hook and stabbed at the glowing coals. "Perhaps he feeds on pain and wants to create more of it."

"Perhaps, but I suspect that he has other goals in mind as well," Lady Beth said thoughtfully. "No Guardian has ever been a cabinet minister before; members of the Families tend to avoid such public positions. Do you suppose he craves worldly power?"

"Unquestionably." Simon analyzed some of the lower levels of Drayton's mind that he hadn't noticed consciously at the time. "But he wants more than power for power's sake. He has some other goal. One that is dark and twisted."

"Some sexual perversion?"

He almost laughed at the incongruity between Lady Beth's question and her demure countenance. "If so, I didn't sense that in him. His interests lie elsewhere."

"Do sit down before you pace a hole in my carpet, Simon." Lady Bethany leaned back in her chair. "I shall see if I can reach him and learn something."

"Be careful." As Simon took a seat opposite his hostess, he thought of the devastation he'd experienced at Drayton's hands. "He is dangerously unpredictable."

Lady Beth ignored his warning rather than point out that she was, after all, head of the British Guardian Council and one of the most powerful sorceresses in the land. She had a particular talent for communicating across long distances, so she might be able to touch Drayton's mind better than Simon had.

"There he is, in London," she murmured. "My, what a dank, unpleasant mind. He . . ." Power surged viciously in the room. Lady Bethany made a strangled sound, then crumpled into a small heap on the carpet.

Simon leaped to his feet, swearing. Drayton had felt Lady Bethany's mind touch and was striking back. The fury Simon had suppressed since his defeat at Drayton's hands surged through him, multiplied by the rage he felt on Lady Beth's behalf. His focus narrow as a steel blade, he followed Drayton's energy back to the source and struck with all his power.

For an instant Drayton staggered under Simon's attack. Then he hit back. Simon erected a shield to deflect the energy bolt, which was much weaker than the energy Drayton had commanded when he held Meg captive.

Intent on gathering his power for another strike, Simon didn't recognize that the transformation spell had been reactivated until his legs collapsed and he crashed to the floor. Searing pain blazed through him as bones lengthened and muscles were wrenched into new shapes. His vision distorted as his eyes changed, and flames streamed from the fireplace to join the burning pyre that engulfed him.

The destruction of his clothing, the change in balance and perspective, were familiar this time, and more frightening for that reason. After an endless time, the burning gradually faded and he scrambled to his feet—his *hooves*—again. His unicorn body felt—comfortable, and the reduced scope of his mind more natural, but he *hated* that he had been helpless to stop the transformation even though Drayton had been weaker than he. Grimly he controlled his fear, grateful that he was among friends who would recognize what had happened.

Two steps brought him to Lady Bethany's side. Her face was as white as her hair and he saw a bruise forming on her cheek where she'd hit the floor.

He nuzzled her gently. She didn't respond, but at least she was breathing. He nudged her again. Nothing. He supposed he could use his teeth to tug on the bell rope to summon a servant, but what would a servant make of a unicorn in the morning room and the lady of the house unconscious?

On impulse, he lowered his head and laid his horn against her cheek. Her eyes flickered open at the first touch. After a blink of surprise, she focused her gaze on him. "I see that Drayton was able to invoke the spell again."

Simon opened his mouth to reply and only succeeded in breathing warm air onto Lady Beth's face. She gave a shaky laugh and pushed herself to a sitting position. "Can you understand what I'm saying? If so, tap your right . . . hoof once."

It took him a moment to recall the difference between right and left, but after he had that straight in his mind, he tapped the carpet.

"Good." Moving slowly, Lady Bethany attempted to stand. Seeing that she was having trouble, Simon bit into the neck of her gown and lifted.

"Thank you, Simon." When she was on her feet again, she smoothed out her rumpled gown. "Even as a unicorn, you are a gentleman. Do you mind if I touch your horn? Tap twice if you don't want me to."

He considered. Having someone touch his horn was a strangely intimate act, but this was Lady Beth, who had been like a mother to him. He tapped once for yes.

She reached up and clasped the horn. "Fascinating. I can feel a power unlike any I've ever known. The aches I got from falling are fading as I speak. You said earlier that you couldn't do magic in this body, but as a unicorn, you *are* magic."

He snorted, wanting to convey that being a magical creature was not an improvement over normal life. She smiled a little. "Let me see if I can touch your mind. Two taps if you would rather I didn't."

He tapped once. A moment later he felt her calm strength flow through him, but when he tried to form words and speak directly, he couldn't.

She shook her head in frustration. "I can sense some of your feelings and I imagine the reverse is true, but very vague." Releasing the horn, she said, "No matter. What is important is returning you to yourself. If I touch my blood to yours, I should have enough magic to restore you. Is that satisfactory?"

He tapped the floor once. Lady Bethany opened the sewing basket beside her chair and brought out a needle. Straightening, she studied him. "You are very beautiful as a unicorn, Simon. Of course, you are very beautiful as a man."

She laughed when he snorted with disgust, then moved in with her needle. The sting on his hindquarters was so slight he hardly noticed it. She pricked the middle finger of her left hand and squeezed out a drop of bright blood, then closed her eyes and summoned her magic.

When the air around her began to shimmer with power, she touched her finger to his flank, her blood to his. A wave of itchy magic swept through him, but his body remained obstinately stable. He was still a unicorn.

She tried again. Though Simon again felt the magic, it had no effect on him. Under her breath, she muttered a word sweet little old ladies weren't supposed to know. "I'm sorry, Simon. This isn't working."

He swung his head, pointing his horn toward the upper floor, where Meg rested. Perhaps the legends were right and only the blood of a virgin would do.

"You're right," Lady Beth said, as if he'd spoken aloud. "I'll go get her."

She was moving toward the door when it swung open and Meg slipped inside, her expression tense. Dark hair tumbled loose around her shoulders and her bare toes were visible under her white nightgown. The plain gray shawl tossed hastily over her shoulders did nothing to disguise her enchanting self. She was the loveliest creature he'd ever seen. Full of longing, Simon bounded across the room and almost knocked her over with his enthusiastic welcome.

Half laughing and half in tears, she wrapped her arms around his neck and rested her forehead against his mane. "I knew something was wrong. Can I help?"

"I hope so," Lady Bethany said. "I tried my blood and all the magic I could summon to reverse the transformation spell, but it didn't work. Of course, at my age I can barely remember what it was like to be a virgin."

Meg blushed and stepped back from Simon. "I don't know what I did before, but I'll do my best. Do you have a knife?"

"Try my needle." The older woman handed it over. "It does less damage. I'll get you a knife if this doesn't work."

Simon rubbed his head against Meg again, feeling strangely ambivalent. He wanted to be restored to himself, but his rapturous pleasure at her nearness was intoxicating. When had he ever felt this happy?

"Forgive me, my lord." Simon's tail twitched as Meg stabbed more deeply than Lady Beth had. Then she peeled off the bandage applied over her grazed finger and broke open the scab that had formed, pressing till blood flowed.

Lightly she touched his flank—and the world fell apart again. He pitched to the floor, once more feeling the agony of transformation. The air warped around him. As his spine twisted, he saw Meg and Lady Beth stumbling backward, blasted by the energy.

He emerged from blackness as Lady Beth laid a blanket over him. The floor was cold and hard, and he was so weak that he doubted he could sit up. He *hated* being helpless in front of others. "How long was I unconscious?" he asked, trying to keep his voice steady.

"Not long. A few moments." She touched his cheek. "Are you all right?"

"Well enough." By sheer will, he managed to sit up and wrap the blanket around himself. The wool was scratchy against his bare skin. Seeing the ruined garments he'd been wearing, he said dryly, "Drayton's spell is playing havoc with my wardrobe."

"Not to mention playing havoc with your body." Moving slowly, Lady Beth got to her feet. "It can't be healthy to suffer such wrenching changes."

She was right; Simon felt as if he'd aged twenty years. Meg knelt beside him with a glass in each hand. Her eyes were dark with concern. "Water or brandy?"

"Both." He took the water glass and emptied it in one swallow. After handing her the empty glass, he started on the brandy more slowly. "Thank you."

Meg sat back on her heels and smiled a little. Her complexion was silken smooth and begged to be touched. He looked away, not pleased to note that despite his restoration he still found Meg to be the most alluring female he'd ever seen. He hoped the effect passed soon. It wouldn't do for him to nuzzle her now that he was a man again, though the thought was tempting. "Meg, did you feel Drayton's energy earlier? He attacked Lady Bethany as well as reactivated the transformation spell he'd laid on me."

Her face tightened. "So that wasn't my imagination. I woke out of a sound sleep feeling as if he was . . . was coming after me."

Simon checked the silvery thread of energy that connected her to Drayton. The block he'd created still held, but it had taken a beating. The renegade mage had managed to damage all three of them. "We'll have to come up with a better shield for you."

"Yes, and we also need to decide how to handle Drayton, but not tonight." Lady Beth headed toward the door. "We all need rest. I don't think he'll try anything more until he's recovered from your energy blast. Good night, my dears."

Simon was glad he'd done some damage to his enemy. He just wished he'd done more.

Feeling stronger, he managed to get to his feet without letting the blanket slip or his brandy glass spill. It was a measure of his fatigue that he was hardly bothered by the impropriety of wearing only an itchy blanket in the presence of a nubile young female.

After Lady Bethany left, Meg moved toward the door, then paused. "My lord . . . what happens now?"

"There's a range of possibilities." Guessing that she was tired but too tense to go back to sleep, he settled into a chair. "Join me in a brandy if you'd like to talk."

She moved to the side table that held drinks and glasses and poured herself a blend of brandy and water, then settled in the chair opposite him. She was graceful even in her fatigue. Trying not to stare, he said, "What happens next is London."

"So you and Lady Bethany will pursue Drayton to London." Meg turned the glass in her hands. "Do . . . do you think that she will allow me to stay on here for a while? I have nowhere else to go."

"You'll come to London with us, of course. You are no longer alone in the world, Meg—you are part of the Families." He grimaced. "You are also part of this tangle with Drayton, so you need to be in London."

She relaxed a little. "Very well. But I wonder—do Guardians always live with the fear of mental attacks?"

He laughed ruefully. "Usually our lives are much like the lives of anyone else. I have estates to manage, a seat in Parliament, and personal interests like the Royal Society as well as my Guardian responsibilities. Lady Bethany has a large and devoted family and is involved with charitable works. Being a Guardian is not usually so dramatic as what you've witnessed in the last few days."

"If you hadn't confronted Lord Drayton, I would still be a mindless slave, so I can't complain about the consequences." She sipped at her watered brandy, made a face, then swallowed more. "How will you stop Drayton? And can I do anything to help?"

Simon frowned. "I think he will be called to account for his actions in a hearing before the Guardian Council."

"Why does that disturb you?"

He noted how adept she was becoming at reading emotions. "As enforcer of Guardian law, I have a fair amount of latitude in deciding what must be done and how to do it. I am careful and never confront a renegade unless I'm sure of his guilt. But because the situation with Drayton has exploded in our faces, he will now have a chance to state his case to the full council, and he's a master of lies and half-truths."

Her brows arched. "Your council won't support you even though you risked your life to enforce Guardian law?"

"Most will support me." He hesitated, wondering if he should get into the politics of the Families. But she would need to know. "Usually Guardians deal harmoniously with each other. But my family has a long tradition of enforcing our rules, and that is an occupation that can create enemies."

Her eyes narrowed. "You are saying that some council members will be prejudiced against you?"

"All are honorable people, but let's say that one or two would lean over backwards to believe someone who accused me of doing my job badly."

"Surely Drayton cannot be allowed to continue injuring people!" Her mouth twisted. "Or perhaps he can, since he is rich and powerful."

"Most Guardians are prosperous. It's useful sensing which side to choose during political unrest, for example." Though even the best of them had had trouble predicting the outcome of the recent Jacobite rebellion. "Based on what Drayton has done, I think it would take several master mages working together to strip him of his powers. But struggles between mages can be dangerous, and no one will be eager to attack him unless it's clearly necessary. So if any council members have doubts about how dangerous Drayton is, he won't be sanctioned."

She sat up straight in her chair. "But you and I and Lady Bethany can all attest to his crimes!"

He had a bad feeling about facing Drayton in front of the council, but that might be only his fatigue and sense of failure talking. "We shall see. I usually assume the worst, so perhaps I shall be pleasantly surprised."

Her eyes shifted from soft gray green to cool ice. "You and Lady Bethany say I have power." Effortlessly she created a sphere of mage light, then tossed it into the air. "Teach me how to use it. I want to be able to defend myself against anyone. And I want to learn how to fight back, like you do."

He controlled his surprise. "It takes special skills to be a hunter and enforcer. Some can be learned, but most are innate."

"Then we shall see if I have them." Her eyes narrowed. "I will never be helpless again."

"Defense is easier than attack. The simplest method is to imagine an impenetrable shield of white light around you, but it's most effective if invoked before you are under attack. With practice, you should be able to maintain a light shield at all times without conscious thought. It can be equipped with an automatic trigger to bring it to full strength if you're assaulted. The fact that Drayton has an energy hook in you will compromise the shield to some extent, but it will still be useful."

Her gaze became unfocussed as she thought about it. "Thank you. I shall practice shielding."

As Simon studied the dense, rich power that glowed around her, he was glad that he was not her enemy.

Chapter EIGHT

After the long day and midnight drama, Meg slept as if she'd been drugged with laudanum, yet she woke at dawn tingling with curiosity. The knowledge that she had magical power made her want to learn how to use it.

The previous night had proved that even Falconer and Lady Bethany might not be able to protect her from Lord Drayton. For a few moments he had surrounded her with suffocating power and ordered her to come to him. She had been perilously close to responding, even though the spell that had rendered her nearly mindless had been broken. If he'd been a little stronger—or if the shield Falconer had created had been a little weaker—she might have fallen under his control again. For her own safety, she must learn how to wield her magic.

After washing with bracingly cold water, she investigated the wardrobe. Lady Bethany's granddaughters must be well dressed and wealthy to leave such fine clothes behind. Meg picked the plainest of the garments, a soft green gown that she could don without the help of a maid.

She lit the room with mage light, then wondered where to begin her experiments. She knew so little about Guardian powers. She could call horses, but that was easy, something she'd done as long as she could remember. Mage light wasn't difficult, either. So—what should she try next?

Shielding would be good. She sat relaxed in the upholstered chair and closed her eyes, the better to concentrate on creating a cocoon of white light that extended several inches beyond her body. This proved to be much harder than mage light—the shield tended to bulge or dissolve when she wasn't paying full attention. Eventually she managed to stabilize the light and maintain it without great effort. Not that she felt any safer. Falconer could tell her if she was doing it right.

He had mentioned an energy line that connected her to Drayton. Wondering if she could find it, she turned her inner eye to the shield of white light, exploring the outside inch by inch. It seemed sound enough. Experimentally she took a mental poke at the shield. It yielded a little but she couldn't penetrate it no matter how hard she pushed.

Perhaps Drayton's hook had failed? No, damnation, there was the thread Falconer had told her about. A wisp of glinting light, it connected to her midriff from behind her back. She guessed the line was intended to be overlooked.

Savagely she imagined a silver knife and slashed at the thread. The knife bounced back, unable to cut through the fragile-looking line. She tried several more times before giving up. If Falconer couldn't do it, she wouldn't be able to.

Opening her eyes, she glanced around the room. Her mage lights had gone out while she was working on the shield. Though the sky was becoming light, the room was still dark. Perhaps she could create a spell that would keep a light glowing without constant attention from her. Perhaps an energy line such as the one that Drayton used?

She created two new mage lights and tossed them into the air, mentally commanding, *Stay!* Then she visualized a thread of energy running to each. A little experimentation proved that only a very small trickle of power was needed. Satisfied with the results, she turned her attention elsewhere.

What might a Guardian be able to do? She certainly didn't want to see if she could investigate Drayton—and she'd never again call him "the lord," as she'd done when she was his slave. He was only a man, and an evil one at that.

Was it possible to move objects with mental power? The mahogany desk had a quill pen resting on the polished surface. She concentrated on it as hard as she could. She was about to give up when she felt a mental shift, as if a key had settled into a lock. Slowly the quill rose to balance on its tip. In her delight, she lost concentration and the goose feather flopped onto the desk. She tried again, and this time lifting was easier. How long could she keep the quill upright?

Her head was throbbing from concentration when the door opened and a young maid entered. "Hot chocolate, miss?"

"Oh, please!" Meg took the steaming cup from the tray gratefully. "What time do people break their fast at White Manor?"

"About half an hour from now, miss. You'll hear a faint gong, not so loud as to disturb someone sleeping. That means food has been set out in the room where you had your supper last night." As she left, the maid paused to straighten the quill, which had fallen crookedly across the desk.

Tired from her efforts, Meg was content to sip her chocolate and watch the sky brighten outside. Already she felt less powerless. She'd been successful in her attempt to keep the lights glowing—above her head, they were as bright as when she'd created them. A good thing the maid hadn't noticed!

Closing her eyes, she let her mind drift, trying to see if any of her early life might come into focus. Nothing—her memories still began with Lord Drayton in the meadow. Her failure reduced some of the pleasure she'd felt over her new accomplishments. It was a relief to hear a distant gong and head down to breakfast. She only got lost once.

Falconer and Lady Bethany were already seated and eating. Meg paused in the door to study them. Cool and controlled, Falconer looked like a society gentleman who'd never had a serious thought in his life. Lady Beth seemed no more than a sweet, harmless old lady whose concerns began and ended with tea and gossip. Both were improbable sorcerers. The whole idea of sorcery was improbable, but Meg could not deny the evidence of her eyes.

Her hostess glanced up. "Help yourself to anything on the sideboard and join us. We're ready to start developing plans." She blinked. "Dear, did you know that two spheres of mage light are bobbing over your head?"

Meg glanced up, her face scarlet. She'd forgotten about the energy threads, and the globes had followed her like well-trained dogs. She cut the threads and mentally snuffed the globes. The lights vanished. "Sorry, my lady."

Lady Bethany looked amused rather than upset. "I can see that your education is going to be very interesting to observe."

Meg served herself coddled eggs from a chafing dish, adding toast and a cup of tea before she sat on Lady Bethany's side of the table, away from Falconer. Her feelings about him were . . . complicated.

"You're right, Simon," Lady Bethany said, continuing the conversation that had been in process when Meg entered the room. "We have no choice but to summon Drayton to a hearing before the council. We shall have to rely on the council's good judgment to recognize the danger he represents."

"I wish I had more faith in their judgment," Falconer said dryly. "But you're right that we can do nothing else. To London we shall go, to give evidence against him."

Meg swallowed her toast with difficulty as her mouth went dry. "Will I have to see Lord Drayton again?"

"I'm afraid so, but by the time of the hearing, you should be able to protect yourself from him," Lady Bethany said reassuringly.

"This morning I practiced the shielding Lord Falconer showed me." Meg visualized the white light cocoon. "Am I doing it right?"

She felt a gentle, nonphysical prod, and realized that Falconer was testing the shield. He pushed again, harder, increasing the pressure. She countered by concentrating more on the shield.

The pressure stopped. "Very good, Meg." Falconer glanced at Lady Bethany. "She needs to be told things only once. I've never known such quickness."

"Gwynne Owens was much the same," Lady Bethany said thoughtfully. "Both she and Meg came into their power late, as grown women. Apparently that's easier than the fumbling most of us experience as our magic develops gradually."

"Perhaps Drayton's continual drawing on her power strengthened it and taught her focus even though she was in thrall," Falconer suggested.

Meg squirmed a lot as the two mages studied her. "I did some experiments this morning. Am I doing this right?"

She glanced around the table for a small object to lift with her mind. There was nothing like the quill, so she concentrated on the silver spoon she'd used to stir sugar into her tea. It rose raggedly into the air. It was two feet above the table when Falconer breathed, "My God!"

Meg's concentration broke and the spoon plummeted and hit her teacup. The fragile porcelain shattered and tea splashed in all directions, staining the white linen tablecloth. Lady Bethany had taken her in, fed and clothed her, and in return Meg was breaking her china! She grabbed her napkin and started blotting up tea. "I'm so sorry!"

"No need to apologize." Lady Bethany's delicate fingers touched Meg's wrist. "You have just demonstrated a most unusual ability, child. Being able to lift solid objects by pure mental energy is extraordinarily rare."

"Duncan moves weather, but that's not the same," Falconer said. "That a novice could lift a spoon with no training is . . . remarkable."

She blushed again at the admiration in his gaze. They might consider her a woman grown, but she felt like a girl in the schoolroom.

Lady Bethany suggested, "Simon, when you've both finished eating, why not go for a walk with Meg in the garden? You can give her an idea of the different kinds of magic we know of. Though her experiments so far have been harmless, that might not always be the case."

"A good idea." Humor glinted in his eyes. "Though I do look forward to seeing what Meg might develop on her own."

Simon welcomed the opportunity to walk in the garden with Meg. Besides teaching her about Guardian power, he could test his self-control where she was concerned. Granted, she was a lovely young woman, but his attraction wouldn't be so intense if not for their unicorn-virgin bond. The sooner he learned to control his attraction, the better.

Though the night had been cool, the morning was pleasantly warm, with the richness of spring in the air. Lady Beth had found a pretty bonnet for Meg to preserve her complexion. Meg had accepted the bonnet demurely, though Simon suspected that she had been a bareheaded hoyden at Castle Drayton.

As they stepped into the spacious garden, Meg asked, "Before we discuss magic, I have a question. You mentioned the Royal Society. What is that?"

"A group of men who are interested in natural philosophy. The society is over a hundred years old." His voice turned dry. "Drayton is also a fellow of the society. We share an interest in mathematics and mechanics."

Her brows arched. "Do you see him often?"

"Not very. We have never been friends." Though neither had they been enemies, until now.

"Mathematics and mechanics," she mused. "The very opposite of magic."

He hadn't thought of it that way. "Perhaps it's how I maintain internal balance. The study of natural philosophy is a matter of the mind. Magic comes from somewhere else entirely."

"Where?"

The simplest questions were always the hardest. "Ultimately magic comes from nature, though no one understands the underlying rules, or why some people have the gift of shaping magic and others don't."

"So it's a mystery. Then I shall concentrate on the *how* and not worry about the *why*. What sorts of magic should I avoid?"

He started with the most dangerous. "Do not conjure spirits and demons, which are nonhuman entities of great and unpredictable power. Mages who are too curious or ambitious sometimes do this, and the results are never good."

"Spirits and demons? Are you serious?" she asked incredulously.

"Entirely." He hoped he wasn't giving her ideas. "But that sort of magic is rare and usually involves complicated rituals. It's not something you're likely to stumble on by accident. It's quite another matter to sense a ghost and strike up a conversation. That's usually harmless and sometimes educational."

She glanced at him askance, her eyes more green than gray. "Now I am certain you're joking!"

"Word of honor, I am not." He gestured toward the far corner of the garden. "A ghost sometimes lingers by a ruin nearby. Shall we see if it's there today?"

Meg's fingers tightened on his arm, but she nodded. As they approached a mound of old tumbled stones, which had been planted with flowers and shrubs to look picturesque, Simon said, "Open your mind. If you sense a presence that seems human, describe it to me."

She nodded again, her eyes wide. They halted by the edge of the stones, and for a long moment there was no sound but the breeze rippling leaves and an occasional bird trill. "It's female," Meg murmured. "An older woman. The stones were part of a gardener's cottage, and she was wife to a gardener who lived here. She was crippled, and on sunny days her husband would bring her out and put her in a chair so she could enjoy the sunshine and flowers."

He nodded. "That's her. Can you ask her a question?"

"I can try." Meg closed her eyes, then exhaled softly. "I asked her why she is here, and she said that it's because she was happy in this garden, sharing a cup of tea with her husband. On sunny days when her husband is busy with his—his 'celestial garden,' I suppose would be the best term—she likes to come back and remember." Meg curtseyed. "Thank you, Mrs. Jones. I shall be sure to call again if I can."

Simon also sent a greeting to the ghost, whom he'd met before, then guided Meg away. As they moved into the cutting garden, she asked, "Are all spirits so pleasant?"

He shook his head. "Not usually. That's why I thought that starting with Mrs. Jones was a good idea. Ghosts are often angry, occasionally vengeful. Sometimes they are lost or sad, eager to tell their stories to anyone who can hear them. I've had the experience of listening to a ghost's tale, then sensing the ghost vanish into the light."

"By 'the light,' do you mean the presence of God?" Meg asked in a hushed voice.

"Perhaps. I'm not sure." But he did find that occasional glimpse of light comforting. "Even an angry ghost is unlikely to hurt you, particularly if you're shielded. Often they are wounded spirits who can be set free once they are healed of whatever torments them. Some Guardians take it as their mission to find such wounded spirits and help them so they can move to a better place."

"That sounds like a worthy occupation." Meg looked hopefully around the garden. "Are there any more ghosts at White Manor?"

"I don't think so. Lady Bethany doesn't allow wounded spirits here. She has a special gift for communications of all types, which is why she's on the Guardian Council. The nine council members communicate by means of enchanted quartz spheres that enable them to meet together even if they are in different places." He guided them to a bench set under a pleasantly private tree. "We've discussed ghosts and the dangers of conjuring dark spirits. It is equally dangerous to intrude uninvited on the mind and spirit of another mage."

She shivered. "In other words, I shouldn't try to probe Lord Drayton's mind? Don't worry—I don't want to come near him either mentally or physically."

Simon bent and plucked a violet that had sprouted by the leg of the garden bench. It was pretty and delicate, like Meg. Though she was less delicate than she appeared. "You've heard Lady Bethany and me speak of many forms of magic. It must be confusing. Is there anything we've mentioned you would like to know more about?"

She pulled off her bonnet and looked up to the sky. "You said that your friend Duncan Macrae saved us by conjuring a storm. How is that done?"

"Most Guardians can move a cloud or freshen a breeze, but a true weather mage can sense the winds and temperatures for vast distances, and then shape them to his will. That is what happened the night we escaped from the castle. Duncan was able to build the existing storm into a major tempest to cover our flight into the forest."

Her brow furrowed and he could see that she was trying to sense the weather. One of the clouds above accelerated faster than its fellows for a minute, then vanished.

"I moved a cloud, but I can't seem to feel larger patterns," she said. "Perhaps I will do better with practice."

"It's possible, but the most powerful weather mages are invariably male. Some magics are more often found in men, and others in women."

"What are some of the female abilities?"

"Women tend to be stronger healers and they read emotions better. There is also the enchantress, a sorceress whose allure can turn male brains to rubble." He studied the violet and thought of Gwynne Owens, wife to Duncan Macrae. As beautiful as she was intelligent, Gwynne could make monks riot if she chose to turn on the full force of her power. "Luckily for men, there are few enchantresses."

"Is there no male equivalent of the enchantress?"

"Some men have a powerful ability to attract women, but that magic doesn't seem as strong as the female version. Or perhaps females are wiser when it comes to attraction." Certainly he didn't feel very wise when he gazed at Meg. Though he knew how wrong it was to have such feelings for a girl under his protection, the desire to touch her was increasing, not fading.

He reminded himself that she wasn't a girl but a woman. Her softly molded features had an innocence that must come from losing so many of her growing years, and in some ways she was like a fourteen-year-old girl. But when he looked into her eyes, he saw a depth of pain that no one could experience and still be a child.

Without conscious volition, his hand moved and tucked the violet behind her ear. It was an effort to pull his hand away rather than trace the line of her ear or cup the blossom-smooth curve of her cheek. "Don't think only of magic, Meg. Take time to enjoy life, as you weren't allowed to do for the last ten years."

Her gaze narrowed, and the energy between them thickened with sensual awareness. No, Meg wasn't a girl at all. She was a woman in her prime who was hungry for experience, and who looked at him with eyes that mirrored his longing.

He leaned forward, his conscience screaming, *This is a mistake!* But it would only be a kiss. One simple kiss . . .

Her soft lips were inexperienced but willing. Desire surged through him like a tidal wave and shattered his vaunted self-control. He wanted to bury himself in her, soothe the ragged edges of his spirit in gentle feminine strength. He slid his arms around her, marveling at her supple warmth as he deepened the kiss. "Meg," he whispered. "Brave Meg, the warrior maiden."

She didn't stop kissing him, but she placed her hand in the center of his chest in an uncertain attempt to keep him from going too fast. The simple gesture broke through the flood of his yearning, reminding him of all the reasons he should keep his distance. Not only was she under his protection, but an innocent who had already been robbed of too much by a heedless Guardian.

Passion turned to fury with himself. He pulled away. "I'm sorry, Meg. I shouldn't have done that."

Her hand slid from his chest to his wrist, holding him from withdrawing as she stared at him with confusion. He had taken a piece of her innocence with his kiss, and he hated himself for that.

It took a moment for him to recognize that magic was crackling around him and that the boundaries of his human form were weakening. Drayton's cursed spell was flaring to life. "Damnation, not again!" he said helplessly.

Meg's expression changed to swift comprehension. She raised his hand and bit his third finger hard, drawing blood. As the pain jolted him, she ripped the bandage from her wounded finger and broke the scab to release crimson blood.

She pressed her finger to his, and Drayton's spell dissolved, harmless once again. Heart hammering, Simon moistened his dry lips. Even as a near-miss, Drayton's spell was draining. "Thank God for your quick thinking, Meg." Carefully he removed his hand from hers.

"It's like walking on thin ice, isn't it?" she asked, her face pale. "At any moment it might crack beneath you."

Before he could reply, Lady Bethany appeared, breathing hard. "Thank heaven you're all right, Simon! I felt a rush of magic and thought to find you a unicorn again."

"Not this time, but only because Meg acted so quickly." He rose to give Lady Beth his seat, then described what had happened.

"Perhaps you really will need to keep a vial of virgin blood with you if the spell can activate at random," Lady Bethany said, troubled. "Meg, would you be willing to contribute?"

Before Meg could answer, Simon said, "The spell isn't being triggered randomly. I was angry both times the spell reactivated. I think that anger—the loss of control—weakens me to the point where the spell can take over." He paced back and forth, his muscles tense. "I suspect that the more often I transform to the unicorn form, the more beastlike my spirit will become, and the easier it will be for the spell to overpower me."

Meg looked away from him. "You were angry with me, Lord Falconer?"

"No!" Though he wasn't proud of revealing his weakness to Lady Beth, it couldn't be avoided. "Lady Beth, I kissed Meg. I think that the lingering effect of the unicorn-virgin bond is undermining my sense of what is proper. I was so angry with myself for behaving badly that Drayton's spell started to overcome me."

"So anger is the key?" Lady Beth's brow furrowed. "Forgive me for asking, Simon, but I must know. You're sure it was anger that made you vulnerable, not desire?"

He thought back to those disturbing moments. "It was definitely anger. I've been attracted powerfully to Meg for some time, and even when I kissed her, Drayton's spell didn't manifest. Only when I came to my senses and became furious with myself did the spell come alive."

Lady Bethany looked from Simon to Meg and back again. "The two of you will have to stay very close together in London. Meg, you have the ability to stop Simon from transforming. Simon, you have the strength to shield her from Drayton's power. I'm wondering if the best solution is for the two of you to marry."

Chapter NINE

Meg's jaw dropped. "You think we should *marry*?"

Stopped in his tracks, Lord Falconer looked equally stunned, a fallen angel who had just hit the earth hard. Only Lady Bethany remained calm. "You needn't look so shocked. Simon, Meg can protect you from the transformation spell, as she just proved, and you can protect her from Lord Drayton."

"That can be done short of marriage!" he retorted.

"Marriage is the most common way for a man and women to be together, and you do need to be together. Remember how you managed to call Duncan Macrae when you needed help? You shouldn't have been able to reach so far, even in a crisis." Lady Bethany's glance moved to Meg. "My guess is that you managed because you were with Meg and she enhanced your natural abilities. You both have tremendous power, which means you need mates of comparable abilities."

"You forget that Meg's virginity has been vital to saving me," Falconer said dryly. "That's the antithesis of marriage."

Lady Bethany brushed that aside with an airy gesture. "You wouldn't be able to consummate the marriage until this problem with Drayton is resolved, but that's only a matter of time."

"I wish I had your confidence," he said soberly.

As the two Guardians talked, Meg stared at Falconer, trying to imagine him as a husband. *Her* husband! Sunlight filtering through the branches of the tree touched his hair with silver gilt. Though he wore plain garments borrowed from someone in the White Manor household, he was unmistakably an aristocrat: powerful, wellborn, and confident. How could a girl with no family, not even a name, be a suitable wife?

For the first time, she recognized that despite his aura of authority, he wasn't old, probably not much above thirty. He had treated her kindly, which Lord Drayton certainly never had. And he was fearsomely attractive. . . .

Suppressing that thought, she said, "I can't imagine that Lord Falconer would wish to tie himself to a nobody who is ignorant of the world. Surely he must have his choice of every wealthy, wellborn woman in Britain."

"You'd be surprised," Falconer murmured. "Don't undervalue yourself, Meg. For mundanes, property is of vital importance at every level of society, whether that means a dowry of ten pounds or ten thousand. But among the Families, power is a dowry greater than gold. I don't think there is another unwed Guardian girl in England who is your equal in magical ability. This makes you highly desirable."

"Exactly," her ladyship said approvingly. "You're well suited, and Simon, it's high time you took a wife."

His mouth curved into a smile. "This isn't about Drayton and the dangers he represents. It's because you enjoy playing matchmaker."

Her eyes twinkled. "Yes, but you must admit my record in this area is enviable."

Falconer's brief humor vanished. "I'll grant you that, but it would be unconscionable to press Meg into marriage now. She has lost half her life to Drayton's wickedness. She needs time to learn who and what she is. She will be a great sorceress, which means she will have many choices when, and if, she decides to marry."

"There may not be much time," Lady Bethany said gravely. "Lord Drayton has an energy hook in each of you. Alone, you are vulnerable. Together, you are stronger than he. Meg, do you want to face Drayton without training and protection?"

Meg shuddered. "Of course not, but can't Lord Falconer and I stay close to each other without marriage? I could be a servant in his household."

The older woman shook her head. "You will need to go out into society, and you can do that only as his wife."

Meg gazed helplessly at Lord Falconer, thinking how fascinating he was, and how impossible marriage would be. "My lord, this cannot be. You are right that I can't marry when I know nothing of myself. I want to find my family, if I have one. I . . . I want time to grow up. To understand my place in the world."

He frowned. "All that is true, and yet Lady Beth is also right. Perhaps we should consider this rather than rejecting the idea out of hand."

She stared, shocked that he was serious. "You've told me much about the Guardians, but not that they are mad." She rose, her clenched hands buried in her skirts. "I see no reason to linger and discover that madness is contagious."

She swept away and lost herself quickly in a succession of vine-covered arbors. Imagining herself as Lady Falconer was as absurd as the idea of her marrying a . . . a unicorn. He and she were as unlike as if they were different species of beast. She could never enter the world of London society—the very thought was terrifying.

The arbor walk ended in a small garden with a fountain in the center. Water poured from the mouth of a jar held by a naked cherub and birds splashed in the pool below the statue. It all looked so peaceful. So normal. She sank onto a bench and buried her face in trembling hands. Though Falconer had said that female Guardians were good at sensing emotions, Meg didn't even understand her own feelings, much less those of anyone else.

Her life had begun only a few days before, when Falconer had lifted the clouds from her mind, yet she was being forced to behave like an adult, to make choices that would affect the rest of her life. It wasn't fair!

Which was a very childish thought, she recognized wryly. She should be grateful that she was freed from Drayton's slavery and that she now had two powerful allies. She owed them a great deal.

But surely she also owed something to herself. What kind of life did she want?

More than anything, she wanted to be strong. It was good to be protected, but even better would be the ability to defend herself against a villain like Drayton without aid. That meant learning how to use the tantalizing magical abilities that seemed to be part of her. She wanted to be a woman equal to a man, which seemed possible among the Guardians if Lady Bethany was typical.

Next to safety, she wanted to belong somewhere—to be part of a circle of family and friends. Though she had been welcomed into the Guardians by Falconer and Lady Bethany, she still yearned to find the family that had produced her. She wanted a home where she was accepted by right of blood, not by charity.

If Falconer was right that her magical power made her a desirable bride in Guardian circles, did that mean that marriage between them might someday be seen as a reasonable match? Perhaps. But not now—she felt that in her bones. To accept Lady Bethany's suggestion would be to lose her chance to find strength and equality.

If they were ever to wed—and privately she admitted that the idea was . . . appealing—it must be after she became a woman secure in herself and her power. She might never be Falconer's equal, but she must be her best self, or she would always be humble and unsure around him.

The fault would not be his—she would abase herself without any help. It was too easy to think of herself as profoundly unworthy of him. If she was Falconer's wife, he would always treat her with consideration, but how could he respect a bride who was ignorant and had no idea how to move in society?

Life had been much easier when she was a simpleton.

When Simon started after Meg, Lady Bethany caught his wrist. "Give her time to think, Simon. Of course the idea is startling, but it's hardly outrageous."

He frowned as he seated himself beside her. "Oddly enough, I find that I am still capable of feeling outrage. Despite her years, Meg is a child emotionally. To coerce her into marriage would be wicked."

"I find it interesting that neither of you said that the idea of marrying the other was personally distasteful." Lady Beth smoothed her skirts over her knees. "Do you find her attractive?"

Simon started to protest, then resigned himself to speaking the truth. With Lady Beth, there was really no other choice. "Of course I find her attractive, but my wits have been scrambled by a spell and I find myself wanting to lay my head in her lap."

She laughed. "Are you sure that's entirely because of Drayton's magic?"

"No, but it's hardly fair to enter into a marriage when I can't separate real attraction from the magical kind." His mouth twisted humorlessly. "Women tend to find men of the Malmain family difficult at the best of times. Meg mustn't be coerced when she has no idea what she would be getting into."

"The fact that your parents' marriage failed doesn't mean that yours will suffer the same fate," she said softly.

"Failed" was such a mild word to describe the living hell that was his parents' union. "No, but you can't blame me for being wary. I think that my cousin and his boys would be worthy heirs to the Falconer title if I leave no son to inherit."

"Lawrence is a fine man but he hasn't half your power, and his sons don't, either. In your generation, only you have the full Malmain gift. The title is of no consequence, but the Families need you to pass on your power."

"There is never a guarantee that children will match their parents' abilities."

"True, but mating powerful mages does improve the odds." She shook her head. "We're wandering from the subject. I wasn't merely matchmaking when I suggested the two of you wed, Simon. Drayton is truly dangerous. I sense that his goal is one that can change the course of British history. Perhaps the world." Her quiet voice was chilling.

Simon went still as her words resonated with the hammer impact of truth. "Do you have some sense of what he plans?"

She sighed. "Looking at the future is like standing on a hill and peering at a foggy landscape. A few scattered hilltops can be seen thrusting from the mist, and perhaps some shadowy shapes are dimly visible. When I look at Drayton, I see the image of a lever and fulcrum. He wants to apply leverage that will shift the world."

Simon considered interpretations. "That sounds like a goal greater than personal power. Surely it must be political. As part of the government, he is in a position to affect great changes. A war? An assassination?"

She shook her head. "There is an . . . unexpected quality to what he wants. So unexpected that I can't even guess. I wish I could tell you more."

"Perhaps it will come in time." He would ponder the question himself. Most Guardians had some sense of possible futures and occasionally flashes of true knowledge, but accurate foretelling was rare.

Lady Bethany toyed with the wedding band she still wore despite years of widowhood. "I feel that you and Meg must work together to thwart Drayton's aims, but quite apart from that, I believe that you are meant to be with each other."

His gaze sharpened. "The way you thought Duncan and Gwynne belonged together? They're happy now, but getting there was the very devil, and they started out better suited than Meg and me."

"In worldly terms they suited, but magically speaking they appeared to be badly mismatched." Lady Beth spread her hands. "Every marriage is unique. You and Meg have much to offer each other. Think about that."

The tender warmth of Meg's essence echoed in his mind. Thinking about marrying her would be easy.

It would be much harder *not* to think about it.

Meg stalked from the gardens into the fields beyond. When she saw horses in a pasture, she climbed onto the fence and mentally tested their natures. She had always done this, she realized, but never with such consciousness or depth. Horses were soothingly simple compared to humans.

On impulse, she called a sweet-natured chestnut mare and slid onto the horse's back from the fence. As she hitched her skirts above her knee, the mare danced with pleasure. "Shall we have a good gallop, sweeting?"

Knowing the mare wanted to run, she used her mind to spur them across the field. When they reached the far fence, the mare soared over, her mane whipping Meg's face. Meg had never felt so much at one with her mount. Why had she bothered with bridle and saddle all these years when she could control a horse with only her mind?

Spirits rising, she spent the day exploring the rolling hills of White Manor on horseback. This time alone in nature was like the best part of life at Drayton Castle, when she was free to wander as she chose. By the time she returned to the house, it was near the dinner hour and she had decided on her course of action.

A bath and another handsome gown awaited. Lady Bethany must have a granddaughter very close to Meg's size. The young maid, Nell, appeared and helped her dress and style her hair. Before leaving, the girl said, "Her ladyship sent these for you to wear if you like, miss." She drew a box containing a delicate garnet necklace and matching earrings from her apron pocket.

"How lovely!" The garnets would complement the red in the floral print of her gown. Meg fastened the necklace around her neck. "I can't wear the earrings, though. My ears have never been pierced."

"I can pierce them for you, miss."

"Thank you, Nell," Meg said gratefully. "Tomorrow would be a good time."

She checked her appearance. Anyone who didn't know better would think she was well bred. Girding herself, she headed down to the small salon, where Nell said family and guests gathered before dinner. She hoped Lord Falconer and Lady Bethany wouldn't be too angry with her for running away from the morning's conversation.

She needn't have worried. The two of them were chatting easily, Falconer braced by the mantel, while her ladyship relaxed on the sofa. Lady Bethany looked up at Meg's entrance. "Good evening, my dear. You look very fine. Did you have a pleasant day?"

Relieved, Meg said, "Very. It was calming to explore the estate."

Falconer asked, "Would you like some sherry?"

She accepted but eyed the stemmed glass warily. "I don't know if I like sherry."

"There's only one way to find out. Be careful, though. It's much stronger than ale or small beer." His blue eyes were warm. Not like a lover's, but friendly.

She sipped at the wine and managed not to sputter at its strength.

After a second sip, she decided she liked the sweet, nutty flavor. Even a small amount made her feel more relaxed. "I've made up my mind. I won't marry you, Lord Falconer, but if you and Lady Bethany wish it, I will pretend to be your wife for as long as is needful to stop Lord Drayton from his wickedness. After I leave London, you can tell people that I died in the country of a fever or in childbirth. That will leave both of us free."

After a moment of shock, Falconer said caustically, "Should I mourn your death greatly? Or shall I act greatly relieved to be free of you?"

Meg felt his anger with her inner senses more than from his tone. Uneasily she recognized that she was asking him and Lady Bethany to lie to everyone they knew. "I'm sorry. I don't like the dishonesty, but it would keep the two of us together in a way that isn't permanent."

"You can't appear in society as Simon's wife, then show up again later as a single woman," Lady Bethany pointed out. "People would be bound to notice."

"I have no desire to return to London society after this affair is settled." Meg's long ride had clarified her thinking. "My greatest wish is to locate my family. I will put this aside for now, but as soon as my role has been played, I will leave London. I think my family must be somewhere in the border country between England and Wales, and I will look as long as I must to find them."

"What if you have no family?" Falconer asked quietly.

"I have to believe that somewhere people missed me when I was gone, and will be happy to have me back." Meg looked away, ashamed of the quaver in her voice.

"There are Guardians who will be able to help in your quest," Falconer said, tactfully ignoring her distress. "I might be able to help, myself. I'm a good finder."

She supposed that was part of being a hunter and enforcer. If he would turn his formidable talents toward looking for her family, she would have a chance of success. But that must wait. "If you don't want me to pretend to be your wife, we could have a false betrothal and break it later."

"As Simon's betrothed, you couldn't live under the same roof." Lady Bethany frowned. "Marriage is the only solution."

"No!" Anger burned through Meg and exploded into words. "I have been Lord Drayton's puppet for half my life. I will not be yours merely because you treat me more kindly than he did!"

A volatile mix of energies crackled through the room too swiftly for her to analyze them, and the two Guardians stared at Meg as if she had turned into a unicorn herself. She clamped a hand over her mouth, shocked by her own rage.

After a charged silence, Lord Falconer said, "Meg is correct, Lady Beth. The fact that our intentions are honorable does not give us the right to coerce her."

After a moment, the older woman nodded. "I'm sorry, Meg. Coercion was not my intention, but that was the effect." A faint smile curved her lips. "I would rather not stir your temper again." She gestured at the vase on the table beside her. The lilac stems clustered there had withered to brown husks.

Unnerved, Meg touched one of the dry flowers. Brittle blossoms fell to the tabletop. "Did I do that?"

"Most of it," Falconer replied. "The shields Lady Beth and I pulled up for protection didn't help. When you lost your temper, you blasted energy in all directions." His gaze rested on the dead lilacs. "The sooner we begin your education, the better. Now that Drayton's spell has been lifted, your emotions have come alive, and that has . . . consequences."

"Indeed." Lady Bethany eyed the lilacs briefly before shifting her attention to Meg. "If you refuse to have a real marriage, I suppose we must settle for a pretend one."

"Either that or let me be a servant." Though ashamed of her loss of control, Meg wasn't sorry that they had given up the idea of her wedding Falconer.

"A pretend marriage is the best of a poor set of choices." The earl's eyes narrowed as he studied Meg's face. "We can solve the problem of her reappearing later as a single woman by altering her appearance. Drayton changed her drastically, but something much subtler will do. If you ever choose to return to society, you can do so with your natural appearance and claim to be my late wife's younger sister. You would need another Christian name, but that's a minor matter."

Gaze intense, he touched her cheekbone. She felt a tingle of what she now recognized as magic. Turning to a mirror on the opposite wall, she frowned at what she saw. It was hard to define how he had changed her appearance. Perhaps her features were a bit more regular and her eyes larger, but if so, the differences were small.

Yet she no longer looked like herself. She hated that, even though he had made her more attractive. "Falsifying myself makes no sense when I am trying to discover who I really am. Better that I use my real face and voice now. There will be time enough to change my appearance if I ever decide to return to London."

"Very well, if that is your preference." He glanced at Lady Bethany. "Are we all in agreement? Meg shall live with me at Falconer House and we shall pretend to be happy newlyweds while we seek to discover Drayton's goal, then frustrate him in achieving it. When that is accomplished, Meg is free to leave London, and we will do our best to help her find her family."

"We shall have to agree on a story of how you two met and married," Lady Bethany observed. "Perhaps you met some years ago, and when you met again here at White Manor, you were instantly smitten. If so, you must discuss all the details of how and where. What you wore on your wedding day, Meg. Simon, you must attempt to look at least a little besotted—it's expected of newlyweds."

He nodded, unenthusiastic but resigned. "We can work out our stories over the next few days, before we go to London."

The cool discussion of deception made Meg uncomfortable, but she had no choice. She owed her companions a great deal and she was glad to do what she could to repay the debt, as long as marriage wasn't required. "I hope that I shall also receive instruction in the uses of magical power."

"That goes without saying. You will have your choice of the best teachers of the Families." Falconer took her hand, bowing over it with consummate grace. "May we have a fulfilling and happy false marriage, my dear Meg."

She managed to smile and reply lightly, and hoped that she would not regret turning down the opportunity to be truly his wife.

Chapter TEN

Meg stared out the carriage window, fascinated and repulsed by the teeming, filthy, smelly London streets. "I didn't know there were so many people in all of England!" She watched as two carts filled with produce got their wheels locked together. The drivers vaulted out and started screaming at each other. As the carriage continued along the cobblestone street, a vendor grinned and waved a piece of gingerbread at her. Through the glass, she could hear the woman call, "Fresh hot gingerbread for my lady!"

The carriage passed a small crowd that had formed around a juggler who was keeping five knives in the air. It had rained earlier, and filthy water ran down the gutters. Well-dressed matrons picked their way across the street wearing wooden pattens that kept them above the worst of the muck.

As Meg stared at the continually changing scenes, Falconer took her hand. "Are you using your shields? Being amidst so many people is an immense mental assault."

Meg felt cool, soothing energy flow from him to her. "I became careless about my shielding," she admitted as she corrected the lapse. "How do all these people endure being right on top of each other?"

"Habit," he said succinctly. "I think London is proof that most people have at least a touch of power. True Londoners use that power to block out the worst of the tumult, and feel bored and ill-used if forced to visit the country."

Meg laughed. "Now I understand why most Guardians spend a good deal of time in the country. It must be hard to do magic in such a clamor of energies."

"One becomes accustomed, but it is an adjustment every time I return to the city," Falconer admitted. "Luckily, my house is in Mayfair, which is rather quieter."

To Meg's relief, he was right. After her raucous introduction to the city, the streets became wider and quieter, the houses larger and more imposing, until eventually they pulled up in front of a grand mansion on a square. Falconer stepped from the mud-splattered coach and offered Meg his hand. "Welcome to your new home, my lady."

Meg took his hand and climbed down to the cobblestone street. Despite the high-intensity education about London social life she had received in the last several days, she was tempted to turn and bolt. "Falconer House is very grand," she ventured.

"Larger than necessary, but it's been in the family for some time so I suppose I must keep it." He tucked her hand in his elbow and led her up the stairs to the house. "I shall be glad to put off borrowed clothing and wear my own."

Meg glanced down at her handsome traveling gown. She would have to offer deep apologies if ever she met the granddaughter whose wardrobe she had pillaged. "I would like that, too."

"Shall I have a mantua-maker attend you here, or would you rather go out to a salon for fittings and fabric selections? You need a wardrobe worthy of a countess."

"That will cost you a fortune."

"I *have* a fortune. Several of them, in fact," he said, amused. "You must dress the part, Meg, or it will reflect badly on me."

She sighed. "Very well, but no more fittings and garments than necessary. I suppose it will be easier to have the seamstress come here, but I do need to go out regularly. Can I ride in London?"

"There are several parks that are good for riding, but you must always be accompanied by me or a groom."

She started to protest, then subsided. "I suppose I have no choice but to live in this cage I've agreed to."

"There is always a choice, Meg," he said seriously. "Sometimes the choices are poor, but there is always more than one way to proceed. At least in this case, you won't have to pretend to be a countess for long."

"How long?" she asked. "Weeks? Months? Years?"

"Weeks or months, perhaps. Not years."

Before Meg could reply, the great double doors swung open to reveal a dramatic foyer. Once more she suppressed an urge to bolt. Falconer had been born to such wealth. Meg hadn't, of that she was sure.

The liveried and powdered servant who had opened the doors bowed deeply. "Welcome home, my lord. There was some concern about the delay in your return." The man darted a curious glance at Meg.

"I had a good reason, Hardwick. Please summon the rest of the staff to meet the new Lady Falconer." Falconer bestowed a fond smile on Meg.

Hardwick couldn't quite conceal his surprise, though he did his best. "It will be my pleasure." He bowed again, this time to Meg, then left to summon the staff.

"This won't take long." Falconer loosened Meg's grip on his arm. "I'm sure the blood will start flowing again soon."

She smiled wryly. "It's hard to relax knowing I don't belong here, my lord."

He regarded her with his penetrating blue eyes. "Perhaps it would help if you call me Simon, at least when the situation is informal. Then you can forget that I'm a lord."

His suggestion made sense. "Very well . . . Simon."

A silvery gray hound came racing into the hall, toenails scratching frantically. He was about to throw himself on his master when Falconer said, "Down, Otto."

Quivering with excitement, the dog sat, its gaze fixed on Falconer, who bent to ruffle the long ears. "Sorry to be away so long, old fellow. Meet your new mistress. Meg, Otto. Otto, Meg."

She found herself regarded by huge, spookily intelligent eyes. The hound solemnly offered her a paw. "The pleasure is mine, Otto," she said as she shook the paw, then scratched the handsome head.

"He'll remember and defend you now," Falconer remarked.

The servants began to assemble, bright-eyed with curiosity about Falconer's new "wife." Scullery maids and chambermaids. A grand cook, an even grander valet. Footmen, hall boys, and so many others that Meg lost track of the names. And this was only one of Falconer's residences! She did make a special note of Falconer's secretary, Jack Landon, a quiet young man who was also a Guardian. He ran the household, and as soon as possible, she would beg him to continue doing so.

Falconer—Simon—himself escorted her to her new rooms, Otto pattering behind them. Not only did she have a magnificent bedroom, but also a sitting room and a dressing room. "I shall get lost in here." She removed her bonnet and rubbed tiredly at her temples.

"What do you think of London?"

She grimaced. "Mad. Beautiful and terrifying. Full of raw, brawling life. I couldn't understand the cries of most of the street vendors. It's like a new language."

"It won't take long for your shields to strengthen so that you'll only notice the voice of the city if you deliberately listen to it."

"I hope you're right. At the moment, I feel as if a hive of insects is buzzing in my head."

"Why not rest through the afternoon," he suggested. "There will be a mound of urgent business on my desk, so I'll busy myself with that until we dine."

"Very well. Then perhaps I'll explore the house."

He smiled. "Just pull a bell rope if you get lost. Until later, my lady." Otto beside him, he withdrew.

Meg did lie down briefly, but her mind was too active for her to rest, so she rose and began exploring her new home. Occasionally she met servants and inclined her head in a friendly way, but she didn't ask any for directions. It was more interesting to wander.

And she did, from the kitchens to the attics. Though she avoided Simon's study, where she heard the murmurs of him and his secretary, there were plenty of other things to discover. The house was richly furnished, but it had an air of disuse, as if it longed for more people to move through the high-ceilinged rooms or to dance in the long gallery.

At the back of the second floor, she found a small room containing a frame and sewing box that had been used by Simon's mother many years ago. Meg scooped up a handful of the richly colored silk thread and had a faint, clear sense that she had done embroidery in the past, but she had never enjoyed it. She tried to envision a scene when she had embroidered—a place, a time, a teacher—but with no success. She returned the silks to the box, frustrated.

At length she ended in the library, thinking she could at least practice her reading, which was improving swiftly now that she was no longer bespelled. She was absorbed in a volume on gardening when a footman entered the room and presented a silver tray with a card placed precisely in the middle. Remembering that this was how visitors made their presence known, she took the card and read "The Honorable Jean Macrae." There were Macraes among the Guardians. "Please show the lady in."

She expected an older woman like Lady Bethany, so she was surprised when a petite redhead of about Meg's age was shown into the library. "Forgive my calling without a formal introduction," the newcomer said with a charming hint of Scotland in her voice, "but your husband and my brother have been lifelong friends so I am perishing of curiosity to meet Simon's bride."

Remembering the storm that saved her and the unicorn, Meg said, "Is your brother Duncan Macrae?"

The visitor nodded. "You've heard of him, I see."

"Please sit down, Miss Macrae. Shall I ring for refreshments?"

"Later, perhaps. And please, call me Jean. We Scots are an informal lot." Jean perched on the sofa. "I'm staying with Lady Bethany. When she returned today from a mad dash to the country, she suggested that I call on you."

"Are you here to teach me?" Meg assumed her visitor must be a Guardian, but didn't want to be specific until she was sure.

Jean grinned. "Though Lady Beth is assembling a team of tutors for you, I would be useful only as an example of what not to do. Lady Beth thought we might offer support to each other, since I am also new to London."

So Lady Bethany had sent this charming young woman to be a friend. Beginning to relax, Meg asked, "Why are you a bad example?"

"I have some power, but I've never learned to use it well. I was always busy running the estate, since no one else in the family was of a practical turn of mind." Jean shrugged. "My brother was so gifted that I decided it was easier to concentrate on cattle and cottages."

"I'm told I have a great deal of power, but I need to learn to use it. My . . . my husband has been teaching me the basics, but he'll be busy now that we're back in London. I look forward to having other tutors as well." Meg thought of the flowers that she'd accidentally turned into dry husks. "I hope that happens before I do damage!"

Jean nodded vigorously. "Magic is alarming, isn't it? We Guardians are supposed to be blessed, but it seems to me that power is usually more trouble than it's worth." She paused. "There are times when it's useful, though."

Meg felt a distinct wave of pain from Jean as she spoke. There was more to Jean Macrae than a saucy hat and green eyes. "Some dreadful thing happened to you," Meg said slowly. "Or should I pretend not to have noticed?"

"You really are talented." Jean glanced away, her expression flat. "I lost my sweetheart in the Rising. At the Battle of Culloden Moor."

"I'm so sorry," Meg said, feeling the sorrow of that death as vividly as if it were her own. Even as simple Mad Meggie, she had heard the stories of Bonnie Prince Charlie and the bloody battles that surrounded his rebellion.

"Aren't you going to ask which side he fought for?" Jean said dryly. "Most people do."

"Grief is grief," Meg replied. "The politics don't matter to me."

"That's . . . refreshing. The politics matter a great deal to most people." Jean began twisting a ring on her right hand. "Ever since Robbie's death, my family has been trying to persuade me to come to London. In theory, to broaden my horizons. In truth, they want me to cease mourning and look for a husband. I wasn't ready to come to London until now, and I still have no interest in the husband." Her smile returned. "But London is definitely entertaining."

Meg decided that she and Jean had a great deal in common. They each had experiences that set them apart from other young women, and neither of them was keen on matrimony. "Shall we get into trouble together?"

Jean burst into laughter, her shadows lifting. "What a splendid idea. Duncan and Simon shall be sorry we met."

"Already I am shuddering," Falconer said as he entered the library, tall and devastatingly elegant in what was clearly a costume tailored for him rather than borrowed. "Hello, Jean. It's good to see you."

"Simon!" Unintimidated by his grandeur, Jean bounced to her feet and stood on her toes to kiss his cheek. "It's been too long since you visited us at Dunrath."

He smiled down at her. "I shall refrain from pointing out how long it has taken for you to get the courage to come to London."

Jean laughed. "London doesn't require courage, merely an ability to ignore noise and smells."

Meg found herself envying the easy banter between Jean and Falconer. Her relationship with him was far more . . . complicated.

Jean continued, "Lady Beth is enlisting teachers for Meg. Mrs. Evans for healing, Lady Sterling for communicating, Sir Jasper Polmarric for illusions—the best mages now in London. She thinks they will help Meg get a sense of her strengths and weaknesses."

"Will you give Meg a lesson or two on protection?" Falconer asked. "You're particularly good in that area, I believe."

Jean's fair complexion pinkened. "I thought you didn't know about that."

"I do my best to cultivate a reputation for omniscience," he said gravely while Meg wondered what the byplay was about. Something to do with the rebellion, she guessed.

Firmly burying the topic, Jean said, "I'll be happy to discuss protection with Meg, but first I must warn you that Lady Bethany is planning a ball in honor of your marriage."

Falconer sighed. "I was afraid of that. Meg, do you think you can face a vast crowd of people anxious to admire you?"

In that moment, Meg truly understood why Falconer had been so reluctant to accept a mock marriage. They were living a lie. They were lying to Jean right now, they would lie to dozens, even hundreds, of people who wished them well. No wonder Falconer hadn't wanted to do this—it felt wretched. In the abstract, Meg hadn't minded, but she found that she hated lying to a generous, good-hearted person like Jean.

Yet she saw no other alternative, since she still had no desire to marry, not even Lord Falconer. So she must lie. "I hope Lady Bethany's lessons in London manners will prevent me from disgracing you."

"It will not be so difficult," Falconer promised. "Beauty is the best and oldest protection, so you will be much admired."

He thought her beautiful? Though she told herself that was only lingering unicorn magic talking, Falconer's words gave Meg a warm glow. "A splendid gown will help."

"And you shall have that." Falconer glanced at Jean as he prepared to leave. "Will you dine with us later?"

"I don't want to wear out my welcome the first day," Jean said. "But if Meg is interested, I will give her a lesson on protection now."

"I would like that. London makes me crave as much protection as I can find. Until later, my lord." Meg gave Falconer her warmest smile, hoping she looked like a besotted bride. She must have succeeded, since he blinked before inclining his head and taking his leave.

When they were private again, Jean asked, "What have you been taught so far?"

"Well—how to talk to a ghost. And how to shield myself." Meg thought. "And how to create globes of light. Though I wasn't really taught that. I saw Lord Falconer do it, and found it wasn't hard."

Jean's brows arched. "Excellent. I assume Simon explained that the underlying principles of magic are nature and willpower. Spells are useful because they concentrate will and magic. A good spell can help you achieve something for which you haven't much natural ability. For example, there are only a few truly powerful healers, but any Guardian can learn time-tested healing spells that will reduce bleeding and inflammation. When Mrs. Evans tutors you, she'll teach you the most effective spells and help you discern how much natural healing ability you have."

Meg nodded. Healing would always be valuable, though she suspected she didn't have much talent in that area. "Is protection more than the shielding I've learned?"

"Shielding is protecting yourself from magical attacks. Protection is a broader subject and usually implies protecting other people," Jean explained. "For example, say you are trying to save a group that is being pursued by enemy soldiers who want to kill them, and you're traveling through hill country with few places to hide so many men."

Meg doubted that the example was chosen at random. "What would one do in such circumstances—make them invisible?"

"That's almost impossible. Much easier is a look-away spell, which makes pursuers disinclined to look at the person or object you've bespelled."

Meg thought of the escape from the castle. If she'd known this magic, they might not have been wounded. "If this spell makes it possible to hide in plain sight, I most certainly want to learn it."

"There are limits, but it's surprisingly effective." Jean's eyes narrowed. "Can you tell me what is hanging on that wall?"

"Well . . ." Meg examined the wall in question. "There are two paintings of the countryside. And . . ." She hesitated, realizing something wasn't right. What? She forced herself to concentrate. "How remarkable! There's a framed map of the world to the left, but I didn't notice that at first."

"That's what a don't-see spell can do. I'll show you how to create one later." Jean gave a pleased smile. "When hiding my . . . my imaginary group of men, I did more. Would do more. Having men lie down and use whatever cover they can find, even if it's only a shrub or a rock, is surprisingly effective because a good protection spell can multiply the effect far beyond the shrub's physical size."

"If I understand correctly, an illusion spell could create a different hillside. Wouldn't that be better than a don't-look spell or increasing the hiding power of shrubs?"

"Convincing illusion spells require a great deal of magic, and they're difficult to maintain for long," Jean explained. "The rule of thumb is to choose the solution that requires the least power. You never know when you might need it for something else."

Meg frowned. "Falconer said that Drayton had put an illusion spell on me to make me ugly, and he used my power to maintain it."

"That was clever of him. How did you look?"

Meg hesitated, trying to remember. If she let her energy flow . . . yes, it went into a familiar pattern. "Like this."

"Goodness! The changes are small—the texture of your skin, the planes of your face, the dullness of your hair—but the effect is enormous. You look like a different person entirely." Jean considered. "There may be times when creating this false appearance quickly could be useful."

"No, thank you," Meg said dryly as she returned to her natural self. "I'll invent my own ugliness if ever that is needful. I want nothing of Drayton's around me."

"Understandable." Jean stood. "Self-defense spells protect from physical harm. My brother's wife, Gwynne, is a master of those. Ask her to show you how to do them when she and Duncan come to London. Some self-defense spells strike at the attacker, others are designed to prevent harm. I'll create one of those so you can strike with your magic. You'll find that it's like hitting soft glass with your mind. Very odd."

"I don't want to hit you," Meg said doubtfully.

"You won't hurt me, I promise," Jean said firmly. "You need to practice with power, not just listen to me chatter. Go ahead, visualize striking me with power."

Meg closed her eyes and imagined gathering power into a glowing white club. When the image felt strong, she opened her eyes and mentally whacked Jean with it.

The imaginary club swept forward, and Jean was knocked sprawling.

"Dear God!" Horrified, Meg knelt beside the other woman. "I'm so sorry!"

"I'm fine, truly." Jean pushed herself to a sitting position and shook her head. "The protection spell spared me from real injury, but I'm amazed that you had the power to knock me down."

Meg offered her hand to help Jean up. "I don't want to do this again—I can't bear the thought of hurting someone. You're right that magic is more trouble than it's worth!"

"You can't stop now! This is just getting interesting." Jean grinned. "Instead of me being a bad influence, you're becoming a good influence on me. I actually want to study more magic!"

Chapter ELEVEN

"David, it's time for you to call on Lord Falconer."

David White glanced up from his workbench. "There's no more reason to believe he'll be at home today than any of the other days since he failed to appear for our original appointment, Sarah."

"Earls do not break appointments, my love. They are called to higher duties and with luck they'll turn up eventually," his wife said pragmatically. "At least Falconer responded favorably to your original letter, and he has a reputation as a fair man. He's our best hope."

"At this point, he's our only hope." David stood and studied his appearance ruefully. He looked like a tradesman who was down on his luck, which was not far from the truth. He must hope that his ideas would attract the earl's attention and patronage, for without a patron, David would be unable to continue his work.

As he pulled on his coat, he glanced around the cluttered room and wondered how much longer the landlord would allow them to stay before eviction. Mr. Scully had been impressed by the letter bearing Falconer's own seal, but not impressed enough to allow them to stay much longer without paying rent.

Sarah brushed his dark blue coat to neatness, handed him his hat, then kissed him lightly. "Have faith, David. Someone will see the value of your ideas."

"It's amazing how many people think that steam engines are already as good as they can be," he said with a sigh. "So I hope I find that someone before we starve. I know you can stretch a sixpence until it squeals, but first you need sixpence to stretch."

"Mrs. Lewis gave me some more sewing and that will take care of food for another week."

He hated seeing Sarah, with her fine mind, reduced to seamstress work, but without it they wouldn't be eating. Impulsively he wrapped his arms around her. Short and pale and unremarkable, Sarah never attracted a second glance from men on the street. Yet the luckiest day of his life had been when she agreed to be his wife. "Someday I'll be able to keep you in silk and lace, Sarah, I swear it."

She chuckled. "One step at a time. First the rent, then the equipment you need. Silk and lace can wait." She handed him his portfolio of papers and design drawings.

Though very worn, the leather portfolio was good quality, one of Sarah's finds at a ragman's stall. "I am so lucky to have you, Sarah."

"I know." Her eyes twinkled. "Now go forth, and let's hope that Lord Falconer has decided to return to London."

He set off on the long walk across London as he had done every day for a week. Despite Sarah's encouragement, it was hard to maintain hope. He had already approached manufacturers, mine owners, and the handful of aristocrats who patronized mechanical development. None had shown more than passing interest in his designs.

Building a model would take time even with sufficient funds. If Falconer rejected him, he would have no choice but to look for a job to support himself and Sarah. Despite his mechanical skills, he had never had formal training, so it would be hard to find decent employment in London, which was governed by strict guild rules. He would have to take what work he could find and labor long hours for little money, leaving him with neither time nor funds to work on his engine.

He cut off the familiar circle of his thoughts. His passion for mechanics was a demanding mistress, but he would have it no other way, and he was blessed to have a wife who supported him in his ambitions. Someday he would build a better steam engine, even if it took his whole life.

Tired and dusty, he finally reached Falconer House and rapped on the door. The heavy brass knocker was forged in the shape of a wicked-looking falcon. As always, several minutes passed before the door was opened by a stone-faced footman who made no sign of having seen David daily for the last week.

"I have an appointment with Lord Falconer," David said, as polite as he'd been the first day but no longer hopeful.

He was so accustomed to failure that it took a moment to register when the footman said, "I shall inquire if his lordship is in." The footman stepped back to allow David to enter.

Startled, David stepped across the threshold into a magnificent two-story entry. So the earl had come back to London. Would he have time to see a petitioner so soon after his return?

The footman led David to a spartan reception room, then withdrew. David paced the floor and mentally reviewed the points he wished to make if he had a chance to speak with the earl. He would list the potential uses of a better steam engine, the savings in fuel and labor. . . .

After waiting so long, now it seemed too short a time until the footman returned. "His lordship will see you."

Heart pounding, David followed the servant upstairs and to the back of the spacious house. There the footman opened a door and announced, "Mr. White, my lord."

David took a deep breath, then entered a handsomely furnished study. The earl sat at a desk scattered with papers. As the footman closed the door, Falconer stood and inclined his head politely. His fine-boned face was aristocratic and he dressed with the richness of a fop or a courtier, but his deep blue eyes seemed to see right through David. "Mr. White. I'm sorry to have missed our original appointment. I was unexpectedly delayed in the country and only returned yesterday afternoon."

An earl was expressing regrets? David was so shocked that he immediately forgot the speech he had prepared. It didn't help that seeing Falconer made him acutely aware of his shabby clothing and rough Birmingham accent. "It is no matter, my lord," he stammered.

"Pray be seated, Mr. White." The earl settled in his chair again. "You said you have a design for a more efficient steam engine. Do you have plans to show me?"

Reminded of his portfolio, David pulled out a pair of drawings and spread them on the earl's desk. "I do, my lord. As you surely know, the Newcomen engine is often used in mines to pump out water, but it is most wasteful, requiring large amounts of coal. I believe that efficiency could be greatly improved with a better-fitted piston and cylinder. Also, much heat is lost each time cold water is injected into the cylinder." Forgetting his nerves, he opened the drawing of his proposed engine.

Falconer studied the design with the care of a man who knew what he was looking at. "How much more efficient do you think your design will be?"

David produced a sheaf of paper. "Here are the calculations made for my piston and steam engine." At the top of the first page was a brief written summary, since few people would understand the mathematics involved.

Falconer scanned the pages before saying, "Your calculations seem sound, but there is often a gap between theory and practice." His eyes narrowed. "The calculations were done in a different hand from the drawings. Did you consult a mathematician?"

No one else had noticed. Warily David said, "The calculations were done by my wife, who is very skilled with numbers."

Falconer's brows arched. "She is talented indeed."

"Her father was a mathematician." Sarah had been raised in her father's home as something between a daughter and a servant, learning mathematics while carrying coal and scrubbing pots in the scullery. She had been left penniless when he died. The unfairness of that was another reason why David wanted to give her the best of everything.

The earl returned to the drawings. "While your theory is sound, fabricating these pistons will require a degree of precision metalworking that may exceed what current tools can do."

Again, no one had noticed. "Very wise of you to recognize that, my lord," David admitted. "In fact, I have a design for a precision lathe that will be able to create the pistons needed for my steam engine." He produced the lathe drawings he had brought along just in case.

"So first you must build the lathe." Falconer studied the drawing with a bemused expression. "You're an ambitious man, Mr. White."

"I propose nothing that is not possible, my lord." Expensive, but possible. David clenched his hands below the edge of the desk, both hopeful and anxious.

Falconer leaned back in his chair. "How much would you need to build a precision lathe, then create a working model of your new steam engine?"

David produced the estimate he had prepared with Sarah and handed it across the desk, giving thanks that the earl was actually considering his proposal.

"More of your wife's work, I see. I should like to meet this paragon." The earl skimmed the pages, raising his brows when he reached the total. "One could support a family in comfort for five years for this."

Seeing hope slip away, David moved forward in his chair, words tumbling from him. "The cost will be earned back a hundredfold, my lord. The lathe alone will pay for everything else once it is built and can be brought to market. As for the steam engine—my lord, it will transform the world. There are countless applications for an efficient source of power. Not just for pumping water, but for spinning and weaving machines. Someday it will be used to heat houses and move ships and power wagons and—"

Falconer raised one hand to stop the words. "All of what you say is possible, but change of such magnitude takes time. Just as you need to build a better lathe before you can build a better steam engine, there are many other areas of mechanics that must be developed to achieve your vision. There will also be resistance to such changes, for they will affect society in far-ranging ways. Jobs will be created and lost, fortunes will be built and ruined. Your engine will open Pandora's box."

David hesitated, recognizing that he had never considered such long-term effects. "My lord, I am not a learned man, and I have not thought of such matters. But I believe that a better steam engine will benefit many people, and I know that I can build it. If that brings about unexpected changes, so be it. There is much about our world that can bear changing." He bit off his words when he realized that they might sound subversive to a man who resided comfortably at the top of English society. What did an earl know about heavy labor and grinding poverty and the filthy depths of coal mines?

Instead of throwing David out, Falconer became very still. "There is truth in what you say, Mr. White." His gaze sharpened. "And if you do not build a better engine, someone else will. All over Britain and Europe, men like you are experimenting with new machines just as natural philosophers explore the secrets of nature. We are living in a time of great intellectual ferment, and the implications are both grand and terrifying."

David smiled a little. "I like the idea of being part of an age of great intellectual ferment. Usually I think of myself as a tinkerer with more ideas than I have time or money to build."

"How did you become interested in machines?"

"My father was a button-maker in Birmingham, so I learned how to shape metal as soon as I could walk. I liked finding solutions to problems, so later I went to work for a military engineer. I learned much from him." It was a simplified explanation for living a life where he hungered for knowledge. Learning was not easily come by for a button-maker's son, but David had persevered. Even if Falconer refused to fund the engine, David would continue working, thinking, and experimenting until the day he died.

The earl squared up the piled papers. "I am impressed by you and your ideas, Mr. White. I will begin by funding your lathe. When that is completed, we can look at further funding for the steam engine itself."

David caught his breath, stunned. Just like that, his dreams had fallen into his hands. "Th . . . thank you, my lord! You will not regret this, I swear it!"

"I'm sure I won't." Falconer tapped the feather of his quill pen on the desk as he thought. "We shall need a contract. I propose that any profits from your inventions be split equally between us. You will have the final say on mechanical decisions, while I will have the last word on business decisions. Is that satisfactory?"

It was generous—many patrons would demand a much higher share of the profits, and David would be happy to turn over the business decisions to a man who understood them. "Very satisfactory."

"Shall we have another meeting a week from today? I will have the contracts drawn up. Give me your direction and I'll have a copy sent to you before we next meet so you can look it over." He smiled faintly. "Bring your wife. I should like to meet her."

"She will be honored to do so, Lord Falconer." David stood and returned his papers to the portfolio, fingers trembling with reaction. After years of work, hope, and despair, it was hard to believe he would finally have the materials and money he needed.

"As a token of our new partnership, will you allow me to advance you some funds?" Falconer asked tactfully. "I'm sure there are things you will wish to buy immediately."

David was unsurprised that the earl had deduced his poverty. Since a man in his position couldn't afford false pride, he was grateful for the offer rather than indignant. "You are most generous, my lord."

Falconer opened a drawer in his desk. After a few muffled clinks, he handed a small purse across the desk. "Until next week."

From the weight of the purse, David guessed there was enough money to pay the rent, fill the pantry with food, and still have money left over. As he dropped the purse in an inside pocket for safety, the study door opened and a lovely young woman entered. From the elegance of her dress, David guessed that she was a family member.

"Simon . . ." She stopped when she saw that Falconer was not alone. "I'm sorry, I didn't realize you had company."

She started to withdraw, but the earl stopped her. "Allow me to present Mr. David White. He is about to leave, but you might see him here again since we will be doing business together. Mr. White, this is Lady Falconer."

The young woman's blush made David suspect that the marriage was very recent. She was a lovely creature, with a slender, shapely figure and dark hair. Her air of innocence was very different from the earl's worldly demeanor, yet her great gray green eyes observed with a perception equal to her husband's. David bowed, wishing he were less clumsy. "I am honored to meet you, Lady Falconer."

"The pleasure is mine." Her smile was dazzling, but what really struck David was Falconer's expression. Though hardly a muscle moved in the earl's face, it was clear that he doted on his young wife. David was surprised, then oddly touched as he recognized that he and the earl had something in common: they loved their wives. It made Falconer seem less remote and intimidating.

David bowed again, this time to the earl, and took his leave. He was anxious to share the good news with Sarah. Though he didn't want to examine the contents of the purse on a public street, in the privacy of an alley he pulled out a single coin. It was a gold sovereign. He tried to remember the last time he had held one in his hand. And now he had a purseful!

Bubbling with excitement, he stopped at a bakeshop and bought a steak and kidney pie and an apple tart. Barely able to manage both along with his portfolio, he returned to their shabby dwelling, which was the back half of a sagging brick cottage. Half a block away, he bought a nosegay of pink and purple flowers from a peddler. They would both enjoy a good meal tonight, but Sarah deserved something that was special and pretty just for her.

As he fumbled the key into the lock, the door swung open. As soon as she saw his face, Sarah knew. "Lord Falconer is interested!"

He deposited food and portfolio on the pine kitchen table, then swept Sarah into his arms. "Yes! He said he was impressed by me and my ideas, and he wants to meet my paragon of a wife." He kissed Sarah long and hard before handing her the nosegay with a flourish. "This isn't silk or lace, my love, but it's the beginning of a better life."

Her expression crumpled, and to his horror, she began to sob uncontrollably. "Sarah, sweetheart, what's wrong?" He pulled her to sit on the edge of the bed, which was only half a dozen steps from the door, and wrapped her in his arms. She buried her face against his shoulder and continued to weep. He guessed that these were tears of relief, and their intensity hinted at how fearful she had been. "You must have been fair worried about money, even more than I knew."

"Not only money." She accepted his handkerchief and used it to wipe her eyes and blow her adorably pink nose. "I am increasing, David. I have been afraid to tell you when things were so difficult."

"Dear Lord in heaven! We're going to have a child?" Awed, he cupped her soft breasts. Why had he not noticed that they were fuller? "Oh, Sarah. I have found a patron today, but you have created a miracle."

She gave a hiccup of laughter. "A very common miracle, but since we have been married five years with no sign of a babe, I was beginning to think I was b . . . barren. A failure at a wife's first duty."

The thought horrified him. "Even if we never had children, I count myself the luckiest man in Christendom to have you by my side."

She leaned forward and kissed him very gently. "And I am the luckiest woman in Christendom to have you for a husband."

David felt that his heart would burst with love. "Since you're increasing, you must be hungry. Shall we dine while the meat pie is still warm?"

Her smile turned provocative. "Later, my dearest husband." She leaned forward for another kiss. "Much, much later."

Chapter TWELVE

After the door closed behind Simon's visitor, Meg observed, "That's an interesting man. He will do great things. What kind of business are you in together?" She halted, uncertain. "Of course, that's none of my affair."

"Even if you are not quite my wife, you have the right to ask me anything, Meg." Simon watched as she moved around the room with restless grace. Though she wore a fashionable gown borrowed from Lady Bethany's granddaughter, she seemed like a wild fawn ready to take flight at any moment.

No, not a fawn, for that suggested fragility. Meg might be slender and youthful-looking, but her steely strength was visible to anyone with the perception to see. "Mr. White is a genius in matters mechanical. He needed a patron to underwrite the costs of developing a better steam engine. I have agreed to give him the funding he needs. What are your impressions of him?"

"He is a good man as well as a genius, and he has the potential to make fortunes for both of you." Meg frowned as she analyzed what she had sensed of the inventor's character. "But there is danger near him. Some unexpected event threatens his life." She shivered. "I don't like thinking that nice man might die soon!"

"It is an article of faith among Guardians that magic always has a price. Seeing dark possibilities is one of them." Simon reviewed what he had sensed during his meeting with the inventor. "I share your feelings about Mr. White. He has great ability. He is also part of the knot that you and I must untangle, and there is danger in that."

Meg subsided into the chair opposite Simon in a froth of skirts and petticoats. "I assume you mean the situation with Drayton, but what kind of knot is involved?"

"I have no idea. Partial knowledge is also part of the cost of magic. The most frustrating part." In the country, he hadn't noticed how brown her skin had become from running wild around Castle Drayton. Ladies were supposed to have fair, delicate complexions, not the tanned skin of a field laborer, yet on Meg, the color was warm and alluring. She made other women look pallid and only half alive.

Damning the way the unicorn spell tangled his thoughts, he gestured to a note on the table. "Lady Bethany writes that the council will meet to consider the charges against Drayton a fortnight from today. Seven of the nine councillors will be present in person, and the other two will participate with their talking spheres."

Meg tilted her head quizzically. "What is a talking sphere?"

He kept forgetting how her education had been neglected. "It's a palm-sized ball made of crystal. Each sphere is charged with a powerful spell that allows council members to speak to each other even when they are at opposite ends of Britain."

"How useful! Can anyone with power use the spheres?"

"Even among mages, not everyone has the gift. A prime qualification for being on the council is the ability to use a sphere well."

"Can you?"

"Yes, though not at well as Lady Bethany. The balls were made and charged with magic by an ancestress of hers over two hundred years ago."

Meg leaned forward, her expression intent. "If Lord Drayton is judged guilty, what will happen to him?"

"The first punishment of a Guardian who misuses power is to be ostracized by other members of the Families, but Drayton is well beyond that. If he is declared renegade, the council members will strip away his magic." Simon thought without pleasure about how that was done. "However, that will not happen unless the council agrees unanimously that it is necessary."

"Agreement must be unanimous? That can't be easy to obtain." Meg bit her lip. "In other words, Drayton might be allowed to continue his wicked ways. How can the council permit that if most people are aware of how dangerous he is?"

"In the distant past, where legend and history blend together, mages fought each other, and the devastation was appalling." It was time for another lesson. "May I touch your mind with memories of what happened? That will explain better than words why we are so careful of each other."

When Meg nodded, Simon leaned forward and touched the fingertips of his right hand to the center of her forehead. Though not necessary, physical contact increased the vividness of the memories that had been burned in his brain when he was a student.

Two mages battling with magic until one's shielding broke. The man's flesh melting from his bones as his screams pierced through time. A backlash of weather magic that sent a torrent down the Thames and drowned countless innocent mundanes who lived along the river. A poisonous blast of magic failed to kill its target, but turned infants in the womb to monsters.

Meg immediately gasped and leaned away. "How dreadful! So much pain and grief and guilt remained even among those who survived."

"A special spell was created to assure that every Guardian child is given these memories. The hope is that experiencing the emotions of deadly conflicts will prevent future mage wars." He smiled wryly. "Not that we are always in perfect harmony. Mages can be a stubborn lot, and sometimes the conflicts are major, as with Drayton. But we have managed to avoid full-scale battle for a very long time."

Meg rubbed her forehead as if it ached from the infusion of memories. "Was the destruction among Guardians only, or were ordinary people also injured?"

"It is said that the Black Plague that devastated Europe was the result of a battle among the mages of Russia. I don't know if it's true. I don't *want* it to be true." He sighed. "But . . . it's possible."

"So Guardians allow each other great leeway, until a rogue behaves so badly that all agree that they must band together to stop him."

He nodded. "The council is the key to maintaining peace. But to keep it from becoming tyrannical, there must be complete agreement that a mage is dangerous."

"I understand the principle, but it still frightens me to think that Drayton may go unpunished."

"Even if the council is not ready to condemn him, you will be safe. I swear it."

She looked away. "I trust your intentions, but you may be promising more than you should."

Her doubt stung. No one had ever before suggested that Simon was not up to the challenge of protecting those in need. But she was right. So far, Drayton had defeated him.

So far.

The seamstress made a minute adjustment to Meg's sleeve. Stepping back, she said in a voice of carefully cultivated awe, "You look magnificent, my lady."

Meg gazed at herself in the long mirror. She did look rather fine in her new riding habit, though it was hard to believe that polished image was really her.

In the week she had been in London, Meg's wardrobe and education had both improved markedly. The seamstresses and mantua-makers and milliners had all worked long hours to ensure the new countess was suitably attired. The jacket of the riding habit had been tailored by a man, since it was believed that males did the best job. Naturally, the Countess of Falconer's habit had been made by the very best habit-maker in London.

Though her wardrobe flourished, Meg's patience had frayed. "Thank you. I shall be much envied," she said to the seamstress who had delivered the habit and assisted in donning the garment. "My maid will see you out."

Meg's newly hired lady's maid, Molly, an expert who had worked for another Guardian lady, took charge of the seamstress and guided her from the room. By prearrangement, she would give the woman a generous gratuity for her services.

Meg had learned her way around the sprawling house, learned the names of the servants she saw most, and learned not to flinch when called "my lady." She could now refer to Simon as "my husband" without looking guilty. She could even contemplate attending a ball without panicking, much.

But if she didn't get out of this house for something other than a visit to the shops or a walk with Jean Macrae, she would *explode.* Catching up her trailing skirts, she left her suite and stalked down to the study where Falconer spent most of his waking hours. She knocked but didn't wait for an answer before she swept into the study. "You said there are places to ride in London. Do I need to ask your permission to have a groom take me to one?"

He glanced up from the documents spread across his deck. "From the gleam in your eyes, if I said you needed permission to go riding, I would become the target of something very dire."

She had to laugh. "Very likely. I simply must get out for a gallop, or I fear for the consequences. What is the procedure for me to ride? I assume you have some decent horseflesh available."

"Just send a message to the stables to let them know when you want a horse and groom to be ready. I had a mount brought from my country place for your use, and my mother's sidesaddle has been oiled and conditioned."

Meg sighed. "I guessed that a sidesaddle would be required. Only lowbred hoydens would ride astride even though one has better control of the horse that way."

"With your riding ability, you could stand on your head on your mount's withers and still be in control." He stood and stretched. "I'm feeling as confined as you. If I have to read one more document, I might set it on fire from sheer irritation. Would you mind if I escorted you myself?"

She felt a rush of surprised pleasure. Though they took meals together, she had seen very little of Simon since they arrived in London. "I would enjoy that."

"If you order the horses, I'll change into riding clothes and meet you at the stables." He circled the desk. "You look quite devastating in your new habit. That shade of green suits you."

Blushing with pleasure, she thanked him and left to make the arrangements, including a stop by the kitchen to get apples. She expected it would take Simon time to change, but he appeared promptly in the stable yard, his appearance as immaculate as always. "How do you manage to look so elegant?" she asked as they walked toward the horses, which were being held by two grooms.

"The practical use of magic." He gestured toward the horses. "I'll ride Shadow. I thought you would like Oakleaf."

Meg mentally greeted Shadow before she approached the handsome golden chestnut Simon had provided. She reached out with both her hand and her mind and found that Oakleaf was a lively gelding, young and playful but with no vice in him. He was in a mood to run, just like Meg. As he ate the apple she offered, she told him silently that if he behaved, he could have a good gallop soon. He responded with bouncing enthusiasm. Smiling, she said, "He'll do very well."

Simon bent forward to help her into the saddle. She set her left foot in his laced hands, her hand resting on his shoulder. For an instant, they both froze. This was the closest they had been since he had kissed her at White Manor, and she could feel the sizzle of attraction between them. Could smell the tang of spicy cologne and the deeper scent of a strong, healthy male body.

Nervous, she made the upward leap toward the saddle, aided by Simon lifting her at the same time. He stepped back while she arranged her legs and her skirts. It occurred to her to wonder if sidesaddles had been invented to encourage flirtation. Still another reason to prefer riding astride.

She loosened Oakleaf's reins and he did a little skipping dance, working off energy but not attempting to dislodge his new rider. His pleasure flooded through Meg. "What a splendid horse! Where are we going?"

"Hyde Park. It's the largest park in London and less than ten minutes' ride away." Simon swung into his saddle and side by side they trotted into the street. Despite Oakleaf's high spirits, he behaved well in the crowded streets around the park.

The horse wasn't a usual lady's mount, so she gave Simon credit for understanding her riding skill. Of course, she had ridden *him,* so he would know. She suppressed a smile at the thought. His time as a unicorn seemed like a dream. It was impossible to think of this elegant, controlled London lord as a beast from legend.

The greenery of the park was a sight for her city-wearied eyes. Once they entered, Simon led the way to a broad, tree-lined track with only a single other rider visible in the distance. "Welcome to Rotten Row. Since the hour is unfashionable, you can gallop to your heart's content."

She gave Oakleaf his head and they bolted forward like an arrow shot from a bow. Heavens, how she had needed this! She raced to the far end of the track, then spun Oakleaf in a tight turn and blazed back again. For the moment, she was Meggie again, and free.

As Oakleaf slowed to a more moderate pace, she thought of how much she had changed in the last fortnight. Though she was no longer in thrall to Lord Drayton, society and responsibility had created new constraints. Perhaps there was no such thing as true freedom. At least now she had choices.

She turned for a second time and cantered along the track until she intercepted Simon, who was also slowing down after giving Shadow free rein. "I think I may come here every day."

"Early morning is very pleasant." He turned Shadow and the horses fell into step as they moved toward the far end of Rotten Row. "How are the lessons going?"

"Lady Bethany has provided me with an overall framework of understanding what is possible, while her tutors have all been very patient. I have only a small trace of healing ability, but Lady Sterling says I have a talent for scrying and communicating and Jean says I'm doing well with protection magic. It's all most interesting."

He glanced sideways, his eyes narrowed. "It feels as if you have better control over your power now. Lady Beth says you've impressed your tutors greatly."

She rode for a dozen paces in silence, wondering why compliments had such a powerful effect on her. The answer appeared as soon as she thought of the question: for too many years, she had been treated as if she was worthless. It was exciting and also alarming to have people speak well of her. "The more I build my strength, the sooner I will be safe. Sometimes at night, I . . . I can feel Lord Drayton tugging at me."

After a silence, Simon said, "So can I. Though he can't break our shields, the invisible hooks he has planted make it possible for him to poke. He hasn't caused harm, has he?"

"No, he's more like a stinging insect. Harmless but irritating." She shivered. "I'll be so glad when next week's hearing is over. If the council strips him of power, surely he will no longer be able to sting."

"You would be free of him. I may not, because of the nature of the spell." He shrugged. "If I don't lose my temper for the rest of my life, I should have no more problems with the unicorn spell."

She gave him a startled glance. "Surely you're joking!"

"I'm not. Luckily I am not prone to anger." He frowned. "Though my control over my temper has been shaken by living in beast form. I imagine that will pass in time."

"I'm glad I won't have to live my life without ever losing my temper. I'd have hooves and a horn in no time!"

He laughed. "I expect you would deal with life as a unicorn better than I, but fortunately you won't have to. Do be careful about your temper, though. You might not turn into a unicorn, but when a Guardian is careless with anger, the results can be dangerous."

She thought about the flowers she had withered, and was grateful that she had done no worse damage. But she felt no anger now. She opened her mind to the emotions of the horses and Simon himself. All of them were enjoying the day, and feeling the pleasure of other beings increased her own pleasure.

As Simon had said, her sensitivity to the city's mental noise had faded after the first few days, and now she hardly noticed it at all. Experimentally she reached out to the other living creatures in the park. Birds had sparkling energies like bright chips of quartz. The darting black squirrels had minds as quick as their supple bodies.

She reached further to test the moods of the people in the park. Most were happy, or at least glad to be enjoying the pleasant day, but some were worried or feeling other, darker emotions. She was relieved she couldn't go any more deeply than surface feelings.

A blast of terror and pain shot through her. Woven around that pain were sick, gloating thoughts that rejoiced in doing harm. She gasped and tightened her grip on the reins as scalding emotions tumbled through her.

Simon swung around to look at her. "What's wrong?"

She tried to sort out the jumbled impressions. "Some creature is being hurt. *There!*"

Spotting two boys under the trees lining Rotten Row, she commanded Oakleaf toward them at full speed. The animal gave a thin scream. She didn't realize that she had mentally struck at the boys until she felt Simon deflecting her blow.

" 'Ey, look!" One of the boys shouted a warning as he saw the horse thundering down on them. Abandoning their victim, they bolted into the trees.

Furiously Meg aimed another mental blow at them as she reined in her horse, then tumbled from her saddle. On the ground lay a bloody scrap of orange fur—a young cat, hardly more than a kitten. It was still alive—she could feel its agony.

Tears in her eyes, she dropped to her knees and gently lifted the broken body. "I wish I were a healer!"

Hoping the simple spells she had learned would help, she calmed herself and invoked the enchantment designed for overall healing. The little cat stirred and licked at her hand, but its head fell back again. One eye was a bloody mess and its breath came in ragged gasps. The white of broken bones poked through the soft fur.

"It's too late, Meg," Simon said gently. He had knelt beside her, his sympathy palpable. "This poor creature is hurt too badly to survive."

"How can people be so cruel?" By now, the tears were streaming down her face. "Why did you stop me from hitting those horrible boys?"

"A punishment should suit the crime. What they did was vile, but they weren't more than ten or twelve. Crippling them for life seemed a little harsh."

She supposed he was right, though at the moment crippling those monster boys seemed like a good idea. The kitten drew another anguished breath and Meg knew it was on the verge of death. "Can't you do anything, Simon?" she begged as she held the injured cat toward him. "You have so much power and training."

He let her place the small body in his hands. "I have no healing power, Meg. It doesn't go with hunting skills. I know only the spells you do."

"Then use them! Maybe you can do them better than I." She pulled off her gloves so they wouldn't interfere with the healing spells, then cupped her hands under his. Maybe their combined power could make a difference.

"I'll try." He gazed down at the injured animal, his expression abstracted. Energy began pulsing through him. To her shock, his hands heated up. She released him, startled and uneasy. Waves of brightness resonated between his palms, surrounding and permeating the injured cat until its outlines blurred.

The energy burned for what seemed a long time, then began to fade. When the last of the light vanished, the cat drew a deep breath, then another. No longer was it gasping for air, and the jagged bones had disappeared. It rolled over and sat up, looking around curiously. Still balanced in Simon's hands, it began to groom itself, licking the blood from its fur. Both golden eyes were intact. It was a skinny little thing, but it now looked perfectly healthy.

"Dear heaven," Meg whispered. "I thought you had no healing power."

"I didn't." From his expression, Simon was as shaken as Meg. "I've never been able to do anything but routine healing spells." He scratched the young cat's head with one finger. It began to purr.

"This must be startling, but surely in a good way?"

"The healing power must come from having been a unicorn," he said slowly. "Unicorn horn was a legendary source of healing. I was able to help Lady Bethany when she collapsed after Drayton's attack. Apparently some of that energy stayed with me."

"What a miraculous gift! Think of the lives you can save."

He shook his head. "Not necessarily. It takes less energy to heal a small creature than a large one. Very few Guardians have the power to do a major healing on a human. Also, I suspect that this healing energy is temporary and will fade in time."

If true, that was unfortunate. "Even if you never do a larger healing, saving this little cat is worthwhile."

His gaze locked with hers. "Any tender heart would sorrow to see an innocent creature tortured, but your reaction went beyond that. Why?"

She thought about that, realizing that her fury had been out of proportion. "Because I was helpless for so long, and I can't bear to see something helpless abused."

He nodded with understanding. As he knelt opposite her, he seemed carved from sunlight, his blond hair shining with gold and silver and bronze threads, his face chiseled with the symmetry of an antique statue. Though his expression had the calm of classical sculpture, she could sense profound disquiet in him. If being a unicorn had granted him healing energy, what other changes had the magic wrought? For a man who had spent a lifetime exploring and cultivating his powers, developing surprising new abilities must be unnerving, to say the least.

She reached out with her mind as she would to an anxious horse—and touched magic. Light danced between them, and deep, deep longing. She felt as if she were falling into those blue, perceptive eyes that had seen things beyond her imagination. This was treacherous closeness, more potent than the touching when he helped her mount her horse. She felt an ancient, very human magic in her desire to be closer yet. Would it be shocking if she kissed him?

He met her halfway, his lips coming to rest on hers. Her eyes closed as she drank him in, her mouth opening under his. What did it matter if this was real attraction or a result of the unicorn spell? It was real enough. . . .

The cat jumped onto Meg's forearm and raced up to her shoulder, the little claws like needles. Meg jumped and broke the kiss.

Seeing his darkening expression, she said, "Please don't get angry with yourself. I don't want to have to bite you again."

After a startled instant, he laughed and sat back on his heels. "Thank you for reminding me of the consequences. I must simply accept that I will continue to be attracted to you, no matter how unwise it is."

She cuddled the cat against her shoulder. It had a remarkable purr for such a small creature. "I'm having trouble remembering why acting on attraction is unwise."

"I feel it would be wrong to exploit your innocence, and you want to preserve your freedom while you discover your true self," he said succinctly. "Plus, there is the power of your virginity, which is too valuable just now to waste on mere pleasure."

"I suppose you're right." His reasons were sound. Yet as her gaze lingered on his warm, expressive mouth, she realized how frail the logic of the mind could be when compared to the passion of the body. Grasping at a change of topic, she said, "I'm taking this little fellow home. Is that all right?"

"I'll have a word with Otto and tell him that the cat is not to be chased. Have you a name for him yet?"

"Lucky," she decided. "Because he is."

Simon smiled. "Why do I think that Lucky will be the first of your own private menagerie?"

She smiled back. "Because he is."

Chapter THIRTEEN

"Mr. and Mrs. David White have arrived," the footman announced.

"Send them up." Simon stretched, glad to have an excuse to push the paperwork aside. An earl with vast holdings faced a never-ending stream of documents and decisions, even with first-rate employees handling the brunt of the work.

White and his wife entered the study, the man's hand protectively behind her waist. She looked very small next to her husband's gangling height, but the intelligence in her eyes was unmistakable. Simon was intrigued to see light glowing gently around her abdomen, the sign of a new life growing inside her. In the past, he would not have noticed such a thing unless he looked for it. Perhaps greater sensitivity to physical states was another manifestation of unicorn healing magic?

Since she was also painfully nervous, Simon rose and bowed. "It's a pleasure to meet you, Mrs. White. I'm glad you chose to accept my invitation."

"David made me come," she said, then blushed.

"It's true that earls are fearsome creatures," Simon said, amused. "But perhaps we can talk later as mathematician to mathematician. I was impressed with your work."

Her eyes widened. "I . . . I should like that. David can build anything, but he's not so strong on mathematics."

"Then we shall talk theory later. Please, be seated. Have you had time to read the contracts?"

White nodded. "Yes, and they seem very fair. I will be happy to sign."

"Very well. I'll call in my secretary later and he and Mrs. White can also sign as witnesses. So much for the legalities. Is your current workshop adequate, or will you need another?"

"I've been working in our sitting room, and that's well enough for now."

Simon frowned. "Surely Mrs. White shouldn't be exposed to noise and mechanical work in her present condition."

She gasped and turned beet red. "How did you know?"

Knowing was easy, but it was unlike him to blurt out such a thing. The unicorn energy was still uncontrolled, which was disturbing. "There is a glow about women who are increasing," he said, assuming they would take that comment as metaphor rather than literal reality. "I am serious about a separate workshop. You have done wonders with minimal resources, Mr. White, but scrimping is no longer necessary. You need a decent workshop and tools, near your home but not in it. God forbid you should have a steam boiler explosion in your sitting room!"

Mrs. White looked alarmed. "His lordship is right, my dear. Didn't your friend Bobby say that a house and separate shed are available on his street?"

"That would be perfect, Sarah. But . . ." White turned to Simon. "My friend Bobby lives in a neighborhood with many craftsmen who have come to London from Birmingham, my lord. There would be plenty of mechanical help when I need it, but renting there would cost easily three times what I'm paying now. I'm not sure that's the best use of your money."

Rarely did people worry about spending an earl's money. White's concern was refreshing. "You need to receive a salary separate from the costs of developing your project—money you can spend on yourself and your household without wondering whether I would approve." Simon nodded toward Mrs. White. "I suspect you are an excellent manager."

"She's the best, my lord," White said proudly. His expression turned thoughtful. "There is something I would like to do, but I was doubtful about whether I should. You've heard of Lord Drayton's great technology forum?"

Simon's instincts went on full alert. "No, I haven't, but I've been out of London a great deal. Tell me about this forum."

White leaned forward eagerly. "Lord Drayton wants to bring together men from mechanics and manufactory and natural philosophy so we can talk and learn. He's inviting professors from the universities, experimenters, inventors. And not just men of Britain! They say he's inviting the best, most forward-thinking minds of Europe and even America. What an opportunity it will be to talk to men who are building the future!"

Simon arched his brows, concealing his intense interest. "Is Drayton doing this in connection with his post with the government, or as a private gentleman?"

"I'm not sure," White admitted. "But the forum will be held in two months at a great house in Hertfordshire and it will last a week. That's a fair piece of time to take away from my work, but it's close enough to London that it wouldn't be expensive for me to attend. Since you and Lord Drayton are both fellows of the Royal Society, I expect you're friends and you'll be going to the forum, too?"

"I have not received an invitation," Simon said dryly. "It's a very interesting idea, and I think you should by all means attend. But how will you feel if you meet a man who is already building a better steam engine?"

"I'll learn what he's doing, and make one that is better yet," White said with a grin. "There's no shortage of good ideas, and we can all learn from each other. A number of my Birmingham friends will be going. We're the best makers in Britain, you know."

There had to be power involved with bringing together so many men who were active in developing new machines, and surely Drayton was planning to gather that power to himself. "Send notice that you will be attending, Mr. White. And please keep me informed as plans for the forum develop."

"It will be my pleasure, sir."

"Enough of discussing the world. Now it's time to discuss your work. I had a couple of thoughts about the design that I wanted to talk over with you." Simon drew out his notes. Though he hadn't the mechanical skills of White, he did know something of machinery and he was intrigued by the project. "About the lathe . . ."

Mrs. White made a small sound, and Simon glanced up to see that she was looking a little green. "Are you unwell, Mrs. White?"

"Increasing is a great nuisance, my lord." She stood. "Perhaps some fresh air."

Simon sensed her nausea, but also a deeper source of unease, even fear. Perhaps Meg could find out what the problem was. She was nearby and should be between tutors, so he sent her a mental call. They had become good at calling each other. Within moments she entered the study, looking delicious in a pale green gown.

Her glance encompassed the room. "Good day, Mr. White. I'm sorry to interrupt, Falconer, I only wished to say hello."

"I'm glad you did. Mrs. White could use some fresh air. If you're free, perhaps you could take her out to the garden?"

"I'd be happy to." Meg gave Mrs. White a dazzling smile. Simon felt the impact even though it wasn't directed at him. "I could use some fresh air also."

Murmuring apologies for causing trouble, Mrs. White left with Meg. Turning to White, Simon said, "Now about that lathe . . ."

Meg had begun the day with lessons in magic, and a tiring business it was. After her morning tutor left, Meg collapsed on her bed, exhausted by the concentration required in her lesson on the use of wands and other instruments for focusing power. "It would be less tiring to ride all day, Lucky," she said to the cat, who was curled up beside her on the bed.

Lucky raised his head and regarded her with worried golden eyes. After only a day in Falconer House, he was still frightened of almost everything and everyone except Meg. He was even nervous around Simon, who had healed him. Meg suspected that the half-grown cat would be wary of all males for some time to come since it had been boys who had almost killed him.

She stroked his soft fur, thinking how much his appearance had improved since the day before. He had been frantic when she brought him home, until she used calming magic on him. Simon had commented that she was unusually gifted in working with animals. Meg didn't know about that, but when she communicated with a creature, it never took long to achieve harmony.

Though so far Lucky had stayed in the safety of Meg's rooms, he'd moved from under the bed to on top of it. He'd also cleaned his smudged fur with his own rough little tongue, so his appearance was presentable. He liked the fact that he could eat whenever he wanted, and he had immediately figured out the use of the box of sand one of the Falconer footmen had provided.

Meg scratched the round little head and was rewarded with a purr. Thank heaven Simon had been able to heal the little fellow. Lucky's presence brightened Meg's life.

Her lazy thoughts were interrupted by a clear sense that Simon wanted her to join him. There was no feeling of emergency, but she did feel that promptness would be appreciated. She liked the way they could communicate mentally. It wasn't like hearing him speak, but it wasn't hard to get the sense of what he wanted.

She gave Lucky one last stroke before sliding from the bed and donning her slippers. After smoothing her voluminous green skirts, she presented herself to Simon in his study. As soon as she entered, she saw that the inventor's wife was looking unwell, and it wasn't hard to guess why.

Wanting fresh air herself, Meg led Mrs. White down to the garden. As they stepped into the sun, she remarked, "Isn't this a lovely garden? It seems larger than it is. Since I grew up in the country, I like coming here to see grass and flowers."

"'Tis very pretty," Mrs. White agreed. "I've lived in towns and cities my whole life, but like you, I enjoy the greenery. My husband and I will be moving to a new house soon and it has a bit of garden. I shall like that."

Meg guided the other woman to a bench shaded by a rose-covered arbor. "Shall I order some refreshments?"

Mrs. White clapped a hand to her midriff, looking unwell. "That's the last thing I need! Though I thank you for the thought, Lady Falconer." She closed her eyes and took several deep breaths. "I'm with child, so this is all normal according to the lady next door. She says I should be feeling better in another month or two."

There had been occasional pregnant maids at Castle Drayton, so Meg knew that was probably true. She had learned a great deal by watching the people around her, being so "simple" that her presence was ignored. "Is this your first child, Mrs. White?"

The woman nodded, her eyes still closed. Meg frowned, feeling a tug of something not quite right. Mrs. White was more than physically unwell. Something else was troubling her. "Forgive me for prying, but is there something wrong?"

Mrs. White opened her eyes. They were a lovely tear-washed gray. "I'm afraid I will die in childbed," she blurted out. "My mother did. I daren't say so to David because it would worry him, but what will happen to him if I die? He's wonderful clever, but has not a lick of common sense." She put her head into her hands and burst into tears.

Meg laid a hand on her shoulder. "No wonder you're upset! Not to mention that carrying a child makes one want to cry even if there's nothing wrong."

"Do you have children?"

"No!" Meg said, startled by a thought that seemed very alien. "Falconer and I have only just wed. But I've known other women in the family way, and tears always can be very close to the surface."

Mrs. White pulled a handkerchief from her pocket and used it to blot her eyes and blow her nose. "I'm sorry to inflict the tears on you, my lady. It's just . . . I wish so much that my mother were alive! I would feel less afraid, and I'd have her to cry on."

Guessing that Mrs. White needed a friend, Meg said, "Bother the title. I haven't been a lady for very long. My name is Meg, and better you should cry in front of me than your husband. The poor man looked worried enough when you left the room."

The other woman laughed a little. "The prospect of fatherhood has him awed and terrified. And I am Sarah, my lady." She halted. "I'm sorry about the 'my lady.'"

Meg chuckled. "I smile whenever I hear the title. My mother always thought I was a proper hoyden." And where did that come from, she wondered in amazement. Perhaps her memory was starting to return?

Yet she could remember nothing of her mother, or when such words had been said. She just knew they were true.

Putting that aside to consider later, she said more seriously, "It is normal to have fears when carrying a child, yet I feel sure that you will be delivered safely. A little boy."

Sarah stared at her. "Are you just saying that to make me feel better?"

No, Meg had had a flash of foreknowledge. Eerily, she had the sense that Sarah might go on to have two more healthy children, but only if her husband survived the danger that hovered around him.

The knowledge was deeply disquieting. Making her voice light, she said, "There have been midwives in my family, so all the females have a gift for seeing when a birth will go easily." Unlike her hoyden comment, this was pure invention, but a harmless one. "As to whether it will be a boy or girl—well, I was just guessing at that, but the odds are equal that I'll be right!"

Sarah laughed. "But you're not guessing about the delivery?"

Meg took Sarah's hand. "I swear that you will bear this child with no danger to you or your son. Please trust me, because fear can undermine your health."

"I . . . I want to believe you."

"Perhaps your mother in heaven is inspiring my words," Meg said softly. "How old were you when you lost her?"

"Seven." Sarah's hand tightened on Meg's. "She died with my newborn sister. I can still hear her screams. . . ."

"She must have been a loving woman for you to remember her so fondly." Meg added a calming spell to her words. She'd learned the spell from Mrs. Evans, the healer. It was much the same as what she did when she was soothing animals. Wanting to distract Sarah from her grief, she continued, "Where did you grow up?"

"In Cambridge. My father was a professor of mathematics." Sarah's smile was brittle. "Since professors can't marry, I'm illegitimate. My mother was my father's housekeeper. After she died, he didn't quite know what to do with me, until he found that I had a talent for mathematics. Not that a woman can do much with the knowledge, but I enjoyed learning, and now I can help David."

"You had an unusual upbringing, Sarah, but you seem to have used it well. Is your father still alive?"

Sarah shook her head. "He died when I was nineteen. He was too vague to have made a will naming me his heir, so his brothers swooped down and took everything. Being merciful, they bought me a coach ticket to Birmingham, where my mother had a sister I'd never met."

"Dear heavens, how despicable of your uncles! I hope your aunt was kind?"

"Yes, though she had children of her own and didn't need another mouth to feed." Sarah smiled and her face lit up as if she'd swallowed a candle. "But then I met David, so it was all worthwhile. He was willing to take me without a dowry, and no woman could have a better husband."

"You are both blessed," Meg said softly.

"So we are." Sarah clenched her hands together in her lap. "There is something I think you and Lord Falconer should know. David and I are Dissenters, my lady. Neither of us will change even if it means that Lord Falconer rescinds his funding."

It took a moment for Meg to understand Sarah's concern. Dissenters from the Church of England were banned from many activities, including public office and attending the most famous schools and universities. Some employers wouldn't hire people who were chapel, not church. Somewhere in her lost past, such questions were important, though she couldn't remember any details. "I can't see how that would affect your husband's ability to build a steam engine or yours to do calculations."

Sarah relaxed. "You don't mind?"

" 'In my father's house are many mansions,' " Meg quoted, and then wondered where that had come from. "I think God is more concerned with how we live our lives than in the details of how we worship Him."

Sarah's gaze was level. "I could never have imagined a countess like you."

"Well, I haven't been one for very long." Was still not one, in fact. "Perhaps in time I will become haughty and intolerant."

Sarah laughed. "I can't imagine that, either. Thank you for your kindness, Meg."

"You seem to be feeling better. I've heard that tea and dry toast go down easily when one's stomach is delicate. Does that sound appealing?"

"Actually, it does," Sarah said with surprise. "In fact, now that I'm feeling better, I'm ravenous."

"Then we shall see that you are fed. Both of you." Meg ushered Sarah back to the house. She hoped that today she had made another friend.

Chapter FOURTEEN

After Sarah and Meg shared tea and cakes, Meg returned the other woman to Simon's study, where the men were still happily discussing things mechanical. Simon gave her a warm smile that made her embarrassingly aware of the brief kiss they'd shared the day before. She wasn't sure whether to be glad or sorry that Lucky had interrupted them before matters had gone too far. The attraction between them was the sweetest thing she'd experienced since waking up to herself, but it was best not explored. Especially not in a public park, where anyone might ride by!

Thoughtfully she returned to her rooms and settled into the comfortable wing chair she used for meditation. It was time to explore the interesting bits of knowledge that had floated into her mind when she spoke with Sarah.

It was surprisingly difficult to slow down a mind, she had discovered. To concentrate, she started by focusing on the quill pen on her desk. It was much easier to lift now than in the beginning. She could move slightly larger objects, too, but suspected that this particular ability would never be more than a parlor trick. It would be much more useful if she could lift a book and bring it across the room to read, but she doubted she would ever be able to manage that much weight.

When her thoughts were as still as she could make them, she let the word "hoyden" float into her consciousness. Immediately she found what seemed like a true memory of her mother calling her that in a loving, rueful way. Filled with hope, Meg tried to conjure a face, a tone of voice, a location—anything to expand the memory. She failed, yet she had a powerful sense that more memories lay just on the other side of an invisible barrier. Maddeningly, she couldn't reach them.

Might that barrier be part of Drayton's magic? She explored the mental block and found that it had a stretchy quality, like fabric. There was some flex, but the block was impenetrable and it seemed to extend in all directions. She let her mind drift along the barrier—and ran smack into Drayton's consciousness.

She gasped, feeling as if she had fallen into a pit full of vipers. A faint thread of connection with Drayton was always present, but he couldn't reach her through it, so usually she could ignore him. Now she had blundered right into his mind.

He reacted with surprise that changed swiftly into a vicious hunger, as if he were a wolf and she were a rabbit that had fallen at his feet. His energy exploded around her, thick and suffocating.

She pulled away frantically, fleeing to the safety of her own mind while she invoked every shield she had been taught. She added layers until he felt distant, no longer a threat, but she had the ghastly sense that he was sniffing around her borders, looking for a chink in her defenses.

Lucky bounced onto Meg's lap and almost broke her concentration. After a rattled moment, she steadied her shields, at the same time cuddling the cat close. His physical warmth and affection helped counter Drayton's assault.

As his siege continued, a faint burn of power began flowing into her. Not Drayton—something friendly. Simon? No, the flavor of the power was nothing like him.

Lord, she was absorbing feline energy from Lucky! Though slight, the flavor was ancient and feral. Gradually it filled her, like wine pouring into a goblet. The next time Drayton prodded her, she slashed out with a predator's fierceness, raging to tear his spirit to ribbons. He vanished between one heartbeat and the next.

Disoriented, she opened her eyes. Surely he hadn't disappeared from existence? No, she could still feel the faint thread that connected them, but he had broken the larger connection to her mind when she attacked him.

How had she used Lucky's energy? He was just a small cat, so it wasn't a lot of power. Maybe Lucky had inspired something inside her? Or maybe some essential feline wildness had briefly transformed her? The more she learned of magic, the more questions she had.

For the moment, she was too drained to think about answers. She set Lucky on the floor and got to her feet, swaying. It took all her remaining strength to reach her bed. Too tired to push aside the covers, she flopped onto her back on top of them. The cat jumped up beside her and curled into a ball above her right shoulder. His purr rumbled in her ear.

She closed her eyes, thinking that in a week she would meet Drayton face-to-face at the council hearing. Please God, he would be condemned and stripped of his power.

She would never feel safe as long as he was alive and a mage.

"Meg? Are you there?" Simon knocked on her door, wondering if she might have fallen asleep. It was past the time they usually met for a predinner drink.

Uneasiness tugged at him. When there was no answer, he opened the door and entered her bedroom. Meg was sprawled on her bed, so still and pale that he wondered if she was dead. No, he felt the pulse of her energy, but this was not a healthy sleep.

The little cat was curled up beside her, and it glanced up with worried golden eyes as Simon sat on the edge of the bed. When he took Meg's hand, it was icy cold. "Meg, wake up!" Though he pitched his voice to penetrate, there was no response.

"Meg!" As he scanned her with inner vision, he placed his hands on the sides of her head and channeled warmth and what he hoped was his newfound healing energy. Though she stirred, she didn't wake. He found the unbreakable thread of connection to Drayton, but the knot he'd tied still held. He could find no other energy hooks buried in her, nor were there any signs of physical injury.

Her eyelids flickered and opened. She stared up at him from point-blank range, her changeable eyes winter gray. "What . . . ?"

"You fell into a trance of some sort and I needed to warm you," he explained, still cradling her head with his hands. "Did Drayton do this?"

"As I visited with Sarah, I had a memory of my mother so I meditated on that. I found a . . . a sort of barrier to the past. When I tried to explore it, I was suddenly right in Drayton's mind." She managed a rusty laugh. "Exactly what you warned me not to do."

"No wonder you went into a trance," he said grimly. "Drayton created the original barrier, so studying it took you to him. Did he steal your energy again?"

Her brow furrowed. "I don't think so. I retreated and threw up my shields, though he was still there, like a fox outside a chicken coop. Then Lucky jumped on my lap and I started to feel his energy joining with mine. I became . . . very feline. The next time I felt Drayton closing in, I . . . I leaped on him like a tiger." Her smile was uneven but real. "There really aren't good words to describe how magic works, are there? Of course I wasn't a tiger, I just slashed at him mentally. He vanished immediately. I got the impression that he was shocked and perhaps somewhat worried."

"Apparently you were able to merge with some cosmic essence of cat energy and use it to drive Drayton away. Maybe it's a form of wild magic. Dealing with it unexpectedly left you drained." Since she was better, he released her head and placed his left hand over her midriff, just above one of the body's seven energy centers. "Do you still feel catlike?"

She considered. "No. I've always loved cats and I sense them well, but the same is true with most animals. Except insects—it's hard to tune oneself to an ant or a beetle."

Gently he massaged her midriff with a circular motion. "You don't feel a desire to purr or chase a string?"

She caught her breath, her eyes widening. "What you're doing makes me want to purr, but I don't think that's a result of mentally sharing feline energy."

He paused in his massaging to touch her cheek. "You're much warmer now. Do you feel better?"

She stretched with a sinuousness that made his mouth dry. "Much better. I can feel your energy flowing through me like a tonic of sunshine."

Knowing he must get away from her, he started to rise. She caught his hand. "Please don't go away. It felt good to have you touch me." She swallowed. "I miss being touched. When I first went to Castle Drayton, there was a cook who would sometimes hug me." Her mouth twisted wryly. "She always said 'poor little mite.' But a hug from pity was better than none at all."

Wary but unable to resist her invitation, he let her tug him down so that he was lying next to her, on his side. Meg wasn't the only one who hungered to be touched. He placed his hand on her midriff again, feeding in more energy since hers was still low. "We must talk to Lady Bethany about this ability to channel animal energy. There should be a way for you to use it without exhausting yourself."

She raised her opposite arm to pet Lucky. "I wonder if I have to be touching an animal to resonate with the energy. Is Otto nearby? I could try with him."

"Not today. You need to recover." He continued making lazy circles on her midriff, acutely aware of the softness of her body and the lavender scent of her silky, unpowdered hair. "Even with you gone, Drayton still seems to have more power than I would expect. Do you know if he had any other energy slaves like you?"

She caught her breath, startled. "Not that I know of, but it's possible. Maybe here in London? That would help keep him strong." She started to push herself up. "How can we find out if there are others? If so, they must be freed!"

Simon pressed her gently back to the bed. "You're right that we need to investigate that—I don't know why I didn't think of it before. But not just now. You need the rest, and I'm enjoying being this close to you."

"I like it, too." She turned her face for a kiss. She was delicious, a unique, alluring blend of innocence and power. He wanted to inhale her essence, make them one together. His hand slid to her breast. Even through layers of gown and undergarments, he could feel the erotic softness.

"Ah, Simon . . ." She raised her hand to his neck, the skin cool against his increasing heat. His heartbeat quickened.

"We shouldn't be doing this," he murmured, but he continued to caress her, his hand moving from one breast to the other, then gradually down her body until he reached the juncture of her thighs. Warmth pulsed under her petticoats. Using the heel of his hand, he rubbed rhythmically. Her hips began rocking, rising to meet him as her breathing roughened.

Intoxicated by her responsiveness, he lost himself in the moment, carried along by pure sensation. The taste of her mouth, mingled scents of lavender and desire, her soft, eager sounds. He was so tired of being alone. . . .

She cried out and shudders ran through her. When they ended, she opened startled eyes and stared at him. "What happened?"

Her question snapped him from his sensual daze. What the devil had he been thinking? He *hadn't* been thinking, of course—that was the problem. "It was an introduction to the delights of the flesh, my dear."

"Am I no longer a virgin?" She frowned. "That was not like what animals do when they mate."

"As I said, it was an introduction." His body was hard and burning for release, but his control was intact again. He pulled her against him, stroking her back as she buried her face against his shoulder. "One I should not have performed, but at least I came to my senses before taking your virginity."

Voice muffled, she said, "Now I understand why the stallions got so excited when the mares went into heat."

He laughed, grateful that she released the tension with a quip. "All male creatures tend to lose their wits when an attractive, willing female is nearby. It's not to our credit."

After a long silence, she said, "How much of a virgin do I have to be in order to save you from transforming into a unicorn?"

"I don't know." As she had recognized, today he had taken a kind of virginity from her. Now she understood something of what pleasure her body might feel, and how a man's touch could affect her. "Different peoples define virginity differently, I've heard. In some lands, a woman is a virgin until she bears a child. I have no idea how unicorns define virginity."

She studied his face. "You don't seem to have the mindless reaction that you had in unicorn form. I hope that doesn't mean I am no longer virgin enough to be useful."

"More likely it means that I find you attractive in the way of a man." Lightly he kissed her forehead. "If I had been in unicorn mode, I don't think I would have been able to control myself, so perhaps the effect of being a beast is waning. I hope so."

"If the unicorn influence fades, will you no longer have healing ability?"

He smiled ruefully. "I have no idea, Meg. We are in unknown territory, magically speaking. I'll be glad when Gwynne Owens arrives in London. As a scholar of obscure Guardian lore, she might have some knowledge of what I can expect."

"If the council rules against Drayton next week, your troubles will be over." She smiled. "And I can start searching for my family."

She was right—but in his bones, he knew it would not be so simple.

Chapter FIFTEEN

Meg dressed with care, wearing the most dignified of her new ensembles. Then she sat in her wing chair and meditated to calm herself. Lastly, she erected her shields and checked that they were at maximum strength. Nonetheless, when Simon knocked at her door, her heart almost leaped out of her chest. "Come in," she managed to say.

He entered and offered his arm. "Courage, my dear. Drayton will not be allowed to harm you. I swear it." He smiled without humor. "Even if it takes the combined efforts of several of us to block him."

"I trust you and Lady Bethany to protect me, but just seeing him . . ." She shuddered as she took his arm. "I might be violently ill."

"If that happens, try to be sick on him."

A bubble of laughter escaped her. "That's a pleasing thought. Shall we be off?"

He escorted her from the room and down the stairs. "There is no way to avoid facing Drayton, but if luck is with us, this unpleasantness will be over today. If not—well, it may take time, but Drayton will be stopped."

She clung to that thought, and to Simon's arm, as his carriage rattled through the streets of London to Sterling House, the town residence of a leading Guardian family. The large ballroom was convenient for important meetings.

As he helped her from the carriage, Simon murmured, "Remember that you are a beautiful woman with immense power—more than Drayton has in his own right. You are in every way superior to him."

"I do like it when you say I'm beautiful, even though I don't believe it."

"Believe." He smiled down with a warmth that made her fears recede.

Head high, she accompanied Simon inside. As soon as they crossed the threshold, she felt a crush of energy. She glanced around the foyer. "What's wrong here?"

"A damping spell makes it almost impossible to wield most kinds of magic within the house," he replied. "During council meetings that might rouse passions, it's good policy to prevent anyone from working a spell we might all regret. You should be able to sense emotions to some extent, but destructive magic is impossible."

That was wise, but the field made her feel suffocated. She hadn't realized how much she had become accustomed to seeing the world with inner senses as well as the outer ones.

They ascended to the ballroom. At least two dozen men and women were milling about the room, chatting and nibbling on refreshments. Two or three had taken seats at the tables, which were set in a U shape. Facing the tables were rows of chairs. Simon observed, "Members of every Guardian family are here to observe the proceedings."

She studied the group—and froze when her gaze found Lord Drayton. Richly dressed in gray and white satin, he was laughing with a small group of men. He must have felt her presence, because as soon as she looked at him, he swung around to stare at her. His familiar, saturnine face triggered a wave of paralyzing fear. She wanted to run, yet couldn't have moved to save her life.

When he saw her, his eyes lit with malicious pleasure and he started across the room, glittering like the courtier he was. Simon squeezed her arm, hard, and she managed to look away from Drayton. Her heart was pounding. Damnation, she had known that seeing him would make her wits go awry! She looked helplessly at Simon, wondering if there was anything he could do here, where most magic was suppressed.

Expression like ice, Simon ostentatiously turned his back, giving Drayton the cut direct and taking Meg with him. She heard several people gasp at what was the most powerful expression of disapproval available in polite society. Meg could feel emotions of shock, interest, a dash of amusement from a man—and rapier-sharp fury from Drayton.

How did she know about the cut direct? It wasn't something she had learned in the last fortnight. Before she could ponder that unexpected bit of knowledge, Lady Bethany approached them. "You look lovely in that shade of blue, Meg. Welcome to your first council meeting. Let me introduce you to the other councillors."

Radiating calm, she took Meg's hand. Two of the six councillors were among Meg's tutors. The very grand Lady Sterling, mistress of this house, had been surprisingly amusing when she taught Meg techniques of communication. Though the elderly Sir Jasper Polmarric was wheelchair-bound, his lessons on illusion were fascinating.

A chime sounded, and Polmarric wheeled his chair behind the tables, taking the central position. "It is time to begin this meeting," he said in a surprisingly powerful voice. "Please be seated."

Simon led Meg to one end of the first row of chairs. "Two council members can't attend, so Lady Sterling will use her talking sphere to transmit sight and sound to them. Her magic is one of the few that the damping spell will allow. Usually Lady Beth would preside over a meeting, but not today, since she is one of the complainants. Sir Jasper is the senior member, so he will preside in her place."

Meg scanned the serious faces of the councillors as they took their seats behind the tables. Paper and pencils were at every place in case members wanted to take notes. Lady Sterling sat at the far left end of the U, one hand resting on the quartz sphere in front of her on a velvet-covered stand.

Meg asked, "Does being a Guardian also make one a good judge?"

"Not necessarily, but councillors are chosen because they are mature and have a reputation for fairness and honesty. Still, they are individuals who have opinions of their own." His gaze moved to a lean man with salt and pepper hair and a flinty expression. "Some will agree that Drayton is a menace. Others . . . will be harder to convince."

When everyone was seated, Drayton at the opposite side of the room from Meg and Simon, Polmarric said, "We meet today under grave circumstances. Lord Drayton has been charged of criminal misuse of his powers by two other Guardians. Drayton, do you wish to say anything before testimony is given?"

Drayton rose, a polished man of the world who was baffled by the charges against him. "Sir Jasper, I truly do not understand why I have been called before this council. While there was a contretemps with Lord Falconer, I have done nothing to justify this hearing. Let the plaintiffs speak so that I may refute them."

Sir Jasper turned to Simon. "Lord Falconer, you are the chief plaintiff. Please describe what has led you to place such serious charges against a fellow Guardian."

Simon rose, his expression cool and detached. "As all of you know, my family has a tradition of enforcing the council's will. My chief mission is to ensure that no Guardians misuse their powers to injure the innocent, or to bring harm on the Families. I was first alerted to the presence of a rogue mage during the late rebellion, when I detected signs of a powerful sorcerer who was encouraging greater strife. There was no partisanship. Rather, his goal seemed to be to increase the amount of fear and danger.

"I tracked his energy signature until I lost him near Shrewsbury. I believe the rogue realized I was hunting him, because his activity ceased for some months. I maintained a watch, and eventually he began to make trouble again. It took three years for me to build a case, because the rogue manifested very rarely. As I put the pieces together, it became clear that my quarry was Lord Drayton."

Speaking without notes, he listed the instances of improper behavior, demonstrating why he had concluded that Drayton was to blame. When he finished, he produced copies of a foolscap sheet that summarized his points. Meg had noticed that he'd brought a small folio, but hadn't realized what it contained. A young woman distributed the sheets to the council members, also handing one to Drayton.

After the members had glanced at the sheet, Simon continued, "When I visited Drayton's home to confront him, he confirmed his guilt by transforming me into a unicorn against my will. He then attempted to murder me by ritual magic in order to claim the magic of the unicorn horn. If I had been unable to escape, I would not be standing here today, and Drayton would be an even greater menace than he is now."

Gasps filled the room. Meg guessed that it was a mix of shock that the powerful Lord Falconer could be overcome by magic and horror that one Guardian wished to murder another. She also realized that under Simon's controlled mask, he loathed showing his weakness. Despite the damping spell, she was learning how to read the emotions of those around her.

"This is grave indeed," Sir Jasper said. "Have you finished your statement, Lord Falconer? If so, it is Lord Drayton's turn to rebut your charges."

Simon nodded and sat down. Meg touched his hand. His fingers curled around hers in a hard clasp before letting go. An enforcer of Guardian law did not publicly hold hands with a female, even if she was allegedly his wife. But she knew that he had taken comfort in that brief contact.

Drayton rose again, his expression all injured innocence. "If that was Falconer's interpretation of what happened, no wonder he thinks so ill of me! I can't comment on the renegade mage he was hunting. As most of you know, my power is moderate at best, so I was unable to sense any rogues. I am even more incapable of creating the kind of chaos this rogue was conjuring." He made a rueful face. "Really, Falconer, I'm flattered that you think so highly of my powers!"

His words generated smiles and a few chuckles. Meg realized unhappily that Drayton had a relaxed, affable manner that must disarm people who didn't know him. Simon's manner was supremely competent, but also somewhat intimidating, which might count against him in these circumstances.

Drayton turned toward Simon, his expression regretful. "I was startled when you entered my castle bristling with accusations. Especially since you broke in like a thief in the night rather than calling at a civilized hour to discuss your suspicions." He paused a moment to let that sink in for his audience. "Because you entered my study unannounced, you walked into the middle of a magical experiment I was attempting. I found the spell in an old grimoire and decided to try it. It was supposed to increase personal power, so I have no idea how it managed to turn you into a unicorn. Either I made mistakes, or your untimely interruption caused it to go wildly awry."

"There was indeed a spell in your study," Simon said dryly. "Two, in fact. One was the transformation spell; the other, the ritual magic death spell. Both had been prepared and held ready for activation when I walked in. You don't give yourself enough credit, Drayton. It was a masterfully conceived trap."

"I certainly wish I had the power you claim I have!" Drayton said. "There was one spell only, and that incomplete. While I regret that it affected you in such a dramatic way, there was nothing illegal in my experimentation. Guardians are encouraged to try new magic to expand the sum of our knowledge."

"And your death threat?"

The other man shrugged. "You were confused at finding yourself a unicorn. Terrified, even. I don't think you were able to understand human language. I tried to calm you, promising you that I would do my best to undo the spell, but you panicked and smashed your way out of the castle. I sent men after you into the forest. They braved a dreadful storm to try to bring you back to safety, but you had vanished. While this must have been very frightening, you really can't blame me for the consequences of your surprise visit." Having finished his rebuttal, he sat down.

With growing anger, Meg saw how Drayton was casting Simon as both bully and weakling, with himself as an unjustly accused innocent. When Sir Jasper turned to her, she was ready to speak.

"Lady Falconer, please give your statement concerning Lord Drayton."

As she stood, she called on the feline energy she had learned from Lucky. She had practiced in the last few days, and found that a small amount made her braver and more alert. "I was only thirteen or fourteen when Drayton kidnapped me and removed my memory of home and family. For ten years I lived at Castle Drayton, largely ignored and treated as a simpleton."

Her eyes narrowed as she studied Drayton, refusing to let fear rule her. "The only exceptions were when Lord Drayton brutally invaded my mind. It wasn't until Lord Falconer rescued me and released the mind-block spells that I understood what had been done to me. I have a great deal of natural power. Drayton recognized that and treated me as his slave, stealing my power for his own purposes. He may not have a great deal of innate power, but he didn't need it, because he could use mine."

A shiver of mental revulsion went through the audience. Entering another Guardian's mind without permission was a major offense against propriety. Sometimes two mages who were very close would agree to share power, but taking power by force was brutally painful for the victim, and an even greater offense.

Perhaps Drayton could also sense sympathies shifting against him because he immediately got to his feet again. "Child, child, your anger wounds me," he said with compassion. "I found you on an isolated road, injured and near death from a head wound. The result of a fall, perhaps. Of course I couldn't leave you there to die, so I took you to my home and summoned a surgeon. Though he saved your life, your brain was damaged by the injury. You knew nothing but your first name, and you could barely speak. I did my best to find your family, but without success. I could hardly turn you loose in the world to become prey to every passing tinker, so I kept you in my own household under the care of my housekeeper."

"For a girl who allegedly lost her wits from a head injury, Lady Falconer is remarkably articulate," Sir Jasper observed.

"I am amazed and delighted at how well she has recovered." Drayton smiled at Meg warmly. "To be honest, I didn't think much about you. I'm a busy man, and whenever I happened to see you around the castle, you seemed well fed and well cared for, so I assumed my housekeeper was doing a good job.

"However, on several occasions I tried to heal your mind. That may be what caused you to feel that I was assaulting you emotionally. I am truly sorry that the experience was so unpleasant for you—I would have stopped if I had realized that. Perhaps you were affected so strongly because of your own power and the sensitivity that goes with it, but I wasn't aware that you were so magically gifted. As I've mentioned, my own power is limited. It was clear that my attempts at healing were ineffective, but that wasn't surprising since brain injuries are said to be impossible for even the most gifted healers. Nonetheless, I did try."

"You weren't attempting healing," Meg snapped. "It was mind rape."

Though some councillors flinched at her words, the man with salt and pepper hair said, "Now that you are well, tell us your name and place of birth."

Meg clenched her hands, hating that she couldn't answer. "I don't know. I remember nothing before Lord Drayton abducted me. That day I remember clearly. He said that I didn't know what I was, and wiped away my past. My rational mind was largely paralyzed until Lord Falconer rescued me."

The councillor leaned back in his chair. "Your experience suggests a head injury, so it's not surprising that your memories may be unclear."

"They are *not* unclear! I may not remember my childhood, but what happened since is vivid."

She could see that her protestations didn't convince Salt and Pepper. She sat down again, bleakly aware that a single dissenter could save Drayton's lying neck.

Sir Jasper turned to Lady Bethany. "You also have placed a charge against Lord Drayton. Please give your statement."

Lady Beth stood at her place behind the table. In the slanting afternoon sun, she was as pretty and petite as a china figurine. "I became involved with the situation when Falconer and Meg appeared at my country home. Clearly both had endured a considerable ordeal. When Falconer had recovered, we discussed what had happened. I attempted to investigate Lord Drayton's energy—not to enter his mind, but merely to get a general sense of where he was. He struck such a fierce blow in return that I collapsed. If Falconer had not acted promptly, I might not have survived."

Her words produced another powerful emotional reaction in the audience. Falconer might be feared and Meg was a stranger, but Lady Bethany was well known and well loved among the Families.

Drayton sprang to his feet again. "Lady Bethany, I am horrified to think that I might have injured you! I remember the incident, but only now do I realize who was the source of that mental invasion. I was distressed by what had happened with Lord Falconer. When an unknown mind attacked mine, I reacted as if a wasp had landed at my hand. I hit back instinctively." He smiled ruefully. "You do not know your own strength, my lady. What might have seemed a gentle touch to you felt like an assault to me."

"You also do not know your strength, Lord Drayton," Lady Bethany said dryly. "I've never experienced such a powerful mental attack."

His expression turned solicitous. "Though your magic is as great as ever, with age bodies become more frail. Perhaps that is why my defense seemed so powerful. If only I had known it was you! But mind-touch has never been a talent of mine."

It didn't take power to recognize that Lady Bethany wasn't pleased by the suggestion that she was feeble, but she held her tongue. So did Simon, barely, though Meg sensed his rising anger and feared that he might shape shift, until she realized that the damping spell prevented that.

She leaned over and whispered, "What about the energy hook he has in me? If the councillors see that, wouldn't it be proof that he's lying?"

He shook his head. "The damping spell makes it impossible to see something so subtle."

"What if the damping spell is dropped?"

"Even then, only a handful of people in this room would have the ability to see the hook, and not all of them are councillors." His mouth twisted humorlessly. "Not to mention that if the spell is dropped, I would probably try to kill Drayton, if I didn't turn into a unicorn first."

He wasn't joking, either. "At least with the spell in place, you can allow yourself to feel anger," she offered.

"Not only feel it, but express it." A dangerous glint in his eyes, he stood and raised his voice so it thundered through the room. "You are eloquent, Drayton, but honeyed words do not change the truth. You assaulted me and threatened murder, you enslaved an innocent girl and stole her power, and you struck down one of the most honored members of the Families, claiming you didn't know your own strength. One of your glib explanations might be true, but all of them? No. They only prove how adept you are at lying."

After a moment of shock, Drayton exploded with fury. "How *dare* you! If this were not a council meeting, I would call you out! Falconers have been hunters for too long—you think yourself superior to the average Guardian. Sir, you are *not.* I am a royal minister, a confidant of the king, yet you had the audacity to invade my home, kidnap an unfortunate girl under my protection, and incite Lady Bethany to attempt an illegal invasion of my mind. For too long your arrogance has been allowed to go unchecked, but no longer will you be allowed to persecute your fellows."

His gaze swept the row of councillors, meeting the eyes of each in turn. "You are my friends, my family, my fellow Guardians. Think hard before you condemn me based on one man whose unlawful invasion of my home caused all the subsequent accusations. Particularly when he is a man of great power who has too long gone unquestioned."

Meg was becoming skilled at reading emotions through the damping spell, and she recognized with dread how effective Drayton's performance had been. The brute had done a masterly job of turning everything inside out.

The meeting continued for another hour. As councillors questioned Drayton and his three accusers, it was obvious that Drayton had cast enough doubt to undermine Simon's accusations. Meg tried to explain the twilight state in which she had existed under Drayton's control, but the image he'd painted of her as a brain-injured girl had taken root. Most of the councillors did not take her testimony seriously.

When the councillors had no more questions, the vote was taken. Lady Bethany was called first. Voice clear and strong, she said, "Even if I had not personally experienced Lord Drayton's attack, I would still accept Lord Falconer's word. In the years we have worked together, I have never once known him to lie, mislead, or exaggerate. I vote guilty."

Sir Jasper Polmarric was next. "To strip away the magic of a fellow Guardian is the most grievous punishment we can impose. Never should it be done lightly. Nonetheless, what I have heard here today has persuaded me that Lord Drayton has gravely misused his power. I say guilty."

Salt and Pepper, whose name turned out to be Lord Halliburton, was next. "Falconer, you have failed to make your case beyond a reasonable doubt. Indeed, if Drayton chose to bring charges against you, I would be willing to hear them. As enforcer of Guardian law, you above all must be above suspicion. I say not proven."

Meg released her breath in a rush. They had lost, and Drayton would walk out of this house with his power unchecked. The final vote was four "guilty" to five "not proven." The older councillors, who had worked with Simon for years, were uniformly behind him, but the younger members were less supportive.

Based on the emotions she was reading, Meg guessed that two of the dissenters genuinely felt the case against Drayton was insufficiently proven. Two more had voted with distinct satisfaction that they could justify opposing the infamous Falconer. The fifth councillor, she couldn't read, since it was a man not present at the meeting. His vote was relayed through Lady Sterling, who had supported Simon.

With the voting finished, Sir Jasper said, "The greater the power, the greater the need to act according to the rule of law. This decision is binding upon all parties to this hearing. Any attempt to injure opposing parties would be viewed as a major crime against Guardian law. Do you all accept this verdict and the authority of this council?"

"I do." It was a chorus of replies from Drayton, Simon, and Lady Bethany. Meg was unable to make herself agree, but Sir Jasper overlooked that, probably because she was new and uneducated in Guardian ways.

Expression gloomy, Sir Jasper said, "I declare this hearing adjourned."

The ballroom broke into a buzz of conversation. Several younger Guardians surrounded Drayton and offered congratulations. Meg felt clearly that too many in this room were taking pleasure in seeing Simon humbled. Drayton's affability had proved more powerful than the truth.

She stared down at her knotted hands, and felt afraid. Very afraid.

Chapter SIXTEEN

Simon moved a few steps away to talk to Lady Sterling, who looked worried. Meg stayed in her chair, her gaze down as she struggled to compose herself. Then a shadow fell across her and a chillingly familiar voice said, "You've improved remarkably, Meg. Foolish of me to overlook your great potential."

"Damn you!" Heart pounding, Meg leaped to her feet. Even with her standing, Drayton loomed over her. Like everything else he'd said today, his comment to her sounded innocent but was double-sided.

As she looked into his face, she saw something new: raw, angry desire. Now that she was no longer a ragged simpleton, he wanted her for more than her power.

As her fear escalated, she tried drawing on feline energy to make her braver, but it didn't work. He was too close, his presence too overpowering. Then she tried to think of a suitably searing retort, again without success. Magic wouldn't operate here, so she couldn't strike him with her power. Should she give him the cut direct? No, Simon had already done that, and besides, that was too civilized a reaction for the mixture of fear, loathing, and fury that she felt.

According to Drayton, Meg was a brain-injured child, so why not act like one? As swift as thought, she slapped his cheek as hard as she could. "You lie brilliantly, Drayton," she said through gritted teeth. "But the truth will ultimately win."

His jaw dropped and his cheek flared red from the impact of her blow. Pivoting on her heel, she walked away. Simon had turned at the sound of the slap and in two strides he was beside her. Under his breath, he said, "My sentiments exactly, Meg."

Everyone was staring at her. Let them. Slapping Drayton might be childish, but it had relieved a little of her frustration. She took Simon's arm. "It's time to leave."

Tall, elegant Lady Sterling came up to them. "Would you like some privacy to compose yourselves before you return home?"

"An excellent idea," Simon replied. "Essential, in fact."

They followed Lady Sterling from the ballroom and up another flight to a small sitting room. "Stay as long as you like." Lady Sterling regarded them both sympathetically. "I'm sorry the hearing went so badly. Drayton is a liar through and through, but a very skilled one."

Simon grimaced. "I knew it would be difficult to convince all nine councillors beyond doubt, but I didn't think the results would be this bad."

Unable to keep silent longer, Meg said bitterly, "What will it take to persuade them that Drayton is evil? A murder committed in front of the whole council?"

"No, but it will take more than one person's word against Drayton's, when he has a plausible alternative explanation to what really happened. Plausible doubt is a great blessing to the accused." A glint of amusement showed in her ladyship's blue eyes. "Lady Falconer, officially I must disapprove of your slapping Drayton, but privately, it did my heart good to see it. Sometimes I worry that the Families are overcivilized. The proof of that is that we are allowing a predator to walk free."

Simon shook his head. "Guardian misdeeds can have catastrophic effects. Strict laws are necessary so that we know we will not be persecuted unjustly. At the same time, we all know that no matter how much power we have, we will be unable to resist the combined power of the council if we are judged to be rogues. The law saves us from ourselves."

"This is why you're such a fine enforcer, Falconer. You truly believe in the law. Which is why it's also impossible to believe that you would lie when accusing a man of criminal abuse of power." Lady Sterling opened the door to leave. "I'll tell my husband to keep the damping spell in force until you leave. As to Drayton—well, when matters come to a head, you know that you can call on us both if necessary."

"I do, and I'm very grateful for that."

After Lady Sterling left, Meg sank onto the sofa, rubbing her arms with nervous fingers. Just thinking of Drayton made her feel unclean. Simon frowned. "Did he say something to you before you slapped him?"

"Only that he had overlooked my potentials. But . . . the way he *looked* at me!" She shuddered. The more she thought about being touched by him, the more she loathed the idea.

Simon swore and caught her left hand in his. "He can't take you against your will, Meg. You have too much power. No matter how much he lusts for you, he won't be able to break through your shields."

She sighed and rested her cheek against the back of his hand, soothed by his touch. "What if he manages to activate the spell that takes away my mind and will?"

"He will not get that chance."

She appreciated the reassurance, although she knew that even Simon could not absolutely guarantee her safety. "I shall have to continue practicing my shielding and defense techniques."

His fingers tightened around hers. "No matter how much I want to protect you, there is no substitute for being a fierce fighter yourself. Jean Macrae speaks highly of your defensive skills."

"I hope I never have to use them against Drayton." She hesitated. "He had such power over me for so long that it's hard not to become paralyzed when he looks at me. I have a horrible fear that if he came after me when there was no one around, I might not be able to lift a hand to him."

"I understand how he has that effect on you, but I think that if such a situation should arise, you would surprise yourself." With his other hand, he caressed her head, his touch gentle. "You survived meeting him today with colors flying. Next time it will be easier."

She sighed. "Given how small society is, I suppose there will be a next time."

"Probably it will be at Lady Bethany's ball." He smiled. "Invoke the lioness energy before you go, and he will shrink like a terrified mouse."

She had to laugh. Releasing his hand, she said, "You give me strength, Simon. I know that you must have faced much worse than Drayton."

"There is more than one way for a situation to be difficult." He began to pace around the room, his restless power blatantly visible under his well-tailored surface. "It's damned unnerving to know that if I can't get my temper under control, I'll turn into a wild beast."

She relaxed into the sofa, tired now that her tension was unwinding. "I assume the damping spell is what has spared you from transforming into a unicorn?"

"Yes, which is why Lady Sterling will ensure that the spell is maintained until I master my anger." He stopped to stare out the window at the mews behind the house, his hands locked behind his back. "Which will take time. I am furious with Drayton for the damage he has done and his insults to you and Lady Beth. I am almost equally angry with myself for how I presented the evidence, and for losing my temper. I had thought the effects of the unicorn form were wearing off, but apparently not. My judgment and self-discipline have both been weakened."

Though his voice was expressionless, she could feel the bleakness in his soul, as well as his suppressed fury. "You are too hard on yourself. Drayton is wickedly clever, and Guardian law makes it difficult to condemn a rogue to the maximum punishment. You are not to blame for either of those things."

"I am to blame for being a man that some people prefer not to believe."

"As you said once, those who enforce the law are not always popular. The experienced councillors all supported you." She frowned, sensing that there was more to this discussion than was obvious. "I have trouble believing that you have ever done anything to cause other Guardians to condemn you."

There was a long silence before he replied. "I haven't. But an old scandal has tainted the family name."

She studied his broad shoulders, rigid under the subtle shimmer of his brocade coat. "That's not your fault, either."

"Perhaps not. But there are many who believe that the sins of the fathers are visited on their sons."

Guessing that he hadn't used that phrase by accident, she asked, "What did your father do?"

After another silence, he said flatly, "My esteemed sire murdered my mother, then killed himself. I was sixteen."

Meg gasped, understanding that this explained much about Simon. "How horrible! Why did he do it?"

"Among Guardians, adultery is rare unless the marriage is a complete failure. Intimacy makes such emotional demands on us that it is not done lightly. There are exceptions. My mother was one. She liked the casual immorality of aristocratic society. My father was . . . old-fashioned and possessive. Finally he stopped her in the only way he knew, and could not live with the consequences."

"H . . . how did he do it?"

"By magic. A wicked perversion of all his great talents."

An image flashed through Meg's mind of a man and a woman making love, the man with Simon's silky fair hair, the woman voluptuous and provocative. In a way impossible to describe, the image contained passion, fury, death, and soul-destroying despair.

And Simon was the one who had found his parents' lifeless bodies. The scent of twisted magic had hung over them.

Aching, she rose and came up behind him, wrapping her arms around his waist and resting her head against his shoulder. "How damnable it was to leave you to face those consequences when you were only a boy."

"The madness that drove him to murder was not the product of a rational mind." He turned and enfolded her in his arms. "It was a long time ago. Lady Bethany took me into her household. Lord and Lady Sterling and Sir Jasper Polmarric were particularly kind. As I've said before, the Guardians take care of their own."

She wondered if he had seen the ghosts of his parents, but it wasn't a question she could ask. She had admired his strength before. Now she admired it even more.

And her admiration wasn't only of the mind. The physical pleasure of his touch loosened her badly strung nerves. Perhaps the effect could be mutual. "I know that we can't make love, but I want to feel your hands. I want you to take away the memory of the way Drayton looked at me." Rising on her toes, she brushed her lips against his.

His embrace transformed from comfort to passion as his fierce kiss tilted her head back. She responded breathlessly, whimpering with pleasure as his hands slid over her with leisurely thoroughness. Every fiber of her came alive as sensation drowned all memory of Drayton's fetid lust.

"You're not quite tall enough," he murmured as he drew her across the room. He sat on the sofa and pulled her onto his lap. "Isn't this better?"

"Much," she breathed. As their kisses deepened, she shifted position so that she was straddling him, her skirts shimmering around them. Their bodies pressed together in a wickedly provocative imitation of intercourse. Intoxicated, she leaned into him, hardly noticing as they sank down until they were lying along the sofa, with her on top.

Hazily she wished that there were no garments between them, but mere fabric couldn't block passion. She rolled her pelvis against him, unconsciously longing for more. He began driving his hips against her. Panting, she matched his rhythm as flesh called to flesh.

This time when her body convulsed she recognized what was happening. He groaned and caught her hips, thrusting against her over and over until the tension suddenly rushed from his body.

Meg gasped for breath as she lay sprawled along his hard, muscled body. If a simulation of lovemaking could be so intense, what would the real thing be like? The question brought an image of lying skin to skin with Simon. She shivered with delight at the thought.

"Are you cold?" He caressed her back and hips with both hands, spreading warmth and contentment.

"No." She rubbed her cheek against his shoulder. "I was just wondering what it would be like to be lovers in truth."

"I think we already are, even though we have not been fully intimate." He smoothed back her hair, which was tumbling down from its formal arrangement. "I tell you things I tell no one else. When you are not near, I wish you were."

She kissed him again, her lips clinging with lingering sweetness rather than passion. "If lovers speak private words meant only for each other, then lovers we are." She smiled, liking the sound of that. "I have a lover. That makes me sound terribly grown-up."

Her comment was a mistake—she knew it when his lips tightened.

"I am not fourteen, Simon," she said firmly. "I may not have the experience of most women my age, but that is being remedied quickly."

"That does not change the fact that I am taking advantage of your innocence," he said, his eyes troubled.

"Nonsense. It was I who took advantage of you," she said briskly. "And if what we did was less than wise—well, I'm no longer bothered by the thought of Drayton's lust, and you no longer feel angry."

"Point taken." He levered himself up, keeping her within the circle of his arm. "But I hope we don't have to find out if you are still virgin enough to save me from being trapped as a unicorn. The answer is getting more doubtful."

"I have trouble worrying about that now." She rested against him, eyes closed as she wondered if she had ever been happier. Not that she could remember. "Why does the idea of being lovers feel so right when the idea of marriage feels so wrong?"

"Because marriage is a commitment till death does us part. You're not ready for that now. I don't know if I will ever be ready." His fingers skimmed her cheek with gossamer tenderness. "And yet—after Drayton is vanquished and you leave London to find your family . . . I hope you'll come back."

"I will," she whispered. She was beginning to suspect that she would always come back to him, and that was a thought as alarming as it was irresistible.

Chapter SEVENTEEN

David's gaze roamed over the newly outfitted shop, from the tools hanging on the wall to the cabinet holding small bits of hardware to the long table where components for his new model engine rested. Along the wall stood working models of three engines that he'd painstakingly built. "Isn't this the prettiest sight you've ever seen?"

Sarah laughed. "I wouldn't go that far, love, but it's a splendid workshop, to be sure. And outfitted at a bargain price."

"I didn't want to waste Lord Falconer's money." He grinned. "I want his lordship to be willing to give me more later."

Sarah laid a hand on his arm. "All well and good, but now it's time to come to the house and have a bite to eat. You should start work with a full stomach."

"As my lady wishes." Laughing, he slid his arm around her waist and gave her a kiss. "You're right—the shop isn't the prettiest sight I've ever seen. You are."

His wife's eyes sparkled. "If you think such a foolish compliment will get you an extra egg for your tea—it will."

He rested a hand on her still-flat belly. "You've always been lovely, Sarah, but now you glow, just like his lordship said."

She threw her arms around his neck with sudden fierceness. "We are so lucky! God grant that we always be so."

Silently he agreed as he hugged her back. Sometimes he dreamed that he would become a famous inventor and that he and Sarah would live in a fine house in the country, with children and grandchildren underfoot. Other nights, he had nightmares of dying suddenly, maybe a fever or run over by a wagon, and Sarah being left penniless to support their child. His wishes and his fears, both vividly expressed at night as he lay with his wife in his arms. He wanted to believe that the dream of long life and prosperity was the true one.

The door swung open. "Mr. White? Oh, sorry!" Blushing beet red at the sight of David and Sarah, the young man pulled off his cap and backpedaled from the door.

Keeping an arm around Sarah, David said, "I'm David White. What can I do for you?"

The tall, gangling youth said with a Scottish accent, "My name is Peter Nicholson, sir. My cousin William, who lives just around the corner, said you are developing a new steam engine. I . . . I was wondering if you might need some help. Sir." He swallowed hard, a prominent Adam's apple bobbing.

David's brows arched. "News travels quickly. What is your experience?"

"I worked for an instrument-maker in Greenwich, sir. And my father was a blacksmith, so I know how to forge."

"Those are useful skills." David thought about it. An assistant would be valuable, but he hadn't planned on paying wages so soon. "I couldn't afford to pay much, nor can I give you an apprenticeship since I have no Guild membership myself. Also, an assistant of mine can't be afraid to get his hands dirty."

The youth raised his hands, showing the calluses and ingrained soil of a working man. "I come of honest craftsmen, sir. My hands are my best tools."

David glanced at Sarah, who was the expert at judging character. She gave a slight nod. "Then we shall deal well together, Mr. Nicholson."

"You'll have me, then?" The youth's face lit up like a lantern. "Oh, thank you, sir! 'Tis said that you've solved the problem of Newcomen's engine."

"Not yet, but I hope to. His engine burns far too much fuel, so it's not practical for much more than pumping water out of mines." He waved at his row of models. "I have a model of Newcomen's beam engine. Shall I explain its flaws?"

"Yes, *sir!*" Nicholson crossed the workshop and reverently touched the scale model that had been David's first serious attempt to understand steam engines.

"I'll bring over bread and ale and cheese," Sarah said philosophically. "I swear that if the house wasn't at the other end of the garden, you'd soon starve."

"You shall be my savior." David smiled, then turned his attention to his worktable and his new employee. With four skilled hands, they could work twice as fast.

Meg sat quietly in her favorite wing chair while she examined her surroundings with inner vision. She was practicing the detection of trace magic both old and new. She had no trouble locating the thread that bound her to Drayton, curse his black soul. She checked it daily to ensure that the block was still holding. So far, so good. Simon did good work.

Much more complicated was identifying other traces of magic in a house that had been home to Guardians since it was built. Her rooms had belonged to every Falconer countess, so she could clearly sense the energy of five or six different women. Strongest were the traces of Simon's mother. She seemed to have been a charming, lighthearted female. A pity those traits had contributed to her death.

After Meg scanned the sitting room around her, she moved mentally to the adjacent bedroom. Furious embarrassment flooded her when she reached the bed. A *lot* of magic had taken place there, most of a highly personal nature.

One of her tutors had said that she was exceptionally gifted at detecting traces of magic. Meg supposed that there were times that would be useful, but now it was mostly a nuisance. She damped down her sensitivity so that she didn't feel all of the room's previous residents. With the tutor's help, she was seeking to find a level where she wouldn't be distracted by too many magical traces but would notice anything unusual that bore further investigation.

Jean Macrae was going to call at noon. Meg was glancing at the clock when Jean bounced into the room a few minutes early. Meg rose to give her friend a hug, glad to be distracted.

"Tell me about the hearing!" Jean said as she dropped onto the sofa. "Did you really slap Drayton?"

"Yes, and I'm not sorry. But it probably wasn't the wisest thing to do." Meg returned to her wing chair. "As a countess, I'm a failure."

"Did Simon complain?"

"He was rather glad I did it," Meg admitted. "Why do you want to know more about the hearing? You've had two days to tease details out of Lady Bethany."

"Her version is rather restrained," Jean explained. "How did Drayton react when he saw you? What did he say to make you slap him?"

Thinking about Drayton sobered Meg. After describing her view of events, she said, "My first instinct was to learn more defensive spells, but what I really need is the strength to use the ones I have. His presence turned me into a terrified hare. Is there anything I can do to prevent that?"

Jean frowned. "Though I don't know how to prevent the initial panic, it's possible for you to create a way to break free. I haven't had to do this myself, but I've read about the technique. The key is to choose some sort of charm. It can be physical, like a ring, or mental, like a word or image. Then you decide what spells you want to link to it. For example, you might want to combine a shielding spell, a self-defense strike, and a damping spell."

"Could I learn a damping spell like the one on Sterling House?" Meg asked, surprised.

"No one can match Lord Sterling for damping spells, but I'm sure that you could learn to dampen magic in the area right around you, at least long enough to reduce any assaults from another mage."

Meg thought about snuffing Drayton like a candle. The vision was gratifying. "Where do I start?"

"You practice each spell until you can invoke the power without having to consciously construct the spell. Then you mentally attach each spell to your charm or trigger word. The goal is to know the spells so thoroughly that all you need do is think 'Protect!' or rub your ring or whatever method you choose to invoke the charm. Then all three spells will be cast. If you do this correctly, you can trigger protection even if your will is almost paralyzed. Once your defenses are activated, your willpower should recover quickly."

"This sounds perfect. Can you teach me the damping spell?"

"Yes, though I'm no expert. The other spells you know already. Just remember that it's not easy to link all these spells together and trigger them at once. It takes patience and a very strong mage to activate three at a time. Luckily you have enough power to do this, but a great deal of practice will be required."

"Then I shall practice." Meg looked down at the plain gold band Simon had given her as part of their marriage charade. Somehow it seemed wrong to choose a charm that was inherently false. A word would be better, and it couldn't be taken away from her. "Does the word need to be unusual, or will something as simple as 'protect' work?"

"I don't think it matters if it's a word that you use often, as long as it suggests protection to you. What turns it into a trigger is desperate need. Your thoughts have power, and that power is what will activate all the spells."

What meant protection to her? Meg thought about it for only a moment before realizing that the answer was obvious. Her protection charm would be the word "Simon." "Should the spells trigger at exactly the same instant, or one after another?"

Jean frowned. "I don't know—the subject wasn't addressed in the essays I've read. Now that you raise the subject, I suspect it would be better to trigger them one after another so that each gets a separate burst of power."

"The personal shield should be first. Then what—the damping spell?"

"I think the self-defense spell. You don't want to risk the damping spell backfiring on your own magic."

It all made sense. "Then let us begin." Meg's mouth twisted. "I don't suppose I'll be lucky enough to avoid meeting Drayton again. Next time it happens, I want to be prepared."

To snuff him like a candle . . .

Chapter EIGHTEEN

"Glorious!" Meg's call reached Simon as he cantered forward to meet her. They rode together every morning and always started with a wild, reckless gallop to burn off the horses' energy. He usually stayed a couple of lengths behind because he enjoyed watching her blaze through the soft morning air. She was a magnificent horsewoman. Being able to enter a horse's mind was obviously a plus.

Laughing, she brought her horse into step with his. "A run like that drives Lord Drayton from my mind. Or at least reminds me that he's just a nasty little ferret, of no real significance."

Drayton did have significance, but Simon didn't ruin Meg's exhilaration by contradicting her. "I shall probably see him at tonight's meeting of the Royal Society. You might want to invite Jean Macrae over for dinner to bear you company."

Meg brushed at the strands of dark hair that had escaped from the ribbon tied at her nape. "Why do you wish to attend if Drayton will be there?"

"It is wise to know one's enemy," he replied. "Tonight's lecturer is a professor from the University of Leipzig. He's speaking on electricity, a special interest of mine, so it would be odd if I didn't attend when I'm in London." He shrugged. "Since I must see Drayton sooner or later, it might as well be tonight. I'm curious to see how he'll behave toward me."

Meg frowned. "He will taunt you about not proving your case before the council. Don't let him provoke you into losing your temper."

"I will do my best not to become enraged." He chuckled. "If I turned into a unicorn at the lecture, it would be a demonstration that would impress even the most jaded member of the Royal Society."

"Much better to bore them. Shall I give you virgin's blood for safety's sake?"

He grimaced. "I know we've joked about that, but there is something profoundly barbaric in the thought of carrying a vial of your blood."

"Rubbing it into a cut would look odd in the midst of a meeting of natural philosophers." She stretched out her hand. "Remember that I am only a mind-touch away if needed."

He took her hand. That was safe enough since they were on horseback. At home, they avoided touching or drawing too close, since the results would be unpredictable.

Actually, the results were highly predictable. Sexual tension hummed between them and every time they succumbed to it, if only for a kiss, the attraction became even more unruly. If not for the need for her to remain a virgin—and their mutual qualms about a deeper relationship—they would be lovers already.

Sometimes he wondered where this unusual relationship would take them. And then he would try to think of something else.

Simon paused in the doorway leading into the lecture hall of the Royal Society. He liked that most members were mundanes. There was more to the world than magic.

His mouth tightened when he recognized Drayton in a group near the speaker's podium. Usually Simon found satisfaction in confronting his suspect after he finished an investigation, but that wasn't the case with Drayton. The rogue mage was so closely connected with Meg that even Simon's best efforts at protection couldn't completely guarantee her safety from the man. The thought was deeply troubling.

Drayton must be attuned to Simon's energy, because he broke off his conversation and turned to face the door. He smiled with pure pleasure and crossed the hall to Simon, saying amiably, "Good to see you,

Falconer. I guessed that a presentation on electricity would bring you here." He accompanied his commonplace words with a massive energy attack.

Simon's shields sprang into effect, but it was harder to control his shocked reaction. Bloody hell, was Drayton *insane*? He had to know that he couldn't do any real damage, and he risked catching the attention of others. Most mundanes had at least a trace of power, and a major blast of energy would not go unnoticed. Already men were glancing in their direction. *Damn* the man!

A familiar blurring sensation flowed through Simon, and his shock turned to horror. The unicorn spell was reactivating.

No! Instinctively he reached for Meg, needing her strength and magical innocence. When he touched her mind, her flash of surprise changed to quick understanding. She flooded him with her energy, as pure as it was powerful. After an instant of nausea, his normal form stabilized. He sent a swift thanks and reassurance to Meg, thinking wryly that he would resent his dependence if he didn't need her so much.

Could Drayton have known that provoking Simon's anger would trigger the transformation spell? No, the rogue was merely harassing him, confident that Simon wouldn't make a scene in front of mundanes. If his assault hadn't been so outrageous, Simon wouldn't have become angry enough to trigger the spell.

Only seconds had passed since Drayton's attack, so Simon replied blandly, "Electricity is a tremendous power, if we ever learn to harness it." On the magical plane he returned a fierce, narrowly targeted blast, rather like slamming a door on a snake that was trying to slither inside. "My own experiments have been most interesting."

Drayton's eyes lit with pleasure at the skirmishing. "I suppose you bought a Leyden jar to play with." He returned another blow.

"I didn't buy one. I built it after I read an article describing how they work." Tired of Drayton's games, Simon altered his shields so that the next attack would bounce back on the attacker. Few people could master the attack-repulsion spell. It was worth reminding Drayton that Simon was one of them.

Drayton attacked again, then gasped as his own power ricocheted back into him.

Simon said coolly, "You might not want a Leyden jar. They can be . . . quite shocking."

"Not half as shocking as I am." Drayton's eyes glittered with anger, but he didn't attempt another attack. Instead, he surrounded the two of them in a spell that would make their words unclear to listeners. It would also discourage anyone from joining them. "You are going to get exactly what you deserve, Falconer. I will personally destroy you."

Something dark and hungry lurked under the other man's words. Simon frowned. "I expect to be resented by lawbreakers, but it's more than that with you. Why?"

"You know why."

"Actually, I don't. Is there some history I should be aware of?"

Drayton's brows arched. "I suppose it's no surprise that your father never spoke of an incident that was so shameful. He accused my father of breaking the Guardian laws and stripped away his power." His eyes narrowed to slits. "My father killed himself rather than live without his magic."

Simon was rocked by the news, but he kept that from his voice. "My father would never take the power of a mage who was innocent of misusing it."

Drayton's laughter was chilling. "Any more than he would murder your mother and kill himself? You're a fool, Falconer."

His words struck harder than his earlier magical attack. News of the Falconer murder-suicide had been covered up and very few people knew of it. Hearing Drayton gave Simon a sudden unprovable conviction that the other man had been involved in the double death. He had wanted vengeance against Simon's father, and perhaps he had found a magical way to wreak it.

Putting aside the thought for later, he said, "My father kept his files private, so there's no special meaning in the fact that he didn't mention your father's case. But he would never have been able to punish your father unjustly—the council would have known and held him to account. Your father had to have been doing something that merited punishment."

An odd glint showed in Drayton's eyes. "My father was experimenting with older spells. As we are encouraged to do. Your father judged and destroyed him."

The pieces of the puzzle clicked together in Simon's mind. "Your father's experiment involved stealing the magic of others, didn't it? That must be what started you on your crimes. No wonder my father hunted him down and stripped away his power. As I shall do with you."

Drayton's smile was feral and full of teeth. "After you are dead, I will have Meggie again. My illusion spell was so good that I never noticed what a toothsome morsel she had turned into. I need a wife to bear me sons, and when I put her into thrall again, she will be the wife of any man's dreams. Lovely, obedient, and a whore in bed if I ask that of her."

Instead of rage, Simon reacted with ice-cold control. "I have never taken pleasure in destroying a fellow Guardian, but for you I will make an exception. When I strip your power away, I will do it slowly so that you suffer as each particle is ripped from your soul. You will scream and beg, and I will be glad of it."

He pivoted and stalked away to find a seat since the lecture was about to start. In a distant corner of his mind, he recognized that the danger of hatred was that it could turn a man into a mirror of what one hated. Because Drayton was brutal, Simon was discovering brutality in himself.

That was another thing to ponder later.

During a pleasant evening with Jean, Meg monitored Simon with a corner of her mind. She had sensed disturbed emotions for a time after his call for help, but they didn't rise again to the level of triggering the transformation spell. Eventually his mind settled into concentration. She guessed that the lecture had begun and it was engrossing.

Long, too. After Jean was sent home in the Falconer carriage, Meg retired early with a good book. Now that she had regained the ability to read, she raced through books as if trying to make up for all the years she'd missed. When she wasn't practicing magic, she read all kinds of volumes from Falconer House's impressive library. She'd found that mage lights were much better for reading than candles, and they didn't run the risk of burning the house down.

She had set her book aside and fallen asleep when something brought her abruptly awake. A noise in the street? No, Simon had returned. She concentrated on him, and decided that he was safely bipedal but troubled.

And he wasn't going to bed, blast him. She tossed and turned and punched her pillow restlessly, unable to separate herself from his overactive mind for what seemed like hours. Gradually it occurred to her that his energy was different from usual. Though she'd seen him in a range of moods, tonight his mind had the tenor of a . . . a ringing blade.

She rose to don slippers and robe, then went into the corridors with mage light in hand. Finding Simon was easy—his energy flared like the sun. She bypassed his bedchamber, where any sensible man would be at this hour. He was downstairs, probably in his study.

Wrong. When she opened the door, the study was empty. She frowned. He was very close, but where if not here? She sharpened her magical vision—then blinked when the image of a door shimmered into place at the far corner of the study. How long had Simon been concealing that door from her and the rest of the world? Crafty devil!

The door had been disguised with the strongest look-away spell she'd ever seen. She marveled at its construction as she turned the knob. The door opened soundlessly, which made sense. It would be silly to waste magic on a door that squealed.

The chamber revealed was surprisingly large—how did Simon manage to hide so much space in the house?—and was some sort of workroom. Two long tables bore strange devices as well as occasional scorch marks, and cabinets and shelves held tools, journals, and glass jars of mysterious substances.

As Meg examined her surroundings, Simon rose from a desk at the right end of the room, setting aside a journal as he did. "Good evening, Meg. I'm sorry I woke you."

The night was warm and he had removed his coat and waistcoat. Meg found it unnervingly erotic to see him in dishabille. His shoulders looked much broader in white linen than when disguised by fashionable tailoring, and the mage light above him struck silver and gold highlights in his fair hair.

She fought an impulse to cross the room and wrap herself around him. Vivid sensory memories of the touch of his lips and body briefly overwhelmed her. Passion was altogether too distracting. Would it become less so if they became lovers? That was hard to imagine.

She drew a deep, slow breath. Erotic fascination was a daily, even hourly, occurrence when she was near Simon. In some ways she might be childlike because of her lost years, but in this area, she had jumped directly into feverish womanhood. But she wasn't here to seduce him. Though if he tried to seduce her, she wouldn't protest.

She gave her head a sharp shake. "Simon, is something wrong?"

"Not really." He gestured at the room. "I just realized that I never brought you here to my laboratory. I do experiments here, mostly with electricity. I also have odd mechanical devices that amuse me. Have you ever seen an orrery before?" He gestured to a nest of wire loops with balls of different sizes fastened to them. "It's a model of our solar system. See, when I put a mage light in the center to represent the sun, I can turn the crank and one can observe the motions of the planets."

He began to crank and the model planets moved. "This is a particularly fine orrery. It has all the planets of our system. See Saturn all the way out here with his shining rings?"

It took a major effort to tear her gaze away. Reminding herself that she hadn't come to look at gentlemen's toys, she said, "I heard you worrying and it kept me awake. What mischief did Drayton cause? I gather that before your meeting began, he made you dangerously angry. You still look . . . dangerous."

He abandoned the orrery and rubbed the side of his head, tangling the thick blond hair. "Sorry. There are two kinds of anger. The fierce, red blazing kind comes from the heart. Much rarer is the cold white rage than comes from the head. Talking to Drayton triggered the latter."

White rage. She nodded, understanding the distinction. "So red rage is what threatens to transform you into a beast. What does white rage do? I want to know because I don't ever wish to become the target of that."

He smiled faintly, his tension easing a little. "You won't. It takes evil like Drayton's to cause such cold fury."

"I'm guessing that his insults included me. What else did he say?" She studied a mechanism of wheels and suspended balls, wondering what on earth it did. The question was more intriguing than wondering what Drayton was thinking about her.

"He was insulting and threatening on a number of subjects. Most interesting is what he told me about his father. The elder Drayton was also a rogue mage, and he was stripped of his power by my father. This lends a particularly personal note to Drayton's desire to bring me to a nasty end."

She caught her breath. "You didn't know this?"

He shook his head. "Records are kept private whenever possible. Punishment is rare, actually. Usually only a quiet suggestion is needed if someone has crossed the line of magical ethics. Though I speak of stripping away the magic of renegades, I've actually done that only rarely. Twice on the Continent I helped administer justice when a local mage had gone rogue. Only once have I stripped away the power of a Briton, and that was a poor mad old member of the Polmarric family whose lost wits were endangering him and those around him."

He touched the journal he'd been studying when she entered the room. "My father had to administer justice in earnest, fighting an unrepentant renegade the whole time. Can you guess what crime the last Lord Drayton committed?"

Though Meg wasn't gifted in clairvoyance, the answer was obvious. "He was stealing the magic of others."

"Exactly. From my father's case notes, it's clear that he was less ambitious than his son, or less skilled. He didn't imprison magically gifted children, but he regularly drew energy from Guardians around him. That included his wife and son, and the notes don't suggest that he asked permission first."

Meg winced. "No wonder Drayton thinks such behavior is normal."

"He knows better. There is no excuse except for his lust for power," Simon said dryly. "The case notes are intriguing, not to mention alarming. Apparently the elder Drayton speculated that it might be possible to develop a device that would store magical power. He made some experiments in that direction, but never succeeded, though he was adept at forcibly taking power from people around him."

She gasped. "If Drayton developed a storage device, he'd be unstoppable."

"Precisely." Simon set the journal on a stack of similar volumes, squaring the edges meticulously. "The principle underlying Guardian justice is that no single mage, no matter how powerful, is stronger than the combined council. That principle has been a sufficient deterrent for generations. But if Drayton could store power until he had enough to overwhelm our most powerful mages even when they're working together . . ." He shook his head.

She remembered the searing horror of the ancient mage war that Simon had shown her, and shuddered. "Do you suppose he joined the Royal Society to find out how to design and build such a device?"

"It's certainly possible, though I cannot imagine how a mechanical object could hold magical energy." Simon frowned. "Using living creatures seems more likely. Perhaps a group of magically talented individuals placed in thrall could be spelled to hold more power than they have inherently."

Meg thought back to her time with Drayton. "If that was his plan, I don't think he has succeeded. At least, not yet. Whenever he stole my power, he used it straightaway. There was no storage."

Simon's voice softened. "I'm sorry. This must be unpleasant for you to discuss."

"Not as unpleasant as experiencing it." She shivered as she remembered the helpless horror of Drayton's mind rape, and wondered again if he had others enslaved to his will. "Even if he hasn't found a way to store magical energy, he might still be able to defeat the combined council if he has enough people in thrall. We *must* find out if he has others."

"I've been investigating, but so far I haven't found signs that he has links to other captives." Simon's brows drew together. "It's almost unimaginable that he would be able to find and abduct other mages with power that is anything like yours. There simply aren't many with such power to begin with, and most are members of the Families who couldn't be easily abducted, so I think Drayton's threat is limited, at least for now."

"He may not have enthralled anyone with as much power as I have, but he might have a dozen with lesser power." Meg forced herself to face unpleasant necessity. "You are famous for your ability to trace magic, especially its illegal use, but I have experience with Drayton that you lack. Perhaps I can do better than you in finding if he has others in thrall."

"You may be right, but it would be a dangerous search. Look at what happened when you explored the memory block and ended up in Drayton's mind." Simon retrieved his coat and wrapped it around her shoulders. "You look cold. I wish I could believe you are merely chilled, but it's a warm night."

She pulled the coat tight around her shoulders, inhaling the reassuring scents of cologne and healthy male. "I loathe the idea of poking around Drayton's mind, but I think I can do it more effectively than anyone else."

"We'll be seeing Drayton soon at Lady Bethany's ball. Why not wait and investigate him there?" Simon suggested. "In the midst of a crowd, many of whom are Guardians with strong magical auras, he is less likely to notice your probing. Plus, I'll be there. If I lend you my energy, perhaps you can learn more than either of us can alone."

"I like that idea. What is the technique for borrowing another person's power?" She shivered again. "I'm an expert at supplying it, but not at taking."

"The technique is simple." Simon took her right hand and raised it to his lips. His kiss vibrated through every fiber of her being. "But not a task for tonight. Sharing power voluntarily is a very intimate process. In our present moods, if we try we will surely end by becoming lovers in truth."

She gazed at him, pulse pounding. "Would that be so bad?"

"Until Drayton is defeated, yes. I need you more for the magical power of your virginity than as a lover." His smile was wry. "Which is saying a great deal."

"Until later, then," she whispered.

"When Drayton is gone, the rules of society will still exist, Meg," he said gravely. "When I am with you I tend to forget, but honor, propriety, and reputation matter."

She laughed. "Are you trying to tell me that society has no illicit lovers? Even I know better than that."

"Reputation always matters, especially for innocent young ladies."

"I am a false countess who has been in thrall to a monster, so I am already far outside the rules of normal society," she said with a humorless smile. "If I survive our struggle with Drayton, I want to leave London to discover the girl I once was, but before that happens, I want to know what it is to be a woman. Will you grant me that?"

He drew an unsteady breath. "Nothing would please me more, and you know that, you minx. But sharing bodies and souls is more complicated than you think."

"I will worry about that later." Their hands were still clasped, so she squeezed his. "For now, I want to know that there will be a reward for all this struggle and unwanted self-discipline. If I were still Meggie and you had kissed me, I would have given myself to you in a haystack. To be honest, I think there is much to be said for that kind of simplicity." An unwelcome thought struck her. "Unless—is your heart given to another and you don't wish to betray her?"

He shook his head. "My life has been much duller than you might imagine. If you truly wish this, of course I will honor your wishes and consider myself blessed. But you may change your mind between now and the time when Drayton is brought down."

"I won't." She rested her cheek against the back of his hand before letting it go. The prospect of abandoning propriety and discovering the sins of the flesh with Simon was yet another incentive to destroy Drayton as soon as possible.

Chapter NINETEEN

The principle of a steam engine was simple. A coal-fired boiler heated water till it produced steam that flowed into a cylinder. Cooling the steam created a partial vacuum so that normal air pressure rammed the piston down into the cylinder. A crossbeam translated that movement into power, usually to operate a water pump. David knew the principles inside and out. It was the details that were tricky, especially when a man was trying to build a better engine.

Burning coal had already raised the water in the boiler to the boiling point, so David nervously checked over the other components of his model. The insulated cylinder and pump looked fine, as did the condenser and piping that connected the components.

Nonetheless, David worried. This was a jury-rigged engine, thrown together as quickly as possible to test his theory that a separate condenser would be far more efficient at cooling steam than Newcomen's method of spraying cold water in the cylinder, which wasted huge amounts of heat. Sarah had calculated that only one percent of the energy was used effectively. Surely David could build an engine that did better than that.

"This engine will work a fair treat, sir," Peter Nicholson assured him.

The youth had proved to be an apt assistant, willing to labor long hours and having deft hands for mechanical work. He was as excited as David, and he wasn't the only one. A dozen other mechanics, craftsmen, and urchins from the neighborhood were crowded into the workshop to see the test. Their fellowship and support made David feel like part of a community for the first time since his childhood.

"Let 'er rip," Gaffer Lewis said around his pipe. "If 'er don't work, ye'll just have to build another."

There was general laughter. All of these men had experienced failures as well as successes. They would celebrate if David's engine worked, and offer sympathy and practical advice if it didn't.

Sarah should be here, too. Without her calculations and patient explanations, David never would have fully grasped the principles of heat, steam, and evaporation. But he had sent her back to the house earlier, before the boiler was stoked up. Though the chance of an accident was slim, neither of them wanted to risk the health of the precious babe she carried.

"Start the engine, Peter," David ordered.

Peter complied with a dramatic flourish, pulling down the handle that opened the valve and allowed steam to rush into the cylinder. With hisses and clanks, the piston rammed into the cylinder. A cheer broke out from the watchers as the crossbeam began pumping up and down. "She works, sir!" Peter said jubilantly as the pounding piston found a steady, powerful rhythm.

"That she does!" David watched the hammering crossbeam and exulted in the clamor of his engine. Even without measuring, he knew that his engine would be able to pump water from a flooded mine far more efficiently than the Newcomen engine. And how many other uses might clever men find for such a source of power?

He frowned as a high-pitched hiss joined the sounds of bubbling water and clanging metal. Could there be a leak? He moved toward the engine to turn it off.

Kaboom! The cylinder exploded and chunks of brass flew about the room.

"Bloody hell!" David dived behind the worktable for protection. Even as metal smashed into walls and furniture and the sharp sound of shattering glass filled the room, the other men were doing the same. Thank God Sarah wasn't here!

When the only sound left was the hissing of the boiler as it pumped steam into the room, David cautiously raised himself to a crouch. "Is everyone all right?"

Voices spoke up attesting to their safety. Peter's head appeared above the other table. "We were lucky," he said, his voice unsteady. As the man closest to the engine, he had been at the greatest risk.

"Very lucky." The dry, cultivated voice came from near the doorway. "But your engine does indeed work. Congratulations, Mr. White."

Recognizing the voice with a sinking heart, David scrambled to his feet. "Lord Falconer? I didn't know you were coming today. I'm sorry for . . . for this." He waved a hand to indicate his workshop. As near as he could tell, the window facing the house was broken and tools had been knocked to the floor, but the damage didn't look too bad. The model engine was a disaster of fractured metal and twisted pipes, though.

"You mentioned in your last note that you would be testing today, and I didn't want to miss that." Falconer was dressed plainly, more like an advocate than a lord, but his aristocratic presence was unmistakable. When he crossed the room, the other men withdrew warily. They weren't used to seeing earls in workshops.

Falconer eyed the wreckage critically. "Where did you get the cylinder? It looks like cast metal rather than a machined piece."

"You're right, my lord. I borrowed the cylinder from Jeb Hitchen here." David nodded at a silver-haired man, a metal caster from two streets over. "I'm sorry, Jeb, I'll replace it."

Hitchen shrugged. "There must have been a weakness in the casting or it wouldn't have failed. 'Twas worth it to see your engine working."

"The pressure was too high for that cylinder." David forced himself to meet the earl's gaze. "I was impatient to see if the design worked, so I cobbled this model together. If I'd taken the time to build the lathe and machine a cylinder properly, this wouldn't have happened. At least, I hope it wouldn't," he added punctiliously.

Falconer gave a surprising grin. "If I'd spent as long developing this engine as you, I'd be impatient, too. But now that you know the principle is sound, perhaps you should spend more time on the next model. And add a pressure relief valve."

"Yes, sir!" David said fervently. He touched the chain that connected the crossbeam to the piston. "But 'twas a pretty sight while it worked, wasn't it?"

"That it was."

"David, what happened?" Sarah had arrived, drawn by the noise. She stopped in her tracks, her eyes widening as she looked at the ruined engine. "Oh, dear!"

"No harm was done," Lord Falconer said. "And your husband has proved that he can take the steam engine to a whole new level of efficiency." He glanced at David. "Though you might want to experiment using lower pressures at first."

"Aye." Now that alarm over the explosion had died down, David realized that his design had succeeded. It had worked! Today, in a small way, the world had changed, and he was a step closer to dressing Sarah in silk and lace.

Falconer was studying the engine with interest. "Mind if I take a closer look? It looks as if you've made some refinements on your original plans."

"I did, sir. See how cold water circulates in the jacket of the condenser?" As David explained, Falconer and the other men gathered around, asking questions and tossing out opinions. In no time at all, the neighborhood craftsmen had forgotten they had an earl among them. What mattered was that Falconer had the makings of a fair to middling engineer.

When the library door opened, Meg didn't bother looking up from her book. "You can set the tea tray on the table, Hardwick."

"Yes, ma'am," a deep voice said.

Startled, Meg glanced up to see Simon placing the tray on the table. "I saw Hardwick coming this way with the tea, so I had him double everything." Simon poured two cups of China tea and handed one to Meg. "Having spent a vigorous afternoon discussing David White's steam engine, I felt in need of sustenance."

Meg laughed as she stirred sugar into the delicate porcelain cup. "I take it you decided to watch the test. Did it go well?"

"Well enough, except that it exploded after two or three minutes."

Meg halted, the teacup halfway to her mouth. "Was anyone hurt?"

"No, but there would have been a few injuries if I hadn't been there." Simon sat in the chair opposite. "Now I know why intuition was urging me to go see the test. I arrived just as the engine was started. When it exploded, I was able to shield everyone from injury. There's quite a community of engineers and inventors nearby, so he had a good audience."

"Is Mr. White's design flawed?"

"No, he just built this model in haste to see how it would work. I suggested that he build his next model to higher standards of quality. He agreed rather fervently."

"I wonder if today's explosion was the possible death I saw for Mr. White?" Meg said thoughtfully. "I'd like to think the danger is past now."

Simon hesitated. "Perhaps. But my feeling is that there might be other threats in the future."

Before Meg could ask Simon to elaborate, his secretary, Jack Landon, opened the library door. "Sorry to disturb you, sir, but you have visitors you'll want to see as soon as possible."

Landon stepped aside to allow a couple to enter the library. Simon rose and went to meet his guests with a broad grin. "Duncan, you're in London ahead of schedule!"

The other man laughed as they shook hands. "You're losing your touch, Simon. You should have known when I would arrive before I left Scotland!"

Meg studied Macrae with interest. He bore little resemblance to his petite, redheaded sister. Tall and dark and broad, he radiated force. It was easy to imagine him calling a lightning strike if he was displeased. Simon looked lean and elegant by comparison, but there was an interesting sense of balance between the two men.

"Where is my godson, Gwynne?" Simon asked as he kissed the cheek of the woman obscured behind Macrae's large frame.

"With Jean and Lady Bethany, being spoiled abominably," she said with a laugh.

Simon turned to Meg. "Here are Duncan Macrae and Gwynne

Owens, of whom you've heard so much. They are more formally known as Lord and Lady Ballister, though it pains Duncan to admit to an English title."

Gwynne Owens moved around her husband to approach Meg with a smile. "I'm pleased to meet you, Lady Falconer."

Meg's jaw dropped when she had a clear view of the other woman. "I . . . I'm sorry to stare," she stammered. "I had heard that you are an enchantress, but I didn't truly understand what that meant."

Though Meg had known an enchantress could steal male wits, no one had mentioned that Gwynne Owens could rivet the attention of females as well. Meg managed enough objectivity to realize that despite shimmering red-gold hair and a splendidly female figure, the other woman wasn't truly beautiful. But she had a magnetism that drew the eye, and her strong, less than perfect features were memorable in a way that mere beauty was not.

Gwynne made a face at Meg's expression. "I think I had better reduce my allure. This is an interesting power to have, Lady Falconer, but often a nuisance."

Meg sensed the other woman make a subtle magical shift. While there was no visible change in Gwynne's appearance, she was no longer as compelling. Attractive and interesting, but it was possible to look away from her. "How . . . interesting." Meg tried to sound matter-of-fact. "I would ask how that is done, but I'll never need to know."

"Don't underestimate yourself, Lady Falconer." Duncan bowed with a grace surprising in a man so broadly built. "You also have a touch of the enchantress in you."

"I noticed that rather quickly myself," Simon agreed. "Though Meg is fortunate enough not to have so much allure that it causes trouble." He smiled at Gwynne, and Meg realized that he was more than fond of his friend's wife. Not in an improper way, but he was not immune to her magnetism.

Simon continued, "Meg, Duncan and I have matters to discuss. Will you mind if he and I withdraw to my study while you and Gwynne become better acquainted?"

"I would like that," she said sincerely.

"As would I." Gwynne made a shooing motion with her hand. "You gentlemen can take yourselves off now. Lady Falconer and I have much to learn about each other."

As the men left, Gwynne turned to Meg. "Jean told me of your experiences. Though our situations were different, there are similarities. I came into my power late and in a great rush, while you were denied real access to your power until you were a grown woman. Jean thought I might have some useful insights on adjusting to power as an adult." She smiled. "Though she also says that you are mastering your powers with amazing dexterity, so perhaps my thoughts aren't needed."

"I'm interested in anything you have to say that might be useful, but please, call me Meg. I am not yet accustomed to being a countess."

"It's healthier not to become attached to titles, I think." Gwynne subsided gracefully onto the sofa. "In Scotland, everything is more informal, so call me Gwynne. No one calls me Lady Ballister except when we visit London."

Meg's attention was caught by the way the other woman's skirts fell into flawless folds. "Is it part of enchantress magic that even your gown behaves perfectly?"

Gwynne eyed her elegant gown with surprise. "Perhaps. To be honest, I never noticed that before. Magic is so full of quirks and corners. It's been three years since I came into my power, and I still feel like a novice sometimes. Is it that way for you?"

"I . . . I don't know if that is how I would describe it." Meg searched for the right words. "My magic doesn't seem new or strange, though using it is a constant surprise. I have more trouble with the idea of being a Guardian. Everyone has been so kind, and yet I feel as if I'm an outsider. Not one of you. I . . . I'm sorry if that sounds rude."

"No need to apologize." Gwynne tilted her head consideringly. "I think one's sense of self depends on how one is raised. I had no power to speak of, but I grew up in the heart of the Guardian establishment. Though my mother was a mundane, I always felt like a member of the Families, albeit an untalented member. You're the opposite. Magic has pulsed through your veins since you reached womanhood, yet the society of Guardians is new to you. It will become more comfortable with time."

"What if I am not a real Guardian?" Meg asked softly. "Simon and Lady Bethany seem to think I am, but what if I find my family and I'm not of Guardian blood?"

"To be a Guardian is to have power and swear to use it on behalf of others. You are already a Guardian, even if you are not of the Lineage. Isabel de Cortes, an ancestor of Duncan's, was one of the greatest mages of her time and she came from a family of Spanish mundanes." Gwynne paused. "Now that I think of it, have you taken the oath yet, or has that been forgotten amidst all the turmoil?"

Meg blinked, startled. "I have sworn no oath. No one has asked me to."

"That will have to be taken care of, after you've studied the oath and have time to think about the implications," Gwynne said seriously. "The vows are a magical binding and should not be made casually. Not that the oath itself compels obedience—there have always been rogues like Drayton who have forsworn themselves and committed crimes. You should . . ." She stopped with a wry smile. "As a scholar, I'm quite prepared to give you a boringly long lecture on the subject, so don't encourage me!"

"I would like to hear your lecture, but first I have a favor to ask." Meg moved forward to the edge of the chair. "Jean says you're one of the finest scryers in Britain. Would you be willing to see if you can discover something about my family?"

"Of course." Gwynne reached into a pocket hidden in a seam of her overskirt and pulled out a velvet drawstring pouch. Inside was a smoky, translucent disk set in a silver frame. "This was Isabel de Cortes's own scrying glass," she explained. "It's made of obsidian and I can feel her energy in it still."

Meg admired but didn't touch. Her tutors had taught that scrying glasses were very personal. "Jean says that one day you will sit on the council."

"Perhaps. Scrying is a particular gift of mine," Gwynne admitted. "But Simon is also extremely good. If he has been unable to learn anything about your family, I don't know if I can do better."

"Please try." Thinking it might help to know more, Meg added,

"I'm reasonably sure that I come from the borderland between England and Wales. I . . . I can almost remember my mother. She thought I was a proper hoyden. But I can recall no more."

Gwynne smiled at the description before she relaxed, her gaze resting lightly on the obsidian disk. Then she swore under her breath. "The path is blocked. I can feel Drayton's energy. He's a nasty piece of work."

Meg exhaled, disappointed but not surprised. "He has separated me from my past in all ways. Have you ever met him?"

"Once or twice at social affairs. He seemed . . . neutral. A certain superficial charm, but not particularly interesting or powerful. However, that was before I came into my own power, so it's not surprising that I had no sense of his darker side."

"Most of the council members don't consider him a threat, so you were not alone," Meg said bitterly. "He claims that I was an injured, addled girl whom he rescued and sheltered from the goodness of his heart. The idea makes me want to *spit.*"

"It's insult to injury," Gwynne agreed. She contemplated the scrying glass again. "I can't see your past directly, but perhaps I can find out something by looking more broadly." Her gaze slipped out of focus. "There are no details, but I do feel that you have strong family connections. You're no orphan. When and if you find your way home, you will be welcomed." She glanced up from the glass. "I hope that helps."

Meg closed her eyes, blinking against the sting of tears. *You will be welcomed.* "That does help. Thank you."

Tactfully ignoring the tears, Gwynne said, "According to Jean, you have the ability to move physical objects?"

"Yes, but it's a small talent of little practical value." Though Meg still couldn't raise much weight, it took much less effort to do it. Only a moment's concentration was needed to lift her quill pen from the table. She swooped it over to Lucky, who was snoozing in an upholstered chair. Sleeping was his favorite activity.

Carefully Meg used the feather end of the quill to tickle his nose. The small cat woke with a start, then leaped on the quill, tail lashing, and wrestled it to the chair seat.

Gwynne laughed. "How marvelous! Duncan can move clouds and shape winds, but I don't know if he could lift a solid object like that."

She leaned forward to scratch Lucky's head. "I have a cat, too, but he's half Scottish wildcat and quite fearsome."

"Lucky is a lover, not a fighter," Meg said as the cat rolled onto his back, purring and paws waving under Gwynne's expert ministrations. "I'm told I have great power, but I don't seem to have any distinctive talents, like you and Duncan and Simon."

"Not everyone does, but you do have a vast amount of sheer, raw magic. When you can fully command it, you will be formidable."

"Which is why I was so important to Lord Drayton," Meg said glumly. "He used me as his reservoir."

"He doesn't have you now, and he will live to regret what he has done. I guarantee it." Gwynne smiled, her tone lighter. "Are you ready for that lecture on the Guardian oath now?"

"Yes, although what I need most is dancing lessons," Meg said ruefully. "Lady Bethany's ball is almost here, and I've been worried into knots about it. What to wear. How to face so many curious Guardians who will know more about me than I know about them. Worst of all, worry about seeing Lord Drayton again."

"How dreadful to face your first ball with so much on your mind!" Gwynne exclaimed. "May I help in some way?"

Impressed by the other woman's generosity, Meg said, "Despite my complaints, the gown is no longer a problem, since Lady Bethany made sure that I now have one that is quite lovely. I met Drayton at the council hearing and survived, and plenty of Guardians looked me over there, so that's not so bad. But now my mind has enough space to worry about the fact that I can't dance! My first grand ball, I'm a guest of honor, and I can't even manage a simple country dance." She had seen Drayton's tenants dancing at harvest festivals, but no one had included Mad Meggie in the festivities. "Since it takes months to learn proper dancing, I shall restrict myself to conversation."

"That won't do! This is your ball, and you should enjoy it," Gwynne said firmly. "With magic, I should be able to teach you the basics of dancing. There is a specific kind of mind-touch that allows one person to send memories or knowledge to another. Simon could do this for you, but better you receive the lesson from a woman since that's the part you'll be dancing." She lifted her hand. "With your permission?"

"Please."

Gwynne placed her palm on Meg's forehead and closed her eyes. A rush of energy poured through Meg, sparkling with brightness like golden fish leaping through a rippling stream, except that the flashing glints were images and words instead of fish. *Left hand turn . . . back to back . . . grand chain . . . down the middle and back . . .* "Oh, my," she breathed, enjoying the vibrant cascade.

Gwynne maintained contact for what seemed like a long time, with interesting, subtle shifts in the energy she was sending. When she took her hand away, she said, "That seemed to work rather well. Do you feel that you've learned anything?"

"Did you send four different dances?" Meg asked. "I feel as if my mind is full of shadow dances, but they aren't quite real."

"That's because dancing is so physical. I gave you only a few of the most common dances, though from knowing those, you will be able to pick up others easily." Gwynne looked thoughtful. "You need a session of real dancing so that what is in your head can become fixed in your body as well."

"The ball is tomorrow night!" Meg said, not feeling any more qualified to dance than she had before the lesson.

"Don't worry, I'll press Duncan and Simon into service when they're through talking. Simon is the best dancer in London. He could take a chair as a partner and make it look graceful." Gwynne settled back on the sofa. "Ready for that lecture on the oath?"

Meg was. If she was going to pledge her power to the service of others, she needed to understand what she was getting herself into.

Chapter TWENTY

When they reached the privacy of the study, Duncan asked, "What the devil have you been up to, Simon? Your letters were entirely too discreet."

"Drayton is a dangerous rogue who lusts after power, and I think he's plotting to take control of the British Guardians. Is that indiscreet enough?" Simon dropped into the chair behind his desk, glad to be able to reveal his worst fears to his best friend.

Duncan whistled softly. "You're sure of that? No one has tried such a thing since the mage wars. Is it even possible to dominate so many independent mages?"

"If a rogue controlled enough power, I think it would be possible, and everything Drayton has done has been to increase his power. He wouldn't have to dominate everyone—those who opposed him the most might meet with untimely ends. Others might find themselves favored. Guardians are human, after all, with all the weakness of our breed. A combination of threats and rewards would be very effective." Simon lifted the dagger that he used for cutting seals on letters, turning it idly in his hands. "I can't even imagine what kind of power Drayton would have if he'd murdered me and obtained the unicorn horn. It might be all he needs."

Duncan winced at the blunt statement. "What was it like to be a unicorn?"

Other Guardians wondered that, too, but only a close friend would dare ask. A shiver of wildness flickered over Simon's skin as he remembered the exhilaration of racing the wind. Of being free of all bonds and doubts. "There was a degree of liberty that was . . . not without a certain appeal," he said in his driest tone. "But overall, it was much less amusing than one would imagine."

Duncan nodded acceptance, able to draw his own conclusions about what was left unsaid. "I wonder if he will try to cast the transformation spell on another powerful mage, since he has failed with you."

Simon had also wondered about that. "Possibly, but it would be difficult. The spell is very complex and it would have to be constructed in advance. Then he would have to lure a very powerful mage into his trap. Since I was hunting him, I walked into the spell, but I think that other mages of unusual power will be very wary of entering space controlled by Drayton."

"I certainly wouldn't go near his home," Duncan agreed. "By the way, you never mentioned how you regained your own form."

"Meg." Simon considered saying more, but didn't feel like getting into the highly personal areas of virginity and his sham marriage. "Her power is quite . . . extraordinary."

"I could feel magic burning in her." Duncan smiled. "Your lady is already a force to be reckoned with. When she is fully trained, she will be one of the great mages of our day. And she's a lovely, sweet lass as well. I congratulate you on your marriage."

Simon was tempted to tell the whole complicated truth—that Meg was everything Duncan said, except that she was not his. But this was a matter too private to discuss even with a close friend. He settled for saying, "Thank you. Meeting her as I did was perhaps the greatest stroke of good fortune in my life." That, at least, was the truth.

"Drayton stole Meg's power and he tried to take your life to obtain unicorn magic. In what other ways has he sought power?"

"His father tried to find ways to store magic before he was stripped of his own power. Though the father was unsuccessful, the son might be trying the same thing. It would explain why Drayton is a member of the Royal Society. Meg suspects that Drayton might have others in thrall as he held her, though that is unproven." Simon's mouth twisted. "Of course, his rank in the royal government is another kind of power. My instinct says that he will strive to possess any power he thinks he can grasp."

"And the devil is still running around loose despite all his crimes." Duncan looked thunderous. "Damn the council for acquitting him of all charges! Are they blind? How dare they dismiss the testimony of you, your wife, and Lady Bethany!"

"Our law demands that conviction must be beyond doubt. Drayton was most plausible. Even you would have been half-convinced by his defense. All of his lies had a grain of truth, which made them convincing."

"Can we afford laws that let dangerous mages go free?"

Simon studied his dagger, imagining it stabbed into Drayton's heart. He set the weapon aside. "We Falconers have cause to be grateful that the accused always receives the benefit of the doubt, but the current stalemate is disturbing. My fear is that Drayton will do nothing overt until he is in a position to destroy our most powerful mages in one great strike. The rest he will dominate, intimidate, or keep in thrall."

"Surely you don't think he can do that!" Duncan said, aghast.

"I think it's possible. Remember, when I confronted him, he had enhanced his natural abilities to the point where I was unable to take him down. He has lost Meg, which is a huge blow, but if he can place other latent mages in thrall, or if he finds a way to store magical power until he is ready to use it, there is no telling what he will do."

"You will not let Drayton go so far." It was a statement, not a question.

"No," Simon admitted. "I'm watching him. If I suspect he is about to strike, I will act. I'm tempted to act even before that, but the cost of that would be very high."

His friend frowned. "You and Drayton have been enjoined by the council to leave each other alone. If you act against their orders and without unmistakable evidence of criminal behavior, you will be condemned and stripped of your power."

"I know." Simon drew a deep breath. "I may have no choice."

Duncan swore again. "I hope to God matters don't come to that."

"So do I." Knowing Drayton's father had committed suicide after losing his power had made Simon wonder if he would want to go on living if he was no longer a mage. How could he bear losing the exhilaration of magic? He couldn't imagine. Didn't want to imagine.

But he would do what he must do. Honor demanded no less.

When Simon and Duncan had caught up with each other's news, they returned to the library. The ladies were laughing together, Meg's sleek dark hair contrasting with Gwynne's glorious sunset tresses.

Simon had been very fond of Gwynne since he met her as a shy but learned child bride in her first marriage. When she married Duncan and came into her enchantress power, he had been captivated by her shimmering charm. For that reason he had kept his distance, since even a casual, affectionate touch from Gwynne affected him too much.

Yet now it was Meg that drew and held his attention. She hadn't lost the quality of innocence created by her strange life at Castle Drayton, but every day he could see more strength as she became grounded in her magic.

He was beginning to suspect that her magic was wild, not Guardian. She was too fey, too much a child of earth and air. No, not a child: a woman. What would she become when she was fully grown into her power?

Observing Simon's intent gaze, Duncan said with a laugh, "I never thought I'd see you as a besotted husband. I'm glad to be proved wrong." His warm glance went to his wife. "Shall we leave the newlyweds to their privacy?"

"Not yet." Gwynne stood, looking purposeful. "Meg needs dance practice before the ball, and with two couples, we can make a decent job of it. As I recall, Jack Landon plays the harpsichord rather well. Would he be willing to accompany us?"

"I'm sure he will." Simon suffered an attack of conscience. "I'm sorry, Meg. I've been so busy I forgot you need lessons in dancing as well as magic."

"No need to apologize." Meg rose and crossed the room with a smile that started deep in her sea-mist eyes. He could drown in those eyes. . . .

She continued, "Gwynne gave me a dancing lesson with mind-touch and says that with some dancing practice, I'll be able to manage."

"I should have thought of that. It's a perfect method for teaching a specific skill like dancing." As he tucked Meg's hand in his elbow, he admired the pure line of her profile. Duncan had been right that she had a touch of enchantress in her. More than a touch. "Now let's find Jack Landon."

When located, in his office, the secretary said, "I'll be happy to play rather than do the household accounts." He stood with a grin. "As Simon knows, I took this job because of the excellent harpsichord. But I do ask that I be allowed a dance with my lovely mistress, if Lady Ballister will take a turn at playing."

Meg tried not to blush at Jack's compliment. Jean had warned her that such gallantries were routinely offered by gentlemen on social occasions, but Meg was not yet accustomed. The group trailed off to the music room, with Gwynne and Jack discussing what dances would be best for Meg.

"Start with 'Heart's Ease,'" Gwynne suggested. "It's very simple, a longways dance for just two couples. I'll call the steps, Meg. When I was the Countess of Brecon, I had to attend a vast number of balls, so I know far too many dances."

She looked expectantly at Meg. As Jack Landon began to play and the first crystal pure notes from the harpsichord filled the room, Meg found herself moving to stand next to Gwynne. When she was in position, the men came to stand opposite. Ah, right, this was longways, when men and women lined up in two rows facing each other. Her foot tapped as the music called to her.

Simon bowed, then smiled with a warmth that almost made her fall over her own feet. "Dance with me, my lady?"

She dropped him a curtsey. "It will be my very great pleasure, my lord."

Gwynne called, "Meet and fall back once, then again."

Meg moved forward and back, her feet moving lightly with no conscious effort on her part. The movements seemed familiar and natural as she followed Gwynne's commands.

"Now a two-handed turn. Since you must be able to converse and dance at the same time," Gwynne said after a few minutes had passed, "I'll ask how you feel about your dancing, Meg. You appear most accomplished."

Turning with Simon's strong, warm hands in her clasp, Meg replied, "It's rather like donning new clothing. The shadow dances in my mind and I are coming together. Becoming one."

"Dancing is the most intimate two people can be in public," Simon murmured as he released her fingers with flattering regret. "It is flirtation, courtship, and promise as well as simple pleasure."

Dancing was also, she realized, a surrogate for making love. That was why heat purred through her veins as she and Simon crossed and turned, their bodies moving in harmony with the music and each other. Her lesson had included the knowledge that holding each other's gaze was important and now she did it as naturally as she breathed.

Though they had talked and kissed and rode together, through dance she found another kind of communication, one that was as potent as sharing magic. Even when Gwynne called a dance that Meg hadn't been taught, it was easy to follow Simon.

She also realized how much tension usually bound him, because now that was gone. He wasn't worrying about Drayton or other criminals; he was simply a dancer enjoying himself. This was a kind of magic available to everyone, mage and mundane alike, and the pleasure of it sparkled through her like bubbles.

"Time for the ultimate test, Meg," Gwynne announced as they finished the fourth dance. "The minuet."

Meg's feet suddenly became clumsy. "That's said to be very difficult."

"You've managed the other dances perfectly, and you can do the minuet as well. It was the last of the dances I taught you through mind-touch. Jack, are you ready?"

The delicate notes of a minuet began to play. Meg stiffened, then forced herself not to think of her feet as she did the lead-in figure. Simon turned her three-quarters of the way around, then they separated

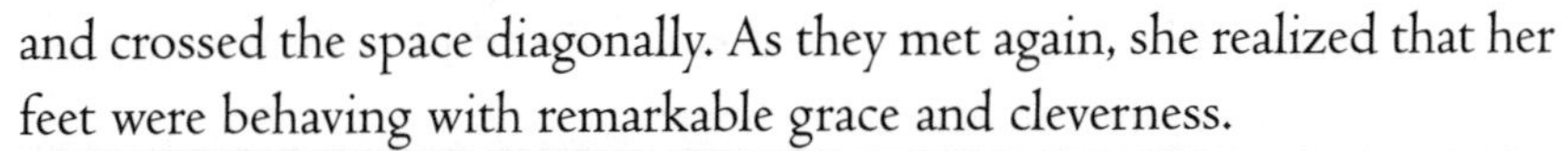

and crossed the space diagonally. As they met again, she realized that her feet were behaving with remarkable grace and cleverness.

In fact, as she skipped sideways, she realized that her movements were exactly the same as Gwynne's. Laughing, she said, "We had best not dance side by side at the ball, or the other guests might notice that I am a mere copycat of you."

"You will develop your own style soon enough," Gwynne replied. "You're doing beautifully. A credit to your teacher."

Though Duncan was a good dancer, surprisingly light on his feet, it was Simon who made Meg giddy whenever their hands touched. "How sad that I never danced before," she said breathlessly after they finished the second dance, which was more complicated than the first. "I was missing so much!"

"Both you and Gwynne deserve great credit," Simon said. "You're a superb rider, and that's also a skill that requires strength and movement and grace. But you could never have become a good dancer so quickly without Gwynne's lesson."

"I've never had a student learn so quickly." Gwynne ended her minuet by holding Duncan's hand as they bowed their respects to an invisible audience. The movement was echoed exactly by Meg.

As they caught their breaths, Jack Landon rose from the harpsichord. "Now it is my turn." He bowed to Meg. "My lady, will you honor me with this dance?"

"It will be my pleasure, sir." As Gwynne sat down at the harpsichord and struck up a country dance tune, Meg discovered that the secretary was also a fine dancer, but he wasn't Simon. Neither was Duncan when he took a turn dancing with her. But she definitely enjoyed dancing.

When Gwynne declared the session over and Simon rang for refreshments, Meg said, "Thank you all. Now that I've seen four fine dancers perform, I'm even more aware of what a disaster it would have been if I'd gone to the ball without any preparation! I would have disgraced you, Simon."

"Never," he said, his gaze holding hers. "Every man there will envy me my bride. Except perhaps Duncan. You will be a great success, my dear."

To her surprise, she realized that she believed him. Perhaps he had cast a spell to inspire confidence on her.

She was even ready to face Lord Drayton. This time, she would be ready for him.

Sarah shook her head when she looked at the pathetic crumbs of bread, cheese, and pickled onions scattered across the worktable. "I can't believe the way that you and your friends eat! A mouse would starve on the leftovers. A good thing that we've been able to hire a maid and there's a cook shop round the corner."

David laughed and kissed his wife on the end of her nose. "Inventing is hungry work, my love. Your reminding us to eat is almost as important as your mathematical calculations. Almost, but not quite. There's not another wife in the kingdom who can match all the things you do so well."

She blushed adorably. "And there is surely not another husband would appreciate the mathematics as much as the food."

"Many can cook but few can calculate." He set an empty crock and the used tankards on a tray. He would carry it back to the house himself. Mustn't allow Sarah to work too hard. She laughed at his fretting over her, but she enjoyed it, too.

Sarah gazed around the workshop, which was lit by slanting rays of late-afternoon sun. "Someday we will look back at these days as our golden age. I'm so happy it's almost frightening. And don't talk about silk and lace. Such would be a pleasure to own, but what more do we need than what we have now?"

He set down the tray and considered. "I'll be happy when my lathe is finished, but you're right. We have each other, good friends, my work is going well." He laid a gentle hand over her belly, feeling the subtle swell of pregnancy. "Your work is going even better, for you are creating a miracle." Superstition touched him. "Shall we say a prayer of thanksgiving? I don't want the Heavenly Father to think we are taking our blessings for granted."

Sarah smiled. "Shall you begin the prayer, or shall I?"

Before David could answer, the door to the workshop opened. It was locked only at night, and David was used to his craftsmen friends wandering in to look over his shoulder and make comments both raucous and helpful. But the man standing in the doorway, the light behind him, was no mechanic. For a moment the elegant clothing made David think it was Lord Falconer.

The next moment he realized that the newcomer was a stranger, though surely another nobleman. His long face bore the lines of authority and his magnificent wig and embroidered garments wouldn't have looked out of place at court. He strolled across the shop. "You are Mr. David White?"

"Indeed I am, sir. And this is Mrs. White. How may I serve you?"

"I am Drayton." The gentleman gave the briefest of nods to Sarah before he paused to study the lathe that was under construction. "You wrote a letter expressing interest in attending my forum on technology and natural philosophy."

David's eyes widened. "Yes, my lord! I wrote your secretary, but I never dreamed that you would call on me in person."

Drayton studied him with cool interest. "Your description of your work interested me, so I made inquiries. I'm told that you are at work designing a new steam engine that will revolutionize industry in Britain."

"I . . . I would never make such claims, my lord," David stammered. "Much work remains to be done. Though I believe the principles are sound, turning principle into reliable practice is a hit-or-miss matter that takes much time."

"You are modest, Mr. White, but all my sources of information indicate that you are well on your way to achieving great success." An odd smile flickered over his lips. "That is why I wished to call on you in person, to make my own judgment. You have the ability to change the world. If you are successful, men will talk of the White steam engine for centuries to come."

Profoundly embarrassed by the compliment, David changed the subject. "Does this mean you will allow me to attend your forum?"

"More than that." Drayton's gaze moved from the lathe to the remains of the trial steam engine. He seemed to be drinking in the workshop, almost like a hound scenting the wind. "I insist that you attend as my guest and that you give a presentation on your work."

The thought was equally flattering and alarming. "It may be too soon to discuss my work in public, Lord Drayton."

"If you fear that your work will be stolen, I can help you with the patent office. But I must insist that you speak about at least the general outlines of your work. The best mechanical minds in the country will be present and the potential of sparking new ideas is immense."

David glanced at Sarah. She looked like he felt—both impressed and nervous. "My wife would be the best to give an overview of my work. She is an uncommon mathematician and without her I would be no more than a blacksmith banging on metal."

"Indeed?" Lord Drayton turned the full force of his attention on Sarah, his expression faintly surprised. "Then I hope she accompanies you to the forum. She will find much to interest her. Nonetheless, you may wish to give the speech yourself, since a female lecturer would be so distracting that her words would go unappreciated."

"He's right, love," Sarah said in her soft voice. "I have no desire to stand up and speak before critical strangers, but I would like to attend and listen with you."

"Well enough. The two of you can prepare the presentation together, but you will present it alone, Mr. White. Will you have a working model?"

David didn't recall agreeing to speak, but he supposed that men like Lord Drayton assumed agreement. "I may have a model by then, my lord, but I make no promises."

"Would more hands make the work go faster? I should be happy to underwrite the cost."

Startled, David considered that briefly. "Thank you, my lord, but the work requires experienced hands. I have an assistant now. Training another in the time available would take more work than it's worth."

"You know your own business best." Drayton frowned. "The kind of work you do is expensive and for a long time there will be no money coming in. If you are in need of a patron, I should be delighted to stand you in that stead."

David was beginning to wonder if he was dreaming this whole encounter. Mere weeks ago, he and Sarah had barely been able to put food on the table, and now a second nobleman wished to sponsor him? "Your lordship's generosity is truly magnificent, but I already have an investment partner."

Drayton snorted. "Let me guess. Would that be Lord Falconer?"

"Indeed it is, sir. How did you guess?"

"Falconer and I have . . . interests in common." The glint in Drayton's dark eyes made ice look temperate. "He has won this round, but there will be others. My secretary will send you more information about the forum and the patent process. Good day, Mr. White. Mrs. White." This time his nod to her was a little deeper and more respectful. He turned and left as abruptly as he had arrived.

David sank onto a bench. "Am I dreaming, or did we just have another lord here offering us money and fame?"

"You weren't dreaming." Sarah stared after the vanished Drayton.

"If Falconer decides to cease funding my work, it's good to know that another patron is ready and waiting."

Sarah frowned. "I wouldn't want to be beholden to that one, David. Nor do I want to become caught in a competition between two noblemen."

"I like Falconer better myself," David admitted. "But if he withdraws his support, Drayton's offer could prove useful."

Sarah's face set in stubborn lines, something David had seen only once or twice before. "We will not have Drayton as a patron, David. If we need another investor later, we can find someone else. A merchant, not a lord. I wouldn't want Drayton's money."

Startled by her vehemence, he said peaceably, "As you wish, my love."

It was the megrims of pregnancy affecting her, he decided. She would come around if they ever needed Drayton's support.

Chapter TWENTY-ONE

Meg stared at herself in the mirror, trying to reconcile the image of a terrifyingly grand lady with Mad Meggie. The sumptuous silk brocade gown was patterned with roses and opened in front to reveal a deep rose-colored petticoat. The stomacher was covered with intricate gold embroidery and gemstones, and the skirts were so wide that if not for the hinged panniers, she couldn't have passed through a doorway without turning sideways. Even her hair powder had a subtle undertone of rose to harmonize with the gown. In short, she looked like a total stranger.

Wishing her confidence matched her splendid facade, she said to her lady's maid, "Thank you, Molly. You have made me appear to be a genuine society lady."

"You *are* a genuine society lady," a deep voice said from the doorway. "A very beautiful one."

As she turned to the door, Simon entered her boudoir. She caught her breath. He was always handsome, but in full evening dress of blue velvet and satin, he was mesmerizing. Though his white wig made him seem distant and intimidatingly fashionable, the effect was softened by his hound Otto, who padded beside him on silent paws. Trying not to gape, she said, "Thank you, but credit for my appearance goes to Lady Bethany, the modiste, and Molly."

He set a velvet covered box on a table. "They only gilded an already lovely lily."

She made a face. "Am I going to have to spend the evening deciphering complicated compliments?"

He laughed. "Without question. Every man who sees you will be trying to come up with new ways of saying how beautiful you are. Expect poetry. Just don't expect it to be good poetry."

She would prefer to be invisible, but didn't know any spells for that. "I assume that as a mere uneducated female, I don't have to be clever in return."

"All you need do is smile and the gentlemen will be falling at your feet. I do hope that none of them challenge me to a duel to win your favor."

As Meg smiled at his banter, Otto decided to sniff at Lucky, who was curled in a ball under the vanity table. Taking instant offense, Lucky hissed and scrambled for safety on top of the nearest high object, which happened to be Meg.

"Oh, no!" Molly wailed as the cat raced upward, tiny claws digging into the embroidered rose silk. "That little beast will ruin your gown!"

"No, he won't." Simon swooped in and captured Lucky just as the cat was about to latch on to the wide fall of lace that spilled around Meg's wrist. "The claw marks won't be visible amidst all the embroidery."

Laughing, Meg scratched her cat's head, the only part of him not caged by Simon's hands. "He doesn't seem to understand that Otto is forbidden to hurt him."

"If a creature fifty times my size was sniffing me like a beefsteak, I'd be nervous, too," Simon observed.

Meg dismissed Molly before the maid could start worrying about orange cat hairs getting on the gown. When she and Simon were private, his light manner dropped away. "Of course you're worried about your first ball. Any woman would be. But remember that you are going to this event with a goal—to discern whether Drayton has other captives. The conversation and dancing will take care of themselves."

His words settled Meg's nerves. She turned to examine herself in the mirror again. "This incredibly expensive costume is armor, isn't it? A way to disguise myself so I can learn what I need to know." The thought made her feel strong instead of uncertain and vulnerable.

"Exactly. We have discussed how you intend to proceed. I will never be far away. This will be your best opportunity to discover the truth."

Their gazes met in the mirror. His words made her feel that they were warriors together. "And if we find others in thrall?"

"Then we will free them." Simon raised Lucky and stroked the purring cat's soft fur along Meg's bare throat. "You need some jewelry for a finishing touch."

Shivers ran through her at the wanton sensuality of the gesture. "I don't think that Lucky can be trusted to stay perched on my shoulder," she said breathlessly.

"Cats tend not to be good ornaments." He brushed the silky cat along Meg's cheek with teasing delicacy. "So we had best keep Lucky out of Otto's reach."

Simon placed the cat on the vanity table, where he retreated to settle among bottles of potions and perfumes. Then Simon retrieved his velvet box, which was wide and flat, with a double lid. "You can wear the Falconer diamonds. They are rather famous." He flipped up the right-hand lid.

Meg gasped at the brilliance of the gems that sparkled from necklace, earrings, and bracelets. She took a closer look. "A tiara?"

"For the most formal occasions only," he explained. "I understand it gives the wearer a fearsome headache."

She rested her fingertips on the centerpiece of the necklace, which was an amazingly large square-cut diamond. The gem was framed and supported by gold settings and three strands of smaller diamonds that sparkled with beauty. The stone carried traces of several different women's energy. The strongest signature was of a swift, restless, mercurial temperament. A woman of charm and volatility. "This set belonged to your mother?"

"She was the most recent owner."

Meg withdrew her hand. "These are beautiful, but I . . . I'd rather not wear them."

"She wasn't wearing these when she died," he said quietly.

"I didn't think so—there is no pain energy caught in the stones. But it seems wrong to wear family jewels when I'm not a real member of your family."

"I thought you might feel that way." He closed that lid and opened the other side. "Here is an alternative."

A blaze of scarlet met her eyes. This suite of jewelry was made of rubies and lighter in style than the diamonds. To her eyes, the pieces were far more beautiful than the family jewels. She skimmed her fingers over the necklace and earrings. "This is new, isn't it? I can feel only trace energy impressions, all of them male, probably the gem cutters and jewelers." She frowned. "There's also some strong magic bound up in the stones."

"You're very perceptive. I bought this set new as a gift for you. The magic is a protection spell."

"No!" she exclaimed. "You mustn't give me anything so valuable. You've given me far too much already."

"You saved my life. That is worth more than rubies to me. Think how undignified it would be if my unicorn head ended up mounted above Drayton's fireplace." He took the necklace from its velvet nest. "The spell might not be needed, but it won't hurt to have more protection available. Would you like to see how this looks?"

Meg wavered between her wish not to be even more beholden and a purely female desire to wear jewels that were so much to her taste. Desire won. "Please."

He fastened the necklace around her throat. The image of them in the mirror was unreal, a reflection of two impossibly handsome people. Yet the gold was cool against her skin and his warm fingertips sent excitement shivering through her. Her heartbeat quickened. "You're trying to distract me from my nerves, aren't you?"

"That's part of it." He bent and pressed his lips to the bare flesh just above the rubies. "But not everything I do is calculated. You are entrancing, Meg. I am having some trouble remembering that we should be leaving for the ball right now."

Though tempted to close her eyes and lean back against him in wanton invitation, she managed to say, "Duty calls."

"I'm glad that one of us remembers duty." He kissed her on the pulse point below her jaw, then stepped away. In the mirror, she saw the mask of control drop into place.

She put on the earrings, which moved with scarlet vivacity when she turned her head, then donned the matched bracelets. Last of all she raised her fan and opened it for Simon to see the painted image. "Jean gave me this to commemorate my first ball."

He smiled ruefully when he saw the scene depicted. "A unicorn hunt with the beast laying his head in the virgin's lap. Jean has a wicked sense of humor."

Meg studied the fan. "This makes it all look so peaceful. No fierceness in this unicorn. No murderous hunters. No sense of wonder."

"Is that what you felt, Meg?"

She thought back to the moment when an impossible, ethereally beautiful creature laid his shimmering head in her lap, the twisted horn reflecting subtle rainbow highlights. "It was the most remarkable moment of my life." It was also the beginning of the end of Mad Meggie, and thank God for that.

"Whatever fate brought us together, it truly was remarkable." He offered his arm. "Shall we venture forth to dazzle society and steal Drayton's secrets?"

She laid her hand on the exquisitely soft blue velvet of his coat. "This time, I will not let him captivate my will." But though her words were emphatic, in her heart she was less sure. Drayton was connected to her energy, and she was still vulnerable to him.

But surely that connection ran both ways, and he could be vulnerable to her. She intended to find out.

Meg's first ball was everything she had expected, and a great deal more. The guests were a mixture of mundanes and Guardians, and they sparkled with color and vivacity. The Guardians, perhaps, sparkled a little bit more. She also loved the music, which was played by a group of professional musicians whose skill far exceeded anything she'd ever heard.

She was less fond of the scents of too many perfumes, candles, and bodies heated by dancing. She simply wasn't used to being around so many people, and the weight of their minds was a good test of her shielding. Luckily, she had been trained well.

After several dance sets, Simon headed off to get them cool drinks, leaving Meg to relax in a chair at one edge of the ballroom. Jean Macrae approached and took the chair next to her. In a room filled with white wigs and powdered hair, Jean's blazing red locks stood out. They had greeted each other earlier, but hadn't had a chance to talk.

"That was a beautiful minuet you and Simon performed." Jean's eyes twinkled. "Your dance style is remarkably like Gwynne's."

Meg laughed. "Thank heaven for her lesson! I thought I'd perish of shyness when I found out that everyone was going to watch us. I think that Simon must have used a calming spell to get me through the first steps."

"Very likely. He's a practical man." Jean made a wry face. "You look so lovely and polished that I heard two Guardian women say that you couldn't possibly have spent ten years in thrall. Sometimes one can't win no matter what one does."

"I choose to take that comment as a compliment," Meg said. "But people can be very tiresome."

"Especially for a powerful magic holder like you. There are several ladies' retiring rooms upstairs if you need to take a break from all the people."

"I'm almost ready now." Meg raised her fan and wafted cool air over her face.

"What did Simon say when he saw the fan?"

Meg glanced down at the painted unicorn. "He said you have a wicked sense of humor. I'm not quite sure if that was a compliment."

"Probably not." Jean laughed. "Since he and Duncan are close friends, he is something of a big brother to me. An indulgent if alarming big brother." Her smile faded as her gaze scanned the crowded chamber. "I haven't seen Drayton. Have you?"

Meg shook her head. "No, and I've certainly been watching. I don't think he's here, or I would sense his presence. I don't know whether to be relieved, or sorry that I won't have the chance to face him after girding myself to do so."

"Be relieved. Nothing good can come from that man." Jean wielded her own fan, an elegant trifle decorated with a Chinese scene. "It's amazing how quickly I've progressed from being terrified of balls to acceptance, and now to a certain ennui."

"Does that mean that you've made no progress toward the goal of finding a husband?" Meg said teasingly.

"Not even close. I've met several eligible males who might be willing to make an offer if I encouraged them, but none of them are particularly interesting, and I have no desire to settle for someone who is merely adequate." She frowned. "I've always felt that I wouldn't marry a Guardian, but I've done no better in meeting mundanes than with the Families."

"You still miss your young man?" Meg asked softly.

Jean snapped her fan shut. "I shall always miss him. Robbie and I had known each other our whole lives. Though he was mundane, that . . . never mattered. He was my best friend." The candlelight caught a glint of tears in her eyes.

"I'm sorry."

"So am I." She managed a smile. "But I'm doing my best to get on with my life. It's what Robbie would have wanted, and what I would have wanted for him if I were the one who had died. People can recover from the most horrific things, after all. A couple months ago, you were virtually a slave, and now look at you—you're a beautiful countess, with one of the best men in Britain for a husband."

"Believe me, I remember daily how lucky I am!" Meg rose, feeling the need to get out of the ballroom for a few minutes. "I see that Simon has been waylaid by your brother so I'll visit the retiring room. Tell him I'll be back soon."

"I will, but I may drink your iced punch if you're gone long."

Meg laughed. "Please do." She headed purposefully for the door, not wanting anyone to catch her eye so that she would need to stop and talk. Though she was enjoying herself, Jean had been right about the need to take a break from the crowd.

Because Lady Bethany's home in Richmond was too far out of London for convenience, Lady Sterling had offered the use of Sterling House's spacious ballroom. Tonight there were no damping spells like the ones that had been so suffocating at Drayton's hearing.

Thinking of Drayton sent a shiver through her. It was almost more unnerving to wonder why he wasn't here than it was to confront him.

Chapter
TWENTY-TWO

As Jean had said, several bedchambers on the floor above had been converted to retiring rooms, their doors opened invitingly. In the first, several young mundane girls chatted slanderously among themselves. In the second room, a maid was kneeling to hem a torn flounce on an older woman's gown. The third room was empty, so Meg entered. A screen concealed a chamber pot, while a table offered a basin and pitcher, towels, lavender water for cooling one's temples, and other small luxuries for guests.

For Meg, it was enough to have silence. She perched on a chair, since her corset was not designed to permit lounging.

What if it wasn't possible to bring Drayton to justice? She had volunteered to play the part of Simon's wife until the job was done, but what if the rogue laid low and refrained from causing more trouble? How long would she be willing to stay before setting off on her quest to find her family? Surely Simon would not insist she stay in London indefinitely.

She sighed and trailed her fingers through the bowl of lavender water. Though she didn't want to owe Simon too much, she would have to continue to accept his charity until she found her family. It was hard to see beyond that. Harder yet to guess what she would do with herself if she didn't find her kin. If she could make herself useful to the Guardians, it would make it easier to accept their charity.

"Lady Falconer?"

"Yes?" Meg looked up to see another guest at the door. A few years older than Meg, she was strikingly lovely, with the blue eyes and fair brows of a natural blonde. She was also beautifully gowned, but there was a slackness to her posture as she leaned against the door frame.

"Sorry to disturb you," the woman said, "but I'm perishing of curiosity. Do you mind if I lie down?" Not waiting for an answer, she moved into the room, swaying. Fearing the woman was about to fall, Meg jumped to her feet and caught her arm, guiding her to the bed and helping her to lie down.

"Too much champagne," the woman said apologetically. "I thought it best to come up here and rest until my head clears. Then I saw you. You've probably forgotten, but I'm Lady Arden. We met earlier."

"You're right, I remember hardly any names from the receiving line. Thank you for the reminder," Meg said. "Is there anything I can do for you?"

"No, I'll be all right soon. My particular magical talent is accompanied by the inability to drink wine or beer. Usually I don't mind, but sometimes I succumb to temptation when there is champagne being served." She rubbed her forehead sadly. "It tastes so *good.*"

"I'll leave and let you rest, then."

Meg was heading for the door when Lady Arden said, "If you don't mind, I have a question for you. Simon is wonderfully handsome, of course, but how can you bear to be married to him? Aren't you frightened?"

Meg stared at her. "Frightened? My lord Falconer has been kindness itself."

"I don't remember ever seeing him unkind, but that doesn't mean he isn't frightening." Lady Arden's eyes closed.

"You seem to know him very well," Meg said, curious even though she knew it was improper to gossip about Simon behind his back.

The other woman's eyes flickered open, sadness in the blue depths. "He once asked me to marry him."

"You could have married him and didn't?" Meg exclaimed.

Lady Arden sighed. "The great mages are very alarming men and women. I didn't think I could ever be comfortable as Simon's wife. In fact, he terrified me. Because I was young and not good at saying what I meant, I fear I hurt him with my rejection. I shouldn't have mentioned his . . . his family history."

Meg was fascinated but unsure how to reply. So Simon had wanted to marry this woman. She was very lovely, and Meg guessed that she had a fair amount of power. She would have made a proper Guardian wife. "Do you regret refusing him?"

"Arden and I are better suited." She sighed again, as if being better suited was not, perhaps, enough. "The work Simon does is necessary but difficult, and not always fully appreciated. I am glad for his sake that he has found a wife who is his equal."

"I am not his equal. Not at all." Meg bit her lip. "This is a very strange conversation."

"I'm sorry. It's the champagne speaking." Lady Arden gave a lovely smile. "A man needs a wife who doesn't fear him. I wish you both happy, my dear."

"Th . . . thank you. I hope you're feeling better soon. Good night." Meg made her escape, closing the door behind her so that Lady Arden could rest until the champagne was out of her blood.

How did she feel about meeting a woman Simon had wanted to marry? Meg wasn't sure, but had to admit that he had good taste. Lady Arden seemed to have a warm heart as well as more than her share of beauty. If he still felt the pain of her rejection, it would help explain his disinclination to marry.

In the hallway, she paused to smooth wrinkles from the heavy silk folds of her gown. Ruefully she decided that her appearance must have been what convinced Lady Arden that Mad Meggie was Simon's equal. No wonder Simon and Lady Bethany had been so insistent that she be dressed well. Because she looked well-bred, Meg was perceived as worthy.

Before returning to the ball, she cautiously lowered her mental shields enough to experience the torrent of mental energy that rushed through the house. She had never been under the same roof with so many people, a fair number of them Guardians. It was interesting to listen, though rather overpowering.

Most of the guests were enjoying themselves, but some were unhappy for various personal reasons: health, broken hearts, worries about family. A man was regarding an unsuspecting woman with hungry lust. There were many different flavors of energy, like sampling the spice chest in a pantry. Even at this distance, she recognized the emotional signatures of those she knew well, like Simon and Jean.

Intent on her thoughts, she noticed nothing wrong until a hard hand clamped over her mouth. *Drayton.* She realized it as soon as he touched her. His power flooded through her, intense and completely overwhelming her will and physical strength.

With horror, she realized that she was sliding into thrall. She managed to raise one hand to clasp the ruby necklace, using its protective spell to save herself from total surrender. With the help of the necklace, she managed to retain a spark of awareness of who and what she had become since escaping his control the first time. Yet she was helpless as a wax doll as he dragged her into the empty bedroom a few feet away. Small and spare, it hadn't been designated as a retiring room, but it was well lit by several globes of mage light.

He kicked the door shut, isolating the room from the hall, then turned the key in the lock. "I knew you would walk by, Meggie," he hissed in her ear. "You are mine and I have come to reclaim you."

The spark of selfhood managed to speak. "You *swine!*"

Feebly she struggled against his grip, but every fiber of her being was saturated by his energy. He reeked of arrogance and lust.

How had he overpowered her so easily now that she was shielded and Simon had blocked the energy connection between her and Drayton? Her hazy mind suggested that it was because he was physically touching her, not at a distance. Whatever the reason, the result left her only a hairsbreadth away from Meggie's mindless obedience.

She tried to master her panic. *Use your power.* She had practiced her magic for just such an incident. Surely she should be able to do something to prevent him from kidnapping her out of a house full of people!

He turned her around, maintaining a bruising hold on her arms. She refused to look directly in his eyes, afraid that would increase his power over her. He was dressed in formal evening wear. Since he had been invited, he would have had no trouble entering the house, then finding this spot to watch for her. Most women withdrew to the retiring rooms at some point, so it was an easy guess that she would pass him sooner or later.

"Anything to say for yourself, Meggie?" he said, smiling broadly. "If you're deeply enough in thrall, you'll stop fighting me."

"Never!" She locked panic in a corner of her mind until she could afford to deal with it. First, what magic was Drayton using?

Most obvious was the domination spell he'd controlled her with for so many years. Her mind recognized it all too well and returned to the familiar passivity. Also, she sensed an unusual kind of shielding spell around them. She guessed that it was designed to block any signs of their struggle from other Guardians. The spell would conceal them if he took her from the house, so she must find some way to escape or call for help before that happened.

"You're like a hissing kitten," he observed. "You wave your little paws, but are no threat to me."

The triple defense spell. Belatedly she recalled the three-way protection spell she had developed with Jean's help. It was designed for exactly these circumstances. Even if the shield and striking spells weren't effective, the damping spell should knock out Drayton's protective bubble so that others could recognize that something was wrong and come to her aid.

She was about to invoke the triple spell when she remembered her earlier thought that the connection between her and Drayton ran both ways. This might be her chance to find if he had others in thrall.

Engage him in conversation. That might give her more access to his mind. She managed to gasp, "This time, you will not get away with abducting me. I am no longer a helpless child without friends."

"These so-called friends will accept it when you earnestly tell them that you are leaving your dull husband to return to me, the man you have always loved." He smiled, showing his teeth. "You will be most convincing. No one will interfere. Even if Falconer tries, he will be unable to breach the wards on my London house."

The spark that was Meg flared angrily. "I *won't!*"

"You will do anything I want of you. If I tell you to walk on all fours and whinny like a pony, you will do it and swish your imaginary tail. If I tell you to jump from the garret window of my house and shatter that lovely body on the cobblestones, you will leap with alacrity." His grip on her arms tightened. "Consider yourself fortunate that I want you to be my adoring, obedient consort."

She spat in his face.

He flinched, his expression hardening. "With the right spell, you could be made to believe yourself happy to be in my thrall, but I think I would rather know that somewhere under your perfect behavior, you will hate me even as you spread your legs."

Furious, she reached for the false appearance created by the illusion spell he'd used on her for years. The image in the mirror over the wash-stand blurred, then cleared to show Mad Meggie with slack face, awk-ward body, and drab clothing.

For an instant he was startled. "I'd forgotten how ugly I made you. No wonder I never considered you as a mate." With a blast of raw power, he dissolved the illusion, returning her to her real appearance.

His eyes narrowed. "It occurs to me that it might be better to change your appearance entirely so no one will realize that my new con-sort is the missing Lady Falconer. If I lay a powerful illusion spell on you, I may as well make you the most beautiful woman in Britain. Shall I make you look like Gwynne Owens? No, I can do better than that. You must be blond, of course, but what else?"

Meg felt hammer blows of magic jangle through her. As each blow struck, she saw more changes in the mirror. Her features shifted to per-fect, bland symmetry. Then masses of loose blond hair spilled wantonly over her shoulders. Her bosom enlarged to a startling extent and her gown became a thin night rail that concealed very little of her.

Drayton touched his tongue to his lips. "I've outdone myself. How fortunate that this room has a bed." He put his right hand on her breast, then frowned. "The spell is only superficial now, which means that under the lovely illusion that covers you, you're still locked into corset and stomacher. I must wait until I have time and privacy to make the il-lusion spell change you so profoundly that you will feel as you appear."

"Change your own face when you do so I don't have to look at your vile features!" Meg knew she sounded childish, but it was a struggle to maintain her sense of self. She had no strength left for wit. Using what power she still commanded, she probed Drayton's mind to discover if he had others in thrall.

"Even though you're not yet the woman of my dreams, you'll do for a quick fuck." His eyes hot with desire, he pulled her toward the bed. "We might as well take advantage of the bed before we leave. We'll be done in five minutes, and when we are, you will fight me no longer."

Dear God, she couldn't let him rape her! Lust was loosening his defenses, but not enough to learn what she wanted. Taking a chance, she looked directly into his eyes, hoping that would establish a deeper connection. His dark eyes were a window to the cruelest, most ruthless soul she had ever seen.

He was affected by her gaze, but not the way she wanted. He shoved her onto the bed and dropped on top of her with a rattle of pannier frames, swearing when a metal spoke jabbed him. Then he forced her mouth open with a violent kiss.

She gagged, choking on his disgusting tongue. She must invoke the triple defense spell before this went any further. Grimly she made one last attempt to delve into his mind.

There were others! Perhaps four or five. She recognized the same kind of thread that connected her to him. But where did the threads go? She must follow them if she was to find his victims.

Abruptly he lifted his head and stared down at her. "Well, damn me for a tailor! You're still a virgin. That molly boy Falconer hasn't even been able to take your maidenhead. Oh, this is rich indeed!"

"Simon is a thousand times the man you are!" She spat again, trying to get the taste of him out of her mouth.

He backhanded her across the cheek. "Time you learned manners, wench." His body still pinning her to the bed, he frowned. "I've never sensed that Falconer is a molly boy, so why hasn't he bedded a toothsome morsel like you?" After a moment's consideration, he said slowly, "It must have something to do with the unicorn spell. I reckon he wants to keep a virgin nearby in case he grows a horn again." Drayton gave a rusty crack of laughter. "It will be two horns he'll be wearing—the cuckold's horns."

"It's a sign of your stupidity that you will waste the magical power of virginity by giving in to your lust," she snapped.

He slapped her again. "What a tongue you've developed since you escaped my tender care. But you have a point. There are more useful ways to take that maidenhead. Instead of changing your appearance so no one will know that you're Lady Falconer, you will stay as you are. Once you're under my roof, you will sue Falconer for an annulment on the grounds of impotence. I might as well humiliate him before I destroy him."

She tried to wrench free without success. "No one will believe you!"

"They'll believe the physicians who examine you. Rest assured that the examination will provide you with your share of humiliation." Again he gave her the toothed smile of a predator. "In the meantime, there is much that can be done short of taking your virginity." He ground another kiss into her bruised lips.

She forced herself to control her physical revulsion, using all her crippled power to dive into the rank depths of his mind. She managed to locate the connection threads again, but was unable to follow them to the ends. They vanished into misty space.

She was about to surrender and invoke the defense spell when she remembered that another source of magic was available. She imagined Lucky, then reached for the essence of feline power: subtle, hidden, hunting. Energy sparked incandescently through her mind, illuminating those gossamer trails.

Yes! Five people, all young, all trapped in the horrors of thrall. It took only an instant to memorize the auras and directions. She would know how to find those other poor suffering devils.

Having learned what she needed, at a damnably high price, she gathered her power and her desperation and mentally cried out the word that would trigger the triple defensive spell.

Simon!

Chapter TWENTY-THREE

The group of half a dozen men had been idly discussing politics when the music started again. Most left to claim dance partners. When only Simon and Duncan were left, Duncan said quietly, "You've assumed that Drayton is interested in seizing control over the Guardians. What if his main aim is power within the mundane government? He is already a cabinet minister, and we know of his interest in mechanics and technology. The economy of Britain is on the verge of major change, and if he is at the forefront, he might end up with tremendous worldly power."

"I've considered that," Simon replied. "But he could pursue such goals without causing trouble in the Guardian community, and it would be safer not to break our laws. He already has me monitoring his activities, and others are watching as well. Though he has considerable power, I don't think he is yet capable of taking us all on."

"If he wants to influence the mundane world, he will be able to do so more effectively if he uses magic in ways forbidden by our laws." Duncan frowned. "Strategically, it's to his advantage to enhance his power by whatever means available, use that power to take control of the Guardians so that there will be no one strong enough to oppose him, then use magic to enforce his will in the worldly sphere."

Simon whistled softly. "It's an ugly prospect, but so large in scale that I'm not sure anyone could achieve it."

Duncan shrugged cynically. "He doesn't have to achieve it. He only needs to think he can, and he's arrogant enough for that. Not everyone is as logical as you are."

Simon was silent for a long moment. "You're right. I have been allowing logic to limit my imagination. Drayton's whole nature is illogic."

Before he could say more, Meg's mental voice rang in his mind as she called his name with the power of a great church bell ringing. He gasped, feeling her desperation. How long since he had seen Meg? Perhaps a quarter of an hour? What the devil had happened to her?

Her mental cry was followed an instant later by a wave of damping magic that swept through the laughing crowd. The mundanes were unaffected, but the Guardians all reacted. A man developed a paunch and a woman's wrinkles appeared as their illusion spells were smothered. Though the damping spell dissipated swiftly, it left a confused magical atmosphere in its wake. The woman's skin smoothed out again, but the gentleman remained paunchy, perhaps too shaken to maintain his false appearance.

Spinning on his heel, Simon said grimly, "That was Meg. She's upstairs." He cut through the startled crowd, Duncan at his back as he took the stairs three at a time.

Several females had emerged from retiring rooms into the hall and were looking around in bewilderment. No Meg. He decided to start with the nearest closed door. It was locked. Blocking what he was doing so the mundanes couldn't see, he blew the tumblers open with a furious blast of power, not caring who he might find fornicating on the other side.

He stepped inside, and was horrified to find Meg collapsed on the bed, her eyes closed and her face pale except for reddened marks on her cheeks. The room's window was open and a breeze blew in, rippling the curtains.

While Duncan rushed to the window, Simon went to Meg. Remembering his success with healing the kitten, he gently framed her face and poured in healing energy. Though she wasn't truly unconscious, her mind was disordered, steeped in confusion. As he continued with the healing, he felt her thoughts smooth out.

Her eyelids flickered open to reveal that her changeable eyes were the color of charcoal. "I know where they are," she said huskily.

He caught his breath. "Others that Drayton has in thrall?"

After she nodded, he said, "We'll talk about that later. How are you? Who hurt you?"

"Drayton. Is he still here?" she asked in a strained whisper.

"I don't believe so." Now that he knew who was responsible, fury seared through him. He must find Drayton and smash the rogue with his hooves. . . .

Meg's nails bit into his hand, drawing blood. *"Don't!"* she said fiercely.

The pain pierced his anger, bringing him back to himself. He broke into a cold sweat when he realized how close he had come to transforming. He had hoped that the beast nature was fading, but obviously not. "Thank you."

A brief flare of light came from the window. Duncan swore. "There was a knotted rope hanging out here, but a dissolution spell just made it vanish. Drayton is gone and he left no traces."

Half a dozen people, all Guardians, entered the room. One of the first was Lady Bethany. She sat on the edge of the bed and laid a cool, lavender-scented hand on Meg's forehead. "Did Drayton hurt you?"

"He tried to abduct me again," Meg whispered.

Lord Halliburton pushed into the room in time to hear Meg's words. He scowled. "Once more you are slandering Lord Drayton without proof. Though I know Drayton well, I can't sense a shred of his energy here."

"Lady Falconer's damping spell has removed all traces of magic in the area," Simon said dryly. "What sort of proof would you consider acceptable, Halliburton? Would you believe Drayton guilty of killing chickens if you caught him wringing a rooster's neck?"

Halliburton flushed. "You and Drayton were both ordered not to take action against each other. Getting your wife to accuse him makes you guilty of violating the council's order. I'll have you brought up on charges."

Meg pushed herself to a sitting position and stared at Halliburton, her gaze burning. "I am no one's creature, not even Simon's. Do you doubt my word?"

He fell back a step, startled by the power of her anger. "If . . . if you made up this accusation by yourself, it is you who are guilty of violating the council's order. Everyone involved had to pledge not to cause trouble."

"Don't be a fool, Hally," Lady Bethany said briskly. "Lady Falconer has clearly been assaulted and you have no right to call her a liar or Falconer a conspirator. There may be no absolute evidence that Drayton attacked her—though personally I think it's fair to believe the victim—but neither is there any proof he is innocent. He certainly wasn't downstairs dancing."

Simon suppressed a smile. Leave it to Lady Beth to put matters into perspective.

Lord Sterling, master of the household, entered the room. "Did Lady Falconer cast that damping spell?"

Meg nodded. "I hope I didn't inconvenience anyone."

"Not seriously," Sterling said with a speculative gaze. "That was an impressive piece of magic. Where did you learn it?"

"Jean Macrae taught me the basic spell." Meg swung her feet to the floor and stood, swaying. Simon wrapped an arm around her waist. She was shivering with shock. "I don't think there was anything special about it."

"I am the expert at damping spells who is called on to cast them for events like council hearings. I believe that I have just met my successor, Lady Falconer. Perhaps at some future time we can discuss the fine points of technique." Sterling bowed respectfully, then turned to the other guests who were in the room or hall. "Supper is about to be served downstairs. Shall we adjourn and enjoy it?" Effortlessly he ushered out everyone but Simon and Lady Beth.

"I'm going to take Meg home now," Simon said to Lady Bethany. "I'm sorry to leave early, but Meg needs peace and quiet."

"Of course." The older woman looked troubled. "This obsession of Drayton's concerns me, Meg. What did he say?"

"That he . . . he wants me for his wife." Meg looked ill at the thought. "He considered several possibilities. One was to change my appearance so I would look like the sort of woman who excites him. Lady Falconer would simply disappear. Then he decided that I should stay myself and sue Simon for an annulment. He wanted me to be perfectly obedient, yet hate him in my heart."

Lady Bethany's mouth thinned. "Despicable. Simon, keep her safe."

"I will." He hugged Meg closer. She seemed drained by her experience. "Rest, my dear. Once more, you have defeated Drayton."

After Lady Beth left, he said, "You'll be more comfortable without the panniers." He raised Meg's skirt and untied the frames, then helped her step out when the panniers and attached underpetticoat collapsed to the floor.

Bemused, she said, "I'll trip," as she surveyed the yards of sumptuous brocade pooled around her ankles.

"No, you won't. Relax now. You don't have to think about anything." He scooped her into his arms and headed for the door.

Meg gave a little sigh and turned her face into his shoulder, her eyes drifting shut. He guessed that she wanted the security of being close as much as he did.

To his surprise, Blanche was waiting in the hall, her eyes worried. He reminded himself to think of her as Lady Arden. They saw each other regularly on social occasions, but they hadn't spoken since the day she had vehemently rejected his offer of marriage.

"Is your wife all right?" Blanche asked.

"She will be," he said tersely.

Blanche's gaze went to Meg's face. "I wouldn't have had the strength to be your wife. She does. I'm sorry, Simon."

It was an apology that covered many things. Simon's wariness eased. "When you refused my offer, your instincts were sound even if your words were ill-chosen. We would not have suited well, Blanche. Are you happy?"

"Yes. Fate is often wiser than we are." She gave the entrancing smile that had once won his heart, then drifted toward the stairwell, one hand trailing along the wall for balance. She must have had some champagne and was still recovering. Blanche never had been able to resist a glass of champagne.

The thought brought back other memories of their ill-fated courtship ten years before. Blanche had dazzled him, and at first he had intrigued her as well. As he carried Meg down a back stairwell, he realized that Blanche had been right. Fate had been wise. And if she had refused him clumsily, well, she had been young. So had he.

Youth was greatly overrated.

Lady Beth had already summoned his carriage, and a servant had retrieved his hat and Meg's shawl. It required care to climb into the carriage without waking Meg or banging into the frame, but he managed. Once they were inside, he settled her warm, vibrant weight across his lap and draped the shawl over her shoulders.

As the carriage started for Falconer House, he made sure it was well shielded, then concentrated on Meg. She looked like a sleeping child, yet she had fought off a fully trained mage. He felt a tenderness that almost disabled him. More than anything on earth, he wanted to keep her safe, but if not for her own strength, she would have been stolen away again. If this was war, Drayton was winning. The knowledge was bitter.

He brushed back her hair, wishing that her natural dark, silky locks were free of the heavy powder. She had looked stunning tonight—every inch a fashionable lady. Her ability to adapt and pick up new things was—well, magical. He guessed that she was pulling social knowledge from those around her without even realizing it.

Her eyes opened. "Do you still miss Lady Arden?"

Startled, he asked, "How did you know about her?"

"She told me. I think she wanted to assure herself that I was worthy of you."

"I trust she approved," he said dryly. "Not that it is any of her business."

"She approved." Meg shifted distractingly in his lap. "She seemed very nice. And very beautiful."

Despite the blandness of her tone, the question was obvious. "She is both, and a talented Guardian. She was also right that we were not well suited. I can't imagine that she would rescue a captured unicorn if she had been in thrall for ten years. Nor face down Drayton as you did. You have a warrior heart, Meg."

"That's good, I'm sure."

"You also are beautiful," he said softly. "Inside and out."

After a long, still moment, she tilted her head back, her gaze intent. "Will you kiss me? I want to get the taste of Drayton out of my mouth."

Lightly he touched the bruises forming on her cheeks, channeling more healing energy. "What did he do to you?"

She shrugged. "Shoved me on the bed, made threats, slapped me to teach me obedience, and forced his horrible kisses on me. He realized that I was virgin."

"That was perceptive of him." No wonder Drayton had come up with the idea of forcing Meg to sue for an annulment. Wordlessly Simon bent his lips to hers. His kiss was soft in deference to the physical and emotional battering she had endured. She gave a soft sigh of pleasure, her lips opening under his. Though he felt desire stirring, he kept his exploration of her mouth gentle. She was sweet and intoxicating as honey wine.

He hated knowing that Drayton had used and abused her even though it had stopped well short of rape. His kiss deepened and he caressed her back with both hands, wanting to eliminate any lingering taint left by the brute's touch.

His tongue found a rough spot inside her mouth. From the faint metallic taste of blood, he guessed that the abrasion was a result of Drayton's violence. He licked the area and sent healing until the roughness smoothed out.

Meg shivered with response and locked her arms around his neck. Her urgency transformed his concern, anger and tenderness into feverish passion. He wanted to sink into her, become one, body and soul.

She responded with matching fervor, turning to straddle his lap. Their hips ground together, straining to connect despite the layers of fabric that separated them. He tugged up her voluminous skirts so he could caress her leg. His palm glided up over the silk of her stocking to the warm, bare flesh above.

Her moan vibrated through him, transmitted through their kiss. More than anything on earth, he wanted to increase her pleasure, intoxicate her until they came together in mutual madness. He slid his hand between them, probing gently until he found moist, exquisitely sensitive folds of flesh. At his intimate touch, she cried out and convulsed against him.

He was fumbling with his breeches, frantic to enter her, when he realized what he was doing. Fury and self-revulsion swept through him because he was seducing a woman who had suffered one assault this night. Not only was this despicable in its own right, but he was about to destroy her precious virginity.

His anger was too swift and deep to be subverted this time. Recognizing that Drayton's spell was beginning to rip through him, he shifted Meg to the opposite seat, as far from him as possible. Vast amounts of energy surged into his body, bringing agony along with the wrenching changes. As Meg gasped with surprise, he tried to retreat, but his expanding form rapidly filled the carriage's limited space.

The haze and pain of transformation faded, leaving him panting with distress. His unicorn body was jammed across his seat and his legs bracketed Meg. He tried to move, but his neck was twisted awkwardly along the right side panel and his horn stabbed the quilted ceiling. Though his instinct was to run, he had enough wit left to realize that he daren't move for fear of accidentally injuring Meg, who was trapped within the circle of his solid equine body.

Worst of all, his splayed hind legs flagrantly revealed his rampant desire, and a unicorn was not a small creature. He stared at her helplessly, wishing he were anywhere in the world but here. At the same time, he wanted her more than ever, physical passion compounded by the magical allure of her virgin purity. She was exquisite, both object of desire and a chalice of grace.

Eyes huge but unflinching, Meg's gaze moved over him, lingering briefly as she noted his swollen male flesh. "You really must stop being so angry with yourself when you lose control. Your valet will weep bitter tears when he sees that you've destroyed your magnificent costume." She stroked his foam-streaked neck, calming energy radiating from her hand. It helped, a little.

"Do you understand what I'm saying?" she asked.

He nodded, twisting his neck further.

"I will use the pointed back of an earring to prick your shoulder, then my finger. That should provide enough mingling of blood to restore you."

He nodded again, hoping she could transform him back before he utterly disgraced himself. His whole body felt like one huge, quivering sexual organ.

She unhooked her right earring and leaned forward to prick the shoulder muscle. The quick sting caused a dark droplet to form on his shining white hide. He watched, entranced by her movements, wanting to lay his head against her but unable to move.

She stabbed the middle finger of her left hand. When blood appeared, she touched it to his. Nothing happened for what seemed like a long time, and he began to fear that the magic was gone—that the increasing physical intimacy between them had destroyed the innocence needed to counter Drayton's spell.

Frowning, she rubbed her finger against him, mixing the blood more thoroughly. Metamorphosis was immediate. The heat that had rushed in when his body enlarged now radiated outward in waves as bones and flesh crushed back into human form. The violence of the change pitched him from his seat and he ended half-collapsed across Meg's lap, panting, naked, and covered with sweat.

He was so drained he wasn't sure he could move, yet still he burned with desire. Ashamed, he buried his face against her unyieldingly corseted torso, knowing he should pull away, yet neither able nor willing to do so. "I'm so sorry, Meg," he whispered.

"Poor Simon," she murmured, her voice still honey sweet. "Your transformation is far worse than anything I suffered at Drayton's hands tonight."

Her gentle hands stroked over his bare back and arms, smoothing his jangled aura as if it were fur standing on end. He began to feel calmer, though he still dared not move because that would expose his arousal.

Her supple hand slid down his waist, then under him. Before he realized her intent, she clasped the rigid, pulsing length of his maleness. He gasped as ecstasy shot through him. "Meg . . ."

"I don't think this should take much," she murmured. "Though I've had no more experience with the mating habits of men than with those of unicorns."

She drew her hand upward, squeezing. It was enough. Groaning, he erupted in a violent release that was as shaming as it was rapturous. When his dizziness passed, he found that his arms were clenched around her waist and his face was buried in her lap.

Feeling more beast than man, he let go of her and sat back on his heels, jammed between the seats as tightly as his unicorn form had filled the whole carriage. "I'm sorry, Meg. You . . . you shouldn't have had to deal with my brute male lust."

"Why not?" She wiped her hand on a piece of his ruined velvet coat, then leaned forward and kissed his forehead. "You gave me great pleasure. I wanted to do the same for you. I am a simple country girl, Simon. It is natural for creatures to mate, and I have great difficulty understanding how something that feels so right can be wrong."

He sighed. "When I touch you, I have trouble remembering that, too. But in the calm that comes in the wake of desire, I once more feel that I am taking advantage of your youth and inexperience."

"I'm experienced enough to know that I prefer you to Drayton," she said tartly. "Or to any other man I've met. Isn't that enough?"

He wished he had more and better words. "What would have happened if I had taken your virginity? How would the transformation spell have been countered?"

"There are other virgins in London. Jean Macrae would come in a heartbeat if her help was needed." Meg's mouth quirked up. "Though I must admit that I don't want you looking at another female the way you look at me when you're a unicorn. It is rather wonderful to be adored."

He had to laugh. "You have a splendidly sensible way of dealing with absurdity."

"Thank you, I think." She glanced out the window as the carriage rumbled to a stop. "We're home again. Shall I go inside and get a cloak for you?"

"No need. There are carriage robes under your seat. If you move over here, I'll get one out." After she moved to his side of the carriage, he raised the padded seat and retrieved a woolen blanket. It was scratchy against his bare skin, but covered him well enough. "We'll simply march inside and leave the servants to their own conclusions."

Her laughter was husky and not at all innocent. "I hope word of our wickedness gets back to Drayton and he assumes the worst." She brushed a tender hand through his hair. "And I look forward to the day when we can truly come together."

So did he. Dear God, so did he.

Chapter TWENTY-FOUR

Meg welcomed the familiar tingle of the wards when they entered the house. She had come to appreciate the power and sophistication of Simon's protections. Falconer House was the safest place in London for a mage, and it was a relief to relax her personal shields.

To the footman who had admitted them, Simon said, "Please send a light supper for two to my study." He was as coolly dignified as if he wore a Roman toga rather than a barely adequate plaid blanket. She wondered what the ostlers would think when they cleaned the carriage and found his ruined clothing. They would probably assume she had attacked him like a lioness in heat, which wasn't far from the truth.

As she studied his chiseled, enigmatic profile, she realized that it was increasingly easy to identify man with unicorn and vice versa. Both had lean elegance, power, and heart-stopping beauty. If he had been broad and dark-haired like Duncan Macrae, would his unicorn form have reflected that? An interesting question. A dark, muscular unicorn might be equally impressive, but she doubted she would find one so attractive.

She was amazed that Simon could resist the fierce sexual attraction that bound them. Perhaps she would have more self-discipline when she was a more experienced mage. Or—she swallowed hard when she noticed how the carriage robe exposed his powerful shoulders—perhaps not. It was impossible to imagine not wanting him. She was beginning to suspect that her origins were pure peasant, since her nature was more earthy than refined.

Simon turned to her. "Do you wish to discuss the information about your colleagues tonight, or in the morning when we are rested?"

Her fatigue vanished. "Now."

He smiled faintly. "I guessed as much, which is why I ordered refreshments. We missed the excellent supper at Sterling House. Let us change into more comfortable garments and meet in my study."

She nodded and headed up the stairs. It took time for her maid to remove the complicated evening costume and her hair would not be free of powder until it could be washed, but undoing the elaborate style, brushing out her hair, and donning a comfortable house robe were a great relief.

Simon was already in his study, wearing a loose, blue velvet banyan. The supper he had ordered was on a tray to one side of the room, but for now, he handed her a glass of watered brandy. He must have used magic to determine exactly the right proportion of ingredients because the brandy glowed through her, warm but not burning.

He sipped his own drink, which was considerably darker, then set it aside so he could unroll a large scroll on the desk. "Here's a map of London and the area around it." He set weights on the corners and edges. "Can you show me where Drayton holds the others in thrall?"

"I'm not sure." Eyes narrowed, she bent over the map, tracing the course of the Thames, then the villages that lay outside of London proper. "I don't know any of these places. I know nothing of the city but this neighborhood and the park."

"You don't have to know the city. Trying closing your eyes and using power to locate your lost souls."

Someday she would remember to use magic without having to be reminded. She closed her eyes and held her open hand over the map while she thought back to the energy threads she had discovered deep in Drayton's mind. Without conscious volition, her hand moved to her left and came to rest on the map, her palm glowing with heat. "Here. Four of the five are here." She opened her eyes and saw that her hand touched an area west of London, a little beyond Richmond. "In a manor house outside this village."

Simon studied the spot. "Brentford Abbey?"

"Yes! How did you know that?"

"Because Brentford Abbey is the country house where Drayton is holding his great technology forum. He leased the estate several years ago to have a country retreat that is near enough to London for him to be close to the court and government." Simon frowned. "I haven't investigated the place, but it was once an abbey and it is sited on the intersection of three ley lines. Centuries of prayer and ritual have added great power to the site."

"Wouldn't that have dissipated by now? It's been over two centuries since Henry dissolved the abbeys."

He glanced at her. "You remember that much history? Or is that something you read recently?"

She tried to remember where knowledge of Henry VIII had come from. "I haven't read anything about the Tudor period since you rescued me, so I must have known it already."

"More evidence that you were a well-educated child when Drayton abducted you." His gaze returned to the map. "Some spiritual energy might have faded, but much remains, and ley lines are eternal. The abbey is a perfect place for a renegade mage."

She caught her breath. "Do you suppose he wants to combine the power of the abbey with what he steals from his slaves so he can place the men who come to his forum into thrall?"

"I'm sure he wants to use them in some way, but I don't think he could put them into thrall as he did you. These men will be older than you were, and few if any will have much magical power. Even if he is able to capture their minds in some way, it would be very conspicuous to turn a hundred or more prominent men into simpletons." He smiled faintly. "People would notice."

"What if he only wants to enthrall a few of the most powerful?"

"It's possible that he has developed spells that will put his guests into his power in a way short of the enslavement you suffered," Simon said thoughtfully. "I'll have to think about how that might be done, and how it could be countered. For now, what can you tell me about the four captives he's holding at Brentford Abbey?"

"Two males, two females. I think all are younger than I." Meg's brow furrowed as she concentrated on the phantom essence of what Simon had called "lost souls." "I don't know if any are Guardians—one has an energy unlike any I've sensed before. I would say that none are top-class mages like you or Lady Bethany, but taken together, they command a formidable amount of power."

Simon swore under his breath. "And their power is always at Drayton's disposal. No wonder he can accomplish so much. You said there is a fifth captive. If not at Brentford Abbey, where?"

Meg closed her eyes again and returned to the moment when she had discovered the threads. Four led one way. Now she traced the fifth. "It is a woman. A girl, actually, she's quite young, perhaps fourteen or fifteen. And . . . and she's very close." Instead of using her whole hand, Meg pointed with a single finger as she traced the gossamer connection. "Here."

Simon whistled under his breath. "Drayton House, which is only a few streets away. Can you tell me more about her?"

Meg reached the end of the thread and was startled by what she found. "The girl has a great deal of power. In my inner vision, she glows like a bonfire. I think she is only newly enthralled, and her power might not be fully accessible to Drayton. But it's just a matter of time until he can take it all, as he did with me."

"Drayton is devilishly good at finding victims," Simon said grimly. "We need to free them as soon as possible, both for their sakes and to reduce the power available to him."

Meg looked down at the map. "The girl at Drayton House is so close. Should we free her first? Maybe tonight? Dawn is still hours away."

"Patience, my warrior maiden." Simon rolled up the map and laid it aside, then set the tray of food on the desk. "You've had a tiring night and missed supper at the ball, so have something to eat while we think about how to proceed."

"What is there to think about?" She folded a slice of cold beef and bit off the end. "We free the captives as soon as possible."

"The girl at Drayton House will be the hardest to rescue—Drayton's wards are formidable. They must be studied and counterspells prepared."

"How long will that take? That girl is suffering, Simon!" Meg exclaimed. "I can feel the fear and loneliness under the spell Drayton has laid on her. The others are in like case. They may look like simpletons, but inside, they . . . they *hurt.*" To her horror, she realized that tears were running down her face.

Simon wrapped an arm around her and drew her close. "I know this is misery for you." Softly he stroked her hair. "But we must not let emotion send us running into disaster. Yes, Drayton is abusing them abominably, but he also needs them, so no one will be physically injured. When the time comes to free them, we must be well organized so that we can move swiftly and get them all to a safe place before Drayton can retaliate."

Hearing reserve in his voice, she lifted her head from the comfort of his shoulder. "You're worried about something beyond rescuing the captives, aren't you?"

He sighed. "When Drayton tried to abduct you tonight, it was a declaration of war. I doubt he meant it that way—he probably thought he could steal you away and cover it with clever lies, as he did at the hearing. But you escaped, and a goodly number of the Guardians in London were in Sterling House. Some of them who were neutral or believed Drayton must now be having doubts about his truthfulness. His position is more precarious, which makes him more dangerous."

"We mustn't allow him to keep his slaves a moment longer than necessary," she said flatly. "And surely when we've freed them, their testimony to his crimes will strengthen your position before the council."

"I agree, but rescuing the captives will escalate our undeclared war. I think we can safely extract those in Brentford, if not the girl in London, but as soon as we act, Drayton will strike back at you or me or those we care about. The ruthless have an advantage when it comes to battle."

Meg shuddered at the thought of falling under Drayton's control again. She would rather die than return to slavery. "Despite the risks, we must act. He certainly won't end whatever evil he plans if we ignore him and hope for the best."

"Yes, but I promised to protect you. So far I haven't done a very good job of it." Simon's gaze was bleak. "If you hadn't fought back so effectively, he would have had you tonight. I failed. And as we go forward, the danger to you will increase."

"Does it matter who is responsible for my evading his clutches?" she asked tartly. "What matters is that I did escape him, and God willing, I will again if he tries another abduction. How much of your concern is from pride?"

He dropped his arm from her shoulders and moved away, restlessly prowling the room. "I can't deny that pride is a factor. A stronger one is my sense of myself. If I can't protect the innocent, what good am I?" He swung around, catching her gaze. "But most powerful of all is my concern for you. I . . . I care for you deeply, my warrior maiden. And that is dangerous because it interferes with my judgment."

The power he radiated took her breath away. They were bound in so many ways, but there was something frightening in his saying the words aloud. "I care for you also, my lord. I can't be sorry for it, even if that does complicate my life."

His expression eased at her blunt words. "Lady Beth would probably say that complications *are* life. We must do what is necessary, and hope we can counter the consequences. It is time to think about Brentford Abbey."

She settled in a chair and rolled another piece of beef, then folded it into a piece of bread. Plotting was hungry work. "Do you know anything about it?"

"With your permission, I'll follow your mental connection to the thralls. That will allow me to learn more."

After she nodded agreement, he closed his eyes and located the threads that led from Meg to the thralls. Because of her intense concern with their situation, much information was available to him. "The abbey is very large, which is why its wards are not so powerful as those on Drayton House. It takes more magic to guard a large area. He's using some of his captives' energy to maintain the wards, which reduces the amount of power available to him."

"As he did with me," Meg murmured. "It's particularly wicked to enslave us with our own powers."

"Drayton is a particularly wicked man." Simon shifted his attention from the site to the individuals. "The thralls are quartered in a separate outbuilding. Originally the rooms were monk's cells, so they make a good prison." He frowned. "I feel that since your escape from Castle Drayton, he has tightened his control on his remaining victims."

Intrigued at the detail, she asked, "How do you see so much?"

"The family talent is to read power whether near or far, particularly if there is something wrong about it," he explained. "Magic flows from nature, and properly used, it is harmonious. Disharmonious magic draws my attention. Usually it isn't even necessary to use a scrying glass."

"Is it hard to be a hunter of men?" she asked quietly.

"It's not the magical gift I would have chosen, but someone must do the work." He settled in the opposite chair and began absently shredding a slice of bread into small pieces. "Hardest of all is to hunt a friend."

Startled, she asked, "Has that happened?"

He hesitated before replying. "Duncan is a Scot. During the Rebellion, he was . . . somewhat uncertain about where his deepest loyalties lay. It was a difficult time."

"Yet you're still friends," she said, fascinated but unsure how much she dared ask.

"Luckily he did not do anything irrevocable." Simon sliced a corner of cheese and tossed it to Otto, who lay by the desk with hopeful eyes. "I did not feel compelled to ask awkward questions after the crisis had passed. It was much more satisfying to help rebels escape to America, where they could build new lives. That work Duncan and I did together."

"I think that being a hunter and enforcer would be far too complicated for me," she said frankly. "I'm glad it is not a female gift."

"Not traditionally, but you do have some skills similar to mine," Simon said. "Look how quickly you located the others Drayton has in thrall."

"That is only because I had suffered as they did," she said uncomfortably. "I am no hunter. All I want to do is free Drayton's slaves, and see that he takes no others. Surely we can also rescue the child here in Mayfair." Something about the girl resonated within Meg, perhaps because they had been of a similar age when abducted.

"I hope so, but it will be very difficult to enter his house." Simon tossed more cheese to the dog. "I will see what I can do."

"Is Drayton truly evil?" she asked slowly. "Or is it only that he does evil deeds?"

"I don't know," Simon replied. "I will leave the answer to the theologians. To me, what matters is deeds, not words. No matter how fair a man's words, if his acts are wicked, he is not a good man. As to wicked thoughts—well, we all have them sometimes, I suspect. But I have trouble believing that God will punish us for our thoughts if we don't act on them."

"I should think there is special virtue in resisting wicked thoughts. Where is the virtue in never being tempted?"

He laughed. "You have the makings of a theologian."

"Better a theologian than a slave." She stood, yawning. "Let us discuss how to free the captives of Brentford tomorrow. Perhaps we can even ride out to survey the place?"

"We shall see."

Meaning he didn't want her to go, and she would have to be stubborn. On this issue, she could be very stubborn. It helped that he had a basic sense of fairness.

Hand on the doorknob, she glanced over her shoulder. "My thoughts about you are impious."

Then she fled the room before the warmth in his eyes made her wicked thoughts turn into wicked deeds.

Chapter TWENTY-FIVE

"Time to tether the horses and proceed afoot." Simon guided his mount toward a thicket a safe distance from the narrow lane they'd been traversing. Meg followed silently. She had come down for breakfast this morning ready to ride immediately to reconnoiter Brentford Abbey, and she had been most annoyed with him when she learned that he didn't intend to visit the place until dark.

They had spent a good part of the day arguing whether or not she would accompany him. He'd finally agreed, though reluctantly. While he hadn't done a brilliant job of protecting her so far, she was still safer with him than anywhere else.

Once they were deep in the thicket, he dismounted and fumbled toward a tree to find a good tether point. To his surprise, a faint glow began lighting the area around them, just enough to show shapes of trees, horses, and Meg. Dressed in a boy's black coat and breeches, she was slim and serious as a sword.

"Are you creating the light?" he asked softly. "We don't want anyone in the abbey to see us."

"There's no moon. I didn't want us or the horses to get injured." She swung down from her saddle. "No one will see us. The light is only visible here."

He tested the glow, which covered an area several yards across. "This doesn't feel like regular mage light. What are you doing?"

She gestured vaguely. "I thought it would be useful to have a light that . . . that turns inward rather than outward. So I thought about it and here it is."

Turns inward? He stepped outside of the lighted area, then turned to look. Sure enough, he couldn't see the light, or anything that was inside the area. "Remarkable. Can you make it brighter?"

"Yes, but a stronger light might not stay inside as well. Can you see this?"

After a moment, he perceived a large, faint globe of light around where Meg and the horses stood, though he couldn't see them, only the light. He doubted that the glow would be visible for more than a hundred paces. He stepped into the lighted area, and was startled to find it as bright as day. Blinking, he said, "Clever of you to find a new way to use mage light, Meg. I wish I'd thought of it."

She snapped her fingers and the light dimmed again. "Since I received no lessons in creating mage light, I did much experimentation. This version was useful."

He made a note to try it later. "Shall I go over our approach again?"

"We are here to scout the situation, not perform heroics," she said, a satirical glint in her eyes. "You will use an illusion spell to cover our tracks. I must be on the alert for wards, of which there will probably be several. You won't warn me unless I'm in danger of walking into one, because you want to see how good I am at detecting them. If I'm really lucky, you might allow me to try to create an opening in one. We will decide how many people we need to return with for the rescue—you think we need four, one for each person in thrall—and what kind of transportation will be best."

He had to smile. "Have I been prosing on too much? But with this kind of work, one can never be too prepared." His smile faded. "I thought I was prepared when I called on Castle Drayton, and it wasn't good enough. I'll not get into trouble again through carelessness." Even more, he didn't want to get Meg into trouble.

"Which is why you turn everything into a lesson. I'm grateful for that, Simon," she said seriously. "You're a fine teacher."

"And you are the most alarming of students." He experienced a brief, searing memory of how it had felt the night before when her hands were on him. Alarming indeed . . . He gave a mental shake and set off toward the abbey.

The estate was surrounded by a stone wall about ten feet tall, so they approached a section well away from the gates. Simon led them to a spot where the stonework was rough enough to climb without much trouble. When he reached the top of the wall, he took a secure seat and extended a hand to help Meg. Not needing his aid, she swung lithely up beside him.

Her voice a mere breath, she said, "Wards along the line of the wall are designed to warn of intruders. You've opened a portal so we can pass through unnoticed."

He nodded, pleased at her perception, then turned and lowered himself, hands on the edge of the wall, before dropping to the soft turf. As Meg did the same, he couldn't resist the temptation of reaching up to catch her waist to ease her descent. She didn't speak, but her fingers brushed his hand as he released her. The faintest trail of light was left in the wake of her fingertips. As the light faded, he resolved to spend time exploring this gift of hers. Meg the Lightbringer. Meg who had brought light into his life.

The whole area inside the wall was a park of grassy turf and scattered large trees. The grass and lower branches of the trees were cropped to neatness by the cows and ornamental deer that ranged freely inside the walls. The abbey and its outbuildings were in the center of the park, about half a mile ahead on the crest of a gentle knoll.

He had spent several hours in the afternoon studying the estate, using both scrying glass and hunter's magic. Now he was close enough to confirm his observations. Like Castle Drayton, this estate had guards, but only three. Simon guessed that a leased estate like Brentford Abbey concealed fewer of Drayton's secrets than his family seat, which was far to the west.

Two of the guards were at the main gates, one in front of the house and the other almost opposite. A third guard patrolled the house and outbuildings. The man seemed competent, and Simon hadn't observed a predictable pattern, so they must be careful of him when the time came to rescue the captives.

At least Drayton was no problem. He spent most nights at the London house, including tonight. Of that Simon was sure. To Meg, he said, "I've located the estate's steward, a Guardian who is sleeping in the main house. I've met him a time or two, a fellow named Cox. He hasn't major power, but he does have the abilities of a good watchman. I suspect the wards are set up to alert him instantly if a mage is detected entering the estate."

"Let us wish him a good night's sleep."

Using the deeper shadows of the trees, they zigzagged toward the buildings. They were in an open area between two trees when they heard a deep animal snort. Simon and Meg froze. Whatever it was lurked beneath a tree to the left. Simon probed the energy and realized that the creature was a bull.

A moment later the beast stepped out of the shadows, casting his massive head back and forth until he located the creatures who had wakened him. Head down and tail whipping back and forth, he headed right toward them. Simon swore silently, guessing that the brute was allowed to roam loose in the park for old-fashioned, nonmagical protection.

He was wondering how to handle the bull when Meg moved forward. Simon's heart leaped into his throat. He had to remind himself that her special gift for dealing with animals should include suspicious bulls who were pawing the turf.

She gave a wordless murmur of greeting, and Simon could feel the magic that accompanied the sound. The bull raised his head, his posture no longer so threatening. Meg reached the bull and began rubbing at his neck. Hard, since bulls didn't notice light touches. The beast turned his head and rubbed against her like a horse. Simon almost laughed out loud at the sight. Having felt her soothing energy as a unicorn, he shouldn't be surprised that the bull was just as captivated.

After some friendly scratching, Meg dismissed the bull. He ambled back toward the tree where his harem dozed. Simon joined her. "Well done," he murmured.

She shrugged off the compliment. "He wasn't really angry. Just curious."

He wondered how she would do with a pack of barking watchdogs. They'd probably be eating out of her hands in no time.

They were approaching another set of wards, these circling the buildings proper. Two paces short of the invisible fence, Meg paused for Simon's evaluation. He probed and found the energy much more powerful than the ward around the wall. Besides triggering a warning, there was a nasty spell that would inflict pain in direct proportion to an intruder's magical ability. Probably it would give Simon and Meg a bad headache.

Though the spells were powerful, he thought Meg could handle them, and one learned by doing. He tapped her on the shoulder, which was their prearranged signal for her to attempt the wards. She concentrated on the protective shield with palpable force.

Though she worked more slowly than he, only a minute or so was required for her to open a portal. She stepped through and Simon followed, careful not to brush an edge of energy. When they were both inside, Meg neatly closed the portal.

"Excellent," he whispered.

He felt more than saw her smile before she turned and headed toward the buildings. As they neared, she paused. "What is that energy that pulses through the earth and air? It's like the vibration of a great silent gong."

"Three ley lines intersect here, and that creates a tremendous vortex of earth energy. If Brentford is like other abbeys, the chapel was built where they converge."

Meg's brows arched. "Were the early priests sorcerers?"

"I don't think so, but they understood power and how to harness it for their spiritual purposes." He closed his eyes to better see the great lines of light shimmering up from the earth. Where the three intersected, they would make a six-pointed star with a fountain of energy blazing into the sky. Centuries of prayer and piety had strengthened the earth's natural power, providing a feast for the magically aware. "These ley lines are as strong as any I've ever seen. My guess is that Drayton is trying to harness the power for personal use."

"What if he has succeeded?"

"We would probably know about it, because the power is great. But I've never heard of that happening. The ley lines do energize us, but they will not be harnessed for the petty affairs of men. Luckily." He resumed their course toward the buildings, touching Meg's arm to indicate that they should go to the right.

There was just enough starlight to see the looming shapes of buildings. The main house had started as a church with an attached infirmary, but over the years owners had built additions that turned the place into a sprawling, ungainly warren that covered a substantial amount of ground. Most of the outbuildings were very old, and continued to perform the same functions as they had in the time of the Benedictines: bakery, brew house, dairy, and so forth.

The patrolling guard was near. Simon caught Meg's wrist and drew her into the shadow of the stables, masking them with a don't-look spell until the hulking man had passed and moved on toward the main house. Only when the guard was gone from sight did Simon move forward again, Meg at his side. The blazing power of the energy vortex was distracting, but he forced himself to concentrate on finding the thralls.

There. The captives were in that square structure just ahead of them. Simon's early explorations had suggested that they were held in a building with a garden. Now that he saw their prison with his own eyes, he guessed that the structure was a small cloister, perhaps built when the community grew, or perhaps kept as a retreat, or a refuge for monks who were ill. No windows faced out.

Inside, he knew, there would be a dozen monk's cells, along with a kitchen and a small refectory, all facing the courtyard. The structure was protected by a ferocious set of wards: final proof, if any was needed, that the enthralled captives were inside. Besides a sensitive warning alarm, the wards had the power to knock a mage out or worse.

Within the cloister he felt the dulled fire of the four captives, plus one other presence, a combination keeper and guard who had some magical power. Meg pulled up short just before walking into the wards, then began prowling around the perimeter, Simon beside her as they both analyzed the prison.

When they returned to their starting place, he leaned down and whispered, "When the time comes, I can manage these wards. I think you could, too. We might be able to come as soon as tomorrow night, if we can arrange for two people to help us and secure a refuge by then. Anything more you need to know?"

She shook her head but continued gazing at the building, as if she couldn't bear to tear herself away. Simon touched her arm, and reluctantly she turned to leave.

Anguish blazed through the night, freezing them both in their tracks. Loneliness, despair, and suffocation . . . "A nightmare," Simon whispered after a shaken moment. One of the thralls suffered in his sleep. Simon tried to touch the unhappy mind to send a little peace and hope before they left. *Not much longer, lad. Not much longer.*

Distracted by that, he didn't realize that Meg was opening a portal in the wards until she leaped through it. She was halfway to the door before Simon followed her, swearing again. In her impatience, she hadn't been careful enough at neutralizing the wards, and the alarm had gone off. In the instant before Simon cleaned up Meg's hasty work, Cox might have been alerted.

Just short of the door, he caught Meg's arm and yanked her to a halt. "We leave *now,* Meg," he snapped. "The alarm has been triggered. If we try to free them tonight, we run a serious risk of failing, and God knows what would happen to us if you and I are captured. We might both end up as unicorns slaughtered by ritual magic."

She yanked out of his grasp, her anger crackling around her. "Preparation is all very well, but sometimes one must *act.* It will take time for the steward to wake and determine if there really is a problem. That boy is in agony, and the sooner we get him and the others out, the better. If you won't help, I'll do it alone!"

He weighed the likelihood of success if he tried to remove her by force, and decided that would produce an even greater disaster than proceeding with the rescue. "Very well, but we'll have to move like lightning, and pray that the thralls will come with strangers."

She nodded fiercely before continuing to the door. It was locked. Simon rested a hand on the knob and poured in power. Bits of metal shifted and the lock snapped open. The damned door squealed, the sound painfully loud in the night.

They stepped into a short passageway. Simon sensed the thralls' keeper sleeping in the chamber to their left. The man was stirring, and he was a Guardian with a fair amount of power. Simon was wondering how best to handle him when he felt Meg reach out and use her soothing magic to lull the keeper back to sleep. She was remarkably good at that.

Hoping the effect would last, Simon moved to the end of the passage, guided by a shimmer of Meg's subtle new mage light. The door opened into the courtyard. A covered cloister walk ran around all four sides.

Without pausing, Meg crossed the courtyard and opened the right-hand of two doors. Simon stayed at her heels, all his senses alert for possible danger. She was right that it would take time for Cox to follow up on the alarm, but that time would be only minutes.

They entered a small but comfortably furnished chamber that contained a bed, washstand, and storage chest. Despite the bed, the inhabitant was curled up in a blanket on the floor, his body knotted in misery.

Meg brightened her light, revealing a young African boy lying on his side, tears drying on his dark face. He looked to be seventeen or eighteen. Simon wondered if he had been a slave to some society lady who thought it fashionable to have a black page. As a foreigner without family, he would have been easy prey for Drayton.

Meg knelt by the boy and laid a hand on his shoulder. "Wake and come with us," she said softly, "and you will be free."

The boy's eyes opened, blank from the effects of thrall. He must be the one with magic unlike anything Meg had experienced, for African power pulsed through his veins. Simon had once met an African mage, though he hadn't become well-enough acquainted to learn the differences in magic. But he remembered how she had radiated rich, earthy power, and he sensed an echo of that here.

Meg laid a hand on the boy's forehead. Simon guessed that she was using mind-touch to communicate that she had endured thralldom, and that she and Simon had come to take the boy away from his captivity.

While she worked, Simon examined the boy's energy field. Yes, there was the thread connecting him to Drayton, and it was heavier than the one used on Meg. The rogue was holding his remaining thralls more tightly. Knotting the connector was difficult, but Simon managed and was reasonably sure that he hadn't alerted Drayton in the process.

Though he was unable to sever the thread, the knot should prevent Drayton from controlling the boy or tapping into his energy.

When Meg lowered her hand, the African boy's eyes widened and he scrambled to his feet. "Moses come. But must bring friends. *Must.*"

Tall and slim, Moses had a slight French accent. He had been sleeping in breeches and a shirt, for which Simon was grateful. With the addition of shoes and a coat, he would be ready to go.

"We will take your friends," Meg promised. "Where are they?"

Moses headed toward the door. Simon stopped him with a gesture. "Dress yourself first. Also, is there anything here you wish to take with you?"

Moses stopped, his brow furrowed. Then he slid his feet into shoes set under his chair and pulled on a serviceable blue coat. He cast an uncertain glance around the small room before pulling an object from his coat pocket. It appeared to be a figurine made of carved ivory. Assured that he had it, he slipped the figurine back into his pocket. "Find friends."

"Take us to them," Simon said, trying not to show his impatience. *"Quickly."*

Though the night was still quiet, he knew in his bones that time was running out with terrifying speed.

Chapter TWENTY-SIX

Moses led them to a door in the left-hand cloister walk and entered a cell similar to the one he'd slept in. "Jemmy? Wake now. We must leave. Quickly."

A scraggly little boy jerked awake. Though he looked no more than twelve or thirteen, his blue eyes were much older. Obedient to his friend, Jemmy hopped from under the covers. His naked body showed the burns and scars characteristic of a chimney sweep's climbing boy. He would have been starved to keep him small enough to crawl through the complicated maze of chimneys found in large houses. He was lucky to be alive. Most climbing boys didn't live to adulthood.

Simon tied off the energy connection while Jemmy yanked on his clothing, responding to Moses's urgency. When the boy was dressed, Meg touched his forehead. "You'll be safe soon, Jemmy. Is there anything you want to take with you?"

For the first time, the pinched face showed expression. He reached under the bed and pulled out a carved wooden top. He concealed it in his left coat pocket, his hand staying inside to clutch the top. The poor little devil probably hadn't had a single stroke of good fortune in his life, except perhaps the friendship of Moses. He stayed close to the older boy as they returned to the courtyard and crossed to a door on the opposite cloister.

Moses halted outside the door, expression troubled. "Girls here. Locked."

Simon took hold of the knob and unlocked it magically, thinking that this evening would be a stronger drain on his power than he had anticipated. He opened the door to reveal a double-sized chamber, probably two monks' cells that had been combined. Each end held the same furnishings the boys' had.

The figure in the right-hand bed sat up, revealing a girl about Moses's age with carrot red hair and a thin, freckled face. Even under the dullness of thrall, fear and stubbornness were visible.

Moses said, "Breeda, we go with them." He waved toward Meg and Simon.

"Why?" She looked at the strangers suspiciously.

"We are here to free you." Meg moved forward, her hand raised for mind-touch. Breeda gasped and dodged Meg's hand as if it were a blow. "I won't hurt you," Meg said quietly as she extended her calming magic.

This time Breeda allowed Meg's hand on her forehead. Her expression began to ease under Meg's touch. Simon knotted off the energy connection, then turned to the girl in the other bed.

Moses bent over her. Voice gentle, he said, "Lily, wake now. We be free."

The girl opened dazed eyes. She had pale, limp hair and a colorless face, yet she was also beautiful, in a wraithlike way that looked one step from death. "Moses?" Her voice was nearly inaudible.

Moses helped her sit up. Her nightgown fell in loose folds around a bone-thin body. Simon guessed that Drayton was draining her life force as well as her magical power. Did Drayton know that he was killing her? Did he care? Simon knotted off the energy connection with savage thoroughness. When he did, Lily blinked, her gaze clearing a little. She shrank closer to Moses at the sight of Simon.

"They help us, Lily," the African boy said soothingly. "We leave now."

Lily tried to stand, and failed. If Moses hadn't caught her, she would have fallen to the floor. "I'll help her dress while you men wait in the courtyard," Meg said. "Breeda, after you dress, can you find any things you and Lily want to take with you?"

Breeda nodded and opened a chest as Simon ushered the boys outside. Despite Lily's weakness, it was only a couple of minutes before Meg summoned Simon back inside. "She'll need help," Meg said in a low voice.

"I know." He approached Lily, who sat on the side of the bed in a plain gown and a shawl wrapped around her narrow shoulders. "Lily, you're going for a ride and I'll be your horse." Before she could worry, he scooped her up in his arms. She weighed no more than a child, though he guessed she was about the same age as Moses and Breeda.

She stiffened at first, but a dose of Meg's calm helped her settle down. Simon was already halfway across the courtyard. He had an itchy feeling that this was going too smoothly. Cox must have woken and discovered that the estate had been invaded.

They moved safely past the quarters of the still-sleeping keeper, only to run afoul of the house wards. Though Meg opened a large portal and urged them through the center, Jemmy moved around Moses and clipped the edge of the portal. He cried out before the energy blast knocked him down. He lay unmoving on the ground just outside the wards.

The boy wasn't breathing. Simon's newly developed healer's sense on full alert, he snapped, "Take Lily, Moses."

Wordlessly the boy accepted Lily's weight. Despite his slight build, he was strong enough to hold her while Simon dropped on his knees beside Jemmy. He had to fight the rage that rose in him at the knowledge that this poor child might die after a lifetime of abuse, without ever having a chance to live.

He rolled Jemmy onto his back and placed one hand on the boy's forehead and the other over his heart. The child was absolutely still, with no pulse.

Once Simon had seen the thatcher on the Falconer estate collapse after being struck by lightning. The apprentice had shrieked that his master's heart had stopped just before the thatcher slid from the roof. Perhaps it was the jolt of hitting the ground, but when Simon rushed to help, the thatcher's heart was beating again. He'd recovered with no lasting problems, too.

It had been only seconds since Jemmy's collapse, and his spirit had not yet departed. With a jumble of healing energy, prayer, and visualization, Simon tried to coax Jemmy's heart back into action. He imagined that small heart beating again. He wasn't asking God to heal the dead, only to give this boy another chance. . . .

Thump. Thump. Thump, thump, thump. Simon almost wept with relief when he felt the pulse under his hand. *Thank you,* he said silently. Standing, he said, "Moses, can you carry Jemmy? We must get away from here."

Moses nodded and carefully transferred Lily back to Simon, then bent to pick up his friend. "Where?"

"This way, and as quickly as we can." Simon set off at a fast walk that he should be able to maintain for some time. "Meg, with this party, I think we'll need to risk the rear gate rather than going over the wall."

She nodded in silent agreement and cast one of her new mage lights around the group so no one would fall on the uneven ground. They were heading downhill, which helped a little, and the thralls seemed to understand the need for urgency, but even so, they could manage only a fast walk. Simon surrounded them with the strongest don't-look spell he could project. Magic should buy them a little time, but it wouldn't fool a trained Guardian like the abbey steward for very long.

Breeda stumbled and fell heavily, dropping the bundled shawl that contained personal possessions for her and Lily. Meg stopped and offered a helping hand. "Are you all right?"

"Breeda can walk," the girl said through gritted teeth. She scrambled to her feet without Meg's help and snatched up her bundle before continuing at a faster pace.

Simon wondered what the thralls' lives had been like to create such determination despite the numbing spells laid on them. Meg had been equally determined to free the captives as soon as possible, despite the risks.

Meg increased the level of mage light a little to reduce the chance of other accidents. They zigzagged down the hill, taking advantage of the scattered trees for cover. Then a shout rose from behind, "There they are!"

Breeda gasped and forced herself to move faster while Moses mut-

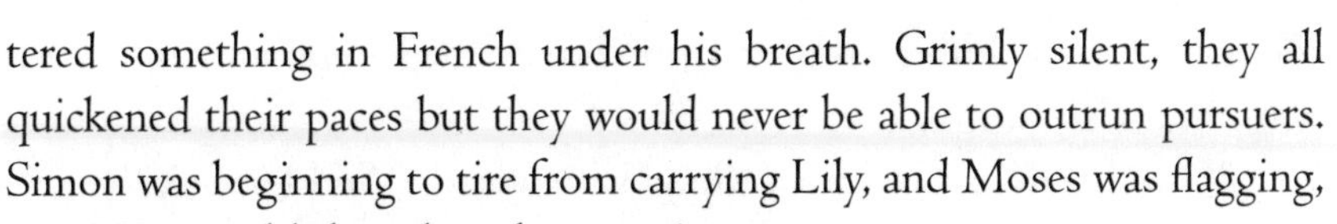

tered something in French under his breath. Grimly silent, they all quickened their paces but they would never be able to outrun pursuers. Simon was beginning to tire from carrying Lily, and Moses was flagging, too. How could they slow the pursuit?

Simon scanned the hunters and decided that the leader must be the steward, Cox. He was accompanied by the man who had slept in the thralls' cloister, who seemed to be a low-level Guardian. The two were supported by half a dozen estate hands, with the Guardians mounted and most of the pursuers carrying firearms. Shotguns, he thought. The situation was eerily like the escape from Castle Drayton, only this time there was no swift unicorn to carry them to safety.

Should he change forms? No, he couldn't carry everyone on his back, and nothing less would save them.

They were almost on the middle wards. He opened a portal large enough to allow them all to rush through without risking another incident like the one that had almost killed Jemmy. When all were on the other side, Meg whirled and closed the portal, then infused the wards with a defensive spell. She used an extravagant amount of power, but her enhancement would provide an unpleasant surprise for Cox and his men.

A minute later there was a howl, then another, as the pursuers hit the wards. The original spell would have allowed mundanes to pass through unaffected, but Meg had changed that. Though Cox should be able to counter what Meg did, it would take time since he had less power.

They were nearing the gatehouse, and the guard must be taken care of. "Meg, can you reach the guard and calm him, maybe put him to sleep?"

"I'll try." Her breath was ragged with exertion. After a long moment, she said, "He was already dozing. I deepened that. With luck he'll sleep until we're gone."

Since she was proving talented at doing spells on the run, he said, "Good. Can you bring our horses to the gate?"

She flashed a quick smile. "Animals are easier than men."

Simon heard a shout of triumph from behind. Cox and his men had breached the wards successfully. Another diversion was needed. Where was that damned bull that had threatened them earlier? "Meg, can you send the bull into their path? You seemed to be on good terms with him. Can you make him angry?"

"I . . . I think so." Her breathing was ragged. "And I should be able to wake up the cows as well."

It wasn't long until a neighing horse, a bellowing bull, and mooing cows gave evidence that Meg had succeeded. If the cattle slowed Cox down long enough . . .

They were almost to the gatehouse, and still no sign of the guard. Panting for breath, Simon led the way to the tall double doors of the gate. When they reached their destination, Jemmy said in a thin voice, "I can stand now."

Gratefully Moses set the smaller boy's feet on the ground, though he continued supporting his friend with one arm. Simon did the same with Lily while he examined the lock. "Lily sorry to be a burden, sir," the girl said in a quavering voice. "Leave Lily so you can run."

"We escape together or not at all," Simon said grimly as he tried to force the lock. He swore to himself. The mechanism shouldn't have presented a problem, but Drayton had laid a complex spell over it. Simon would have to pick his way through layers of convoluted magic before he could open the door.

The hoofbeats were alarmingly near. He glanced over his shoulder and saw two men on horseback and three more loping behind on foot. Cox shouted, "Surrender and I won't hurt any of you. Don't, and die."

That Simon doubted—Cox wouldn't kill Drayton's thralls, and he must have deduced that the rescuers were Guardians. He would try to capture the whole group.

Death here and now might be preferable. Simon made another attempt on the lock, thought he had it, then swore when he failed again.

A shotgun blasted, the pellets peppering them. Breeda cried out as one struck her. Moses stepped toward the attackers and shouted, "No! *No!*"

He raised both arms. Magic gathered around him like a storm, blurring his outlines. Jemmy stumbled away from his friend, eyes wide with fear.

Moses aimed his hands at the pursuers, now only fifty feet away. Red light crackled from his palms and blazed out to strike men and horses. The men collapsed like rag dolls. The horses were unaffected by the magic, but they reared in panic at being suddenly left riderless.

Simon stared at the limp bodies. "My God, Moses, that's quite a trick."

"Thank you, sir." Moses looked pleased and a little embarrassed.

"Are they dead?" Meg asked in a hushed voice.

"I don't think so," Moses said uncertainly.

Meg glanced at Simon. "Can you do that?"

"I don't know. I never tried." He would try to figure out what Moses had done later. For now he had a lock to open. "Can you bring the abbey horses to us?"

Meg nodded and closed her eyes. Her fatigue was etched across her face.

Gazing at the fallen pursuers, Breeda asked, "Go now?"

"As soon as we can." Simon concentrated on the lock again, sending a tendril of magic through the mazelike spell. Meg laid a hand on his arm, and her touch lent strength and focus. There! The lock clicked open. He swung the double doors back, then took Lily's arm and led the refugees into the quiet, grassy lane. Breeda was behind him, feet dragging but chin high, while Moses helped Jemmy.

Meg lingered to call the abbey horses. They approached skittishly, nervous and sweaty but willing to be wooed. She stroked their muzzles, communing silently until they steadied, then collected the reins and walked them toward the gate.

Simon had just decided that they were clear when the burly gatekeeper, woken by the shots, came racing down the staircase inside the wall, a shotgun clutched in his hands. "Stop, thieves!"

Someone who thought them thieves was more likely to kill than Cox, who wouldn't waste mage blood unnecessarily. Simon was about to cast a tangle-foot spell, when Jemmy slid back to the bottom of the steps and stuck a foot in front of the charging gatekeeper. The man pitched heavily to the ground, dropping his shotgun. When he tried to rise, Jemmy grabbed the shotgun and whacked the guard over the head. The fugitives would be well away before the man woke again. Though Jemmy might not talk much, he'd picked up some useful skills in his hard life.

Four horses would make their escape much easier. Simon asked, "Do any of you know how to ride?"

"Lily rides," the girl said. "Walking hard, riding easy."

"Breeda ride." The redhead wiped her sweaty face with her apron. "Some."

It took only a couple of minutes to get everyone mounted. Simon put the two girls on the gentlest mounts after Meg conferred with both horses to request good behavior. Then he lifted Jemmy up in front of him, since he was the lighter of the two boys, while Moses perched behind Meg.

"Where to?" Meg asked after she swung into her saddle and made sure that Moses was securely settled.

"Lady Bethany's house in Richmond. It's only a few miles away." He turned his mount and started retracing their route along the lane. If nothing more happened, they should reach Lady Bethany's before dawn. She would not turn them away. But this draggled party would strain even Lady Beth's legendary calm, Simon suspected.

Chapter TWENTY-SEVEN

By the time they reached Lady Bethany's house, Meg was close to falling from her horse with exhaustion. Luckily Simon seemed tireless and he kept a watchful eye on the whole party.

Unlike White Manor, her ladyship's Richmond house was not an estate, merely a mansion with a few acres of garden running down to the Thames, but even at night it looked gracious and welcoming. When they pulled to a halt by the front steps, Meg bade the horses to stay, then helped Breeda up the steps to the house. Simon carried Lily, but Jemmy was able to manage on his own. The six of them made gypsies look respectable.

Before Meg could wield the knocker, Lady Bethany opened the door, wearing a lace cap and a night robe of oriental silk brocade. "Hello, Meg. Visits at odd hours are becoming quite a habit," she remarked. "Simon, what have you brought me this time?"

"Four thralls kidnapped from Drayton's Brentford Abbey." Simon set Lily down and beckoned the others forward. "You will be safe here. Lady Bethany, allow me to present Moses, Lily, Breeda, and Jemmy."

As the four of them curtseyed or bowed, looking anxious, Lady Beth said warmly, "Welcome to my home. Is anyone hungry, or shall I just put you all to bed?"

"Rest, please," Breeda said. Her freckles stood out against a face pale with fatigue. Her three comrades nodded.

Jean Macrae entered the entry hall, smothering a yawn and also wearing a night robe. "You are having a party and didn't invite me? For shame, Lady Beth."

Lady Bethany turned to Jean and introduced the thralls. "Will you take these young people to bedrooms and get them settled? They've had a hard time."

Thinking the newly freed captives would be nervous in a strange place, Meg suggested, "Jemmy and Moses can share one room and Breeda and Lily another."

Understanding, Lady Bethany nodded. "Jean, you help Lily and Breeda up to the yellow room. Simon, take the young men to the blue room and see they have whatever they need. I'll ring for a man to take care of the horses." She tugged on a bell rope.

Everyone obeyed her ladyship's crisp orders willingly. Within minutes, Meg was in a pretty pink room stripping off her dark breeches and coat so she could don one of Jean's nightgowns. The gown was too short, but no matter. Her hands shook with stress and when she looked in the mirror, her appearance was so haggard that she dimmed her mage light so she wouldn't have to see herself.

She brushed and braided her hair and was washing her face when someone knocked on her door. Why did she know beyond doubt that it was Simon? "Come in."

He entered soundlessly, having shed his boots and coat. Despite his dishabille, he looked as calm and handsome as if he had been at a ball instead of dodging a bull and bullets. "Lady Beth put me in the room next door, so I thought I would see how you are before I go to bed. You had a difficult night."

She gave him a crooked smile. "I presume you also want to scold me for recklessly rescuing the thralls. You have every right to be angry—we could have all been killed. We would have been, if not for you."

He shrugged. "Having seen how eager they were to escape, I better understand your need to free them as soon as possible. We succeeded, which is what matters. Sometimes I am too cautious, so perhaps your impulse was for the best."

She thought of Jemmy's near-lethal encounter with the wards, not to mention the pursuit and the shotguns. "You are generous not to scold. Next time I shall try to be more cautious."

He became more alert. "Next time? Surely you aren't already planning an assault on Drayton's town house. Rescuing the fifth thrall will be far more difficult than invading Brentford Abbey."

"I have no plans yet. I was speaking in more general terms." Though she did want to free that final girl from thralldom as soon as possible. Something about the girl, perhaps her age, demanded action. But this time, she would be less reckless.

Her gaze moved over Simon, admiring his broad shoulders and lean, powerful body. More than anything on earth, she wanted to feel his arms around her to take away the fear and fatigue of the night. And someday she would like to loosen his blond hair. It would feel like living gold in her hands.

Perhaps it was time to give in to another impulse. She crossed the room and walked straight into his arms. As he drew her close, she gave a long sigh of release. He felt so warm and strong and *present.* "I wish you could stay the night. Just to sleep."

He hesitated. "I'd like that, too. If you're sure."

"I'm sure." She tilted her head back to look at him. "If it wouldn't be too . . . too provocative for you."

He smiled wearily. "Believe me, tonight I want nothing but sleep. Preferably with you." He draped an arm around her shoulders and steered her to the bed, then tossed the covers back.

The bed was high and she was summoning the energy to climb into it when he scooped her up and deposited her in the middle of the mattress. She blinked up at him. "Don't you ever run out of strength?"

"With some frequency." He climbed onto the mattress beside her, dousing her mage lights. "But I'm rather good at concealing that." He rolled onto his side and pulled the covers over them before enfolding her in his arms.

When she heard his long, weary exhalation, she recognized that he'd spoken the truth. He also was exhausted, and perhaps he needed this closeness as much as she did. As she relaxed back into him, she murmured, "No wonder people get married."

His low chuckle teased her hair. "There has to be some reason."

His large hand gently stroked her arm and hip. Though there was nothing overtly sexual about his touch, she found that she wanted to melt into him. Become one flesh. How fortunate she was so tired.

In the last moments before sleep claimed her, she said sleepily, "Tomorrow will be an interesting day. I wonder what our thralls will be like when the spells are lifted."

"Not as fierce as you, I hope. I definitely haven't the strength for that."

A smile on her lips, she finally slept.

Meg awoke to sunshine pouring in the windows. It must be nearly noon—and one part of Simon seemed particularly awake. Lazily mischievous, she rubbed her rump against him.

He caught his breath and his arm tightened around her waist. "Time to be up and away, I think." He let go of her and swung from the bed.

"You have entirely too much self-control," she said regretfully. The bed seemed far too empty without him.

"One of us needs it, my wicked maiden," he said with amusement. "Rise and greet the day. Aren't you curious to learn more about the young people you rescued? I don't think any of them have power on the magnitude of yours, but they have significant talents. I'm particularly interested in learning more about Moses."

"Knocking out five men was impressive. I wonder how he did that?"

"He may not know how he did it. He was acting from instinct because his friends were threatened," Simon said thoughtfully. "He may have been using an African magic different from ours."

"Why would African magic be different from English magic?"

"Magic is drawn from the earth, from nature. Africa is a powerful, ancient part of the world. I would not expect an African mage to be exactly the same as one of us."

She sat up, the covers tumbling to her waist. "I wonder if any of them will be able to remember their past."

Simon's gaze went to the loose neckline of her nightgown, which was dipping dangerously low. "Oh, the devil," he muttered. "I've earned something after last night." He leaned over the bed and kissed Meg with devastating thoroughness.

His hair *was* like living gold. She tunneled her fingers into the thick waves as they fell into each other. His kiss was magic, stirring power through her until she felt ready to burst with exaltation. She didn't realize that she was lying on her back with his body pinning her to the mattress until he lifted his head. His eyes were dazed and she recognized that they were a hairsbreadth away from becoming lovers. If he hadn't had the sense to go to bed mostly clothed, they would have already joined.

Simon recognized that also, because he tore himself away from her. "I must stop listening to my lower nature," he panted as he backed toward the door.

Before Meg could respond, he turned and was gone. She touched her lips, wishing they had carried those kisses to their ultimate conclusion.

He had promised that before she left to search for her family, they would become lovers in truth, and he was a man who kept his promises. She wouldn't give him a choice about keeping this one.

As the philosophers said, man was torn between higher and lower nature. Simon's lower nature was definitely winning. When he reached his room, he locked the door and leaned back against it, eyes closed and chest heaving as he struggled to regain control. Whether it was virgin magic or Meg's own sweet, indomitable self, she could bespell him like no other woman ever had. What he had felt for Blanche in his youth was no more than a pale shadow of his attraction to Meg.

Any future they might have wouldn't come until Drayton was stopped. Which meant Simon must get a grip and free the thralls from the spells that bound them. With luck, one of them would have useful information about Drayton. Even if that wasn't the case, at least their power was no longer available to the rogue.

Lust mastered, for the time being, he washed and neatened his appearance as best he could. If he had known they were going on an overnight raid, he would have brought a change of linen.

He met Lady Beth in the breakfast parlor. She had long since eaten, but she sipped at a cup of tea while writing in her journal. Raising her head, she glanced over the top of her spectacles, looking like the mildest of grandmothers. "I've strengthened the wards on the house so Drayton can't reach the thralls, but I've felt his energy sniffing around the boundaries of the property. You do like to keep an old woman challenged."

He made a rude noise. "Don't think you can fool me by playing the part of an innocent old lady. I know you too well."

"I would never claim innocence, but I am certainly an old lady." She brushed at her silvery hair. "Your children are all awake and fed. They're an interesting lot. I wonder who you'll bring to my doorstep next time."

He helped himself to food from the sideboard. "If you didn't have such conveniently located houses, I would turn up on other people's doorsteps." He gave a crooked smile. "I'm grateful to be here. It was a near-run thing."

Between bites of food, he summarized the events of the previous evening. Lady Bethany frowned. "I wish I believed this would be enough to persuade everyone in the council, but I suspect that Drayton would again claim that he had taken in orphans from the goodness of his heart and accuse you of harassing him."

Simon shrugged. "If we deprive him of his power, we reduce the amount of damage he can do. Meg says there's one more thrall at Drayton House, a very powerful one. If we can rescue her, Drayton will be limited to his innate power. That I can handle on my own." He swallowed half a cup of tea in one gulp. "And I will, with or without the council's permission."

Meg appeared in the doorway. Being primly dressed in a borrowed gray gown diminished her appeal not at all. "Good morning." She headed to the sideboard and helped herself to tea and bread and butter. "Do we have a plan of action yet?"

"I looked at the binding spells and it's best if you undo them, Simon," Lady Bethany said. "It will be a delicate business, but you were successful with Meg so you're best suited to do it again. You might want to work with him, Meg. The four of them are very nervous and could use your soothing touch."

"I do want to be there." Meg swallowed the last of her toast. "Who first?"

"Lily," Simon replied. "She has suffered the most from Drayton's draining of her power. She would not have lasted much longer."

Meg stood. "Then let us find her."

"Try the garden," Lady Bethany advised. "The rose arbor, I believe. For the magical work, use the morning room, Simon. That has particularly good energy." She returned to her journal writing, probably recording details of the latest magical dilemma to land in her lap.

Together, Simon and Meg left the house. As Lady Beth had said, the four thralls had settled under the arching trellises of the rose garden. The scent of sun-warmed roses filled the garden, and two hundred paces beyond, the Thames flowed east to London, with an occasional boat gliding by. It was a peaceful place to recover from horror. Simon paused. "You probably noticed that two ley lines intersect here. One is a line that runs through Brentford Abbey while the other is much less powerful, but it's still a significant energy center. It's why Lady Bethany and her husband built their home on this spot. I doubt it's an accident that the thralls have gathered right at the intersection of the lines."

Meg narrowed her eyes to look for the lines, then nodded. "Earth energy seems to be a pure, healthy kind of power. Perhaps it helped them in their captivity and they are still drawn to it."

Lily and Breeda sat on one stone bench with Moses opposite, while Jemmy was curled in a ball at the African boy's feet. Simon observed, "Despite their silence, they are all connected to each other. Can you see that?"

Meg's eyes narrowed thoughtfully. "They have become a family, joined by a web of emotion and caring. That must have helped them survive."

Hearing wistfulness in her voice, he said quietly, "You are no longer alone, Meg."

"Everyone has been very kind." She raised her voice, effectively cutting off the subject. "Good day. I hope you are well?"

"Good morning, my lady. Sir." The thralls stood. They looked much better than they had the night before, though they still had the blank expressions of enthrallment. Breeda and Lily bobbed curtseys, while Moses bowed. Jemmy mimicked him a little clumsily. Simon tried to recall if he'd heard Jemmy say anything. Perhaps the boy couldn't talk? They would find out soon enough.

"Good morning to you. Have you been well cared for?" Simon gestured for them to sit down.

"Free!" Breeda smiled. Her face was full of healthy color this morning. The others nodded their agreement.

"Freedom is only the beginning," Simon said. "Do any of you remember being captured, then having your thoughts changed so that you felt like a different person?"

They all nodded. Lily said with a frown, "The lord did something to Lily. Not sure what, but *wrong*."

"What is wrong can now be set right," he said. "Will you trust me to try?"

Breeda and Jemmy looked uncertain, but Lily and Moses both nodded. "Lily, you're first. We'll go into the morning room." Simon's glance moved from face to face while he projected trust and hope. "You will see how Lily is made right before you decide if you want healing, too. Unlike Drayton, we will not force you."

Meg asked, "Lily, do you need help to reach the house?"

The girl shook her head. "Stronger today."

Indeed she was, able to walk up the slope and into the house without aid. The morning room was pleasant and filled with light—a good place to chase away dark shadows. He guessed that Lady Bethany had performed a great deal of wholesome magic here over the years, because the room radiated positive energy.

Lily was quiet but tense, unsure what would happen. Meg said, "Lily, let's sit on the sofa together. I will be right here while Lord Falconer heals what is wrong."

Lily's eyes widened as she took her seat. "Lord?"

"He can't help being a lord," Meg said, a glint of humor in her eyes. "He is a good lord, not like the wicked lord who imprisoned you. Just relax. You will feel something like a touch in your mind. It will seem strange, but it won't hurt. When he is done, your mind will be right again."

Simon wished he shared her confidence. As Lady Beth had said, this was a delicate operation. The fact that he had succeeded with Meg didn't mean there were no risks now. He set a wooden chair in front of Lily. "I will take your hands. As Meg said, this will feel odd, but it is needful."

Lily nodded. Her hands were cold, but she didn't flinch, just closed her eyes. Simon guessed that she was benefiting from Meg's calming skills.

He approached the bindings on her mind cautiously. There was no illusion spell as had been used on Meg. He wasn't sure if that was because Drayton felt it unnecessary, or if Lily didn't have enough spare power to maintain such a spell.

Whatever the reason, it simplified his task. He probed for the essence of Lily and the spells that overlaid her. The block he'd made in the silver thread connecting her to Drayton was holding well. Simon attempted to cut it, again without success. He wondered how Drayton had made the connection so impervious to separation. Was it a product of great power, or a particularly clever spell from some old grimoire? Once Simon understood the spell, he should be able to develop a countermeasure.

He frowned when he discovered a cluster of threads so gossamer light they were almost undetectable. Cautiously he twanged one and identified it as a connection to Breeda. It was impossible to sort all the threads out, but they seemed to be connections and interconnections among the thralls.

The result was a multilayered web composed of the same indestructible skeins of energy as the more-visible attachment to Drayton. Given the emotional sustenance Lily found with her fellows, he didn't try to knot any of the threads to cut off the energy flow.

Next he turned his attention to the bindings on her intelligence and personality. The spells were similar to those used on Meg, though not identical because they were tuned to Lily's individual nature. He released the dark knots tied around her personality first, and felt a rush of sweet awareness. Then he loosened the bonds around her intelligence, thread by thread, and discovered a steady, empathic mind.

Finally he looked for the silver apple of trapped energy that he had found in Meg. The thread from Drayton led right to it, except that this time it wasn't an apple. More the size of a nutmeg. Guessing that it reflected the fact that Lily had less power, he was gentle when he dissolved the structure with white light, freeing what was caged within.

Lily gasped and her eyes flew open. "Merciful heaven!"

Simon released her hands, glad that her reaction was less intense than Meg's had been. "Do you feel 'right' now?"

She frowned as her mind turned inward. "I am myself again. How?"

He glanced at Meg. "It might be easiest if you tell her the story through mind-touch. Then she can ask whatever questions she has."

Meg nodded and laid her palm on Lily's forehead. It was only a few minutes before the girl—no, she no longer looked like a girl, but a young woman—said slowly, "I see. Lord Drayton was stealing my magic, and taking my soul with it."

"Did you know that you had magic?" Simon asked, intrigued at how calmly she accepted the fact of magic's existence.

She nodded. "My mother made charms for local women who wanted to find love or health or missing possessions. I learned from her. As I grew, it became clear that my charms worked very well—much better than my mother's. She said that I had an unusual amount of magic in my spirit." A shadow fell across her eyes. "But not enough to save my parents and little brother from a putrid fever."

"You remember your past?" Meg asked with surprise.

"Of course," Lily said, surprised by the question. "I'm Lily Winters from Bristol. My father is"—her voice faltered—"rather, he was, an apothecary. My mother said that his doses took care of the body while hers were for the soul."

"Did you remember all this when you were enthralled?"

Lily hesitated. "I . . . I think I knew only my name. I don't remember much of that time. It was like living in a fog from the channel. I don't know how long it lasted."

"Now it is August in the year of our Lord 1748. Does that help?"

"My last memory is a Michaelmas fair in 1746. I was with my cousins, for they took me in after my parents died. I had been in mourning for many months, and the fair was my first return to frivolity. Then I met *him.* Lord Drayton. He seemed a perfect gentleman. When my cousins wanted to watch the racing, he offered to escort me to the Punch and Judy show. I never thought to worry with so many people around. And then . . . and then . . ." Her expression changed as she recognized the enormity of what she had suffered. "That wicked man stole two years of my life!"

"He stole ten of mine," Meg said quietly. "I was held at his family seat, on the edge of Wales. He had no one else enthralled there."

"Oh, my lady!" Lily clasped Meg's hand sympathetically. "How did you bear it?"

"At the time, I knew no better. Since Lord Falconer freed me, I have been *angry.*" Meg tried to keep her voice level. "Unlike you, I remember nothing of my own life."

"Surely that will improve with time," Lily said comfortingly. Her expression changed. "Now it is time to heal my friends."

Chapter TWENTY-EIGHT

Lily seemed restored physically as well as intellectually. Though she was much too thin, her steps were swift and light as she skimmed through the garden to where her friends waited. Simon and Meg followed at a slower pace.

"Was removing the spells difficult?" Meg asked. "I tried to follow what you were doing, but I didn't really understand it."

"It was easier than untangling the spells that bound you. Plus, I had that experience to guide me here." He grimaced. "But it is not a procedure that will ever be routine. Drayton has a wicked talent for enthrallment."

Lily was talking animatedly to the others when Simon and Meg reached the rose garden. When they arrived, four sets of eyes fastened on them. "Free?" Breeda whispered, her expression painful with hope.

Lily slipped an arm around her waist. "Truly free, Breeda. Very soon."

Simon said, "I believe you're next, Moses."

The African boy shook his head. "Breeda first."

The redhead needed no further invitation. Almost vibrating with excitement, she led the way back to the house, her quick steps outpacing those of Simon and Meg. When she settled on the sofa, he could sense her nerves, but also her determination.

Again, Simon found no illusion spell. Drayton probably laid one on Meg because she was the only thrall at the castle, and much of the time he wasn't there. With her looking so unattractive, she hadn't needed extra protection. At the abbey, the thralls had their own small establishment and guardian, so illusion spells weren't needed.

As he loosed the bindings on Breeda, he found a quick, efficient intelligence and a personality that vibrated with energy. Like Lily, she had the gossamer web of connections to her fellow thralls. When he dissolved the silver sphere that trapped her magic, she was still for so long that he wondered if there was more to be done.

Then she opened raging eyes and swore, "May God damn that devil Drayton to hell!" in a distinctly Irish accent.

"I couldn't agree more," Meg said. "How do you feel, Breeda? And what do your remember of your past?"

"Well enough, except for a devil of a fury." She rubbed at her temples. "I'm Bridget O'Malley, Breeda for short, and I came to Bristol to find work because our cottage in Wicklow was full to overflowing. At a hiring fair, his filthy lordship said he would take me on as a kitchen maid. He promised I would be taught to cook, which would be a grand position. Holy Mother of God, I was fool enough to go with him!"

"Don't blame yourself for what made perfect sense at the time," Simon said.

Breeda shook her head. "I didn't have a good feeling about him, but I thought maybe all he wanted was for me to spread my legs a time or two, and that would be a small price to pay for learning to cook. I should have listened to what my liver was trying to tell me."

It sounded as if she had some talent for precognition. As Meg asked more questions, it became clear that Breeda had been enthralled for about three years. Like Lily, she remembered her past clearly now that the spells were lifted. Also like Lily, she accepted the news that she had magic power very calmly. "They say there is fairy blood in the O'Malleys. Most of the women have a touch of it." She frowned. "I had a bit of the sight, and I was sure that going to Bristol would be a fine thing for me. As wrong as I was, mayhap I haven't any magic, after all."

"Despite the thralldom, you may benefit by coming to England," Meg suggested. "After all, you made good friends. Now that you are free of Drayton, you may be able to achieve your dreams."

"Now my one dream is revenge." Breeda stood, her blue eyes piercing as she stared at Simon. "I want to gut Drayton with a fish knife. Where might I find him?"

"I understand the desire, but it is too soon for revenge. He would enthrall you again with no effort at all."

She frowned, too intelligent not to recognize the truth in Simon's words. "He's your enemy, too, isn't he? When you're ready to gut him, can I help?"

"I don't know if that is the fate he'll face, but if I need your aid in bringing him down, I will certainly ask for it." Though Breeda's power was only moderate, there was a warrior edge to her spirit, and Simon suspected she could prove a valuable ally.

He opened the morning room door so they could return to the garden, and they discovered the other three thralls waiting in the corridor. Lily asked, "Breeda?"

"Yes!" The Irish girl threw herself into Lily's arms, almost knocking her slighter friend down. "'Tis a grand thing to be myself again!"

Simon asked Moses, "Are you ready?"

He shook his head. "Jemmy now."

The smaller boy darted into the morning room between Simon and Meg. Any wariness he'd expressed earlier was gone. Simon closed the door, thinking that if the thralls had become a family, Moses was the father who protected and helped the others, putting their needs and desires first.

At Meg's invitation, Jemmy seated himself on the sofa, his feet not reaching the floor. After giving the usual description of what was going to happen, Simon asked, "Jemmy, are you able to speak?"

The boy nodded but didn't say anything. A lad of few words. Perhaps he would be more talkative once he was released from the spells.

Both binding spells and the web of connection threads were unusually dense and difficult to untangle, a result of Jemmy's own nature. Simon confirmed that the boy had led the hardest life of all the thralls, and he had survived by becoming suspicious and defensive. As Simon worked, he added unicorn healing energy to ease some of the deeper wounds the boy had suffered. Jemmy would need far more emotional healing than could be done in one day, but it was a start.

When Simon dissolved the enthrallment spell, Jemmy's eyes shot open. His stature was still that of a boy, but his eyes were ancient. In a surprisingly deep voice and an accent from the London stews, he said, "That bluidy bastard will try to catch us again, and 'e'll kill anyone who gets in the way."

Though Meg was taken aback, Simon said calmly, "He will have a great deal of trouble killing me. My hope is that now that his captives have been taken from him, he will no longer have the power to do great damage."

Jemmy looked doubtful, but didn't argue the point.

Meg asked, "Do you remember your name and your life before you were taken?"

He shrugged his thin shoulders. "Just Jemmy. Me mum sold me to the chimney sweep when I was old enough to climb—maybe four or five. Don't remember more of 'er than that. I was the sweep's best climber for years. It was me that 'e sent into all the fancy houses, till I got too big."

"Then what happened?"

"The sweep was going to drop me since I was too big and 'e said I ate too much. Then that bluidy lord"—Jemmy almost spat on the carpet, then thought better of it—"came up and gave the sweep five quid for me services. Said 'e wanted to train me for a jockey." He looked wistful. "I didn't know much about 'orses, but I liked 'em. I thought I'd like bein' a jockey. Instead . . ." He shrugged with resignation. "Don't know why 'e wanted me. It weren't much of a life, but I ate regular. That's somethin'."

"Not much," Simon said dryly. "You deserve better out of life, Jemmy. As to why Drayton wanted you, it was for your magical power."

Jemmy had trouble believing Simon's explanations of magic, but admitted that he had a knack for finding his way around mazelike chimneys, along with some other skills that were maybe not so common. He was frowning in thought when he opened the door to his friends. Breeda hugged him. He pretended to scoff, but Simon saw that he liked the attention.

When Jemmy had reported on his experience, Moses entered the morning room. Simon was tired—removing enthrallment spells was not light work—but he reckoned that he could manage one more, and it would be cruel to make Moses wait.

"I imagine Lily and Breeda told you what to expect?" Simon asked.

Moses nodded. Though he sat straight on the sofa, his tight lips betrayed his tension. He wanted release as desperately as the others had.

Removing the spells took longer than with the other thralls, and not only because of Simon's fatigue. Moses's energy was deep and exotic and difficult to read. The "flavor" was unlike that of the British Guardians, though Simon recognized similarities to the one African mage he'd met. While Moses's temperament was naturally balanced, Simon sensed a potential for his power to erupt in dangerous ways, as when he had stopped the pursuers at the abbey.

Hence, Simon was prepared when he dissolved the silver sphere that contained Moses's magic and his selfhood. Power surged forth like a lion, and Moses's eyes were wild when the lids snapped open. Meg placed her hand on his hand and squeezed hard. "Steady, Moses," she said. "You are safe here. Safe and whole again."

Moses closed his eyes and took several deep breaths before he mastered himself. When his eyes opened again, they were dark and cool as polished ebony. "I owe you a debt greater than I can repay in this lifetime, my lord and lady." His French-accented speech was clearly that of an educated man.

"Such debts are not repaid, except in service to others," Simon said. "Do you have any memories of your life before Drayton enthralled you?"

Moses considered his answer. "I was born in Zanzibar, which has been a crossroads of African trade for centuries. My father was a powerful merchant, and when I was six he moved the family to Marseilles, where he could order his business in Europe. That is where I grew up and received my education. I was the eldest son, so my father had me tutored in many languages so I could carry the business into the future."

"How did you fall into Drayton's control?"

Moses frowned as he searched for the memories. "His lordship said he wished to do business with my father, to import ivory and other African goods to Britain. My father asked me to escort him to our waterfront warehouse so he could select what he wished to buy. I remember no more than that, except days without end at the abbey. I would have gone mad, if I'd had enough wit left for it."

When Meg asked how long he'd been held in thrall, they established that it had been almost three years, and he was now twenty-one. Like the others, he looked older now that his mind was released from paralysis. Though Moses had not been consciously aware of the existence of magic, he accepted the news calmly, as if it was something he had always known without recognizing it.

Guessing the young man might have a broader perspective than his three fellow victims, Simon asked, "Drayton kidnapped six different magically gifted people that we know of, and he stole their magic for himself whenever he wished. Do you know how he used that stolen power?"

"He wanted to forge us into a weapon to gain still more power," Moses said slowly. "He used to . . . to play our powers together, like a musical instrument."

Simon thought of the web of interconnected energy that was visible in all four of the former thralls, and wondered how Drayton had contributed to its creation. And if the rogue had helped build it, was that a potential problem? "Did you stop the pursuers as we were leaving Brentford Abbey by drawing on the energy of your friends?"

"Exactly so," Moses said, surprised, "though I was not aware of that at the time. I guided the blow, but it contained elements of all of us. My power, Lily's practicality, Breeda's fierceness, and Jemmy's experience at fighting great odds." He looked upset. "I did not mean to kill."

"You didn't," Meg said. "As we left, I looked at the life force in each victim, and that was undiminished. But they did not regain their wits for some time."

"I am glad for that." Moses gave her a level gaze. "You are sad that you do not remember your past as the rest of us do. It will come back to you, I swear it."

It was Meg's turn to be startled. "How did you know that?"

Moses looked uncertain. "I . . . I sometimes know what people are thinking."

"That's a useful talent," Simon observed. "Is that why you were willing to trust us so quickly?"

"Yes. I knew your hearts and words were honest."

Simon and Meg shared a glance. There were many forms of mind-touch, and the ability to read the thoughts of a stranger was perhaps the rarest. He asked, "Were you ever able to read Drayton's thoughts enough to discover his plans for the future? We fear he is plotting great evil. Anything you might have read in his mind would be valuable."

"He thought much about . . . about mechanisms designed to improve on the labor of men." Moses's brows knit as he strained to clarify the memories. "I saw—great chimneys belching black smoke, and devices that move water and spin wool and weave cloth. At least, I think that's what they were—I have seen no such machines in real life."

"Drayton is very interested in such things," Simon agreed. "He is planning a great forum of inventors and engineers so they can exchange ideas and learn what others are doing. It will be held in a week at Brentford Abbey. Do you know about that?"

Moses blinked. "Now that you say it, yes, that was in the wind. Drayton's servants have been very busy with preparations. He wanted us to be ready for this forum, though I don't know how he wished to use us."

"Perhaps it's time we invited the others in to talk," Meg said soberly. "We are all part of this—and I feel that time is in short supply."

Simon moved to open the door and discovered that Lady Bethany and Jean had joined the thralls. "It's time for a council of war, don't you think?" Lady Beth said as she sailed into the morning room.

Meg smiled. "How do you manage to always be right?"

"Years and years of practice, my dear," the older woman said placidly. "Now let's all find seats and get comfortable. There is much to discuss."

The morning room had enough chairs and sofas to accommodate everyone. As Breeda took a seat between Jemmy and Lily, she said hesitantly, "I want to go back to Ireland to my family, but I haven't a penny to bless myself with. May I borrow the fare? I swear I'll pay it back as soon as I can."

Simon was spared having to tell her that was impossible when Jemmy said, "We can't leave here, Breeda, or that bluidy bastard will take us again."

Breeda looked thunderous, but Lady Bethany said, "He's right, my dear. Even in this well-shielded estate, I can't completely guarantee your safety. If you left without powerful magical protection, I think Drayton would recapture you very quickly."

"If you met him face-to-face, you might find that your will has disappeared and you have slid into helpless obedience," Meg said gravely. "That almost happened to me."

The former thralls exchanged glances, and Simon had the impression that they were consulting each other without words. "We appreciate your courage and generosity," Moses said, a stubborn set to his jaw. "But we do not wish to exchange one captivity for another. I, too, want to return to my family as soon as possible."

"I also wished to find my family," Meg said. "But Drayton is so dangerous that I have put my personal desires aside to deal with him. He is enemy to all of us."

"If you fail with Drayton, does that mean I can never go home?" Moses asked.

"If we fail," Simon said dryly, "I would advise all four of you to leave Britain as quickly as possible and hope he doesn't notice you."

His words had a sobering effect on the group. Meg added, "Staying here isn't captivity. You all need training in how to use your magic and how to defend yourselves. I have been given such training since Simon rescued me, and it has been as interesting as it has been valuable." Her eyes narrowed. "Training has made me feel strong."

The former thralls looked thoughtful, and much less belligerent. "Who would train us?" Lily asked.

"I would," Jean said. "I found with Meg that I liked teaching. I think that Lady Bethany and Meg and Lord Falconer would all be willing to help. Among others."

After everyone named nodded agreement, Lady Bethany said, "You may stay here for your training. Unless you prefer to take them into London, Simon?"

He shook his head. "This is a much more pleasant and spacious cage."

"What will we learn?" Breeda asked.

"How to use and control your magic," Simon replied. "How to shield yourself. What your particular talents are, and how to best use them."

Breeda looked at Jemmy. "Could we maybe learn to read?" she asked shyly.

The awkward silence was a reminder of how deprived these two had been. It ended when Jean said warmly, "I'd love to teach you. Reading is a most useful skill."

"When can we begin?" Breeda asked.

"Today if you like."

Breeda gave a satisfied nod.

"Lord Falconer, what do you think Drayton wants?" Moses asked. "He went to great effort and expense to capture and use us. Why?"

They deserved to know, and greater understanding might produce some useful information. "This is speculation on my part, but I think that his aim is to control the most important developments of engineering and industry in Britain," Simon said slowly. "I believe he wants this control for its own sake, and also to increase his wealth."

Meg's brows arched. "He's interested in something as mundane as money?"

"Money is a compelling goal when one doesn't have enough," Simon replied. "In my investigations, I learned that Drayton's financial situation is precarious. He spends lavishly, as if his wealth is limitless, but in fact he's had to go to the moneylenders for huge sums. If he controls the men who are developing the machinery that will change Britain, that will bring him immense wealth, and with wealth comes more power."

"Why did he want us?" Lily asked, her expression puzzled.

"Again, I am only guessing, but I believe he wants to put a light spell of enthrallment on the engineers and natural philosophers who will attend his forum. Not so deep a spell as to make them appear simple, but enough so that they will bend to his will when he commands them."

Meg nodded thoughtfully. "If your friend with the steam engine is typical, he is more interested in his work than in riches. Such men might easily be taken advantage of if Drayton takes away some of their will."

If anything, David was more practical than many inventors. Simon didn't like to think about the havoc Drayton might wreak if he enthralled the best mechanical minds of the nation. "Enthralling so many men, even lightly, will require immense power—more than any one person has. I think he was forging his Brentford captives into his instrument of thralldom, with Guardian and ley line power fueling his weapon."

"Though you're guessing, your theory does conform to what we know," Lady Beth mused.

"Where did I fit into his plans?" Meg asked. "And the girl enthralled in London?"

"I'm not sure, but you and the London girl are the most powerful of his captives. Earth energy is immensely difficult to control—that's why it's almost never used. Perhaps he planned on augmenting his own power with that of you and the London girl to give him the strength to channel the power of the ley lines into the Brentford thralls."

"I start to see how many men could be lightly enthralled," Moses said, his brow furrowing. "When Drayton was in my mind, he tried to . . . to shape my thoughts. Or not exactly my thoughts. Rather, my magic. Though I was unaware of it before, now that power is a presence within me. If the energy I used to strike the five pursuers last night was spun fine, like a web, and thrown broadly . . ."

"It is fortunate that we are away," Lily said with a shudder. "You could do too much damage."

Moses nodded. After collecting the glances of his three fellows, he spoke for them all. "Very well, we shall stay here and learn to use our magic so we may help destroy our enemy. Thus shall we discharge our debt to you."

"In return, I pledge that we will help you achieve your goals when the crisis is past," Simon promised. "Think about how you want to use your freedom."

"I'm glad that's settled." Lady Bethany rose. "It has been a tiring morning. Let us adjourn to the dining room and rebuild our strength." She smiled at her four new guests. "I promised that you will be impressed by what my cook can do. I believe that ginger cakes were being planned. With lemon sauce."

Expressions brighter, the former thralls left, ushered by Jean and Lady Bethany. Simon lingered. Meg stayed also. When they were private, they turned to each other and embraced. She gave a little sigh as she settled against him. "You look tired."

"I've learned that freeing thralls requires great concentration." He rested his chin on her soft hair, thinking how right it felt to hold her. "Did you see the web of connections between them?" When she nodded, he continued, "I'm wondering if those were deliberately forged by Drayton, and if so, do they represent any danger? The threads seemed to be as unbreakable as the connections to him, but perhaps they could be severed if necessary."

Meg thought about it as she rested her head on his shoulder. "I think he might have encouraged the connections for his own purposes, but that doesn't mean they are inherently bad. I felt no darkness in those threads. Only strength and mutual kindness."

"I felt the same." He tightened his hug. "The forum begins in a week. If Drayton is going to try to get them back, he will have to work quickly. With Lady Bethany's permission, perhaps Duncan and Gwynne should move out here for a week or two. They could help with the teaching, and their power added to Lady Beth and Jean should make this house impregnable."

"That's a good idea." She made a face. "Until then, perhaps I should stay here, too. Jean and Lady Beth will need help."

"Staying would be best," he said reluctantly, trying not to think how good it had been to hold her in his arms the night before. "Though I prefer being under the same roof with you, we must be practical and I need to be back in the city." He kissed her forehead, knowing it would be a mistake to do more. "In a fortnight, this should all be over."

"And I'll finally be free to find my family."

"May I go with you and help in the search?"

"Do you mean that?" she said with delight. "I would love to have your aid." Her voice became husky. "And your company, as we celebrate our victory over Drayton."

He wished he could guarantee that victory. But he couldn't escape the knowledge that the scales were closely balanced, and could tip either way.

Chapter TWENTY-NINE

"Mr. White?"

David jerked in surprise, banging the back of his head on the beam of his model engine. Rubbing the bump, he straightened to see Lord Drayton, as soft-footed and vaguely sinister as on his previous visit. Sarah stood several steps behind him, a basket in hand. She gave David an apologetic look for not being able to give more warning.

David set down his wrench and wiped his hands with a rag. "Good day, my lord. I was not expecting you, or I would have been better prepared."

"Then I would not have the opportunity to see you at work," Drayton pointed out. "Is your engine ready for transport to Brentford Abbey? My forum begins in five days."

"I need to make some adjustments to the condenser and the regulator, but it will be ready the day after tomorrow, as I promised. That will give me a day to install the engine and fix anything that might be damaged in transport." Mentally he crossed his fingers that the regulator would hold up to what would be demanded of it. In the future he would hire a machinist to make a more rugged model, but there hadn't been time.

"You are a careful man. I respect that." Drayton studied the engine with narrowed eyes. "Will you grant me a demonstration?"

"It will be my pleasure, sir." David signaled his assistant to add more coal to the embers in the firebox. The fuel flared, raising the temperature of the water in the boiler.

Building the engine had meant backbreaking work for him and Peter Nicholson, and many late meals delivered to the workshop by a tolerant Sarah. Though the theory was sound, actually making an engine work meant trial and error and a fair amount of bashing metal with hammer or wrench.

But the result was worth all the long nights and injured knuckles: his new engine was significantly more efficient than Newcomen's. Mine owners were desperate for better engines to pump water from their mines, and exhibiting his model at Drayton's forum would spread the word of his invention throughout Britain. Orders would flood in, he was sure of it. After David perfected the manufacturing process, Lord Falconer could manage the business while David worked on new inventions. He and Sarah would be able to raise their child with the advantages they had lacked. It was a heady prospect.

Soon the beam was pumping noisily away, a promise of energy for the burgeoning manufacturers of Britain. Drayton watched, face expressionless. "You are talented indeed, Mr. White," he said in a voice pitched to be heard above the clamor. "To be honest, I didn't think you would finish in time for my forum, but I wished to include you if at all possible. Your engine will be one of the important devices exhibited."

The words were satisfying, but Drayton's flat delivery was disconcerting. David thought it was almost as if his lordship resented the engine. Maybe he had wanted to be an inventor himself but lacked the ability or the patience? More likely, the man didn't have the time invention required. David had only a vague idea of what was involved in being a government minister, but the work was surely demanding.

Drayton gave a final nod of approval. "The wagon to transport your engine to Brentford Abbey will arrive first thing in the morning the day after tomorrow and the journey can be accomplished in one day. I imagine you will accompany it?"

"Yes, sir." David disliked leaving Sarah overnight, but once the engine was properly installed, he'd return to London for her. "I forgot to say that the engine should be set on a stone floor because of the weight and power. Do you have such a place?"

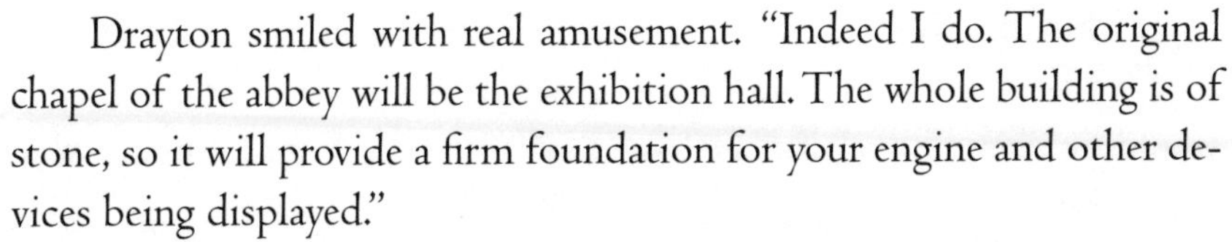

Drayton smiled with real amusement. "Indeed I do. The original chapel of the abbey will be the exhibition hall. The whole building is of stone, so it will provide a firm foundation for your engine and other devices being displayed."

Even though he wasn't Church of England, David was taken aback. "A chapel, sir? That sounds like . . . like sacrilege."

"On the contrary, it's most appropriate." Drayton stared at the still-pumping engine. "In the future, such machines will be worshipped by the common man."

"I would hope not," David said uncertainly. "'Tis just a machine, not the Deity."

Drayton turned from the engine with a cool smile. "I merely jested. The chapel has not been used for worship for many years. I chose it as the exhibition hall because of the space and the solid stone floor." He nodded his head. "Give you good day, Mr. White, Mrs. White. I shall see you at Brentford Abbey."

David murmured a proper farewell, but privately he was glad to see the lord leave. A strange bird was old Drayton. Falconer was also strange in his way, but he was a more comfortable man to have around.

When Drayton was gone, Sarah crossed the shop and set her basket on a clear space on the workbench. "I'll not be going to the abbey with you, David." She patted the barely discernible curve of her abdomen. "It's bad enough being sick every morning. If I had to ride all that way in a wagon, I'd be fit for nothing."

David regarded his wife thoughtfully. "Surely that's not the whole reason."

She shrugged and pulled bread, cheese, knife, and a jar of pickle sauce from the basket. "I would probably be the only woman there, which is bad enough, but I'm not pretty and I'm not a lady and I'll be green from the wagon ride as well. I'd rather not be there than go and be miserable, because if I'm miserable, you will be, too."

"True enough, lass, but is that the all?"

She gave a catch of laughter. "You always know." She spread pickle sauce on a piece of bread, laid on a slab of cheese, and handed it to Peter, who was circling hopefully. "Very well, I'm not comfortable around Lord Drayton. I would rather keep my distance."

"He's an odd duck, for sure, but this is a great opportunity to meet some of the finest minds in Britain, and even other countries. Surely you would like discussing your maths with someone who understands what you're saying."

Her smile wry, she handed him bread and cheese. "There aren't five men in Europe who would be willing to speak with me about mathematics as an equal. One of them is Lord Falconer and you say he won't be at the forum. Likely the other four won't be, either. The guests who are at the abbey will look at me as if I'm a talking mule. Interesting, but useless for a mule's main purpose."

David had to admit she was probably right. "Very well, if you don't wish to go. But—I'll miss you."

"You'll only be gone for a week." She poured ale into two mugs, then assembled two more servings of bread and cheese and took the lid off a small crock of pickled onions. "And you will enjoy yourself more without having to worry about me." She kissed him before popping a pickled onion in her mouth and returning to the house.

David was sorry to think she would miss the excitement of the forum, but he had to admit that he liked the idea of her and the coming child safe in London.

Odd. One would think a country estate would be safe.

Shrugging off a vague sense of apprehension, he turned his attention to his design for a flywheel that would convert the engine's power into rotary motion rather than the up-and-down pumping of the beam. The spinning and weaving business could surely use such power. . . .

Lord Sterling picked a path through the crowded coffeehouse to the table where Simon waited. The coffeehouse was noisy at this hour, which made it a good place for a private conversation. "Good day, Falconer. How is your charming wife?" The wooden spokes of the Windsor chair creaked as he settled into it.

Simon signaled the waiter to bring the coffee tray he'd ordered. "She is still charming, though sadly absent since she's staying with Lady Bethany for a few days. The house is empty without her. I look forward to her return tomorrow."

Sterling smiled fondly. "Sally and I have been married over forty years, and I still don't like it when we're separated for a night."

"If I were married to Lady Sterling, I'd keep her close, too." Simon shook his head. "I can't imagine why a man would want a simpering miss with nothing between her ears when one can have beauty and brains instead."

Sterling chuckled. "You certainly spared yourself from simpering. Your wife is one of the most interesting new talents we have. I look forward to seeing what she can do with magic suppression spells."

The waiter set down a tray containing a coffeepot, two cups, and several small saucers of extra ingredients, then vanished. Simon stirred shaved chocolate, cinnamon, raw Jamaica sugar, and a dollop of heavy cream into his cup. "Speaking of spells . . ."

"Ah, are we getting down to business?" The older man followed Simon's lead in which ingredients to add to his coffee. "I didn't think you had invited me here solely for the purpose of discussing how delightful wives can be."

"I was hoping you would help me study the wards on Drayton House," Simon said bluntly. "They are exceptionally powerful, and I suspect I'm not fully understanding them. You might be able to see some of the mechanisms involved."

"So you intend to invade Drayton House." Sterling sipped his coffee. "Mmm, excellent. Decadent, even. I trust you have a good reason for becoming a burglar?"

"Meg says that there is another thrall held captive there. Last week we liberated four from Brentford Abbey and that was difficult enough. Drayton House will be harder. Given how Meg feels about rescuing Drayton's victims, I fear that she might try to break in as soon as she's back in town, so the more I can do to help her, the better."

"You've set yourself quite a task. I haven't studied Drayton's wards deeply, but they're formidable." Sterling frowned. "So formidable that it's more evidence that he is stealing power from others. Even I might not be able to match them, and this sort of work is my specialty."

"This is not encouraging." Simon pushed his chair back. "Shall we take a look?"

"After we finish our coffee, my boy." Sterling added another spoonful of shaved chocolate to his cup. "At my age, one learns to savor life's moments, since it is never clear how many more one will have."

"I stand corrected, sir."

Sterling grinned. "What a very polite way to wish me to the devil."

Simon had to laugh. "Sorry, is that how I sounded? I am impatient, but a few more minutes won't matter, and the coffee here is the best in London."

They finished their coffee in a leisurely fashion, then left to walk the few blocks to Drayton House. The house faced onto a small square, so they lingered as if watching children play in the tiny park in the middle instead of observing Drayton's home.

Lord Sterling asked, "Is the gentleman, a term I use ironically, at home?"

"No, he's out doing cabinet business, I believe. Definitely not at home." Simon could have ridden directly to Drayton's present location if he chose. The rogue was always in the back of Simon's mind, like an unscratchable itch.

Lord Sterling relaxed, his hands folded on the silver head of his cane and his unfocused gaze on the wide, fashionable house. "Drayton has strengthened the wards since the last time I was here," he murmured. "Mundanes like his servants can enter and leave without being affected, but anyone with power will suffer greatly if Drayton doesn't escort them in himself."

"He had wards of this type at Brentford Abbey, but these appear to be stronger." Simon also studied the house with his inner eye. "Opening a portal will not be easy."

"The inside of the house is virtually opaque. These wards must take a huge amount of power to maintain." Sterling's brows drew together. "Lady Falconer claims that a thrall is imprisoned here. I can't detect any such person—the wards are too strong. Might they be fueled by the thrall's own power?"

"Not only possible but likely. He used Meg's power to fuel an illusion spell that made her look ugly and undesirable."

Sterling's brows arched. "That *would* take a great deal of power, and shows how the devil thinks. If the thrall is there, it explains how Drayton can maintain such strong wards. He's a clever devil."

"The girl is there, all right, in an attic room. I can't sense any more about her, but Meg was right about her existence," Simon said thoughtfully. "It would seem that if we find the thrall and block the energy flow to the wards, it will be much easier to leave the house than it was to get in."

"When the time comes, I would suggest coming and going through the front door. Since Drayton uses that himself, the field might be weakened a little." Sterling's gaze slid out of focus. "These wards have some aspects I've never seen before and can't identify. He may have come up with something specifically aimed at you or your lady, or both. I would be very, very careful."

"Do you know what Drayton's larger purpose might be?" Simon asked. "I know he needs money, but the true goal is surely power of whatever kind he can build or steal."

"Over the last several years, you've been traveling outside of London a good deal," Sterling observed. "When there's a critical vote in the House of Lords, you show up to cast your vote, then vanish, so you must be out of touch with the murkier aspects of politics. You know that Drayton is the minister of state for domestic affairs, but I think he has grander ambitions. I think he wants to be the prime minister."

Simon's brows arched. "The king wouldn't dare set aside Pelham. It would bring the government down."

"This king won't. But he is not a young man. If something should happen to him, the Prince of Wales will inherit."

"The Nauseous Beast? He is so disliked that even men who hate his royal father pray for George to have a long life."

"Frederick is indeed disliked—which is why he has welcomed Drayton's flattery. Our rogue has become one of Wales's chief confidants. If the king dies, his son will be able to choose a new prime minister if he wishes—and he will probably wish so."

Simon whistled softly. "As prime minister, Drayton would have enormous mundane power, including ample opportunities to rebuild his finances. If he also controls the minds of the country's finest engineers—I can't even imagine what he might do."

"Stop him, Falconer," Sterling said gravely. "I'm no seer, but I feel it will be very bad indeed if he is permitted to gather such power into his greedy hands."

"I'll do my best." Though Simon wished he was more confident about what should be done. "Shall we walk by the house and see if we pick up anything else?"

"By all means. I'd like a closer view of the wards."

They strolled around the square, Sterling leaning heavily on his cane, which was a convenient excuse for moving slowly. They had covered half the distance when Simon started feeling unwell, the boundaries of his body blurring. Two more steps and he realized that Drayton's transformation spell was reactivating.

He tried to control the spell, but already it was clouding his mind and sliding poisonously through his blood. The first agonizing pains shot through muscle and bone as they began to soften and stretch. Dizzy and unable to speak, he pivoted and moved away as quickly as his shaky limbs would permit.

Startled, Lord Sterling swung around. "My boy, are you unwell?"

"You almost had the pleasure of sharing your stroll with a unicorn," Simon choked out, grateful that the effect of the spell dropped sharply with distance. Now that he was out of range, he halted and tried to collect himself.

Sterling moved forward and took Simon's arm to guide him back along the street. "Now we know what Drayton added to the wards that are aimed at you."

"This bloody spell has become the bane of my existence," Simon said through gritted teeth. "And there may be no way to lift it. Lady Beth thinks only Drayton can break the spell, and he would see me in hell first."

"What if he dies?"

"That probably won't do me any good. I'll spend the rest of my life trying to avoid becoming so angry that I sprout hooves and horn." If he did change, would he be able to return to himself? Though he had no proof, intuition suggested that Meg was able to control the spell because of the combination of virginity and her great power. Either alone might not be enough—and the virginity would surely be gone soon.

He gave a mental shrug. The spell was only an issue if he survived the coming confrontation with Drayton—and survival was by no means assured.

Chapter THIRTY

As she skipped up the steps of Falconer House, Meg called mentally to Simon. She was reasonably sure he was home, but she'd discovered that wishful thinking could affect her magical judgment.

Not this time, though. As Hardwick let her in, Simon came down the hall steps two at a time. "Meg! I didn't expect you home until tomorrow."

"I received an unexpected offer."

A few steps behind Meg, Duncan Macrae said, "I was coming into town by boat, and Meg was keen to get back to you as soon as possible."

Meg didn't bother to blush since it was true. She caught Simon's hands, needing to touch. She'd been worried about him, unnecessarily it seemed. "It's good to be back."

To her surprise, he bent into a thorough kiss. *He's had unicorn problems again.* That must be what she had sensed. The realization didn't interfere with enjoying the kiss.

A cleared throat interrupted them. "I'll just be going along now," Duncan said with amusement.

Still holding Meg's hands, Simon said, "Thanks for escorting Meg home. I don't want her to be alone as long as Drayton is on the prowl."

"I could say the same of you," Duncan said dryly, "but you wouldn't listen."

"We can't huddle together like sheep until this is over," Simon said reasonably.

"What a pity," Meg murmured as Duncan took his leave.

"You would make a very charming sheep," Simon assured her with a rare, teasing smile. "How are your students doing?"

"Very well. They're all determined to learn as much as possible so they won't be helpless again." She took Simon's arm and guided him into the sitting room off the front hall. "Jean has become their chief tutor, and she does it very well."

"Did any of them remember clues to Drayton's plans?"

"Alas, no." She tugged him down beside her on the sofa. "I'm starting to wonder how common wild magic is. There are the four of them, plus me and the London thrall, so perhaps there are many people around with unrecognized magical abilities."

"Many mundanes have at least a spark of power, and some rather more than that." He put his arm around her shoulders and tucked her close. "Generally the magic manifests as good intuition or the ability to sense other people's emotions, or other traits that aren't so odd as to be noteworthy. Much more unusual are large amounts of power—Guardian-level magic is very rare outside of the Families. The Brentford thralls have a lot of magic compared to most mundanes, but less than the average Guardian."

"Still, isn't it impressive that Drayton found so many?" She settled contentedly against him, very aware that under the still brocade of his coat was a warm, strong, male body. "Six captives, and of those I am well on my way to being a mage, and perhaps the last thrall will be also."

"Remember that these six represent a harvest over at least ten years. I think Drayton has a talent for spotting magical ability in others, or he couldn't have found even six people to enslave." Simon grimaced. "I'm finding that his talents are not unlike mine. Though his power isn't inherently as strong, his illegal enhancements have made him very good at tracking magical energy across distances. He found you that way, and probably his other victims as well. In the back of his mind, he is probably always scanning to locate undeveloped magical potential."

She sighed. "How did I have the misfortune to spend the longest time with him? And alone? I really envy the bond between the Brentford four. I . . . I would have liked to have a kindred spirit near me."

His arm tightened around her. "I'm sorry, Meg. I think he spent years looking for another like you, without success. He did better when he lowered his standards."

It was kind of Simon to use terms designed to make her feel special, but those ten years had been an eternity of pain and emptiness, until a unicorn had appeared to save her. The thought reminded her of what she had sensed when Simon kissed her. "You were almost overcome by the unicorn spell, weren't you? Did you lose your temper?"

He smiled wryly. "I wondered if you would notice. This morning Lord Sterling and I were studying the wards on Drayton House. Sterling thought the wards, which are truly formidable, might have components specially tailored to affect me and possibly you as well. Sure enough, when I was about a hundred paces away, the transformation spell flared up again. If I'd gone a few steps closer, I would have been transformed. Luckily the power of the spell faded when I moved away."

She bit her lip. "If this is true, you won't be able to enter Drayton House and rescue the last thrall."

"Not until I find a way to counter the transformation spell." He lifted her chin with his hand so their gazes met. "Meg, my warrior maiden, the same is true for you. Drayton knows the dimensions of your magic intimately. I would be shocked if he hasn't incorporated that knowledge into his wards. He has to know that you were involved in rescuing the Brentford thralls and that you want to free the girl in Drayton House as well. Please, promise me that you won't rashly try to break in. At the least, you would probably end up in thrall to Drayton again. Perhaps worse."

She closed her eyes, frustrated. "I wish you were wrong. But if we hadn't been very lucky, we could have ended up enthralled or dead."

"Exactly." His eyes narrowed. "You haven't yet promised not to attempt to free the thrall. I agree it must be done, but not until we have some chance of success. For now, we have none. Remember that she will not be injured—she is too valuable. We will rescue her later."

"You have my word." Ruthlessly she tamped down the compulsion she felt to go after the thrall. For some reason, this particular girl haunted her. "Though I desperately want to free her, I'm not a complete fool."

"You're not a fool at all—you're clever, brave, and willing to take risks for the sake of others. These are all admirable traits. They just need to be tempered with some caution."

She felt a flicker of bleakness behind his words. "Speaking of caution, you're going to return to Brentford Abbey for the forum, aren't you? Even though Drayton will be on his own ground and waiting for you. And you think *I'm* reckless!"

"When seasoned enforcers like me do such things, it's called a calculated risk, not recklessness," he said with a hint of humor. "I don't see that I have a choice, Meg. I've been scrying until the stone is tired, and it's clear that Drayton will make a major move during this forum. Whatever he does might be very hard to undo. Much better to prevent him from gaining more power and damaging innocent lives."

She took a deep breath. "I'll go with you. Together we are stronger."

"No!" Simon said forcefully. "You mustn't go near him, Meg. The earth power at Brentford will make Drayton stronger and you more vulnerable. If I need your magic, I can draw on it even with you here. We'll practice the technique before I go to the abbey."

"Very well." She felt shamefully glad to obey him in this. The mere thought of again coming face-to-face with Drayton chilled her. "But I will be at Lady Beth's house. Much closer if you need rescuing."

"Fair enough. We can both return there tomorrow. You can coordinate strategy with Jean and Lady Beth and Gwynne and Duncan."

"Can you take Duncan with you?" she asked. The Scot would surely be a powerful ally in enemy territory.

"For this, no. Duncan's magic is not best suited to this kind of mission. It will be more helpful to have him ready to call in a storm if necessary. He does a wicked whirlwind." Simon gave a half smile. "Besides, if I took him with me and he was injured, Gwynne would have my head. It's best I go alone."

She looked down at her hands, at the false wedding ring. No magical power was required to sense that dark clouds were gathering, and that the outcome was perilous. Even with other Guardians nearby and ready to lend power, Simon might not survive the confrontation with Drayton. Images raced through her mind of him collapsing, or turning into a unicorn and being slaughtered brutally. These were not true foreseeings, she thought, merely fears. If they were true—she didn't want to know. "Do you have anything special that you must do this afternoon, or are you free?"

"I have no essential tasks. What do you have in mind?"

She looked up into his marvelous blue eyes and tried not to think that a week from now, he might be gone forever. "Let's do something frivolous, as if we were two mundanes, perhaps real newlyweds. What are the greatest sights in London?"

A slow smile made him look even more handsome. "Taking visitors to see the lions is traditional. That means the Royal Menagerie in the Tower of London. Though you might not enjoy seeing animals caged."

"They have lions?" Her eyes rounded. "I've always wanted to see a real lion. If they are unhappy at being caged, perhaps I can make them feel better about their fate."

With a laugh, he stood, drawing her to her feet. "Very well, we shall go to see the lions, and for at least this afternoon forget about saving England from a rogue mage."

And she would memorize every carefree moment in case there were no more.

On a sunny summer day, the area between the Thames and the Tower of London was like a street fair, full of laughing visitors, vendors with carts and baskets, and a pair of performing acrobats. Meg scanned the crowd, then the vast, looming walls. "I thought this was a single tower, not a whole great castle."

Simon paid off the boatman and climbed the steps to join her. An elderly lady with a flat, shallow basket of flowers approached them. "A posy for the lady, my lord?"

"Excellent thought." He chose a nosegay of pink and white blossoms and presented it to Meg with a flourish. "For my lady's pleasure."

"Oh, Simon." She sniffed the blossoms, delighted, before tucking them into her bodice. "They're lovely. I've never been given flowers before."

He looked startled. "I suppose you haven't. My poor warrior maiden! You need pampering. Would you like a piece of gingerbread?"

"Please!"

Simon bought two pieces from another vendor and presented the larger to Meg. The fragrant gingerbread was fresh and tasty, and better for being eaten out-of-doors. She couldn't remember ever being so light-hearted. Nor seeing Simon this playful, either. This was what she had wanted for this expedition—normal life among normal people.

Simon guided her to the main entrance to the Tower so she could look inside the grounds. "That large square building is the White Tower. It was built by William the Conqueror, but over time, more towers and barracks and other buildings were added. The Royal Mint is here, though they're running out of space and may have to move."

"No wonder they keep the lions here! This must be the strongest prison in England." She eyed one of the famous ravens of the Tower, which was surprisingly large. It stalked toward her, greedy gaze fixed on the gingerbread. Mentally she said, *I'll give you a piece, but only one. Then you must go away.*

The beady eyes blinked, so she tossed a sizable piece of gingerbread. The raven leaped on it while several of his fellows zoomed in, but he succeeded in securing the tidbit. He must have received Meg's message, because he didn't pester her for more.

"The Tower walls are high and thick, but with people coming and going to see the menagerie and other curiosities, it's not particularly secure." Simon led her from the main gate to the separate menagerie entrance, which was closer to the river. After paying the sixpence for admission, he continued, "It wouldn't surprise me if the crown jewels were stolen again."

Meg frowned as she took his arm to enter the menagerie. "They were stolen once, weren't they? Seventy years or so ago?"

Simon regarded her thoughtfully. "I'm always intrigued by what you know. Do you remember learning about the Tower?"

A day too warm for study, dust motes floating in the air in the summer sun. "I remember a history lesson on a hot day, but no more," she replied. "Not who was teaching or where I was."

"Was it some sort of school? Or a home?"

She tried to recall the image. "The lesson was in a . . . a sitting room, I think. Nice, but not grand like your house or Lady Bethany's. A little shabby, but pleasant."

"Not the home of a laborer." His brow furrowed. "One day it will all come rushing back to you. And that will be soon, I think."

"I hope so." Sometimes it seemed as if her memories were only a heartbeat away, but frustratingly, she lacked the key to reach them.

Simon's gaze became unfocused. "Drayton is close. Very close."

Her fingers bit into his arm. "Might he be following us?"

"I believe he's at the Royal Mint," Simon said slowly. "His government work requires an occasional visit, so this is probably coincidence."

She inhaled slowly, trying to calm her hammering heart. "Does he know that we're here?"

"If I can sense him, he can probably sense us," Simon replied. "But there are a number of stone walls between the menagerie and the mint, and I doubt he would try anything on the spur of the moment. He has bigger plans in mind."

She hoped he was right. They entered the visitor yard, a semicircular structure with cages on each side. The openings were arched stone, with iron bars and a locked iron gate at the front of each cage. As they entered the near end of the semicircular walkway, she wrinkled her nose at the thick, acrid odor. "Interesting smells!"

"Since the lions are fed great slabs of meat every day, their odor is . . . distinctive."

A family group that was in front of the first cage moved away, allowing Meg her first view of a lion. She took one look, and fell in love with the splendidly maned male stretched out lazily in the cage. "He's beautiful!"

On the railing that kept visitors a safe distance from the cages was a brass plate that said "George." She moved to the railing and looked into the beast's great amber eyes. Cautiously she reached out to touch the lion's mind, gasping with delight as she tumbled into the essence of lion energy. The feeling was similar to her previous experience with feline energy, but a thousand times more intense. Raw, powerful, and utterly confident, lion energy made her want to throw back her head and roar.

"Magnificent, aren't they?" Simon murmured beside her. "Lions have always been identified with the British monarchs. Each new sovereign has a lion named after him or her. They all have their own personalities, too. Look at the lioness in the cage to the right."

Meg complied, then exclaimed with horror, "There's a little dog in that cage! Can the keeper get it out before it gets eaten?"

"As a puppy, that spaniel was tossed into the cage by some bravo who wanted to see blood. Instead, the lioness, Sophia, treated it like her own cub. She won't let the keepers take the spaniel away. They live very amiably together, as you can see. She gives the dog part of her daily meat ration."

Fascinated, Meg touched Sophia's mind. There was the same confident power as in the male, but softened. This was a less ferocious creature—unless anyone threatened her cubs, or her spaniel. "Sophia was raised in captivity, I think. She seems very comfortable with it."

"Yes, she was born here at the Tower. When she was a small cub, I had the opportunity to play with her and her brethren." Simon smiled reminiscently. "They were quite like your little Lucky, only bigger."

"I'd like to have a lion cub," she said mischievously as they moved along the curving yard.

"Cats like Lucky, yes. Lion cubs, no. They grow very quickly." Simon's eyes glinted. "Though perhaps we do need a lion. The lion and the unicorn are both part of the royal arms, after all."

Glad he could joke about the unicorn spell, she said a mental hello to each of the cats as they moved slowly by. A tiger eyed the cluster of visitors in front of him as if he sought the most tasty possible dinner. His energy was more tense and solitary than the lions. "Does the menagerie have animals other than great cats?"

"Creatures that don't eat meat, like the elephant and the giraffes, are in another yard. Jackals and hyenas have their own area. There are some splendid birds, too. Eagles and owls and more."

"I want to see them all!"

Taking their time, they moved around the semicircle, admiring each creature in turn. The leopards were cool and quick, the catamounts frisky, and the black Barbary panther looked bored.

They were turning from the panther when magic scorched through the area. Simon swore, "What the devil . . . ?"

With clangs and squealing hinges, the cage doors sprang open. Suddenly alert, the panther pushed at the door of his cage, then leaped onto the railing only an arm's length from Meg. As Simon pulled her back, a woman screamed.

Pandemonium broke loose among the visitors. A man shouted, "Run!" as a lion roared. The deep, terrifying sound was picked up by the other great cats, and blood-chilling roars reverberated from the stone walls, echoing and magnifying.

Seeing that the panther was about to jump into the walkway, Meg reached out mentally. *Go back to your nice safe cage, sweeting, before men come to hurt you.* Lithe and deadly, the panther swung its head around and glared at her. It had . . . very long teeth.

Burying her fear, Meg tried again. *I am on your side, my beautiful panther. I don't want to see you hurt. There is nothing for you here.*

After a long, tense moment, the panther pivoted gracefully on the narrow railing and leaped back into his cage, his sleek body shimmering sensuously.

The other visitors were stampeding to the right, which was the nearest exit from the curving row of cages. Children were snatched up by parents, and a bottleneck of frantic people formed at the exit. An old man fell and disappeared in the press.

"I'll try to clear these people out," Simon snapped. "Can you persuade the other cats to return to their cages?"

"I think so. I'm sure they won't hurt me." Fairly sure.

He squeezed her hand. "Be careful, Meg!"

On his way toward the bottleneck, Simon detoured to help a youth who had tripped and fallen. As a tiger approached with low, stalking movements, the young man stared in horror at his approaching doom.

Meg felt Simon use magic to calm the tiger as he took the boy's arm and pulled him to his feet. "Come along now, but don't run. Running excites hunters." Sweating, the young man obeyed as he headed to the exit, slowly. Simon held the tiger's gaze until it abruptly swung around and returned to its cage.

A low growl behind her turned Meg's attention to the great, restless cats. Shouting in the distance meant that the soldiers who guarded the Tower were coming with guns. She *wouldn't* allow any of these splendid beasts to be slaughtered!

Sophia was out of her cage and pacing. Meg touched the lioness's mind and urged her to return to the safety of her cage. *Your little dog needs you, Your Majesty. One of the other cats might mistake him for a meal.*

Sophia immediately returned to her cage, placing herself between the spaniel and the open door. Something had to be done about the doors.

All of the other visitors had vanished around the curving walkway, leaving Meg alone, so she hitched up her skirts like a tomboy and swung over the railing. Moving along the row of cages, she latched each one shut after its inhabitant returned. The latches were less secure than locking the doors with a key, but they would do until the keepers appeared.

Most of the animals were confused and uneasy at the unexpected opening of the cages, and they returned to their familiar dens gratefully. The exception was a young lion named Frederick who growled at Meg when she touched his mind. She stood absolutely still and tried again. *Truly you are a king. Don't let some stupid two-footer shoot you so he can brag that he killed the king of beasts.*

He turned and slunk into his cage like an angry boy being sent to bed without his supper. Frederick was the last of the escaped cats. As she latched his cage, she had time to wonder how the locks had been opened. There had been magic, some kind of spell. . . .

The spell had to have come from Drayton, and he must have done it to create chaos and distraction. Suddenly cold with fear, she spun on her heel, but it was already too late. Drayton stood an arm's length away.

"You're a clever girl, but not clever enough." Before she could invoke her protection spell, his hands were on her shoulders and he was pouring energy into her. She was weakening . . . paralyzed . . . *gone. . . .*

Simon managed to clear all the frightened visitors from the lion yard with no one seriously hurt. Besides the panicked youth, he rescued the old man who had fallen. The fellow was bruised but not broken. Simon also reunited a small girl child with her frantic parents.

Soldiers raced into the menagerie, clutching their weapons and looking pale at the prospect of confronting wild beasts. Simon used magic to calm them—armed men in a panic were dangerous. "I don't believe anyone was hurt. Some of the cages opened, but most of the animals stayed where they were."

"I hope to God you're right," a keeper said grimly. Flanked by two soldiers, he entered the curving walkway. As Simon followed, a young officer said, "You shouldn't go in there, sir. Not till we know it's safe."

"My wife ran in the opposite direction and I must find her," Simon said, putting enough authority in his voice to silence the officer.

He expected to run into Meg as they followed the curving lion yard. Evidence of her handiwork was evident in the calm animals in their cages. Muttering prayers of gratitude, the keeper used his key to secure the doors.

But of Meg there was no trace. Worried, Simon reached out, and couldn't find her mental signature. "My wife isn't here," he said through tight lips.

The soldiers exchanged a glance, then looked into the nearest cage.

"No! She can't have been caught by one of these beasts." Simon swallowed hard, frightened by the blankness he found when he tried to touch her mind. "There . . . there would be signs."

There weren't. No signs of Meg at all, anywhere in the Tower of London.

Chapter THIRTY-ONE

Meg cried out as pain ripped through her. A familiar, loathed voice said, "You're a sensitive little thing, Meggie. I'll widen the portal." The pain vanished.

Dazed, Meg forced her eyes open and saw Drayton's evil face staring down at her. He was carrying her as if she were a limp doll. She wanted to strike him, but she couldn't move. She couldn't *think.*

He had placed her in thrall again. The spell suffocated, crushing mind and body. Yet . . . not so much as before. Under the leaden weight of Drayton's magic was a spark of Meg, false Countess of Falconer.

"Here. Now that I'm home, I don't need to carry her myself."

Meg shivered as she was transferred to someone else's arms. A strong, blank-faced footman. Was he also in thrall? She tried to use her magic to touch his mind. The effort was immense, like digging herself out of her own grave, but she was able to get some sense of the fellow. His name was Boxley, he found Drayton's household strange and somewhat alarming, but he stolidly did his job without questions. Stupid or enthralled? Some of both, Meg guessed. He had been bespelled enough not to wonder at the strange things he saw, but not so much as to render him useless as a servant.

"Once you're locked up, I'll lift the tangle spell so you can move again." Drayton caressed her cheek with chilling affection. "I have missed having you in my mind, Meggie. I have many reasons for hating

Falconer, but his stealing you is the greatest. Now that I have you back, we'll not be separated again." He rested his hand on her throat, his expression abstracted. "And you are virgin yet. Excellent. Was Falconer such a cold stick, or did he really understand the power of your virginity? I think him a cold stick myself." He dropped his hand and stepped back. "Take her to the attics, Boxley. I'll be right behind you."

The footman carried her along a plain hallway to the bottom of a flight of steps. He was starting to climb when Drayton said with irritation, "Not the servants' stairs, you block! They're so narrow you'll be knocking her head and feet with every step. Use the front staircase."

Wordlessly, the footman turned and headed along the corridor again. Drayton opened a door that let them into a grand front hall. The bouncing as she was carried up endless steps made Meg dizzy. When she saw how far she would fall if dropped, her heartbeat accelerated, but she still couldn't move.

Each flight of steps was narrower than the one before, and by the last, her feet and head were indeed banging on the walls. At least her paralysis also blocked pain.

At the top of the steps, they came into a bare, dim space with a peaked ceiling and several doors. Boxley paused uncertainly.

Drayton arrived, panting from the four flights of steps. "Now, where shall we put my Meggie? With the other one, I think. That's the most secure room. I wonder if you'll understand? Probably not. You're wearing your simpleton face again."

He pulled a key from his pocket and unlocked the door straight ahead. From her odd angle, Meg saw that a similar key hung on a nail beside the door. If this was a prison, it must be opened regularly to feed the prisoner.

Or prisoners. Boxley carried Meg into a narrow, whitewashed room with a slanted ceiling, a single bed, a chair and tiny table, and a washstand. A chamber pot sat in the corner. A small, curtainless window admitted light. It was a servant's room and the rag rug on the floor was the only concession to comfort.

"Put her on the bed. Just don't crush the other one," Drayton ordered.

As the footman laid her on the bed, Meg realized that the rumpled covers next to her concealed a slender body. Surely this was the last thrall. A tingle of excitement burned away some of the fog that engulfed her brain.

"Before I release you, I want to taste your energy again," Drayton murmured. As he stared down at her with avid eyes, she felt the hideously familiar violation of her mind. She tried to invoke the triple protection spell, without success. Since that was impossible, she tried a much simpler mental blow.

His eyes widened. "The kitten has developed a bite. All the better. So kind of Falconer to train you for my service." He skimmed a lazy hand down her body, over her shoulder and breast. "Later, after my forum has achieved my goals, I shall decide whether it is worth losing your virgin power for the sake of possessing that sweet body. Rest now." He straightened and made a swift gesture with his fingers before leading Boxley from the room.

As the key grated in the lock, Meg's paralysis vanished. She sat up and swung her legs to the floor, then almost collapsed as she tried to stand. Her muscles were shaking with reaction from having been immobilized. She spent several moments cautiously stretching her limbs before she tried to stand again.

This time she managed to stay upright before lurching to the washstand, which was three or four paces away. Blessedly, the pitcher was full of water. She felt better when she drank some, then splashed her face.

Turning, she surveyed her prison. The window was so small that even a child might not be able to climb through, and when she looked outside she viewed a sheer fall four stories to the flagstones of the back garden. There would be no escape that way.

As she studied the small room, she realized that even though her mind was clumsy and slow, it worked much better than during the ghastly years at Castle Drayton. She knew who she was and what her powers were, at least when they weren't suppressed. She knew that she had friends.

Simon. He must be frantic with worry. He might guess that Drayton had taken her, because the fiend had been so close, but would he be able to sense that she was alive behind the incredible wards that had hurt her as she entered? Even if he knew she was here, he couldn't come after her because of the transformation spell. Maybe Duncan Macrae could send a whirlwind to tear this evil house down.

Except he wouldn't—no Guardian would risk killing everyone in the household, especially if he wasn't sure she was here. Dratted ethics.

Finally she turned her attention to her companion. The other thrall lay on her side, facing the wall. With the blanket pulled over her, only a tangle of dark hair showed. Was the girl even alive? Yes, the faint rise and fall of the blanket proved that she breathed. Had thralldom put her into a deep sleep?

No, the girl was exhausted, Meg decided after studying her energy field. A monstrous amount of energy had been needed to open all the cages at the menagerie, and Drayton must have drawn that power from this child. No wonder she was drained of both magical power and normal human energy.

From the first time Meg had touched the thread that ran from Drayton to this girl, she had felt powerfully drawn to help. Having her mind and soul blunted hadn't changed that. A pity they were meeting in such circumstances.

She perched on the edge of the bed and pulled the blanket down, then turned the girl onto her back. She was pale, with dark circles under her eyes. Meg brushed the dark hair back, then froze.

Lying on the bed was . . . herself.

Gwynne Owens swept into the drawing room, her beautiful face concerned. "We came as soon as we heard. Have you learned anything new about Meg?"

Simon shook his head. "Nothing. No one seems to have seen her after the lions escaped. I've been scrying to see if I could locate her, but without success. My feelings are clouding my vision to the point where I don't know what I'm seeing." It was a bitter admission for a man who had always prided himself on his cool objectivity.

Duncan, a step behind his wife, said, "She can't have been eaten in five minutes without leaving a trace, so that eliminates the lions. Besides, I'm sure she could magic any great cat into lying on its back and waving its paws in the air for her."

Gwynne settled into a chair, her skirts falling elegantly around her. She asked, "Are you sure that her disappearance is due to Drayton?"

"Yes." Simon rose and began to pace. "And not only because he was at the Tower. My intuition is absolutely sure that Meg fell into his hands. I think he took advantage of the coincidence of us being nearby and approached to see if he might exploit the situation to his benefit. When he saw us in the lion yard, he realized it was a perfect way to distract us, since he knew we wouldn't allow innocent visitors to be mauled. A quick repulsion spell on the cage doors, and chaos was unleashed."

"Jean said that Meg had learned a powerful triple protection spell," Gwynne said. "Would Drayton have been able to overcome that?"

"If he reached her before she could invoke it, he wouldn't have had to." Simon's mouth twisted humorlessly. "When confronting lions, it's easy to overlook the jackal at one's back."

"One must consider the river," Duncan said soberly. "It's right there, after all."

Simon understood what his friend wasn't quite saying. "With a strong don't-look spell to protect him, it would be simple enough for Drayton to put her in the river, but he wouldn't kill her. Not only would he hate to waste someone with so much power, but he's obsessed with her personally. He wouldn't harm her unless he was absolutely certain she could never be his."

"She will never really be his," Gwynne said quietly. "She hates him to the bottom of her soul."

"It isn't her soul that he wants. It's her magic and her body, and those he can have by controlling her mind." Simon stopped his pacing at the window, staring in the direction of Drayton House. "She said she would rather be dead than enthralled again."

The taut silence ended when Gwynne said, "I'll try my hand at scrying. Since I'm not so involved, maybe I can find something useful."

"I hope so. Anything would be better than not knowing anything at all." Simon turned to watch Gwynne pull out her scrying glass, a piece of polished obsidian that had belonged to the most powerful British sorceress of the Elizabethan era. Overall, he and Gwynne had similar scrying ability, but where Meg was concerned, he was useless. God willing, Gwynne would do better.

She frowned over the scrying glass for long minutes. "I'm sure Meg is alive, and it looks like your deductions about how Drayton took her are accurate. He waited until she'd caged the last beast, then attacked her from behind. Her standard shielding wasn't enough to stop him, and she collapsed before she could invoke anything more."

Thank God. "Do you know what he's done with her?"

Gwynne shook her head. "His shielding is so powerful that it's impossible to get a clear reading on him. Once Meg was taken within his shields, she vanished. It appears he left the menagerie and climbed into his carriage outside the Tower. I don't see him moving to the riverbank and . . . and throwing anything in, so he must have taken her to his house. I can't swear to it, though. Drayton House is even more heavily shielded than he is personally. It's a magical sinkhole."

"She's so close, and yet impossibly far." Simon's fists clenched. "Lord Sterling and I investigated the house, and the wards include a component that reactivates the unicorn spell. I can't get close and stay human. Though maybe as a unicorn, I could break in and free her."

His guests exchanged an alarmed glance. "That's a really bad idea," Duncan said. "You said a unicorn mind is not good for quick thinking, and you would need all your wits about you if you stormed Drayton House. I suspect that Drayton may have cast a ritual magic circle inside that will activate the moment you set foot or hoof in it whether he is home or not. He might have taken Meg to bait a trap with you as the quarry."

Simon hadn't thought of that. Drayton wanted Meg for herself, but he probably wanted to lure Simon in as well.

"Simon, promise you won't do anything foolish," Gwynne said gravely. "He won't hurt Meg—she's too valuable. I know you hate leaving her in his control, but better to take your time and be successful when you rescue her."

There was irony in hearing the same arguments Simon had used to persuade Meg not to rush into rescuing the thrall. He didn't like hearing them any more than Meg had.

Duncan added, "You'll have a better chance of taking Drayton down at his forum. Brentford Abbey is warded, but he can't fully protect such a large area, especially when a hundred or more people are wandering about. That will be your chance."

"I know you're right." Simon rubbed his temple wearily, unable to reduce the misery and loss that throbbed through his veins. "I will stalk Drayton at the abbey. But if something happens to me, will you undertake to free Meg? And also the other girl who is being held there?"

"Of course," Duncan said. "It might take time to figure out how to do it, but I give you my word that I will see Meg free, or die trying."

"Men are so dramatic," Gwynne said tartly. "Promise to do your best, and leave life and death to fate."

"Good advice, my love. With luck, it won't come to that." Duncan raised his gaze to Simon. "What are your plans for Drayton's forum, and what can we do to help?"

"Nothing complicated. I plan to use my best illusion spell to disguise myself as an eccentric inventor and hope that so much will be going on that Drayton won't be able to pick me out of the crowd. Since he's lost his Brentford thralls, he is weakened." Though he still had the two strongest, Meg and the London girl. "When I know what he plans to do, I should also know how to stop him." He hoped.

Though if he had the chance, he might simply kill the bastard out of hand.

The first reaction of Meg's sluggish brain was that she was going mad. The unconscious girl in the bed couldn't be her. The resemblance to the face Meg saw in the mirror was mere accident. And yet . . .

The small window admitted so little light that it was hard to see the thrall well. Meg wondered if she could still create mage light. She concentrated on what had first come so easily. *Let there be light.* Nothing. She tried again and again, but was unable to summon the magic spark that must precede visible light.

She was about to give up when she managed to create a bright dot on her palm. As careful as if she were coaxing a small flame to grow larger, she encouraged the light to expand. When it was a satisfactory size and brightness, she placed it on the wall above the bed so that the thrall's face was clearly illuminated.

Light made the resemblance even more uncanny. The thrall had the same heart-shaped face and high cheekbones as Meg, the same pale skin, the same dark hair. But she was much younger than Meg, perhaps fourteen or fifteen, and a closer study of her face showed subtle differences in the shape of nose and mouth. They were not identical, but the resemblance was too striking to be chance.

While waiting for the girl to wake from her magical exhaustion, Meg could study the enthrallment spells. She had been with Simon when he removed the spells from the Brentford thralls, so perhaps she could manage some basic work here.

Slowly she explored the web of enthrallment spells. Though working magic took enormous concentration and complicated work was beyond her, Meg was able to erase some of the bindings on the girl's memory and personality. She examined the silver sphere that encompassed the girl's magic, but she didn't dare try the delicate work that would be required to dissolve it. There was too much risk of causing harm.

Neither did she try to knot off the intangible cord that joined the thrall to Drayton. He would notice that immediately, and punishment would be swift. But Meg did find an interesting connection that ran from the girl's magical center to the fortress of energy that protected the house. Hadn't Simon speculated that the thrall was providing the power to maintain the wards? Apparently he had been right, and that was another reason why the girl was so drained.

Thoughtfully Meg tested the connection to the wards. There was a limberness in it different from the connection to Drayton. If there was a chance to escape, it might be possible to cut that connection and shut down the wards.

By the time she withdrew from the thrall's mind, Meg was sweating and dizzy from the effort. But she had enough energy left to share some if she was careful. She visualized vitality and strength flowing from her center to the thrall's. Soon color returned to the girl's face and she shifted position a little.

Maintaining a bare trickle of energy to the thrall, Meg said softly, "Are you awake? Will you talk to me? Please?"

The girl's lids fluttered up, revealing deep blue eyes quite different from Meg's smoky gray green. At first her expression had the dullness typical of thralls. Then her gaze sharpened. "Megan, is it really you?" she whispered. "Or am I dreaming?"

The words jolted through Meg like lightning. "Do you know who I am?"

The girl raised her hand to Meg's face. "You look just like my sister Megan, who . . . who disappeared ten years ago." Her hand dropped away. "You must be a dream. Everything that has happened to me since that man came has been dream or nightmare."

Meg caught the younger girl's hand and squeezed hard, her heart racing. "That man, Drayton, is a nightmare made flesh, but I am real. I think I must be your sister, but I remember nothing before I was abducted ten long years ago."

The girl sat up and stared incredulously, then picked up Meg's left hand. "That scar on the back of your hand." She bit her lip. "You got it when you pulled me away from an angry dog and it bit you by mistake." She raised her gaze again, tears shining in her eyes. "It really is you."

Meg stared at the scar, so faint that she was barely aware of it, and saw canine teeth sinking into her flesh. Two deep punctures and spurts of blood. "Dear God, I remember. You were too young to know that all dogs aren't friendly."

The girl scrambled to her knees and lurched across the mattress into a hug, the tears streaming down her face. "Oh, Megan, we missed you so dreadfully! You used to sing me to sleep when I was little. Mama and Papa were never the same after you vanished. Once Papa said that not knowing what happened to you was worse than if you had died of a fever. Where did you go? Why didn't you come home?"

Meg smiled crookedly. "Why aren't you home?"

"Oh. Of course." The girl's expression crumpled as the joy of finding her sister was overwhelmed by her captivity. "Oh, Megan, it was horrible. Horrible! I had no will. My very self was shattered. And . . . and *he* would rip into my mind, invading my very soul." She began to weep. "There are no words for what he did."

Meg enfolded the younger girl in her arms. "You don't need words, because I experienced exactly the same, for ten long years. Dear God, I wish I could wipe those memories from your mind!"

For a long time they held each other, her sister's tears gradually diminishing. Gently Meg rocked her, sending the same sort of soothing energy she used with animals. To her surprise, she realized that her own pain was diminishing. By sharing what they had suffered, they became stronger. When the girl stopped shaking, Meg asked, "How did Drayton capture you? How long has he held you in thrall? It's August 1748 now."

The other girl sat up and wiped her face with the back of her hand. "I was feeding the chickens when *he* appeared. He didn't say a word—just placed his hand on my head, and my mind was overpowered. I think he led me through the woods to a road where a carriage waited, but I remember very little after that. It was April when he took me, so it's been about four months."

"Thank heaven it was no longer," Meg said vehemently. "Now tell me everything, little sister. What is your name? What is my name? Where did we live? Who else is in the family?"

"You are Megan Elizabeth Harper, and I am Emma Alice Harper," the younger girl said. "You were the oldest in the family and I was youngest. Between us are two brothers, Harold and Winthrop. Papa is the vicar of St. Austell's church in the village of Lydbury in Shropshire. You remember none of this?"

"Emma," Meg breathed. *"Emma!"* Images tumbled through her mind of a little girl with great blue eyes who followed her big sister everywhere. Emma had turned five and was getting too large to carry. "I used to let you sleep in my bed when there were storms. My dogs and cats slept there, too."

"Yes!" Emma bounced with excitement. "After you . . . went away, they came and slept with me. It was very crowded. You remember now?"

"I'm starting to." The images increased in speed, revealing her tall, scholarly father with his grave smile and his devotion to his congregation. Her mother, the warm center of the household, endlessly patient with her eldest child's tendency to run into the woods and ride the squire's horses. "Did I take lessons from a governess?"

"No, you studied with Papa. He tutored sons of the local gentry to prepare them to go away to school, and you would sit in the corner during the lessons. When the boys left, he would drill you on what you had learned. He said you were smarter than any of the boys." Emma smiled through her tears. "After you vanished, I started going to the lessons, too. Papa said it made him feel better to have a daughter in the corner. Once he said I was as clever as you, and it was the nicest thing anyone ever said to me."

It was too much. Meg buried her face in her hands and began sobbing uncontrollably as the pieces of her past fell into place. Simon had thought her memories might come rushing back all at once, and he had been right. Emma's words had dissolved the barrier between Meg and her past. "I didn't even know my name!" she said raggedly. "All I remembered of my childhood was the name Meg."

She had lost so much, so many years of loving and being loved. The family she had longed for had wanted her equally. Drayton had not only torn her away from her family, he had obliterated her past so she hadn't even had the comfort of memories. *God damn the man to hell!*

"Poor Megan," Emma crooned, rocking Meg in her arms as if she were the younger sister. "Why did he steal both of us?"

There would be time to rage against fate later. Now she needed to explain their situation to her sister—her *sister!*—so that Emma would understand. Then they could plan how to escape. "Some people have the ability to perform magic—to do strange and wonderful things. When Drayton found that I had that ability, he kidnapped me and kept me at his family seat, Castle Drayton. It was perhaps half a day's ride from Lydbury. He probably hoped that someone else in the family was similarly talented, so he kept an eye on us until he was knew you were worth abducting."

Emma stared at her as if she were mad. "Magic? Did that man scramble your wits?"

"He dulled my mind, but he didn't scramble it." Meg reached up to the mage light and detached it from the wall, then offered it to her sister. "Drayton's wicked spells have suppressed most of my magic just now, but I was able to make this mage light."

Emma gasped as the light tingled on her palm. "Magic is mere superstition—and yet, here it is." She fluttered the fingers of her other hand through the light. "What else can magic do?"

Meg turned on the bed and leaned against the wall. "This will take a long time. Let me tell you about the Guardians. . . ."

Chapter
THIRTY-TWO

David gasped when he entered the Brentford Abbey chapel. He had expected a smaller, plainer structure, like the Dissenter chapel where he worshipped. As he gazed at carved stone pillars and stained glass that wouldn't have looked out of place in a cathedral, he said, "'Tis surely sacrilege to bring my engine in here!"

His guide, a rather grand fellow named Cox who seemed to be in charge of organizing the technology forum, said coolly, "My lord Drayton chose this as the exhibition hall because it's the largest space on the abbey grounds." His tone made it clear that his lordship's wishes were law. His glance made it equally clear that he was pained by the fact that inventors were not usually gentlemen of refinement.

David surveyed the broad, echoing space. Even though he didn't approve of popish customs, he had to admit it would have been a rare treat to hear monks singing their prayers here in the old days. "Where should I set up?"

"Down here." Cox led the way to the sanctuary at the head of the church, passing intriguing pieces of equipment and knots of men who worked on them. "If you need help moving your equipment, there are laborers ready to assist."

The spot Cox indicated was right where the high altar had once been. Even though this was no longer a real church, David offered a silent prayer of apology as he studied the other exhibits. He itched for a closer look, but first he must assemble his engine and make sure it was in working condition. It would be humiliating to fail when he had such an opportunity to prove what he could do.

With the help of Peter and several estate laborers, the sections of the engine were loaded onto a low cart and hauled into the chapel. Reassembling the engine was sweaty, dirty work. While Peter arranged for supplies of water and coal, David checked and rechecked every component to make sure there had been no damage in transit. Around him were voices with accents from all over Britain, along with banging and clanks as machinery was assembled. No shortage of curses, either.

Peter filled the firebox with fuel, then lit the coals so the boiler could begin heating. When David stepped back from the engine to wipe the sweat from his face, he realized that he had an audience. An expensively-dressed youth nodded to him. "It appears that your engine has two power strokes, both up and down. Is that correct?"

"Aye, so it is."

Another man said, "Using the piston to control the steam and exhaust is brilliant."

"Thank you." The sharp minds around him made David glad that Falconer had already obtained patents on the designs. "I think it's a good engine."

The youth studied the engine with narrowed eyes. "I'm interested in building canals to carry coal from my mines to Manchester and Salford, where it is needed. Can your engine raise water from deeper shafts than the Newcomen engine?"

"Aye, though I'll have to install one in a mine to be sure how much deeper. My guess is that it will lift water maybe twice as high as the Newcomen engine."

A grizzled man with a Lancashire accent asked, "Have you thought about converting your engine to rotary motion? 'Twould be more useful for us in the textile business."

"I'm working on that now." David glanced the length of the nave. "It looks like there are several kinds of textile equipment here."

"I've brought my new carding machine," another fellow with a Northern accent said. "It will revolutionize the cloth trade."

"If it works," another man said with a touch of malice.

Not wanting to encourage hostility, David said, "I'd like to see what others have invented. That machine there is for spinning, isn't it?"

"So 'tis," the grizzled man said. "I've improved the flyer and bobbin system, so this is the best spinning machine made. Take a look while your boiler is heating."

David followed him, heady with excitement. This was what he'd hoped for—the exchange of ideas by men like him—men with ideas, and no fear of getting their hands dirty. Sarah had been right to stay home—it was not the right atmosphere for a lady. But he would remember everything so he could tell her about it later.

Meg woke when she heard a key turn in the lock. Where . . . ?

Oh, yes, she was in Drayton House, partially enthralled, and sharing a very narrow bed with her younger sister. The joy of having regained her lost life almost made up for the rest.

She had given Emma an overview about magic and the Guardians before they fell into exhausted sleep, curled up against each other like kittens. Her sister had been wide-eyed and somewhat doubtful, but the evidence of the mage light made her willing to accept the possibility that Meg was right, not mad.

The mage light! Drayton mustn't know that she could still do some magic. Swiftly Meg dowsed her light.

But it wasn't Drayton who entered. Two footmen came in, one carrying a tray of food and the other, Boxley, watching the girls suspiciously. Meg looked as dull and helpless as possible, which wasn't hard. If she and Emma were to escape, it would be through guile and magic, not physical force.

The tray was set on the table, then both men withdrew, watching the captives warily. As the key turned in the lock, Emma sat up and covered a yawn with one hand. "When we were small, we shared a bed," she said drowsily. "But it was bigger."

"And we were smaller. No matter. We won't be here long." Meg hoped that was true, since the bed was not built for two. It was barely built for one. Feeling stiff, she rose and investigated the tray. There were two plates of food containing boiled potatoes and onions and a two-inch piece of sausage, plus a small jug of ale and two pears. The sun was low in the sky and the room full of shadows, so she created another mage light to improve the illumination. It was a little easier this time.

"Can I make light, too?" Emma asked.

"I'm sure you could, but Lord Drayton has locked up the part of you that can do magic." Meg took one of the plates and a fork to her sister. "It will need to be unlocked before you can start working with power."

Emma balanced the plate on her lap and took a bite. "But you can make light even though you say he has bespelled you."

"The spell hasn't fully worked on me this time, I think because I'm stronger now." Meg poured two mugs of ale, thinking how quickly she had become accustomed to using magic. It was part of her, and she felt crippled now. "If I had my full power, I could have knocked both of those men down so we could escape. Instead, I can only do very small magics." She handed her sister a mug, then started on her own supper. The food was cold from being carried so far, but the quality was decent. She guessed it was what the servants ate.

"This talk of magic is hard to believe, but I know you wouldn't lie to me." Emma swallowed the last bit of sausage, then crossed the room to put her plate back on the tray. She was almost as tall as Meg, but her slight figure had barely begun to fill out. "I feel safe now that you're here."

Such faith was humbling, and even perhaps justified. Emma was mentally much sharper than the Brentford thralls had been at first, and surely that was a result of Meg's work on the binding spells. Simon was needed to fully free her sister, though.

Her heart constricted. Mustn't think of Simon or she would not be able to function. She tossed one of the pears to her sister. "Now that we've eaten, it's time to think about escape. I'm going to spend some time mentally investigating the house, so you get more rest."

Emma nodded obediently as she resumed sitting on the bed, but she kept her gaze fixed on Meg. It had been like that when they were children—Emma had been her shadow, and the dearest little girl in the world. No wonder Meg had felt such a compulsion to release Drayton's final thrall. On some level, she had recognized her little sister. Just as her presence benefited Emma, Emma's presence was surely making Meg sharper and more focused. She had a sister to protect.

Meg settled as comfortably as possible in the wooden chair, then closed her eyes and cleared her mind. The only area she could reach was within the wards. The effect was odd, like being trapped in a barrel.

The good news was that Drayton wasn't in the house. Probably he had gone out to Brentford Abbey for his forum. The farther away he was, the better.

Not so good was the fact that there were at least six servants in the house, possibly more. Several had rooms on the ground floor, near the kitchen, and two or three more lodged up here in the attic.

If she could manage a don't-look spell, it would help them sneak out of the house. She cleared her mind and tried to invoke the spell. As with the mage light, the level of effort was enormous.

"Meg. Meg! Where are you!" Emma's voice was frantic.

Apparently the spell worked. Meg released it and jumped to her feet. "It's all right, Emma, I'm right here." She crossed to the bed and caught her sister's hands. "I was practicing a spell that might help us escape."

Emma's fingers bit into Meg's hands. "I was afraid I had dreamed you!"

"I'm real, and I won't leave without you." Meg looked into her little sister's blue eyes, remembering that the vivid color came from their mother. The boys, Harry and Winthrop, had those blue eyes, too. Only Meg had her father's dreamy gray green color.

Emma cocked her head to one side, a characteristic even when she was little. "How did you make yourself vanish?"

"I didn't. The don't-look spell makes people not want to look in your direction, but you aren't invisible. A number of things can make the spell ineffective. But it's useful, and easy enough that almost anyone with magic can do one."

Emma frowned. "I found myself looking everywhere except the chair. How odd. If this is magic, it will be most interesting to study."

"The most interesting subject in the world. Now let me go back to thinking about escape." Meg returned to her chair. Would the don't-look spell work on the footmen? Perhaps she could make them think she and Emma had vanished. Then the two of them could slip out the door while the footmen were looking under the bed.

But the room was so small that it would be very difficult to leave without brushing by the guards, and if that happened, the spell would no longer be effective. Perhaps Meg could use the spell, then brain the footmen with the chair or chamber pot? That might work if only one man came, but not for two.

The key. It was light and it hung just outside the door. Did Meg have enough magic to lift it from its nail, then pull it under the ill-fitting door? Moving a physical object took a great deal of energy.

Definitely worth trying. Meg concentrated on the key, wishing that she had noticed it more clearly when she was brought to this room. The top was curly. . . .

Concentrating till her head hurt, she reached the key and tugged at it. She felt it swing back and forth on the nail, but maddeningly, the key wouldn't come off.

A hand came to rest on her shoulder. Emma had been drawn by instinct to help. Meg covered her sister's hand with her own and tried again.

A clink sounded outside the room as the key jumped from the nail and onto the wooden floor. "Thank heaven!" Meg rubbed her head, which felt as if it were bound in fire. "Thank you, Emma. You were able to lend me enough energy to take the key from the hook outside. After I've rested a few minutes, I'll see if I can get it into the room."

Emma dipped one end of a worn towel into the water pitcher, then patted Meg's temples. The cool moisture was soothing. "You look ready to drop."

Meg closed her eyes, enjoying her sister's attention. "Thank you, Emma. I feel much better." In those long ago days in Lydbury, there had always been a link between the two of them. Meg hadn't recognized it as magic. Sometimes she had been exasperated at how little Emma was always tagging along, but now she recognized that they shared an uncommon bond.

Meg turned and stared at the crack under the door. The key was only a few inches away. *Come here, little key. Come to me. . . .*

Scraping erratically, the key jerked into the room. Eyes wide, Emma scooped it up. "You did it! You really can do magic!" She gazed at her sister adoringly.

"You will be able to also, though perhaps not exactly the same kinds of magic." Meg took the key from her sister and turned it in the lock. It moved easily and the door opened a crack to reveal the empty hall. To think that Meg had thought the ability to move small objects was a useless trick!

When Emma moved toward the door, Meg closed and locked it again. "We won't leave now. Better to wait until the middle of the night, when the servants are asleep."

"What if someone who sleeps up here notices that the key is missing?"

"I hadn't thought of that! I'll put a don't-look spell on the nail outside so no one will notice." Meg did so, thinking wryly that Emma's mind was in better shape than her own. "Now I'm ready for some sleep."

Feeling as if she had run ten miles, she lurched to the bed and folded onto it. Emma patted Meg's temples with the moist towel again. "I wish I had lavender water."

"This is good enough," Meg murmured. "I'm so glad to have found you, Emma. For ten years, I felt as if I had no family. I felt so alone."

"You aren't alone now. When you come home to Lydbury, you'll have a welcome that will outshine what we'd give the king himself." Emma used the dry end of the towel to blot excess moisture. "I didn't notice at first, but your gown is very lovely. You look like a grand lady."

Meg's eyes drifted shut. "The Guardians took very good care of me." Today she didn't have the energy to explain how she had become a pretend countess. . . .

Simon was finishing his preparations to leave for Lady Bethany's house in Richmond, then on to Brentford Abbey, when his butler entered the room. "My lord, there is a Mrs. White here to see you. She seems quite . . . overwrought."

David's wife? Wondering what had happened, Simon descended to the small reception room where Hardwick had put the visitor.

Sarah White rose at his entrance, her expression strained. "I'm sorry to disturb you, my lord, but I . . . I'm worried about my husband."

"Good day, Mrs. White. What has you worried?" Simon waved her back to her seat and took the opposite chair. "Is your husband ill? I had thought you planned to go to the forum at Brentford Abbey together."

"That was the intention, but I decided to stay home. I told David I didn't like being around Lord Drayton, but that was . . . less than the truth." She bit her lip. "His lordship terrifies me. I've been having nightmares about him, but they were very vague until this afternoon, when I was napping. This time I saw Lord Drayton k . . . killing my David." She began to cry. "It's surely just the foolish fancy of a woman who is increasing, but it was so real! Please, my lord . . ." Gulping for breath, she managed to ask, "Why would anyone want to murder my husband, who has never harmed a soul in his life?"

Her reddened eyes begged for him to tell her that it was just a bad dream, but he couldn't. Sarah White had a spark of clairvoyance, he guessed, and the ability had been triggered by a threat to the one she loved most. "Lord Drayton is not a good man, Mrs. White, but I can't imagine why he might want to kill your husband. How did he do it—with a sword or a gun?"

She shook her head. "It was one of those strange dream images. Drayton waved his hand and David collapsed. I knew it was a death blow. Dream logic. Or illogic."

Would David White do something to infuriate Drayton? Or was this only a nightmare, inspired by his wife's well-justified suspicions? Intuition suggested that the danger was real—Meg had also been concerned about David's future. "I was already planning to attend the forum incognito. I will look out for your husband as best I can."

"Incognito?" she asked with surprise.

"There is bad blood between Drayton and me." An understatement of massive proportions. "I'm interested in his forum, but prefer not to attend as myself."

"Thank you so much. I know I'm being unreasonable, but it makes me feel much better to know you'll be there." She stood and tried to smile. "Thank you also for . . . for taking me seriously, my lord."

"Any man who didn't would be a fool, Mrs. White."

She inclined her head gratefully before heading for the door. He frowned. "How did you get here?"

"I hired a sedan chair." Her smile turned wry. "With the money you're advancing David. I'll take a chair back."

"It's late and it might be hard to get a safe ride back to your neighborhood. I'll send you in a carriage." He hesitated. "Do you have a friend you can stay with? I don't think you should be alone."

"The other women in the neighborhood have been very kind to me, like sisters and aunts. There is a neighbor who would be willing to take me in, I think."

"Good. I shall feel better knowing you are among friends."

"You really do care, don't you?" she said quietly. "Your wife is a lucky woman."

If he could persuade Meg of that, maybe she would be his wife in truth.

Chapter THIRTY-THREE

An hour or so after dark, two pairs of heavy feet came up the stairs to the attic and went to different rooms. Meg guessed that it was the two footmen who had delivered their meal. She and Emma rested silently in the darkness until Meg thought the servants were asleep. If she had her full power, she could have been sure, but now she suffered from a lack of magical clarity as well as diminished power.

It was time. She climbed from the bed and created a bubble of her mage light that turned inward around each of them. "This light can't be seen by others but it will help you see your way. I'll have a don't-look spell on us as well. When we reach the front door, we'll need to stop so I can cut your connection to the house wards. Otherwise I don't think we can leave without being hurt."

"Would it be easier to do that here?"

Meg was tempted, but she shook her head. "Someone in the house might have enough talent to feel when the wards go down. Drayton almost certainly will know, and even miles away, he might be able to cause trouble. It's safer to leave this till the last possible moment."

Emma nodded acceptance. Meg unlocked the door and stepped into the hall. After Emma joined her, Meg locked the door, taking the key in case it might be useful.

Stepping lightly, she descended the steps, wincing with every creak. But the house was quiet. They used the wider front stairs for the lower floors, since these stairs were less used when Drayton was away from the house.

Meg had been unsure whether to use the front or rear door to leave, but one look at the front door sent her along the passage to the back of the house. The door had a massive lock and there was no key in sight.

The rear door was also locked and probably the butler kept the key, but it was a simpler lock and the attic key worked in it. Meg sighed with relief when she felt the internal components shift open. Now to see if she could disconnect Emma from the wards without doing any damage to her sister.

She wiped damp palms on her skirt and was about to start when she heard steps coming down the corridor, along with the wavering light of a candle. Horrified, she pulled Emma into a corner, dowsed the mage lights, and covered them with the strongest don't-look spell she could manage. Could their escape have been discovered?

The candle-bearer was a pretty young blonde, a parlor maid by the look of her. She wore a low-cut night robe and her hair was artfully loosened about her shoulders. Setting the candle on a table, she began to pace the hall impatiently, her gaze sliding away from the two fugitives. Who was she waiting for?

Heavier steps and another candle approached. This time it was the footman Boxley, his expression eager. "I've been waiting all day to see you, Annie."

The maid gave him a pouty smile. "You said you had something for me?"

"Aye." He set down his candle, then reached into his pocket and produced a long sparkling glass vial that contained perfume. "Sweet as you, this is."

"Oh, Will!" She shook the bottle, then pulled out the stopper to sniff the scent. "It's ever so ladylike!" Gaze holding his, she touched the stopper in the cleft between her breasts. "Doesn't it smell lovely?"

He made a growling noise and buried his face in her cleavage while his large hands cupped her buttocks. Their embrace was so lusty that Meg wondered if she should cover Emma's eyes. At least the hot-blooded lovers weren't paying attention to anyone lurking in the corners.

Boxley's hand was up Annie's skirt when she said throatily, "The carpet in the drawing room is softer than here."

"Aye, 'tis." He straightened, with difficulty, and wrapped his arm around her waist. Taking up his candle with his other hand, he kissed Annie as they set an unsteady course toward the front of the house.

When the lovers were out of sight, Meg produced more mage light. Emma's eyes were wide. "This is not a well-run household!" she whispered indignantly. "Mama would never allow such a thing."

"Lord Drayton is not a good manager," Meg agreed. She placed her hands on Emma's shoulders. "I'm going to try to sever your connection to the house wards now. I don't think this will hurt, but be prepared for strange feelings. Remember, we must be quiet."

Emma nodded obediently. Had Meg ever been quite so cooperative? She didn't think so. Closing her eyes, she slid her perception into the tangle of spells and connections inside her sister. As with the Brentford thralls, she sensed a maze of spiderweb-thin lines, but the connection to the wards was large and easy to find. The cord pulsed with power flowing from Emma into the complex spells that protected the house. Emma must have immense reserves of magic to give so much away and still function.

The connection was maddeningly hard to handle, like a slippery live fish. Meg tried cutting the thread, but it slid away, undamaged. After several futile attempts, accompanied by whimpers from Emma, she decided to try knotting the shining energy line instead. With effort, she managed to grasp the cord in two places, pulled it into a loop, and knotted it. For a metaphor, it seemed very real.

Emma gasped and her eyes shot open. "I feel . . . different."

Meg studied the knot. No power was moving through it. The wards should be down, or at least vastly weakened. "Your power is your own again. Now let's *run.*"

Simon was pulled out of a restless sleep by . . . what? Something was tugging at one of the people or objects he was watching magically. He sorted through the various energy lines, whistling softly when he sensed that the wards on Drayton House had diminished to virtually nothing.

Was Drayton baiting a trap to lure Simon in? Maybe, but he couldn't pass up this chance to break in and free Meg.

Throwing on his clothing, he left the house quietly. Drayton House was only a few blocks away, and it was quicker to go on foot than detour to the stables for a horse or carriage. Praying the wards would stay down, he masked himself with a don't-look spell and ran toward Drayton House. . . .

About half a block away, he almost crashed into two figures racing from the house. They seemed to have come out of nowhere.

He felt the sizzle of a dissolving don't-look spell. "Meg? Meg!" He swept her into his arms with crushing force, dizzy with relief. "You're all right?"

"Oh, Simon!" She clung to him, shaking. Spells were binding her, but they were less severe than the ones strangling her when they'd met. The connection to Drayton was still knotted off, so probably it was physical closeness that had allowed him to partially enthrall her again.

Arm locked around Meg, he turned to her companion. "This is the thrall? I should have known you wouldn't escape without her." He created a sphere of mage light and raised it to cast light on the slender figure.

"Her name is Emma Harper."

Simon gasped as the light delineated a face uncannily like Meg's, but younger and more innocent. The resemblance was unnervingly strong, as if Drayton had managed to duplicate Meg. Choosing the more logical explanation, he said, "Surely this young lady must be your sister."

Meg nodded, her eyes shining. "I have my memories back, Simon! Most of them. My name is Megan Harper, and my father is the vicar of Lydbury in Shropshire. Emma and I have two brothers between us in age, and my parents are alive and well. At least, they were several months ago when Drayton abducted Emma."

Simon bowed to the younger girl. "It is a pleasure to meet my wife's sister, Miss Emma." He scanned her magical field and deftly knotted the connection that ran to Drayton. The other bindings could wait, but not this one.

Emma exclaimed, "You didn't tell me you were married, Meg!"

"There was so much else to talk about." Meg looked back at the house and saw lights coming on. "Let's get away from here!"

Simon agreed. Whoever was head of the household under Drayton had been woken by the collapse of the wards, and reprisal might be on the way. With a girl on each arm, he retraced his steps home, using the time to examine the other spells binding Emma. Meg had done some effective work despite her own reduced magical power. What an intrepid warrior maiden she was!

When they were safe inside his house, he asked, "Do you need food or drink?"

Meg silently consulted with her sister. "That would be nice, but release from the enthrallment spells would be even better."

"Both needs can be satisfied in the kitchen." He led them downstairs and found cider, bread, and cheese. While Emma ate, he applied himself to removing the spells on Meg. It was much easier this time—her own trained strength was fighting to free itself.

Removing the spells on Emma was harder, but practice was making Simon rather good at such work. The silver sphere encapsulating her magic was almost as large as Meg's. This young girl would make a powerful mage.

When the final spell was dissolved, Emma gave a low cry and buried her face in her hands for the space of a dozen heartbeats. When she straightened, her eyes were fully focused. "I feel as if I have regained a part of myself that I didn't know was lost."

"That's exactly what happened." Meg, who was sitting right next to Emma, squeezed her sister's hand.

"When can I go home? Mama and Papa must be so frightened." Emma gave a radiant smile. "They won't believe that I've found you!"

Meg exchanged a glance with Simon. She wanted to return to her family as much as Emma did, but she had made a promise. "We will have to wait a few days before we go. There is business relating to Lord Drayton."

Emma opened her mouth to protest, then subsided. She was a very agreeable girl. Less interesting than Meg, Simon suspected, but agreeable. "They must be notified, of course," he said. "Emma, would you like to write a letter? You might want to avoid too many details that might alarm them. The full story would better wait for when you return home, I think. Meg, do you wish to write a letter? Or perhaps it will be easier if I do."

She nodded gratefully. "I would prefer that. Too many years have passed. I . . . I wouldn't know what to say."

"When the time comes, you'll know," he said quietly. "In the morning, I'll take you both to Lady Bethany's. You shouldn't be alone here when I go to the abbey."

"I'm going with you." Meg's gaze was steely. "The situation has changed, and my place is by your side."

He hesitated, tempted, but disturbed by the potential danger to her. "We'll talk about it in the morning."

Meg shrugged. "There is nothing to talk about. I am going." She stood. "Emma, you can sleep with me tonight. My bed is much larger than the one in Drayton's attic."

Yawning, Emma trailed along beside Meg to the stairs. Simon followed, bemused and amused. He suspected that arguing with a warrior maiden would be futile. Besides, now that all the thralls had been rescued, Drayton's power was drastically lessened. The rogue surely had some other tricks up his sleeve, but if Simon and Meg worked together, they should be able to restore order before real damage was done.

At the door to the countess's bedroom, he drew Meg into a kiss after Emma had gone inside. She came into his arms so willingly that he almost forgot the task that lay ahead. What mattered was having her back again, safe.

Her eyes were dazed with desire when she stepped from his embrace. "How do I explain . . . us to Emma?"

"Don't," he advised. "There will be time for that later." He brushed back her hair, his fingers lingering. If it weren't for Emma, he would suggest they spend the night together. Though perhaps he wasn't tired enough to guarantee that it would be chaste.

If they stopped Drayton the next day, by tomorrow night the way might be free for them to become lovers. The thought was so arousing that he acknowledged that it was just as well that Emma was here to keep them in separate beds. "Sleep well, my warrior maiden."

She flicked her hand and golden light spilled from her palm. As it floated over Simon with tingling promise, she murmured, "I'll dream of you, my lord hunter. And tomorrow we will hunt together."

Drayton paced through the ancient chapel, the vast space illuminated only by the mage light that floated above him. To the left was a wide new loom, to the right a model design for an iron bridge. Beyond that was a water frame, which would move the spinning industry from cottages to great manufacturies. These were machines that would change the world. He had deliberately chosen to put White's wickedly clever steam engine where the high altar had once stood, for it was the king of all the inventions here, capable of powering other machines yet unimagined.

He paused to gaze the length of the nave, imagining how it would look tomorrow when the chapel teemed with people for the official opening of the technology forum. The finest inventors and engineers in Britain would be right here, with a seasoning of men from abroad. A fair number of them were sleeping under his own roof tonight, with others scattered in inns and private homes for several miles around.

Some among his guests would have at least a little power. Would any of them be able to detect the coruscating energy of the three ley lines that intersected beneath the chapel? The power was glorious, as intoxicating as fine French brandy. He had discovered this rare energy while seeking to lease an estate near town. The ley lines had convinced him that the vague ideas in the back of his mind could be made manifest.

A magical alarm jangled in his head. Shocked, he felt the wards on his London house collapse. As he probed all his connections to London, he felt his most precious thralls being wrenched painfully away. His stubborn, treacherous Meggie had found a way to free her little sister and escape—right into the arms of that devil Falconer.

He swore viciously, wishing he had Falconer here now. Drayton had painstakingly created a ritual magic circle in the Lady Chapel behind him, using holy water to lay lines invisible to mundane eyes. When Falconer arrived, the circle would transform and destroy after harvesting the power of the unicorn's horn. That sweet, powerful magic would belong entirely to Drayton, unlike what he borrowed from thralls. Adding Falconer's magic to his own would make him the most powerful mage in history.

He exhaled in a hiss of breath, reminding himself that would happen later. For now, he must be grateful that he didn't need the damnable Harper sisters for what would be done tomorrow.

The time had come to summon his tools. He walked around the carved screen that separated the sanctuary from the Lady Chapel. The most potent energy in the abbey was concentrated here, where so many had prayed for the Blessed Mother's grace and mercy. He had turned the Lady Chapel into an office and workroom, with comfortable chairs, a table, and a locked cabinet for files and magical materials.

He settled in his chair and prepared to work. Convenient that his thralls were only a few miles away. After losing Meggie, Drayton had taken extra precautions with his other power providers. He had thought it was enough that the thread of connection he'd spun between himself and Meggie was unbreakable, but Falconer had figured out a way to block power from moving along the cord.

So Drayton had created a back door into the mind of each of the other five thralls. First he had multiplied the existing connections among the Brentford thralls into a maze of almost invisible lines. Then he had buried in each mind a gossamer thread that ran back to him. No matter what Falconer did to the larger, more visible connections, Drayton had full access to the thralls through his back doors.

Theoretically it was possible for Falconer to detect the secondary connections, but only if he was looking for them. He hadn't looked. Smug as all the Falconers, he thought he had foiled Drayton. Tomorrow he would learn better.

A pity it hadn't been possible to install a back door into Meggie's mind, but the defenses she'd acquired since leaving Castle Drayton had prevented that. She would be recovered by straightforward assault when the time was right.

He started with Moses, arrowing his mind along the nearly undetectable filament that connected him to the African. There he was, sleeping peacefully. Drayton flooded the youth's mind with power, effortlessly re-creating the enthrallment spells. *It is time to return, Moses. You and your friends must come home.*

When he was sure the African was under control again, he moved on to Jemmy. Retrieving his tools was even easier than he'd anticipated. . . .

Moses awoke with a silent scream echoing in his mind. *No, no, no, no . . .* But that was buried so deeply he was hardly aware of it. His orders hammered in his brain. *Time to return, time to return.*

He dressed in the dark and moved through the connecting door to Jemmy's small room. When he shook the younger boy, Jemmy came awake with a whimper, quickly suppressed. Raising his dull gaze to Moses, he said, "Time to return."

Moses nodded. "Jemmy dress and go harness pony cart. Moses will bring girls."

Jemmy nodded obediently and scrambled for his clothes as Moses left the room. Breeda and Lily shared a room, so it was easy to wake them. They climbed from the bed, eyes blank, and prepared to travel back to Brentford Abbey.

And deep in each mind, a voice screamed, *No, no, no, no, no. . . .*

Chapter THIRTY-FOUR

Our four students are gone," Lady Bethany said bluntly when Meg, Simon, and Emma entered her morning room.

Meg gasped. "I thought something was wrong! When I reached out to them on the drive here, I couldn't find them."

Lady Bethany's gaze moved to Emma. "My manners have gone begging. Surely this young lady must be related to you, Meg?"

"Lady Bethany, may I present to you Miss Emma Harper, my younger sister." Even the disturbing news about the Brentford thralls couldn't dim Meg's delight in her newly discovered memories.

Lady Beth's sharp glance showed that she understood the significance of having a last name, but she concentrated her attention on her new guest. "Miss Harper, welcome to my home. Is this your first visit to London?"

Simon said bluntly, "You can speak freely in front of Emma, Lady Beth. She was Drayton's final thrall. Meg rescued Emma and herself last night, and we've explained the situation to her."

Emma nodded gravely. "It's very bad that the other four are gone, isn't it?"

With a sigh, Lady Bethany sank back into her chair and abandoned social pleasantries. "Very bad indeed. We should have moved them farther away. Apparently last night Drayton was able to reactivate the enthrallment spells and order them to return to Brentford Abbey. A pony cart was missing this morning, and I caught a sense of their energies just before they disappeared within the abbey wards."

Simon swore under his breath. "Drayton must have established a second connection in that tangle of energies, and I was stupid enough not to notice."

"Don't you dare lose your temper with yourself," Meg said sharply. "There's no time for that. If there were duplicate connections, we all missed them." She looked around. "Where is Jean?"

"She's in her room, trying to reestablish contact with the thralls. She was closest to them and hoped that she might be able to bring them back to themselves." Lady Beth sighed. "I think it's futile at this distance, but we had to try."

"We have a better task for her—tutoring Emma," Meg said. Before she could say more, a wave of strange energy surged through the room. Meg and Emma would have fallen if Simon hadn't steadied them, and Lady Beth had to grab the arms of her chair to keep her balance. Meg gasped, "What was that?"

"Energy surging along a ley line," Simon said grimly. "The same line is one of the three that pass through Brentford Abbey. Whatever Drayton is planning has begun."

"Then there's no time to waste," Meg said. "We must leave *now.*"

"Meg . . ." Simon stared at her, his eyes appalled. "Now that he has four of his thralls back, it's infinitely more dangerous to go to the abbey. You can't—"

Fiercely she interrupted him. "I can and I *must.* Didn't you tell me that among the Guardians, men and women are equal?"

"She's right," Lady Bethany said before he could reply. "Meg is part and parcel of this situation. She not only *should* be there at the end—I think that it is essential for her to go with you if there is to be any chance of success."

Simon exhaled roughly. "You may be right, but I hate the risk to you, Meg."

Her eyes narrowed. "Have you never taken risks?"

"He does so with great regularity," Lady Beth said. "Don't let your feelings interfere with your logic, Simon. Meg is a powerful mage, and to be a Guardian means a willingness to put the greater good above personal safety."

He exhaled resignedly. "We really must arrange a swearing of oaths for you, Meg. When things are calmer."

"I'd like that," she said, glad he had conceded. "Now it's time for us to be off."

Lady Bethany's brow furrowed. "I believe there is no time to waste, and the fastest way to Brentford Abbey may be riding a unicorn."

After a moment of thought, Simon nodded. "You're right. This time, my clothing will be carried rather than destroyed." He turned to Emma. "Grave matters are afoot, my dear. I hope Meg and I won't be gone long. Until we return, Lady Bethany and Jean Macrae will take good care of you."

Emma bit her lip but nodded. On the verge of tears, Meg hugged her sister. "If . . . if I don't come back, tell Mama and Papa and the boys that I loved them."

"Meg!" Emma cried out as Meg turned to leave the room, but Meg didn't look back. In every fiber of her body, she knew they were running out of time. If she and Simon were to be successful, they must leave now.

And she knew just as surely that if they failed, all Britain would be at risk.

Simon felt strange stripping himself naked in the stable, but it made more sense than transforming inside the house. He folded his garments neatly and tucked them into the canvas bag Lady Beth had provided, then cleared his mind for the transformation. Suppressing his anger against Drayton had been difficult. Releasing it was child's play. All he had to do was think of the rogue abducting Meg from the Royal Menagerie. Rage flooded through him and triggered the unicorn spell.

The change was relatively easy, perhaps because it was the first time he'd transformed willingly. He was now familiar with the process, and the primal horror of feeling his body wrenched into a new shape was lessened. Though the pain wasn't.

In the midst of agony his mind blurred. When it cleared, he found himself alert and poised for battle, his human spirit in harmony with his unicorn body. Lion tail switching restlessly, he trotted from the stable. Meg waited outside, still wearing her morning gown since there had been no time to change.

He had forgotten the impact she had on him when he was in this form. He wanted to swoon at her feet. Lie on his back and wave his hooves in the air. Carry her away to the horizon at the speed of the wind.

The last he could do. He rubbed his head against her, impatient to be off.

She stroked his muzzle with unintended provocation. "I know that you hate being forced into this body and that it's dangerous to you," she said softly. "But merciful heaven, you are beautiful. Perhaps even more beautiful than when you're a man."

He doubted that she would say that if he was in his own form. He rubbed his head against her again, enraptured by her scent. Musky, alluring, entirely female.

"I'll get the bundle with your clothing and then we can be off." She skipped inside the stable while he walked to the mounting block. A few moments later she emerged from the building with the canvas bag slung across her back.

After she mounted, a shiver of magic went through him as she masked them with a don't-look spell. Her strong legs wrapped around his barrel. He wished he could see how her skirts pulled up to reveal her shapely ankles.

Meg settled herself. "Now we *ride.*"

He sprang into a full gallop. Using all his strength was giddily satisfying, and this time he wasn't running with a bullet wound.

He left the road outside Lady Beth's house almost immediately, cutting into a grassy lane. From there he leaped into a field. He had studied the roads and lanes in the area before their previous visit to the abbey. Though this route wasn't the most direct, they would avoid houses and other places where they might be seen.

As before, his maiden rode like a goddess, perfectly balanced despite the lack of saddle and harness. Intoxicated by the wind, her presence, and his own boundless strength, he half forgot the purpose of this ride until she called, "We're nearing the abbey. Time to slow down so you can change back before we go over the wall."

He focused on his path, and was shocked to realize that the wall was just ahead. There was barely time to halt before running into it.

Why stop? Reckless with exhilaration, he collected himself and went headlong at the wall, counting on his maiden to prepare herself for a jump. He was no mere horse but a beast from legend, only a pair of wings short of Pegasus.

Using all the power of his lithe muscles, he hurled himself into the air—and soared over the stone wall with inches to spare. His amazing maiden even managed to open a portal for them to fly through.

As he came down lightly on the other side, Meg said with a squeak, "You are *insane.* Magnificent, but insane. How about trotting over to that little grove so you can change back to yourself?"

Beginning to feel winded, he slowed his pace and did as she suggested. A pair of small deer bolted from the shrubbery as they approached. At least there was no bull.

The grove was a pretty place, quiet and protected, with soft moss in the shadowed depths. Meg slid from his back and regarded him with a frown. "You need a quick rub-down. The canvas bag should work after I remove your clothing."

With swift, economical movements, she did exactly that. The firm pressure of her hands wielding the improvised grooming cloth was startlingly sensual. Beginning to wish it was nighttime rather than high noon, he forced himself to hold still and hoped she would pretend not to notice the state he was in.

Tactfully, she did. "I brought a pin with me. This should be quick." She pricked her finger first, then his shoulder. Interesting how the strangest of events could become routine.

He tried to detach himself a little from the pain of transformation, but he still collapsed gasping on the ground. Beyond the pain was a disturbing sense of wildness, as if he had given too much of himself to the glory of running and not all of his human nature had returned.

That changed when Meg draped his coat over him. The garment

concealed the embarrassing fact that arousal carried through from one state to another. Embarrassment was a very human emotion and it pulled him back to a more normal state of mind.

"Take the time to catch your breath and regain your mental balance," she said. "Once we reach the abbey, we need to be at our best."

He peered through the trees at the estate wall they'd crossed. "I can't believe I was mad enough to jump that wall, and that you were able to keep your seat when I did!"

She chuckled as she sat down beside him. A ray of sunshine illuminated her mischievous expression. "I think your unicorn self knew what you were capable of. It's the closest I'll ever come to flying."

He wondered if it would be possible to transform into a bird. Perhaps an eagle? Or the hunting falcon that was the family crest . . . ? He hastily suppressed the thought. What he needed was less transformation, not more.

Fewer chances for wildness to erode his mind and soul.

Drayton peered around the screen from the Lady Chapel, not wanting to make his appearance until the official opening of the forum, when he would welcome his guests. When he would achieve his goal.

Already the church was teeming with engineers, inventors, professors, and others of a mechanical bent. They struck up eager conversations, discussed the exhibits, and speculated about future inventions. His forum was successful beyond his fondest dreams.

Less than half an hour now until the opening ceremony.

He turned back to the Lady Chapel, where the four thralls were sitting passively in a row. They always chose the same order: Moses, Lily, Jemmy, Breeda, which put the two strongest on the ends. When he walked about the room, their eyes followed him in parallel, like hungry dogs tracking food. He found the effect somewhat unnerving, but no matter. They all did exactly as they were told.

He had already tuned the energies of the thralls so that all would be in readiness when the time came, but he couldn't resist tweaking them once more. Like a finely braided rope, their temperaments and powers blended into one entity far more powerful than the simple sum of its parts.

Restlessly he checked the knob of the door that led outside. Carved to match the rest of the chapel's decoration, the door was easy to overlook but essential to his plans. He was about to look around the screen again when he stopped in his tracks, amazed. Meggie was nearby! Had that fool Falconer brought her with him?

He probed deeper and found that she was within the walls of the estate. This close, and with the thralls and ley lines to power him, he would be able to blast his way back into her mind.

He threw his consciousness along the connection thread. This time when he reached the block Falconer had created, he blazed his way through, disintegrating the barrier as if it had never been.

He drank from her greedily. Ah, God, it was sweet to be inside Meggie again, with her power and fear and virgin innocence. Even her sister had not matched the richness of her magic. And this time his Meggie would not escape. . . .

Simon sat up, keeping the coat over himself. "I'm ready to dress."

Meg obligingly turned away. She'd already seen enough of him to furnish her with pleasing memories for some time to come. She'd liked seeing his lean, muscled body against the silken moss. . . .

She was smiling to herself when horror invaded her. *Drayton.* Brutally he rammed into her mind and spirit. *Meggie, my slave, my tool, my thrall. The time has come to return to me.*

She screamed and collapsed sideways on the mossy ground, clutching her arms around herself. "Dear God, he is here in my mind!"

"Meg!" Simon dropped beside her and cupped her face in his hands so that he could pour bright, healing energy into her.

It helped, but only a little. Drayton was like a poisonous fog spreading his evil through her system. When he stabbed into her magical center, she cried out again, twisting violently as he began drawing out her power. "No, no . . ."

Simon managed to maintain his hold on her, barely. The contact allowed him to slide into her mind, down through the layers of her personality and magic. When he found the silver cord that connected her to Drayton, he tried to knot it several times, but failed. He swore under his breath. "He's draining your power and I can't stop it, probably because you're so close and he's enhanced by the other thralls."

"Kill me," she whispered as she felt the first bindings of enthrallment wrap around her. *"Please."* The thought of being sucked dry and turned into a husk of herself was worse than death.

"No!" Simon said furiously. "Can you get into his mind and find something that might be used against him?"

She convulsed around herself again, but managed to gasp, "I . . . I'll try."

Having a mission, however desperate, helped steady her awareness. Grimly she followed the cord that connected her to Drayton straight into the snake pit of his soul, where greed and selfishness and anger twisted like dank tentacles.

Burying her revulsion, she forced herself to probe deeper. Somewhere in the darkness and stench she caught a glimmer of something that instinct said concerned her. She drew closer, trying to capture that elusive knowledge.

Yes! Opening blind eyes, she whispered, "Make love to me, Simon. Right now!"

"What?" He stared down at her, aghast.

She fumbled for words in the chaos of her mind. "Virginity is a vital part of his connection to me. He . . . he was the first man to become intimate with my mind and power, and that makes the bond almost unbreakable. If you and I become lovers, you will . . . will supercede him. Greater intimacy might make it possible to break the thread. It's why he chose young people as his thralls. Easier to . . . to possess them."

"It may work." Simon's expression turned inward for a moment as he thought through the magical implications. Then his gaze caught hers, his blue eyes hypnotic. "Think only of me. Not him. Not magic. Not about past or future. Think only of me, and how much I love you." He bent into a deep, deep kiss, using his mouth to channel more power into her.

When he said that he loved her, she felt a strengthening of the energy he was sending her. She wanted to say that she loved him, too, but she was beyond words, lost in a maelstrom of evil, with only Simon's touch and spirit anchoring her to herself.

He ran a caressing hand down her body. "There is no one like you, Megan Harper, and I will love you to death and beyond."

Her name was another anchor. She stopped thrashing and clung to the shining power that was Simon. Though he couldn't free her of Drayton's grasp, his strength and love kept her from falling in deeper. How much power could he spare before he became dangerously depleted? This time she managed to say, "I love you, too, Simon. I thank God for the day I met you."

Swift joy touched his eyes before his expression turned bleak. "You're so tense I will have to hurt you, my love. I . . . I don't know if I can make myself do this."

"*Please!* Finally we are coming together. Think of that, not the circumstances." She thrust her pelvis up against him in a mute plea.

He took a deep breath, then said in a voice designed to captivate, "Use the pain to separate yourself from him. You are mine, not his. Only mine." He raised her skirts, fumbling through the layers of fabric to find intimate flesh.

Though his touch was gentle, she found it impossible to feel desire and guessed that he felt the same. "Pretend you are a unicorn," she whispered. "I am your chosen maiden and we will mate like lions, swift and fierce."

His expression changed and she saw the echo of wildness in his eyes. He bent and nipped her throat as if he were a stallion and she were a mare.

She responded by reaching for the lion essence she had discovered in the Tower. *Untamed . . .* Wildness surged between them, and when he thrust into her, the fierce pain was freeing, sharp enough to counter Drayton's poison. She bit Simon's shoulder, tasting blood as she raked her nails down his bare back.

He drove into her mind as he had assaulted her body, penetrating to the very core of her as he reached for the connection to Drayton. He found it—and with one furious wrench, he severed the silver cord.

She arched her back, dazed by her release. "He's gone. *He's gone.* I'm free."

Simon folded over her, exhausted yet still rigid with passion. "Oh, my darling," he whispered. "I am so sorry for hurting you." He began to withdraw.

"No!" She caught him around the waist. "Now that we are joined, let us go beyond the pain into true lovemaking." Her lips touched the bleeding bite she had put on him, this time with tenderness and gratitude.

Using the utmost care, he moved within her a fraction at a time. She sighed with pleasure as her body softened into moist welcome. From the beginning, she had wanted him with the wild child part of herself that had forgotten she was a vicar's daughter, but until now, she hadn't been ready to give herself without reserve.

Desire began to build, blotting out the pain of the last minutes. There was magic between them, shimmering threads of love and trust. And passion, oh, yes, most certainly of passion. She saw the discipline, honor, and pain that had shaped him, and also the lighter threads of humor, kindness, and curiosity.

And with a certainty beyond doubt, she knew that he was hers. Even the ten years she had spent enthralled were not too high a price to pay for such a man's love. If not for Drayton, she would never have met Simon, nor become strong enough to be his mate.

As they rocked faster and faster, exquisite sensations engulfed her, bringing every fiber of her body to shimmering life. "Ah, Simon, my love, this is even better than I dreamed," she breathed. "Why didn't you tell me you were a virgin, too?"

He gave a catch of laughter. "I should have known you would sense that. As to why—I found that I didn't wish to lose myself in a woman's energy unless I loved her. One doesn't dishonor a lady, so Blanche and I never reached this point. Now I'm glad, for there is only you."

Meg guessed that he and his first love might have enjoyed some tantalizing sessions that had taught him the basics of sensuality, but no matter. Now he was hers. "I think the fact that it's the first time for both of us increases the intensity."

Power was rushing through her like a storm wind and gradually she realized it was not only human passion but earth energy, ancient and potent. "The earth is radiant with power. Can you feel it?"

His eyes widened. "You're glowing, Meg. You look like a goddess."

Startled, she realized he was right. Earth energy poured through her and into him like a river of fire. He began moving faster and she followed him, her agile body perfectly tuned to his. They tumbled like otters through a sea of pleasure, a sky full of light. "Simon," she cried. *"Simon!"*

Shattered by rapture, she saw that he was shining also, illuminated by Gaia's power. For an instant, they were truly one.

As their physical bodies convulsed, then gradually stilled, they became separate once more. But not quite. There was a connection between them, a golden cord as warm and rich with life as the sun, as untamed as the great lions. And unlike Drayton's enslaving cord, this bond truly was unbreakable.

Simon rolled to his side and pulled her close. "You no longer have a choice about marriage. We are truly wed now, my countess. Though we had best have a church ceremony to make it official."

She gazed at the leafy canopy above them, knowing that they were mated in the most profound of ways. She hadn't the least desire to struggle against that. The fears that had made her resist marriage at the beginning seemed very far away now, though they had seemed real enough then. She had needed time to ripen into a wife. "I'm glad we won't have to explain to people that we were only pretending."

He cupped her with his hand. "I think I should be able to stop the pain and bleeding." The warmth that flowed from his palm did exactly that, and more. If there wasn't a catastrophe about to take place up the hill, she would have liked another exploration of marital relations.

She sighed. "Time for you to dress, and this time I refuse to look away."

Laughing, he got to his feet and reached for his undergarments. "You have the advantage on me. Next time, I look forward to removing your clothing piece by piece."

But first they must defeat Drayton, or there would be no next time. And now that she was no longer dazed by passion, she felt the gathering danger.

It was time to confront the enemy on his own ground.

Chapter THIRTY-FIVE

"The energy here is stunning," Simon said under his breath. Hand in hand, they had reached the clustered abbey buildings at the crest of the hill. Anyone with even a shred of inner vision could see the power shining from the intersecting ley lines.

"It's a vast, indifferent power," Meg mused. "I doubt it notices us small humans who move through time so quickly."

"If Drayton has found a way to channel this power for his purposes, he will be unstoppable. And he might decimate Britain while learning to control it," Simon said grimly. "Let's hope his reach exceeds his grasp."

The medieval chapel drew the eye with its blazing power. Simon had caught only a distant glimpse of the structure on their previous visit. In full daylight it was an impressive testament to the wealth and power of the Benedictines who'd built the abbey. Perhaps the ley lines had helped draw earthly riches to them.

Simon maintained a don't-look spell designed to conceal both physical bodies and magical signatures, but it hardly seemed necessary. The grounds were eerily quiet. Everyone was in the chapel, he guessed. "There are a huge number of people inside and they're listening to someone speak. What are you finding?"

"The thralls are also inside, bound so tightly I can't touch them. I think they're at the far end of the building, perhaps in a smaller room beyond the nave."

Simon located David White's energy. So far the inventor was hale and hearty. "I think Drayton is in the same place as the thralls, waiting and watching."

They reached the iron-bound doors, twice the height of a tall man's head, but with a normal door inset on the right side. Simon studied Meg's face, looking on all levels. "Are you strong enough for this? Drayton took so much power from you."

"The earth energy replenished me," she said, her gaze steady. "I am as prepared for Drayton as I can be."

From what he sensed, she was telling him the truth. He squeezed her hand before releasing it. "Be careful, my love."

They slipped inside and paused in the shadows, unseen. The center of the nave was lit by tall iron torcheres. There were easily two hundred men present, probably more. Their clothing indicated that they came from all levels of society, from the nobility to roughly clad working men, but they had intelligence and curiosity in common. Standing in clusters around the double row of exhibits that marched down the nave, they watched the speaker declaiming from a pulpit on the left.

Opposite the pulpit stood the distinctive shape of the steam engine, though David himself wasn't visible. Suppressing his personal interest in examining the exhibits, Simon studied the speaker and saw that it was Cox, Drayton's steward for Brentford Abbey.

Finishing his speech, Cox said, "Allow me to present your host and the sponsor of this unprecedented forum, Lord Drayton, minister of state for domestic affairs and the greatest supporter of inventions and industry in all of England!"

Magnificently dressed, Drayton ascended the pulpit steps after Cox left. Simon edged Meg into a small chapel on the right that gave them a view of the proceedings.

If Drayton had been disturbed by the recent battle for Meg's soul, he gave no sign of it. In a polished voice pitched to fill the high, stone-walled space, he said, "It is with the greatest of pleasure that I welcome you, the finest inventors, engineers, and visionaries in Britain. Never before has such a gathering taken place."

Simon stopped listening to the words, closing his eyes to concentrate on the suffocating levels of magic that swirled about the chapel. A major spell waited to be triggered, but when he explored, he found no trace of the bindings that would be needed for a mass enthrallment. Instead, the magic was woven into the fabric of the church itself. The spell seemed designed for . . .

His eyes shot open. "Dear God, Meg, I don't think Drayton intends to enthrall these men. He wants to kill them!"

Meg pressed her hand to her mouth, her eyes wide with shock. "Why?"

Simon reached deeper into the spells, looking for the intent that created them. "He . . . despises machines and factories. He prefers a rural England ruled by a handful of powerful landowners, with the rest of the population helpless and impoverished."

"I remember seeing those attitudes when I was in his foul mind," Meg said slowly as she thought back. "He wants laborers tied to the land and kept ignorant, because that means more power for men like him."

Simon had a swift flash of images—of sooty industrial buildings and great clattering machines, but also of schools and well-dressed, well-fed families. "He's right. Industry will create greater wealth and freedom for the average man." His mouth twisted. "Which is why Drayton hates progress. In his view, the common people are no more than chattel to be used for the benefit of the wellborn. The broader the gap between rich and poor, the happier he will be."

Meg nodded as she looked inward. "I saw that he wants all power for himself, and this is a major step in that direction. Next, I think, he will undermine the Guardian Council, eliminating those who are threats before they realize what he is about. When they no longer protect the legitimate mundane government, he will seize power there."

Meg's words sounded chillingly plausible. Drayton would create a world Simon would not want to know. He must be stopped *now.* "The thralls are the key. Without them, he will be unable to focus the huge amounts of energy needed to turn this building into a charnel house."

Meg finished his thought. "So we need to find and release them without getting killed first. That's straightforward." Silently she glided from the side chapel and started working her way up the nave, staying in the shadows along the right wall. Maintaining the don't-look spell,

Simon followed her. There was no sign that Drayton had noticed them. Having so many personalities and energies crowded into one space was an effective mask from even a powerful mage.

Keeping his remarks short, Drayton said, "In the spirit of this gathering, the next speaker will be one of you—a man whose mechanical skill allows us to master the natural world." He turned and gestured. "Let me present John Harrison, a clock-maker, a Yorkshire man—and the inventor of the chronograph that enables our ships to know their location anywhere on the globe. So far, the Board of Longitude has not yet conceded his success, for they think him a mere mechanic." There was a pause for laughter. "But men of the future like you recognize the quality of Mr. Harrison's work, and the profound effect such mechanical genius will have on our world. Gentlemen, meet John Harrison."

A nervous man in an old-fashioned wig came forward to take his place at the pulpit after Drayton descended. Clutching notes, he climbed the steps and began to speak in a voice that slowly gained confidence.

Ignoring Harrison, Simon and Meg continued their quiet progress. When they reached the front of the church, Simon glanced around, frowning. Where the devil had Drayton gone?

Meg touched his sleeve and indicated the carved wall behind what would have been the altar. When he looked closer, Simon recognized that it was a screen separating another chapel from the main church. It was masked by a don't-look spell, which is why Simon hadn't noticed it at first. Drayton had to be there, because the currents of power in the church had begun streaming in that direction.

Masked by shadows, they moved forward. When Simon had confronted Drayton before, he had failed. He prayed that this time he was better prepared.

As that fool Harrison droned on in the church, Drayton turned to his thralls. "Now, my faithful tools, it is time to channel the earth energy that pulses around us." They stared at him, blank and obedient.

Would Falconer and Meggie appear? Though Falconer had managed to break the connection, Drayton had stolen much of Meggie's power first, and it would take time for her to recover. Maybe they had fled the estate—he felt no clear sense of their presence now. Perhaps that was just as well. If Falconer entered the chapel in the next few minutes he would be killed, and with him the potential to harvest his unicorn magic. Better to capture the man later so the horn wouldn't be destroyed uselessly.

Of course, if Falconer made it to the Lady Chapel, all would be well. Drayton had prepared for that possibility, just in case. He allowed himself a swift moment of pleased contemplation.

Time to block all the church exits except the one beside him. There was no need for wards—a simple locking spell on the doors sufficed. He invoked the spell easily so no one could escape except through the Lady Chapel, and none of the mundanes could see that the chapel existed. He hoped to take the thralls with him since they were useful, but if that was inconvenient—well, tools could be replaced.

Raising his arms, Drayton began concentrating the energy that nature spilled so extravagantly around him. This would be easier if he could use Meggie, but his personal power was sufficient to channel what was needed to the thralls. "In a moment," he murmured as he shaped the glorious, intoxicating power. "In a moment . . ."

David was intrigued by Harrison's work—fancy a clock being used to determine a ship's longitude!—until his eye was caught by movement along the wall of the church. He looked more closely, and thought he saw Lord and Lady Falconer. Surely they couldn't be here! In fact, when he looked again, he couldn't see them. Yet there had been someone oddly familiar skulking in the shadows.

Sarah always said that curiosity was his besetting sin, and she was right. Quietly he began moving after the enigmatic forms that had caught his attention.

They were about to step into the Lady Chapel when Simon caught Meg's wrist and gestured at the floor. She would have missed the shimmering circle, but after he drew it to her attention, she saw that several lines of power were braided together. There were at least two separate spells—and one pulsed with dark, lethal menace.

Instead of stepping into the circle, Simon edged into the chapel in the space between the circle and the wall. Drayton's back was to them as he faced the thralls, who were holding hands. Each of them glowed with a subtle light: blue for Moses, rose pink for Lily, icy gray for Jemmy, and a dark, intense red for Breeda.

Hands tented before him, Drayton was concentrating so much power that it blurred the outlines of him and the thralls. Meg realized that he was shaping ley line energy into a dense funnel.

As she and Simon entered the room, Drayton aimed the funnel toward the thralls and commanded, "Now!"

When the rush of earth energy reached the thralls, it flared into an angry, pulsing crimson that for an instant seemed to suck all the air from the room before it began flowing into the fabric of the church. At the first touch of crimson energy, the spells Drayton had buried in the stone came to life. The chapel began to vibrate.

"Damnation," Simon swore, "he's pulling the whole church down!"

Hearing his voice, Drayton spun about. Despite his surprise, he kept the ley line energy flowing without a pause. Coolly he said, "So you made it here in time."

Meg wondered if he had enough energy to spare from what he was doing to hurl a spell at them. Perhaps not, because when the blow came, it was physical. The rogue leaped across the chapel and swung at Simon with a heavy fist.

Simon eluded the blow but his sideways step brought him dangerously close to the ritual circle on the floor. Eyes glittering with triumph, Drayton grabbed his arm and yanked him forward. The instant Simon's hand crossed the space above the circle, he collapsed in a swirl of magic.

Aghast, Meg saw that the braided spells were the unicorn transformation spell and a ritual death spell. If the spells worked as designed, Simon would be forced into the unicorn form, then slain with magic so Drayton could harvest the power of the horn. Simon's body was contorted as he fought the spells, but darkness was overwhelming him.

"No!" Meg grabbed Simon's leg and dragged him back from the

circle, hoping separation would free him of the dual spells. It didn't—Simon's outlines were shimmering, on the verge of transformation.

"Hold on," she breathed as she knelt and rested her hands on his knee. Thanking heaven that apparently Drayton couldn't spare the power for a magical attack, she poured her own magic into Simon to counter the combined spells. She sent both raw power and the deepest calm she could manage, hoping to balance the treacherous fury Simon must be feeling.

He seemed to stabilize, but the death spell still clutched at him and the vibrations in the church were getting worse. The carved wooden paneling abruptly split, with a shower of splinters and a sound like a gunshot.

Noting the damage, Drayton reached for the knob of a cleverly concealed door. "It is time to take my leave." His smile was colder than winter ice. "I go into a better, purer England."

Feeling helpless, Meg recklessly increased the power she was channeling into Simon. The darkness around him diminished and he managed to choke out, "Stop Drayton, Meg! To save his life, he might stop trying to destroy the church."

She gave Simon a last dose of energy, then rose to confront the rogue. "This time, you devil, you will face the consequences of your evil!"

Knowing Drayton was heavily shielded, she used earth energy to blast the concealed door, fusing it shut. Swearing, Drayton grabbed the knob and tried to force the door open, but Meg had sealed it so securely that a battering ram would be needed.

There was the sound of crashing stone from the main sanctuary. "'Tis an earthquake!" a Yorkshire man called.

A moment later a Londoner yelled, "The bluidy doors won't open!" More stones punctuated the sounds of rising pandemonium.

"End the spell!" Meg pleaded. "Don't murder so many innocents!"

Drayton swung around, his eyes no longer sane. "Innocents? Those swine will destroy England by turning it into a poisoned manufactory where inferior men will no longer know their place. If I must die to prevent that, so be it!"

Knowing he expected a magical assault from her, Meg used the same trick Drayton had used on Simon and launched herself at the rogue in a physical, clawing attack. As she'd hoped, she was unaffected by the ritual circle. She aimed at his eyes, wanting to rip them out as if she were a lioness.

Swearing, Drayton backed away and swung a roundhouse punch at her. His fist connected with her cheek. She cried out as she staggered backward.

David White stepped into the chapel, his face taut. "'Tis hard to find the way in. Now, is there a way out before the building falls down?" He stopped, appalled at the sight of Drayton's blow. "My lord, you should not be hitting a lady!"

"You filthy lowborn mechanic!" Drayton whirled and blasted David with magic.

Without a Guardian's shields, David toppled against the wall, striking his head before he slid to the floor, eyes open and staring. Horrified, Meg started toward him.

Stones fell from the ceiling and bounced in all directions. One clipped Simon's arm. In a ragged voice, he gasped, "First things first, Meg. Can you stabilize the church with the ley line energy?"

If she couldn't, they would all die, not just David. Meg raised her arms and invoked the energy that had flowed through her earlier. *Gaia, Blessed Mother, save this place and these people as you saved me. Lend me the strength I need.*

The rush of power staggered her. This was the Lady Chapel, she realized, where the Mother had been worshipped for centuries at a crossroads of the earth's own energy.

She opened herself entirely, becoming an instrument. Her skin began glowing with white light as she channeled earth energy into the ancient building's stones. Seeing Drayton's fury, she spared a tendril of white fire to curl around him in a binding spell to prevent interference.

Slowly the white light drove away the angry red, like the incoming tide driving back river water in an estuary. The goddess energy blotted out the visible world, till Meg felt suspended in light. Power rolled across the length of the nave. She could feel the earth energy spread into the transepts and up the bell tower, stilling the furious shaking of the structure and the frenzied cacophony of the bells.

When the floor below Meg's feet steadied, she sought the black swirl of energy where Simon lay. Finding it, she extended a hand in his direction. White light gushed forth to obliterate the death spell that Drayton had woven into the circle.

Thank you, Gaia. With the last of her borrowed power, Meg opened all the church doors in the sanctuary so that the panicky guests could flee outside even though that was no longer necessary.

Dimly she heard the cries of relief as she sank to the floor, hollow and strengthless. She felt transparent, as if there were nothing left of her but a fragile shell.

A Guardian needed to be willing to sacrifice herself for the greater good. One needn't have taken the oaths to do that.

Chapter THIRTY-SIX

So much of Simon's strength was tied up in fighting Drayton's magic that he was momentarily dizzy when Meg dissolved the death spell. The transformation spell he could control on his own, which was good since he suspected Meg would be unable to restore him now that she was no longer virgin. If he transformed again, there might be no escape.

He stumbled to his feet as Drayton broke Meg's bindings. The rogue was turning with a feral snarl when Simon focused all his power into an ethereal silver sword. With one fierce slash, he severed the pulsing energy connection between Drayton's ley line power and the thralls. The menacing crimson light vanished instantly.

At that instant Meg crumpled to the floor, her face deathly pale. "Meg!" Simon rushed toward her.

Drayton staggered as the power he had been channeling whipped free, then dissolved and returned to earthbound channels. He made an attempt to recapture it, but without success. He hadn't enough personal magic left to master the ley line energy.

"Damn you!" Face distorted with fury, Drayton spun around and used what remained of his power to blast Simon.

Instinctively Simon threw up a shield to deflect the rogue's bolt. When it ricocheted from the shield toward the thralls, he shouted, "Down!"

Obedient as always, the thralls ducked. Most of the lethal bolt flew over their heads, but Lily cried out, scorched by the edge of Drayton's assault. Moses jerked his head up as his true self struggled with the enthrallment spell.

Simon threw another, stronger binding spell around Drayton. It wouldn't last long, but it would give Simon the time he needed to free the thralls. Hoping Jean Macrae had trained them well in self-defense, he slid into Moses's mind. Since he remembered the pathways from before, it took only moments to release the bindings. At first Moses's expression was dazed, but his expression cleared rapidly.

Simon dropped by Meg and checked her throat for a pulse. It was there, faint but steady. *Thank God.* Though her life was in the balance, at least she lived.

First things first. That meant releasing the other thralls. He could have worked with more elegance if he had the time, but what mattered now was speed and effectiveness. He broke the bindings on Lily, Jemmy, and Breeda in quick succession. Like Moses, they took only a few moments to recover from their enslavement.

David White was the next priority. How long since he had fallen? Not long, surely less than a minute, but if he was to survive, he needed healing immediately.

As Simon crossed the chapel to David, Drayton broke free of the binding spell and exploded into filthy curses. Before he could act, Moses rose from his chair, his black eyes flashing with rage as he glared at Drayton. "You devil!" he growled, cool blue light radiating from him.

He extended one hand to Lily. She clasped his fingers and stood unsteadily, her gentle face remote and rose-pink energy churning about her as she reached for Jemmy. Eyes radiating ice-gray light, the former chimney sweep stood and took Breeda's hand.

Scarlet light brighter than her hair flared from the Irish girl as she rose, her expression lethal. Before Simon could intervene, she pointed her free hand at Drayton and hissed, "Die, damn you! And may your evil soul burn in hell *forever!*"

Magic braided from four diverse souls arrowed across the chapel like a javelin. The weapon of power impaled Drayton. For an instant the rogue stood engulfed in scarlet fire. His voice shattered the air with spine-chilling howls.

Then he was gone, flesh and bone crumbling inward until only a handful of ashes revealed where he had been. Simon stared at the ashes, stunned. He had seen magic do many things, but not reduce a man to nothingness. Was that caused by Moses's African magic? Breeda's berserker rage? Or the blend of all four of them? The last, he suspected. Drayton had forged his own death.

The former thralls released each other's hands, looking stunned. But not, Simon noticed, showing any signs of regret for what they had done.

He dropped beside David and placed one hand on the engineer's forehead and the other on his chest so he could channel his newly acquired healing energy. Long moments passed, but it had no effect. Bleakly Simon realized that David was beyond the reach of Guardian healing energy. Only a miracle might bring him back from the abyss.

A unicorn was pure magic, with healing power that transcended what Simon could do in human form. But if he changed, he risked not being able to return to himself. With Drayton dead, the spell could never be lifted.

No matter. He had promised Sarah to look out for her husband, and David wouldn't be here if not for Simon. Releasing the transformation spell he had been struggling with, Simon bent to all fours and *changed.*

Heat seared in from all directions. Wracking pain distorted his limbs to the edge of madness and he experienced the ghastly knowledge that this time the change might be irreversible.

Pain vanished as he shimmered into magical wildness and rose onto his four powerful legs, secure and confident. Bending his head, he touched the tip of his horn to David's chest above the heart. *Heal. Beat strong for your wife, your unborn children, your ideas. You cannot be spared.*

Energy poured lavishly from the horn as vital seconds ticked away. It was a beginning, but he needed more. *Blessed Mother, grant a miracle for the sake of Sarah, who is soon to be a mother.*

The earth energy gushed through him like an iridescent river, saturated David with light. He felt a faint *thump* from David's chest. Another. Another and another, until there was a solid rhythm. David shuddered all over as he inhaled roughly.

Simon waited a few moments to be sure that his friend was well, then turned, carefully. The chapel was small for a unicorn, six people—and a handful of ashes.

The former thralls were staring at him. Jemmy said, "That beast was 'is lordship, I saw 'im change with my own eyes!"

"He's a unicorn," Lily said. "I . . . I thought there was no such creature."

Breeda edged backwards. "I don't like the looks of that horn."

"He will not hurt us," Moses said, but he also stepped back.

Simon didn't care what they did as long as they didn't interfere. He knelt beside Meg and gently rubbed the length of the horn along her body. Her breathing deepened, but she was still unconscious. She seemed frail as gossamer.

His mate needed more than just the horn. He nuzzled her face. *Wake up, my love. Wake up.* She drew a single slow breath, an even slower exhalation. Too long a pause before she inhaled again.

Beginning to feel frantic, he nuzzled her again. *Meg, don't you dare leave me!* Even in his own mind, he had trouble saying, *I love you and need you to be whole. I need you, beloved. Come back!*

She drew a deeper breath and her eyes fluttered open. "Simon?" She smiled and reached up to caress his muzzle. "We're still here, so we must have won."

Vibrant with relief, he nudged her face again. *Yes.*

Using Simon to brace herself, Meg managed to sit up. "What happened?"

The thralls began a garbled account of events since she had passed out. Giving in to temptation, Simon laid his head on Meg's lap. His slow unicorn mind recognized that even though she was no longer virgin, he was drawn as irresistibly as the first time he'd seen her. Though the other two young women were probably virgins, they didn't attract him in the least. Let them find their own unicorns.

Meg listened gravely to the explanations as one hand delicately caressed Simon's ears. When Jemmy finished the story, she said, "So Drayton is gone. I suppose I should regret the loss of a life, but to be honest, it doesn't trouble me much, considering that he was willing to kill hundreds of men because they didn't fit into his own mad view of the world."

"That was my thought." Breeda's smile was a knife blade. "Though not in such pretty words."

Meg glanced at David, who was stirring. "Moses and Jemmy, can you take Mr. White back into the main church? Find him some water and stay with him until he's recovered. He's a lovely man, but it's best he not be exposed to more magic. Tell him a falling stone knocked him out when the earth shook."

With luck, David would remember nothing of what he had seen in the Lady Chapel. Meg sent a spell to encourage that as Moses and Jemmy lifted David, then carried him into the main sanctuary.

Turning to Lily and Breeda, Meg said, "Drayton is the one who inflicted the unicorn spell on Lord Falconer. In legend, virgins have great power over unicorns, and we found that a touch of my blood to his would return him to his natural form. Unfortunately, now that I am wed I can't do that." No need to mention that she'd only been a bride for an hour or two. "Will one of you share blood with him?"

"Of course," Lily said immediately. "Do you have a knife?"

Simon scrambled to his feet as Meg resorted to an earring wire for a quick stab into his shoulder, then Lily's finger. Gently Lily rubbed her finger against the wound in his shoulder. Blood met blood, and . . . nothing, no matter how hard Lily rubbed.

Grimly Meg realized that she had expected this. "Breeda, are you willing to try?"

The Irish girl flushed. "I'd slice my wrist with a dagger for his lordship, but I . . . I'm no virgin. I was ravished by a drunken soldier when I was thirteen."

No wonder the girl was so fierce. "If you don't mind, let's try it anyhow. You have the blood of a warrior, and perhaps that will help."

Another pinhole was pricked in Simon's shoulder. He bore it stoically, but Breeda's blood was no more effective than Lily's.

"I'm sorry, my lady," the Irish girl said. "Is there anything else I might do?"

Meg shook her head. "I don't think so. Thank you for trying."

Simon began pacing restlessly around the chapel. He had regained his strength, and with it the unicorn wildness he feared. How long could he remain in unicorn form before he irrevocably lost his human nature? He'd already been transformed once today for the ride from Lady Bethany's. Time was running out, like the sands of an hourglass.

Lily asked, "Is there some other way to break the spell?"

"Apparently the only person who can break this sort of spell permanently is the person who created it," Meg said tightly. "Drayton."

Breeda looked stricken. "I didn't know, my lady."

"Don't blame yourself. Even if Drayton were alive, he would have died rather than lift the spell." Meg released her breath, trying to clear her mind. "When Falconer is in human form, it's possible for him to stay that way indefinitely as long as he doesn't lose his temper. But I don't know how to change him back."

"My lady, even if you're not a virgin, you are his wife. Perhaps your blood will still break the spell," Breeda suggested shyly.

It was a worthy idea, but didn't work. After admitting failure, Meg wiped the blood from Simon's shining flank, increasingly anxious. He was radiating nervous energy. If she hadn't sealed the door, she could take him outside. . . . No, that wouldn't be wise, not when over two hundred chattering mechanics and engineers were moving around the main chapel and outdoors. The magical shielding over the Lady Chapel was the only thing that gave them privacy here.

What had Simon once told her about the essence of magic? That it was will. She had used that advice, and her will had served her well.

Taking a deep breath, she walked up to Simon and caught his long head between her hands. "You are going to return to yourself, my lord husband. This marriage has just begun, and I will not let it end so soon."

As she spoke, she visualized Simon in human form. The height, the broad shoulders and long muscles, the shine of his blond hair. He was her friend, her lover, her mentor, and her husband. *Hers.* And she wanted him back.

Deliberately she sought the light-filled space where she had channeled the ley lines and saved the chapel. Energy flowed from her, shimmering with the rich dark tones of the earth. This would always be part of her, she realized, even when she was far from a ley line. By surrendering to the earth energy, she had made it her own.

Return, beloved.

Under her hands, the elegant equine head began to change. Heat roiled outward. She skipped backwards, not wanting to interfere with his transformation. As Lily and Breeda gasped, Simon's form was blurred by raging energy.

The transformation moved more swiftly than usual, and in a few moments he was himself again, albeit sprawled naked on the cold stone floor. He managed an unsteady smile. "You've learned a new trick, my love."

"Thank God!" She dropped onto her knees beside him, tears of relief streaming down her face.

"Here, my lord." Lily lifted Simon's ripped coat from the floor and spread it over him, then tactfully withdrew. "Breeda, let's see how our lads are doing." Together they left the Lady Chapel for the main sanctuary.

After the younger women left, Simon exhaled roughly and wrapped an arm around Meg's waist so he could pull her down next to him. "How did you do that? For you are most certainly no longer virgin."

Laughing, she rested her head on his shoulder, so tired that even sitting up was too much effort. "I willed you to return yourself to your own form." She paused, startled, as she realized her body was refreshing itself from the earth energy around her. This could prove useful in the future. "I believe I can break this spell whenever it's needful. That's not as good as removing the spell altogether, but—good enough, I think." She grinned. "So if you lose your temper and grow a horn, I can bring you back again."

Simon looked thoughtful. "There was something rather splendid about being a unicorn. Because of the danger of being overwhelmed by the animal nature, it would be foolish to spend much time in that form. Yet . . . perhaps on rare occasions it would be . . . amusing to run free again. As long as you can restore me."

Meg kissed him on the forehead, right where the horn would be. "We must experiment with this. I would hate to lose my magnificent unicorn forever."

Simon smiled before turning serious. "Send someone to the main house to steal some clothing for me so I can sort out this technology forum. It's quite a good idea, after all, so it seems a pity to waste the opportunity. People can assume Drayton has gone back to London for some reason."

"And somehow, mysteriously, he will vanish on the way. Highwaymen, no doubt." Meg's gaze turned pensive. "Are all those inventors and mechanics and engineers going to change the world for better or worse?"

"Both," Simon said wryly. "We're on the verge of a great new age, my warrior maiden, and there will be pain and anger and disruption. Change hurts. But ultimately, this new age will benefit the great mass of people. There will be more education, more wealth, more choices for everyone. No longer will bright lads like Jemmy die in chimneys and girls like Breeda become maids because there are no other jobs for a poor farm girl. I can't see the whole shape of the future, but I do know that it will be a better one than if Drayton had his way."

"Good." Meg trailed her fingers through Simon's hair, wondering how long it would take him to get the forum on track. When the disruptions had been smoothed over and the mechanics and engineers given the chance to talk each others' ears off, she and Simon could go back to Lady Beth's and some privacy. A long, long night of privacy. "But since I'm no maid, I can't be your warrior maiden anymore."

"No matter." He laughed and drew her closer. "Now you're my warrior queen."

EPILOGUE

Emma was bouncing in her carriage seat. "We're almost there!"

Meg was bouncing almost as much. "I recognize the stone bridge! The vicarage is just around the next bend!"

Simon smiled at the sisters. A week had passed since the final confrontation with Drayton, and it had been a busy one. Soon Moses would take Lily back to Marseilles to his family, and to become his bride. Jemmy had decided to go with them. He wanted an education, and a chance to ride horses.

Breeda had sailed for Ireland to visit her family, but after that she would join the others in France. The bonds the four of them shared were too powerful for them to go their separate ways. Simon had already written a French Guardian he knew in Marseilles to continue the training of the former thralls.

David White had recovered from Drayton's attack with no damage, and no clear memory of what had happened. Later, though, when he had returned from the forum brimming with ideas, he had confided to Sarah that while he was unconscious he had flown through a tunnel of light. At the end he had found the pure radiance of God.

The Lord had given him the choice of staying in heaven or returning to earth. Of course he chose Sarah and his unborn child, because God would always be waiting. Simon learned the story from Sarah when she called to thank him privately for whatever he had done.

The carriage pulled up in front of the sunlit vicarage. Emma tumbled out without waiting for the guard to lower the steps for her. "Mama, Papa!"

Meg stepped out more slowly, yearning but nervous. Ten years was a long time. Simon climbed out last, thinking it best to stay in the background while the reunion took place. He was an outsider at a family's celebration.

"Emma! Meg!" Suddenly the yard was full of Harpers, two tall young men and the vicar and his wife, not to mention three dogs and several cats. A spaniel old enough to have a gray muzzle leaped at Meg with an ecstatic howl that seemed almost human.

"My darling girl!" Meg's mother embraced her, weeping. "I never believed you were dead, never. This last week while waiting for you to come home has been an eternity."

"Mama, Mama." Tears ran down Meg's face as she hugged her mother with breath-squeezing strength. "For so long I had thought I was alone. How could I have forgotten how blessed I am?"

The Harpers ended in one grand, untidy hug, happiness breaking down their reserve. Simon lingered by the carriage, trying to suppress an unworthy pang of envy as he observed the bonds of love connecting the Harpers. Even at its best, his family had never been so loving. Magic had its limits.

The vicar turned and offered his hand. "Forgive our rudeness, Lord Falconer, and please accept our gratitude. You have given us a gift beyond price. For ten years, I believed my eldest child dead. I never dreamed that she would come home whole and alive and beautiful." He smiled wryly. "Not to mention a countess."

Simon returned the older man's handshake. "I'm sorry I was unable to ask you for your daughter's hand. We are well and truly wed now, but we hope that you will marry us again in front of all your friends and family. As soon as possible, for now that Meg remembers her family, she says she won't feel properly married until you have performed the sacrament."

"It will be my privilege." The vicar's gray green eyes, so like Meg's, were shrewd. "My daughter has chosen well."

Simon saw a spark of power in the older man, and guessed where at least some of the Harper magic came from.

Meg turned and took his arm, her smile radiant despite the tear tracks on her cheeks. "Come, my love, and meet your new family." As she drew him forward, Emma took his other arm.

Suddenly he wasn't an outsider after all.

In later years, near the ancient estate of the lords Falconer, there came to be tales of a mysterious white unicorn that sometimes rode through the night as fast as the wind. On his back he carried a fairy queen whose bright laughter and dark hair rippled through the darkness.

But, of course, they were only tales.

AUTHOR'S NOTE

Though the term "scientist" wasn't coined until the 1830s, the eighteenth century was the Age of Enlightenment, and Western society teemed with theories, experiments, and lots of the Georgian equivalent of garage inventors. From this ferment of ideas and experiments grew the Industrial Revolution.

However, since I was tied to the 1740s because of the events of an earlier, related book, *A Kiss of Fate,* I fudged some of the allusions to inventions that appear in this story. David White's steam engine bears a remarkably strong resemblance to the Watts steam engine, which didn't come along until three decades later. The same is true for some of the famous spinning and weaving inventions, and the great age of canal building hadn't quite begun. But my portrait of an age of invention is real in spirit, if a trifle premature.

There really was a Royal Menagerie in the Tower of London from the thirteenth century until the 1830s, when the remaining animals were transferred to the new Regent's Park Zoo. The medieval collection began with royal gifts from foreign potentates, but over time it turned into a real crowd-pleaser. In the eighteenth century, the Tower of London was the city's biggest tourist draw, so much so that the phrase "going to see the lions" was shorthand for touring London.

The lions were extremely popular, and often a lion was named for the monarch. Some of these lions lived so long that one has to assume new lions were substituted when old ones went to that great savannah in the sky. After all, one wouldn't want a lion named for the king to die prematurely—it made people start wondering how long the monarch would survive. Apparently there is nothing new about political spin!

ABOUT THE AUTHOR

A lifelong reader of science fiction and fantasy, M. J. PUTNEY can still quote Robert Heinlein with no encouragement whatsoever. A graduate of Syracuse University with degrees in eighteenth-century literature and industrial design, she followed a peripatetic path to success as a writer. Now a *New York Times, Wall Street Journal,* and *Publishers Weekly* bestselling author, Putney has been a nine-time finalist in the Romance Writers of America RITA contests and has won two RITAs for her historical novels. Her books have been listed four times by the American Library Association among the top five romances of the year. The chance, with *Stolen Magic,* to combine fantasy with her love of history and romance is an example of real-life magic in action. Visit the author's website at www.mjputney.com.

ABOUT THE TYPE

The text of this book is set in Centaur, originally designed by Bruce Rogers for the Metropolitan Museum in 1914 and released by Monotype in 1929. Modeled on letters cut by the fifteenth-century printer Nicolas Jenson, Centaur has a beauty of line and proportion that has been widely acclaimed since its release. The italic type, originally named Arrighi, was designed by Frederic Warde in 1925. He modeled his letters on those of Ludovico degli Arrighi, a Renaissance scribe whose lettering work is among the finest of the chancery cursives. Arrighi was produced by Monotype as the companion for Centaur in 1929. Centaur is a beautiful typeface for books, and can be used effectively for shorter text as well.